# KEMP

## PASSAGE AT ARMS

Also by Daniel Hall

*Kemp: The Road to Crécy*

# KEMP

## PASSAGE AT ARMS

Daniel Hall

BCA

LONDON NEW YORK SYDNEY TORONTO

This edition published 1997
by BCA
by arrangement with Orion
an imprint of Orion Books Ltd

CN 3108



Typeset at The Spartan Press Ltd,
Lymington, Hants
Printed in Great Britain by
Clays Ltd, St Ives plc

*For Louise*

# CHAPTER ONE

'IT SEEMS HE found his glory, then,' Sir Thomas Holland said bleakly.

Holland was dressed in full armour, the jupon bearing his coat of arms – a white lion on an azure background patterned with *fleurs-de-lys* – slashed and bloody, but the blood was not his own, for the sword-strokes which had rent it had failed to pierce the chain-mail habergeon beneath. The visor of his egg-shaped bascinet, now scratched and dented, was raised to reveal the face of a man in his mid-thirties, clean-shaven, a patch of white silk covering his left eye, the right one dark, piercing and intense, giving his bronzed features a saturnine appearance.

Beside him stood his serjeant-at-arms, a dour Lancastrian named Wat Preston, a stocky man with close-cropped hair and a seamed face, wearing a broad-brimmed 'kettle' helmet and a brigandine jerkin of leather reinforced with steel plates. The rest of the huddle of men was made up of five archers, the remainder of Preston's platoon. Their ages ranged from sixteen to fifty-five, although even the youngest, Limkin Tate, had the look of a battle-scarred veteran about him now. Less well-armoured than Holland, their own clothes were torn and blood-stained, as often as not with their own blood, and all of them had sustained wounds. Their faces were pale and drawn from lack of sleep, their chins covered in stubble. With tired eyes, they gazed down at the body of Holland's squire, and at the broken-off point of a lance in his stomach. He lay with his bloodied sword in his right hand, his left hand clutching Holland's banner to his breast, as if he had died trying to save it from capture. His blue eyes stared blankly up into the misty sky.

The squire had not been the only one to die in the battle. Although mist now shrouded the battlefield, the survivors could see bodies strewn across the hillside, heaped thickest where the fighting had been at its most fierce. Assisted by two heralds and two clerks, three knights now moved amongst the corpses, making a careful tally of the men of quality who had been slain. No one bothered to count the bodies of the dead commoners. There were looters too, working their way steadily across the field of death to rob the dead and the dying alike; human versions of the carrion crows engaged in taking their pick of the spoils.

It had been Martin Kemp's first pitched battle.

Kemp was the second youngest member of the platoon, only a few months older than Tate, a broad-shouldered young man with high cheekbones which gave his lean-jawed face a slightly gaunt look. The pale blond hair beneath his arming cap was cut short, his eyes a cold flint-blue. A rough bandage was tied about his head, dark with dried blood above his left ear. Four months ago he had been a villein, innocent of war, pushing a plough on his lord's demesne.

He had come a long way in four months. He had thought himself a man when he lay with a woman for the first time: Lady Beatrice, the daughter of his lord, Sir John Beaumont. But Beaumont had learned of the liaison, and framed Kemp with the rape and murder of a woman Kemp had never even met. Condemned to death, Kemp had been offered a pardon if he served in the king's army for twelve months.

A month and a half later he killed a man for the first time, a peasant levy on the beach at Saint-Vaast-la-Hougue. Then he realised that loss of innocence came not with carnal knowledge but with the knowledge of what it was like to look into a man's eyes as you robbed him of his life. Loss of innocence was nothing to be proud of, he had realised.

But that had been only the beginning. He had marched through Normandy with the king's army, burning and pillaging towns and villages. He had taken part in the assault of Caen, and in the subsequent sack of the city he realised that he had not yet lost all his innocence, for more of it was torn from his soul when he raped a young woman in a frenzy of blood-lust; and yet more when he saw his best friend murdered by a whore in the town of Oisemont; and more still when he fought for his life in the bloody chaos on the field of Crécy.

In the thick of the action, Kemp had thought the French knights must overwhelm the English line at any moment, for the enemy far outnumbered the English and the Welsh in King Edward's service. Now he realised his platoon had suffered disproportionately high casualties because it had been in the front line where the French almost broke through; all told, only a few hundred English and Welshmen had been killed. The French dead numbered thousands. It had not been a battle; it had been a massacre.

Gazing about at the corpse-strewn hillside, Kemp realised that innocence was not something that could be lost in one fell swoop, but a quality that was ripped away shred by shred. He had left England with high hopes, thinking that war would give him a chance to prove himself worthy of Lady Beatrice's love, despite his humble birth. Last night, at Crécy, he knew he had proved himself as brave as any nobleman; better still, after the battle, he had run into Richard Stamford, Beaumont's squire and Kemp's rival for the love of Beatrice. The two of them had fought, and Kemp had won. It seemed there was nothing to stop him claiming Beatrice's hand.

Except for the woman at Caen.

He had set out to prove himself as chivalrous as the bravest nobleman. Instead he had proved he could be as cruel as the worst of them. He thought of his friends Hal Drayton, Pip Herrick and Jankin Newbolt, all slain in the battle, and John Conyers and Hick Lowesby, badly wounded and even now fighting for their lives in the nearby abbey of Crécy-Grange. None of them had been perfect, but they had been good fellows at heart. Any one of them would have given his life to protect his companions. But Kemp felt as if he had betrayed them just as he had betrayed Beatrice by raping the woman at Caen.

He felt ashamed.

The seven men heard the jingle of harness, and almost as one they looked up to see a herald trotting down the slope towards them, his palfrey picking its way fastidiously amongst the corpses. He reined in and raised his right hand to the brim of his hat in salute to Holland, mimicking the gesture knights used to raise their visors, even though he did not wear a bascinet.

'Sir Thomas? My lord of Warwick presents his compliments, and requests that you rally your company and join him by yonder banner . . .' The herald gestured with one hand before realising that a bank of fog rolling across the battlefield had obscured the

Earl of Warwick's banner. 'Oh! Well, he's over there somewhere, about four hundred yards away . . .'

Holland nodded brusquely, and the herald rode off in search of other scattered units from Warwick's battalion. 'Kemp!'

Kemp forced himself to snap out of his guilt-ridden reverie. 'Sir Thomas?'

'You're good with horses, aren't you? Fetch my courser and lance, and meet the rest of us by Warwick's banner.'

At once Kemp turned back up the face of the ridge to where Holland's warhorse was corralled with the other knights' mounts at the centre of a leaguer formed from the army's baggage wagons. He was beyond exhaustion now, treading on the corpses that lay in his path out of numb obliviousness rather than cold-hearted indifference. While the battlefield itself was deserted but for the dead, dying and the looters, the scene around the leaguer to the rear of where the English lines had stood was one of considerable activity as men loaded booty into the wagons, packed away tents or, like Kemp, fetched their masters' horses.

Holland's warhorse was a dappled-grey courser named Peledargent – 'Silverpelt' – a massive seventeen hands high. It was one of many such beasts corralled in the leaguer, each one clearly branded. Kemp found the wagon in which Holland's tent, saddle and lance were stored, and saddled the horse quickly and efficiently, mounting it himself to return to where Holland waited. At first he rode it at a trot, but he soon gained confidence and as he reached the crest of the ridge he spurred it into a gallop, enjoying the refreshing sensation of the wind on his face and feeling his earlier sense of gloom dispel with the exhilaration of the ride.

He could not fail to find Warwick's red and gold banner, even in the fog, for it stood next to the Earl of Northampton's above a column of about three hundred men on one of the roads leading off the battlefield to the east. His companions stood with the other dismounted archers towards the rear of the column. The other platoon of archers in Holland's company was also there; like Preston's, it had been in the thick of the fighting. Although the two platoons had now merged into one, with only eighteen men it was still under strength.

Despite their exhaustion, Kemp's companions managed a mocking cheer when they saw him ride the courser out of the mist.

'Did Sir Thomas give you permission to ride Peledargent?' asked Daw Oakley, the oldest member of the platoon.

Kemp flushed as he handed the lance to David Brewster – a lean, handsome lad with bright blue eyes – before dismounting. 'I just thought it would be the quickest way of getting here with the horse . . .'

'Ignore him, lad, he's teasing you,' said Preston.

Kemp nodded. 'Where's Sir Thomas, serjeant?'

'Up yonder.' Preston jerked a thumb over his shoulder, towards the head of the column. 'Blabbing with their lordships.'

'Any idea what they want with us, serjeant?' asked Brewster, chewing thoughtfully on a piece of marsh-reed.

'Maybe they want to knight us all for valour,' scoffed Oakley.

Holland strode back from the head of the column, and Kemp held Peledargent's bridle while the knight swung himself into the saddle before taking his lance from Brewster. 'We've been asked to conduct a reconnaissance in force,' the knight told his serjeant, but speaking clearly for the benefit of his men. 'Valois is still out there somewhere, with the rest of his army. His Majesty wants to deal the death-blow.'

'The rest of his army!' muttered a tall, thin man with a face pitted by childhood pox. He had been in Holland's other platoon and Kemp knew him only vaguely. Searching his memory, he came up with a name: Elias Jarrom. 'Then whose corpses did we leave strewn all over that hillside?' demanded Jarrom, gesturing back through the fog.

'There are plenty of bodies there, but there aren't sixty thousand,' growled Holland. 'And that's how many men they reckon Valois had with him. The battle isn't over yet, lads.'

They marched in silence, the thick fog lending the countryside an eerie feel. It was the end of August, and within a couple of hours the hot sun would boil away the mist, but for now the condensation billowed from the mouths and nostrils of men and horses alike.

Riding at the head of the column, the Earl of Warwick reined in, and raised a gloved hand to signal a halt. Behind him, inattentive men bumped into one another. The earl heard swearing and the clattering of dropped weapons. He gestured impatiently for silence. Watching the earl, the men saw he was listening, and they listened as well.

Silence.

Then Kemp heard it too. The tramp of feet, the clop of hooves and the clinking of harness. Faint – some way off through the mist – but unmistakable.

'How many reconnaissance forces did his Majesty send out?' murmured Preston.

'Just the one, Wat,' Holland replied softly. 'Just the one.'

They stared at the fog, in the direction from which the sounds were coming. Whoever was out there was drawing closer.

Dark, half-imagined shapes in the mist were silhouetted with the sun behind them, the fog making them seem unnaturally large.

Then a sudden gust of wind tore a rent in the mist, and there they were: armoured horsemen, riding towards them. And behind those, rank upon rank of foot-soldiers. The fog was lifting now, the men drawing nearer, over five hundred of them. With each passing moment, more and more began to appear.

'Looks like we found the rest of Valois' army,' Brewster remarked.

'Oh, sweet Jesu!' moaned Perkin Inglewood.

The men kept on coming. Seeing Warwick's column, they had turned slightly to meet it, approaching from the column's right at an angle. They were four hundred yards away, moving briskly.

At the head of the English column, Warwick seemed paralysed with indecision. 'All right, we've found the enemy,' hissed Jarrom, his voice taut with fear. 'Why the devil don't he order us to withdraw, and go and send in the cavalry?'

Kemp said nothing. He was irritated by Jarrom's grumbling, but only because it reflected his own fear and tension.

Kemp could see the French column clearly now. The men were poorly armed and armoured, almost certainly peasant levies, possibly even raw recruits who had never been in battle. But they were fresh and clearly rested, and there must have been over a thousand of them, outnumbering Warwick's column three to one as they continued to advance.

Still Warwick seemed to dither. To retreat in such open country would have been fatal if the enemy had been mounted; but only the leaders of this column were on horseback, a handful of noblemen appointed to keep the levies in order. On the other hand, if Warwick meant to stand and fight, he was leaving it to the last moment before ordering his troops to form a defensive position.

Then something astonishing happened. One of the noblemen riding at the head of the French column waved in Warwick's direction. Warwick approached Northampton, and the two of them conversed briefly in terse, low tones. Then Warwick turned, and spoke to one of the men behind them. The man passed it back to the man behind him, and he to the man behind him, so that the order was passed down the whole length of the column towards Kemp and his companions, without the need for trumpet orders.

Kemp stared at the French, less than three hundred yards away now and still advancing slowly but surely. 'Hell's teeth!' he gasped as realisation finally dawned. 'They think we're French! They think we're on their side!'

'They won't think that for ever,' said Oakley.

'Can't they see our bows?' gasped Jarrom. The distinctive longbow was almost unique to English and Welsh troops.

Warwick's order reached Preston's platoon. 'Ready your bows!'

Kemp and his companions hurriedly stripped off their woollen bow-bags and began to tie their bowstrings on to the staves. Kemp went through the oft-practised motions almost mechanically, his eyes fixed on the approaching Frenchmen, now less than two hundred and fifty yards away. Any moment, he knew, they would realise their mistake, and attack.

Warwick raised his marshal's baton above his head and waved it so the gilt head glinted in the thin morning sun. 'Nock!' growled Preston, a command which echoed the whole length of Warwick's column. Kemp had already nocked an arrow to his bow.

The susurration of the serjeants' commands may have reached the ears of the Frenchmen, or they may have seen the archers readying their bows; something made the leaders check and rein in their horses uncertainly.

'Mark!'

As it dawned on the Frenchmen that all was not well, their leaders hesitated. Only two hundred yards now separated the columns, optimum killing range for the longbow. Kemp and his companions chose their targets.

'Draw!'

The bending of two hundred bows merged into a single eldritch creak, the broad shoulders of English yeomen drawing the fletchings of their arrows back to their ears.

The French were in no doubt now. The leaders gestured frantically, trying to get their men to go back, but the untrained peasant levies responded slowly to their commands, bumping into one another in their panic.

'And . . .'

Warwick brought his baton down sharply.

'. . . *loose*!'

A cloud of arrows filled the air, soughing with eerie menace as they whirred towards their targets, arcing down to wreak havoc on the French column. The ranks seemed to stagger under the impact, men falling dead and dying on all sides as the steel arrowheads tore through flesh, muscle and sinew. Voices screamed in agony.

'Nock! Mark! Draw!'

Kemp and his companions little needed the orders. Experienced bowmen by now, they performed the motions with ruthless efficiency. After the repeated charges of French knights and men-at-arms, a mere thousand peasant levies held few fears for such battle-scarred veterans, and it was as if even those fears had been dispelled by their incredulity at their enemies' mistake.

'And . . . loose!'

A second volley ripped through the French ranks, and more men fell screaming. The French tried to run, but tripped over one another in their panic. Those nearest the English ranks had over a hundred yards of open ground to cover before they would be out of range of the lethal arrows.

'Loose at will!'

Kemp and his companions were loosing arrows as fast as they could nock and draw. The air was thick with arrows, each man loosing his next shot before his last had found its target.

'Stop shooting!'.

Kemp had almost exhausted the supply of arrows he kept under his belt anyway. Glancing to his left he saw that Warwick and Northampton had used the few moments' grace the archers had bought them to form up the knights and mounted men-at-arms, and now they charged forward, lances couched, goading their horses into a canter. They rode in tight formation, the heavy horses' hooves falling into a steady rhythm as they pounded the turf.

More than half the French remained standing, but their ranks were broken and they fled for safety, their unprotected backs turned to the English lances. After seeing several of his companions spitted on French lances only a few hours earlier, Kemp was pleased to see the enemy getting a taste of their own medicine.

Warwick and Northampton did not take part in the charge. Warwick surveyed the surrounding countryside, as if the whole thing was a trap, and a body of French horsemen might ride into view at any moment. But if it was a trap, it had been sprung too late. He galloped over to the archers. He saw Kemp, and recognition flickered in his eyes – it had been Warwick, in his capacity as Sheriff of Warwick and Leicester, who granted Kemp his pardon – but he did not acknowledge him. 'Well? What are you waiting for?'

The archers needed no second bidding. Dropping their bows, they rushed forward in an unruly mob, drawing swords and war-hammers as they charged across the grass in the wake of the men-at-arms, whooping with blood-lust, all signs of exhaustion gone.

Some of the French had realised the futility of flight in such open country, and were trying to make a stand. A few clutched swords or spears, but most were armed with sickles, scythes and flails; deadly enough weapons, if one knew how to use them.

Kemp had his broadsword in his hand, a souvenir of the second time he had met Warwick, saving the earl's life on the road from Saint-Vaast-la-Hougue. The sword had belonged to the second man Kemp killed, a nobleman who had been trying to capture the earl. He swept it back over his shoulder, measuring the rapidly diminishing distance between himself and a Frenchman who stood ready to receive his charge with the wickedly curved blade of a scythe.

Kemp swung, all the strength of his broad shoulders behind the blow. The peasant raised his scythe, chopping at Kemp's head, but he mistimed the stroke. Kemp's blade sheared neatly through the wooden handle, the scythe's blade flying off, the sword slashing the man's throat open, filling the air with an angry crimson spray.

Then Kemp was past, still running, but slowing, readying

himself for a second stroke as he charged at a man with a sword. The man tried to parry. Kemp knocked his sword aside with his own blade, and flicked a booted foot into the man's crotch. As the man doubled up, Kemp brought his blade down on the back of the man's head, and for the second time that day he stained the grass with a splash of crimson. Without realising it, Kemp screamed, exultant at his own ability to take life with impunity. He slashed left and right, carving down the French levies like a peasant mowing down hay. All around him his friends fought equally savagely; even Perkin Inglewood, only a few months earlier the timid son of a franklin, cut down the enemy remorselessly, his face twisted into a mask of hate.

'This one's for Hal!' Kemp chopped, slicing through flesh and muscle. 'This one's for Pip!' He slashed open a man's stomach. 'And this one's for Jankin!' He thrust, burying the tip of his sword in a third man's belly.

He heard a sound behind him, and whirled in time to see another French peasant fall at his feet, a forester's axe flying from his hand, the side of his chest slashed wide open to reveal the ribs beneath. 'And that one's for a wooden-headed lubber who hasn't sense enough to watch his own back!' growled Preston, although his broad grin belied the condemnation in his tone. 'You're learning fast, boy, but no one lives for ever.'

Kemp was filled with chagrin. He and Preston looked about, but the nearest remaining Frenchmen were over half a mile away and running hard, a troop of English men-at-arms hot on their heels to guarantee they would not get far.

He glanced at the mangled bodies strewn everywhere. A wounded man tried to crawl away, but Brewster finished him off with a sword-thrust in the back.

In less than five minutes they had butchered the best part of a thousand men.

In a way, it had all been over too quickly. Kemp's blood still raged like fire in his veins yet there was no one left to kill. Then exhaustion caught up with him and he flopped to the ground, panting hard. He thought of the Frenchman who would have slain him in the moment of victory if Preston had not been there. The memory filled him with a terror more unmanning than any fear he had known in the wait before a battle. His stomach lurched and he found himself trembling.

Preston took his costrel from his belt, pulled out the stopper and took a deep draught before offering it to Kemp. Kemp gulped back the water and wiped his lips with his sleeve.

'Are you all right, lad?' asked Preston.

Kemp nodded. 'I always seem to get like this after a battle . . . it'll pass . . .'

'Until the next time,' said Preston. 'It never gets any easier.'

The Earl of Warwick rode by, congratulating the archers. They were too exhausted to do more than nod in acknowledgement but the earl rode on regardless, finally reining in opposite Preston. Kemp struggled to rise, but the earl motioned for him to remain where he lay. 'Rest easy, boy. You've earned it.'

Seeing the earl reminded Kemp of his sword, and he picked it up again, wiping the blood from its blade with a rag before slotting it back into its scabbard.

'Aye,' Warwick said thoughtfully. 'A nobleman's sword, and you wield it nobly.'

Kemp felt sudden bitterness well up within him. 'There's nothing noble about what happened here today, my lord,' he muttered, gesturing at the bodies around them.

He realised he had overstepped the mark as soon as the words passed his lips, but to his surprise Warwick smiled. 'That's the problem with you churls,' he remarked blithely. 'You're far too sensitive for the business of war.'

'Don't you worry, my lord,' growled Preston. 'We'll soon cure him of that.'

Warwick laughed. 'Aye, serjeant, that we will.' He chucked his horse's reins, and rode back to where Northampton waited.

Holland rejoined his men. He had discarded his lance, presumably broken in two, and was now wiping blood from the blade of his sword. He reined in amongst them. 'Time for breakfast,' he said simply.

The next day the king marched north with his army, and a week later they came before the walls of Calais.

'You heard what happened at Caen?' asked Sir Amerigo de Pavia. He was a small, dark-haired man with large, moist eyes bulging from a round face. A Lombard by birth, he had gone to sea as a youth and had drifted on the tides of life guided only by luck and his own opportunism. Those tides had eventually made him captain of one of the Genoese mercenary galleys in the service of Valois. Now he was one of the many Italian mercenaries who found themselves trapped in Calais with the French.

The governor of Calais, Jean de Vienne, did not turn to face de Pavia, but continued to watch the French build their siege lines from his vantage point on the battlements of the town walls.

'The townsfolk slaughtered,' de Pavia continued, 'women raped, houses looted and put to the torch. They say the streets ran red with blood. At least if we surrender, we will be treated honourably.'

'Caen was taken by swift assault,' pointed out de Vienne. 'If King Edward thought Calais could be taken as easily, he would have attacked already.' He gestured to where the English were erecting palisades and digging trenches across the dykes and causeways that ran through the marsh surrounding the town on the landward side. 'Instead he settles down to besiege us. These walls are stouter than those of Caen, and will not fall so easily.'

'Then he will starve us out. How long will the supplies in this town last? One month? Two? And then we go hungry. Not just you and I, my friend, nor your garrison, nor my troops, but the townsfolk. The innocents, Jean. The women, the children, the old men. They will starve too.'

'Naturally I will expel the "useless mouths", Sir Amerigo,' said de Vienne. It was almost standard practice in siege warfare for the defenders to throw out all those who would use up vital supplies without actively contributing to the defence. If the besiegers refused to let them out through their lines, then they would be forced to live in the no man's land between town walls and besiegers' lines, lashed by wind and rain, surviving only on scraps tossed to them by those defenders or besiegers who took pity on them. 'It will not be an order I shall relish giving, but my first duty must be to my king. He has entrusted me with the safe-keeping of this town, and I will not betray that trust. King Philip will come to rescue us.'

'How?' demanded de Pavia. 'You have heard the news: your King Philip was routed at Crécy by the English, his army massacred. There is no one to rescue us, Jean.'

'His son the Duke of Normandy will save us,' said de Vienne. 'Duke Jean is in Gascony at the moment, but he will ride north to relieve us with his army as soon as he learns we are besieged.'

'And how long will that be? What if he does not hear that we are besieged in time?'

'He will hear. I shall send out messengers with the "useless mouths", disguised as the old and infirm. Once past the English lines, they will ride to King Philip and tell him we are besieged.'

De Pavia gazed at the English troops massing beyond the walls. 'They will need to be brave men, to undertake such a perilous enterprise.'

De Vienne nodded.

'Let *me* go,' de Pavia suggested. 'You know that you can trust me, that I will not let you down. I will get through to King Philip.'

De Vienne smiled sadly. 'You are a brave man, to volunteer for the task, Amerigo. But that is why I need you here in Calais, to lead your men and help me defend the town. I will send others, more expendable than yourself.'

De Pavia wondered how else he could get out of the besieged town; for he was damned if he would still be there when Calais fell to the English and the common soldiers rampaged through the town, killing everyone they encountered. He would rather take his chances trying to slip through the enemy lines in disguise.

De Pavia had stood with the Genoese mariners on the decks of the French ships at the battle of Sluys, and fought on while his companions died around him, the arrows of the English longbows inflicting ghastly wounds; but that had been for money. De Pavia was a mercenary, and he would endure any hardship for money. But not for Philip of Valois; the bastard wasn't worth it.

De Vienne expelled over a thousand 'useless mouths' from within the walls of Calais, and King Edward, in magnanimous mood after his stunning victory at Crécy, not only allowed them past the English lines but also gave each one of them a hearty meal before sending them on their way.

Then he settled down to the siege in earnest.

He built a ring of siege works around the town, four hundred yards from the walls, just beyond the range of a crossbow. Then he built a second ring of defences on the other side of his camp, to protect it against any French army which might come to the beleaguered town's relief. He sent letters to England, summoning a fleet of seven hundred ships to blockade the town from the sea, completing his stranglehold, which was currently imperfect:

occasionally French supply ships would slip past the English blockade to revictual the garrison of Calais, increasing the town's chances of holding out until Valois could raise an army to relieve it.

English ships plied the narrow seas constantly, bringing food for King Edward's army, for the English did not control enough of Calais' hinterland for his troops to be able to live off the land; and bringing reinforcements from England. Nor did the reinforcements come from England alone. The ranks of the army were swelled with foot-soldiers sent by the King's Flemish allies and German mercenaries, called 'paucenars' after the mail corselets they wore. By mid-autumn, over ten thousand men were camped in the marshes around Calais. It would take many months to starve out the town's inhabitants, and they would be camped there well into the following year.

It was rare for a campaign to continue through the winter. It did not make much difference to men like Kemp, who had been impressed for service for twelve months; but the men who had been raised under commissions of array were disgruntled that they had not been allowed to return to their farms in time for the harvest. Morale had not been helped by the fact that many of the army's senior knights, having served their statutory forty days and more in the king's service, had been allowed to return home. Many of the common soldiers deserted, slipping back to England on board the supply ships that plied continuously between the English camp before Calais and the ports of Orwell, Sandwich and Plymouth; but they were more than made up for by the fresh reinforcements from England. Morale might be low amongst the bored soldiers sitting before the walls of Calais, but back in England the victory at Crécy had caused an immense wave of public support at every level for the king's war against Valois.

Faced with the prospect of being encamped in the Calais marshes during the harsh months of winter, King Edward decided he needed something better than canvas tents to house himself and his army. And so he ordered that a new town be built from scratch to the west of Calais, and called it Villeneuve-la-Hardie.

Villeneuve was made of wood. A fair-sized mansion, built of timber and brushwood thatch but well-appointed for all that, housed the king and his court. There were timber houses for the king's senior officials and noblemen. A hospital was built for soldiers who contracted camp-fever or dysentery during their sojourn in the swamps, and of those there was no shortage. There were stables for the horses, farriers, tailors, tanners, armourers, bowyers and fletchers, as well as butchers' shops and bakeries, haberdashers' shops and stalls selling cloth. And thousands of cottages thatched with straw and brushwood housed the common soldiers. The town was carefully planned, all its roads radiating from a large market square at the centre, and the king appointed two regular market days each week to which the locals could bring their wares.

Although the French peasantry did not on the whole care whether a Valois or a Plantagenet sat on the throne of France, at first they were wary of the English troops that had rampaged through Normandy and Picardy. But the king made it clear that the laws of his realm would be applied within Villeneuve to protect the local inhabitants, just as he intended that one day those laws would be applied throughout the kingdom of France under his rule. If his claim to the throne of France was just, then the French people were his subjects as much as the English, and entitled to his protection.

And so the local peasantry brought their goods to the market of Villeneuve; tentatively at first, but with growing confidence when the English troops, while not perhaps treating the peasants with respect, at least showed a willingness to pay cash for their produce. With so many thousands of mouths to feed and the regular convoys of supplies that came either overland from Flanders or across the sea from England unable to meet the demand, a huge market begged to be tapped.

Thus the French peasants quickly came to welcome the presence of the English, even if they were a rude and surly people. Not only food was required by the English. The soldiers had purses bulging with plundered coins, and nothing to spend them on. As surely as demand creates its own supply, soon the soldiers had their every need catered for, and before long new buildings began to spring up, taverns and stewhouses; buildings not contained in the original plans of the king's carpenters, but which the king was nevertheless prepared to tolerate because he knew that if his brutal and licentious soldiery was unable to buy wine and women, it would take them.

So the town of Villeneuve-la-Hardie prospered in the shadows of the walls of Calais, where the townsfolk were starving, until its close-packed buildings contained a population far larger than most provincial towns in France, and certainly bigger than any in England.

And, when Villeneuve was nearing completion in November, King Edward sent for the ladies of the court.

'This is no way to win a war,' grumbled Jarrom. 'We should be concentrating on fighting, not women.'

'Hark to Brother Elias here!' snorted Brewster. 'Do you want me to go to that brothel in Villeneuve and tell the fat-titted Flemish wench you spend so much time with to go back to Flanders?'

Kemp, Jarrom and Brewster were standing on the dunes overlooking the beach where the king's ship had landed. Dressed in bright particoloured gowns of silk and velvet, the ladies of the court were disembarking.

'Who's yon fat sow?' wondered Jarrom, as a plump, swarthy woman with dark hair lifted her skirts out of the spume which foamed between the hulls of the beached ships, wading up on to the shore.

Brewster grinned. 'That's the queen. And I think calling her a fat sow might be counted treason.'

The next woman to descend from the ship was much younger, perhaps little older than Kemp himself. She was dressed in a blue gown decorated with trimmings of silver tissue. Her hair was covered, as was the fashion for married women, and all that Kemp could really see was that she was petite and slender, yet somehow he knew that seen close to she would be a beautiful young woman.

'Who's that?' he asked, trying to inject both gruffness and disinterest into his voice.

Brewster grinned. 'Ah, but you've got a good eye for the ladies, Martin. That's Joan of Kent, the Earl of Kent's sister; and the woman behind her is her mother, the Dowager Countess Margaret. The bad news is, Joan's already married.'

Jarrom chuckled. 'Twice, they say.'

'Twice?' Kemp asked incredulously.

Brewster nodded. 'Don't mention her in Sir Thomas's presence.'

'Why not?'

'Because he was her first husband.'

Kemp was astonished. The Sir Thomas Holland he knew was a ruthless warrior, dedicated to the service of the king. It had never occurred to him that Holland might have a wife. 'I don't understand,' he said. 'How can she have married another man, while her first husband still lives?'

'You mean to tell me you don't know the story?' asked Brewster. Kemp shook his head, and Brewster plucked a piece of dune-grass and studied it thoughtfully before continuing. 'A few years ago, Holland fell in love with Joan of Kent; the fairest woman in England, they say . . . or maybe he fell in love with her dowry, for she's one of the richest heiresses in England, and all. Either way, it seems the young lady was impressed by the brave knight's courting, because she agreed to marry him.

'It was a secret marriage, of course. Holland's got no money to speak of, and his family is quite lowly. Sir Thomas and Joan had to get married quickly because he was ordered to fight in Flanders. After that he went straight to fight with the Teutonic knights against the Tartars. Now, while he's in Prussia, the king decides that it's time his young cousin is found a suitable match. And who more suitable than William Montague, the son of his old friend the Earl of Salisbury who helped him overthrow Mortimer all those years ago? So before you can say "bigamy", Joan and Montague are exchanging vows.'

'But didn't Joan tell them she was already married?' protested Kemp.

'Who knows what happened? Maybe she was too scared to confess to having secretly married Sir Thomas. Maybe she thought he was dead, killed by the paynim Tartars. Maybe she did say something, but her parents decided such a doubtful marriage to such an undistinguished young man must be invalid.'

'So what happened when Sir Thomas eventually got back to England?'

Brewster shrugged. 'What could he do? Joan was married to Montague at the king's prompting. Oh, by way of compensation they made Sir Thomas steward of her household – a sinecure to buy his silence, I'm sure, since I can't see a fighting man like Sir Thomas working as a steward in the same household where his wife is living with another husband.' He shook his head with a chuckle.

Kemp was stunned, not knowing what to make of the story, not even sure if any of it could be true. He had always admired Holland as a strong warrior, never imagining that a personal tragedy such as this might lie in his private life.

Jarrom spat. 'Come on,' he said, walking back down the side of the dune in the direction of Villeneuve. 'Let's get some supper before we go on the night watch.'

Preston and his platoon shared a barrack house in Villeneuve – no more than a long, low building of brushwood and thatch twenty-five feet long and fifteen feet wide, somewhere to lay on their pallets at night, with a pit dug in the centre of the floor as a makeshift hearth where they could cook the food they bought from the king's victuallers. When Kemp, Brewster and Jarrom got back, they found the rest of the platoon already there, crowded around one of the beds listening to someone talking. Kemp recognised the Yorkshire accent at once.

'John!'

The huddle of men parted just enough for Kemp and Brewster to see through, and there, sitting on a pallet in one corner, sat John Conyers.

Kemp and Brewster rushed forward and embraced him in turn. 'Christ's wounds, John, we thought you were dead!' exclaimed Brewster.

Conyers grinned. 'It'd take more than a French sword-thrust to put an end to John Conyers,' he boasted. A short, wiry young man, Conyers' dark brown eyes always had a mischievous twinkle. The last time Kemp had seen him, they had been carrying him off the field of Crécy with a stab wound in his stomach. Such an injury was usually as fatal as a thrust to the heart, if slower and more painful, and Kemp and the others had thought him dead. 'I'll admit it was touch and go for a while,' he added, uncharacteristically grave. 'At one point they even fetched a priest to read the last rites over me, but I wouldn't let him. They say that your soul wings its way to heaven the moment the rites are complete.'

'There ain't no chance of your soul going to heaven, Conyers!' jeered Oakley, and Conyers grinned.

'Well, you're here now,' said Brewster, as delighted to see his friend alive as Kemp was. 'That's the important thing. You're fully recovered?'

'More or less.' Conyers hitched up his tunic to show them the scar in his side. 'I still get twinges every now and then. And I can't eat as much as I used to.'

'God's belly! I'd hate to see how much you used to eat before!' said Simon Elliott, one of Jarrom's friends, who had just seen Conyers wolf back two bowls of pottage, some cheese and half a loaf of bread.

'Anything left for us?' asked Kemp, smiling.

Sir Thomas Holland found King Edward in the withdrawing room of his mansion talking to the Earls of Warwick and Northampton. Edward Plantagenet of Windsor, King of England, Duke of Gascony and – by claim, at least – King of France, was a tall and well-made man in his early thirties. His shoulder-length hair and beard were golden-brown, his eyes a piercing blue. His face was proud without being haughty, with sternness written in the firm jaw-line, eyes that sparkled with intelligence, and lips that would be equally swift to curse or smile.

He glanced up at the knight standing awkwardly in the doorway. 'Sir Thomas! How are you? What can I do for you? Come in, man, come in!' He gestured for Holland to join them, evidently joyful at the arrival of his wife, or perhaps one of the other ladies of the court; it was impossible to be sure with his Majesty.

Holland entered hesitantly. 'Your Majesty, by your leave . . . I should like to return to England.'

The king stared at him, 'Return to England? While the French still hold Calais? This is not like you, Sir Thomas. When a fight is in the offing, you are usually the first to step forward.'

Holland smiled thinly. 'Your Majesty is too kind. However, I believe it will be several months before Calais falls to us. In that time I should like to return to England and take care of . . . certain personal affairs. If your Majesty can spare me, of course.'

The king frowned. 'Spare you I can, Sir Thomas, though there are few knights I would like to lose less than yourself. What personal affairs are there that require your personal attention? Cannot I use my own influence to help you?'

When Holland hesitated before answering, the king looked thoughtful. 'Leave us,' he told the two earls.

They swept out of the room, Warwick discreetly closing the door behind him.

The king sat down and gestured for Holland to do likewise. 'This has naught to do with any personal affairs of yours in England, does it, Sir Thomas? It seems to me it can be no coincidence you should make such a request the day after my cousin Joan has arrived here before Calais.'

Holland hung his head. 'It was not ambition that made me marry her, sire.'

'An invalid marriage,' the king reminded him sharply. Then he smiled. 'I know, Sir Thomas. She is a lovely child. Were I not already married myself . . .'

'I thought I could forget about her. That I would find another. But there can be no other like Joan.'

'I can see why the two of you should be attracted to one another,' the king acknowledged. 'Both of your fathers were falsely executed by traitors for remaining loyal to my father at a time when most men subjected their loyalty to expediency.' Holland's father, Lord Robert Holland, had been executed by followers of the Despenser family when they had usurped the royal authority. Joan's father, the Earl of Kent, had been executed for plotting to rescue King Edward the second from Berkeley Castle, where he had been imprisoned after the Conquest by his own queen and her lover, the usurper Roger Mortimer.

'But Joan is my ward, and cannot be married without my permission. I judged Sir William a better match for my cousin. One day he will be Earl of Salisbury, as his father was before him . . .'

'Sir William is not the same man his father was,' asserted Holland, who had been a good friend of William Montague the elder. 'More to the point, she does not love him . . .'

The king thumped his fist against the table in a sudden burst of rage. 'Who she loves is irrelevant! She is a ward of her king, to be dealt with as I choose! And I chose for her to marry Sir William!'

Holland was shaken by the king's sudden anger, but refused to be cowed. 'I love her,' he said simply. 'It is more than I can bear to remain here in Villeneuve, and to see Montague flaunt her as his wife each day . . .'

The king made a visible effort to control himself. 'I know, and I understand. I pity you, Sir Thomas.'

'I do not ask for your pity, sire. All I ask is that I be allowed to return to England . . .'

'Then go!' The king gestured towards the door with an out-flung arm.

Holland hesitated, reluctant to leave with such bad feeling between himself and his monarch. Perhaps on another day he would have a chance to regain his king's favour . . .

On his way out of the mansion he encountered Sir Hugh Despenser, a descendant of the Despensers who had caused so much trouble in the old king's reign. Holland and Despenser had fought together at the battle of Sluys – where Holland had lost his left eye – at the siege of Tournai, and alongside the prince at Crécy, but there was no camaraderie between the two. A burly man in early middle age, Despenser was Montague's brother-in-law, and had backed Montague against Holland from the outset of their quarrel. Walking past with his head bowed in thought, Holland pretended he had not seen Despenser, but the other called out to him.

'You seem glum, Sir Thomas. What's the matter? Have you lost something?'

Holland glanced up with a grimace.

Despenser grinned. 'A wife, perchance?'

Holland turned away, determined not to rise to the bait.

'I'm surprised Sir William and you cannot come to some kind of arrangement,' jeered Despenser. 'Sir William could have her during the week, and you could have her at weekends . . .'

Holland lunged at Despenser, catching him by the throat and driving him back against the wall, but in the same instant Despenser drew his dagger from his belt and held the point against Holland's breast, directly over his heart. Grinning, he shook his head chidingly. Holland glared down at the blade and then released him, backing away quickly.

'Only a churl would strike at an unarmed man, Sir Hugh.'

Despenser did not reply. Still grinning, he replaced his dagger in its sheath and strolled off nonchalantly.

Behind the visor of his steel bascinet, Sir Geoffroi de Chargny's face was coursing with sweat. It was a warm day for February, even on the island of Rhodes, but mild for all that. Despite his full suit of armour, a quilted gambeson beneath his habergeon of chain-mail, he would not have sweated had he been inactive. But de Chargny did not don his armour to remain inactive.

He swung his broadsword once more at his opponent, who caught the stroke on his heater-shaped shield, before riposting with a swipe of his own. De Chargny raised his own similar shield, decorated with his coat-of-arms – three white shields on a crimson background, the same design as the one emblazoned on his jupon – and caught the heavy blow with ease. Then he aimed a thrust at his opponent's stomach and the other was too slow with his shield, barely managing to parry the blow with his broadsword. The thrust had caught him off guard.

De Chargny sensed his advantage and pressed home his attack, aiming a blow at his opponent's bascinet. The other man raised his shield, but the force of the blow was enough to force him down on to one knee. He thrust at de Chargny's midriff, but it was a thrust of desperation, and de Chargny parried it with ease. He slid the edge of his sword down the length of his opponent's blade and hooked the point under the cross-guard with a skilful, well-practised motion. His opponent was wearing articulated steel gauntlets, the same as de Chargny's, but the trick gave de Chargny enough leverage to twist his opponent's sword from his grip. The sword struck the cobbles with a dull clank. As the other man tried to hide underneath his shield de Chargny swung his sword again, striking the edge of the shield, knocking it from his opponent's arm. Then he took one sure-footed step forwards and thrust his sword at his opponent's shoulder. The point of the razor-edged blade split the links of the man's chain-mail habergeon, and the man gave a sob as the cold steel bit into his skin. He sprawled on his back on the cobbles, blood seeping through his habergeon.

De Chargny stood over him, the point of his sword levelled at the fallen man's throat. He hesitated momentarily, to rub in the fact that he had his opponent at his mercy. Then he used the point of his sword to flick back the man's visor. The face thus revealed was a young one, barely out of its mid-teens, the watery pale blue eyes blinking at the bright Mediterranean sunlight that suddenly flooded into his helmet.

De Chargny wiped the blood off the blade of his sword with an old rag and returned it to the scabbard hanging at his hip. Instead of lifting his own visor, he began to unlace the cord which fastened his bascinet to his mail coif. 'I could have killed you,' he said in calm, measured tones – the voice of a man who would never become flustered no matter how adverse the circumstance, a man who could stay cool even in the heat of battle. 'You'll have to do better than that. Your next opponent may not be as merciful as I.'

The young man nodded miserably, accepting the hand which de Chargny offered to help him back on his feet. 'Yes, Father.'

De Chargny finished unfastening his bascinet and lifted it off his head. The face he thus revealed was handsome yet cold, with a thin-lipped mouth framed by a neatly trimmed beard. An aquiline nose gave his whole face a sleek, predatory appearance, and his hooded eyes were the palest blue, full of cold intelligence, watchful, unblinking. The body beneath his armour was tall and lean without an ounce of fat. He moved with elegant, almost fastidious precision, like a bird of prey preening itself after devouring its kill.

As de Chargny and his son began to walk towards the shade of the veranda at the edge of the courtyard, his faithful squire Guilbert hurried forward to relieve them of their helmets. A younger son of a knight from de Chargny's native Burgundy, Guilbert was heavily built, with black curly hair and a tangled beard. His movements were as clumsy as his master's were graceful, but there was so much strength in his tall, powerfully muscled body that few people protested if he inadvertently bumped into them. Guilbert would never rise to the knighthood even if he had been able to afford the financial obligations which the honour imposed. He lacked refinement, money and intelligence; and while very few knights had all three qualities, even fewer had none. But Guilbert did not aspire to a knighthood. He was quite content to serve his master with slavish devotion, while de Chargny in return valued his loyalty and unquestioning obedience.

A wooden table and two benches were set on the veranda, and it was from there, in the shade, that the Dauphin of Vienne, Humbert II, had watched the combat. He applauded as they approached. He was roughly the same age as de Chargny. Normally inclining towards plumpness, a recent savage bout of dysentery had left his sallow skin hanging loosely from his bones.

'Well fought, Sir Geoffroi. And you too, boy,' he added, with a nod in the direction of de Chargny's son. He gestured to where a flagon of diluted wine stood on the table. 'Sit down. Drink. You must be parched.'

De Chargny acknowledged Humbert's praise with a curt nod. It was thanks to Humbert that de Chargny and his son now found themselves on this benighted rock in the eastern Mediterranean. The Order of the Knights of the Hospital of Saint John had made it their home more than half a century earlier after the fall of Acre drove the Crusaders from the Holy Land.

They sat in the courtyard of a fine villa in the old quarter of the town of Rhodes. A short distance down the street was the Grand Harbour, and only eight miles to the north – visible from the town walls on a clear day such as this – was the coast of Anatolia, home of the Turkish pirates who preyed on Christian maritime trade. Foremost of the ports used by these corsairs had been Smyrna, until it fell in a joint attack by the Hospitallers, the Venetians, the Cypriots and the Papacy two and a half years earlier. News of this victory against the infidel Turks had quickly spread throughout Christendom, and had so filled Humbert with crusading ardour that he – with the help of a few flagons of fine Burgundy wine – persuaded Pope Clement to appoint him 'Captain of the Holy Apostolic See and Leader of the Whole Army of Christians Against the Turks'. The title was far more impressive than the desultory crusade that followed.

De Chargny had taken the cross as a young man, swearing that at some point in his life he would wield his sword against the infidels; nevertheless, he had been reluctant to join Humbert's ill-planned, ill-financed campaign. The two of them had known one another socially for several years, and they shared a fascination with chivalric codes and values. When Humbert founded the secular Order of Saint Katherine, it had been a feather in his cap when he persuaded de Chargny – widely acknowledged as one of the world's leading experts on all things chivalrous – to join. The Order of Saint Katherine had failed to prove itself, and de Chargny privately admitted to his friends that Humbert had got him drunk before persuading him to join.

Given this experience, de Chargny had kicked himself for not knowing better than to accept Humbert's offer of a drink or two in May 1345. He had awoken the following morning with a thick head, while Humbert had his promise that he would accompany him on a crusade to consolidate the foot-hold gained in Anatolia by the capture of Smyrna.

De Chargny's doubts about Humbert's tactical and strategic prowess had proved well-founded. They had failed to capture the island of Chios, and once their substantial army had landed in Anatolia, it soon suffered from lack of provisions and disease. They found themselves unable to get to grips with the enemy, and after a few desultory sorties Humbert, by now ravaged with dysentery, had decided to call it a day, returning to the island of Rhodes to spend the winter there; for as even de Chargny acknowledged – without a trace of irony – there was a season for hunting infidels, as surely as there were for hunting and hawking. But Humbert's experiences in Anatolia had dampened his enthusiasm for fighting, and despite an earlier vow to remain in the East for three years, he had written to the Pope requesting permission to end his crusade and return to France. Pope Clement – himself keen on crusading – had sighed, shaking his head wryly, and granted his permission.

Guilbert helped de Chargny's son remove his habergeon, and it was then that Humbert noticed the bloody rent in the fabric of his gambeson. 'But . . . you're wounded!' he protested.

The youth's father made a dismissive gesture. 'A trifle. He must learn not to shrink from the sight of blood – least of all his own – if he is ever to show any prowess as a knight.'

Humbert was unconvinced. 'Were you not using blunted weapons?'

De Chargny turned his unblinking eyes on the Dauphin of Vienne. 'I fight to train for war, not for sport,' he said coldly. 'He will learn nothing now if it is not reinforced with the same fear he will experience when he meets an enemy armed with an unblunted blade for the first time.'

As de Chargny's son left the veranda to have the wound in his shoulder seen to, a servant entered and bowed low both to Humbert and de Chargny. 'Sir Ivo la Zouche is here to see you, Messieurs.'

La Zouche had not waited in the hallway but followed the servant into the courtyard almost immediately. An English knight, dressed in simple pale blue robes, his cloak was emblazoned with the eight-pointed star of the Knights of the Hospital of Saint John. In his right hand he waved a piece of parchment, its edges adorned with a broken wax seal. 'There's a ship just in from Venice, bearing news from the west,' he explained with a grin. 'You owe me fifteen marks, Sir Geoffroi.'

De Chargny was bewildered. 'How so?'

'Those unconfirmed rumours of a great battle in which the English massacred the French, which you wagered could not be true? They've just been confirmed. My brother Roger has written to me – he was there himself.'

De Chargny was stunned.

'The King of Bohemia and the Duke of Lorraine were both killed,' said la Zouche, reading from his letter. 'So were the Counts of Flanders, Alençon, Auxerre, Blois, Vaudémont, Harcourt, Grandpré, the Seigneur de Briquebec . . .'

'All dead?' de Chargny lamented softly. Men with whom he had hunted, feasted, jousted, fought . . . killed by the *English*? 'I cannot believe it.'

'It's all in here.' La Zouche tapped the letter. 'My brother would not deceive me . . .'

'Yet he might seek to deceive me,' hissed de Chargny.

La Zouche reached for the hilt of his sword. 'Are you accusing my brother of deceit?' he demanded.

Humbert leapt to his feet and interposed himself between the two men. 'Friends, please, remember your place! I did not come to the East to see Christian fight Christian. I am sorry, Sir Geoffroi, but I am inclined to believe Sir Ivo's cousin. I fear some terrible calamity has overtaken the subjects of King Philip.'

De Chargny sat down heavily on one of the benches, resting his elbows on the table and rubbing his temples as if some headache ailed him. When he left France there had been a truce between the English and French kings, and while King Edward had been talking of war, de Chargny had dismissed it as nothing more than talk. If he had thought for a moment that the English would be successful in launching a campaign deep into the heart of France, he would never have left. 'How came the flower of French chivalry to be laid low by a handful of barbarians from across the sea?' he asked.

It was a rhetorical question, but la Zouche answered it anyway. 'With bows.'

'Hardly a knightly weapon,' sneered de Chargny.

'It wasn't the knights who used them. It was the yeomen.'

'You mean to tell me that my kinsmen in France were vanquished by a mere rabble of peasants?' he demanded incredulously.

La Zouche shrugged. 'It seems one English yeoman is worth ten French knights.'

De Chargny stood, and then slowly and deliberately tugged off one of his steel gauntlets, flinging it in la Zouche's face. La Zouche staggered under the weight of the blow, clapping a hand to his nose as blood gushed from his nostrils.

'Sir Geoffroi! I must protest!' exclaimed Humbert.

'The nobility of France is a brotherhood of chivalry,' said de Chargny. 'Impugn the honour of one, and you impugn the honour of us all. Impugn the honour of us all, and it is up to each one of us to do all within our power to wipe out the stain.'

'End this quarrel, I beg you!' said Humbert. 'I'm certain Sir Ivo will retract his thoughtless remark, if you will apologise for the blow . . .'

'I'll do no such thing!' growled la Zouche. 'That damned vulture struck me!'

'The insult has been made, the gauntlet thrown,' de Chargny replied calmly. 'This is an affair of honour that can only be settled in the traditional way.'

'Then choose the time, the place and the weapon,' said la Zouche.

'The weapons: our swords,' said de Chargny. 'The place and the time: here and now.'

La Zouche turned pale. 'So soon?'

'My sense of honour demands swift retribution for your insults. If you have no stomach for the fight, Sir Ivo, all you need do is retract your remark and apologise.'

La Zouche clapped his hand to the hilt of his sword. 'Nay – let us end this quarrel swiftly.'

'But this is sheer folly!' protested Humbert. 'Sir Ivo has no armour . . .'

'I shall remove mine,' de Chargny responded, and with Guilbert's help he pulled his habergeon up over his head.

'You would fight unarmoured, with unblunted weapons?' Humbert demanded incredulously. 'Fie! One of you will be slain.'

De Chargny turned his pale eyes on Humbert. 'Aye, that is the idea. A duel *à outrance*: to the death.' He stripped off his armour until he was clad only in his hose and quilted gambeson, Guilbert helping him to buckle his sword-belt back around his waist.

The two men strode out into the centre of the courtyard and drew their swords, turning to face one another, measuring out two sword's lengths between them. La Zouche nodded curtly to indicate that he was ready, and both of them bowed.

Then la Zouche lunged forward, swinging the blade of his broadsword in a wide arc aimed at de Chargny's head. De Chargny brought up his sword, parrying the blow with such sudden and unexpected force that la Zouche was driven back, stumbling. De Chargny followed through swiftly, aiming a stroke at la Zouche's side which the Englishman was hard-pressed to parry, wielding his sword at an awkward angle which barely deflected the blade.

A seasoned campaigner, la Zouche fought with both strength and skill, but he was clearly outclassed by the Frenchman. De Chargny's every movement was swift and economical, graceful and yet with the full strength of his limbs behind each blow. La Zouche was slowly forced back until he lost his footing on the cobbles and slipped. He sprawled on his back, his broadsword flying from his grip to fall several feet from his hand. He reached for it desperately, but de Chargny was swifter, placing one booted foot roughly on la Zouche's outstretched wrist, pinning his arm to the cobbles. La Zouche grunted in pain.

'I yield,' he told de Chargny, who stood over him with the point of his sword levelled at his throat. 'You are the victor. My arms and armour are forfeit.'

'I don't need them,' said de Chargny, and thrust his sword-point into la Zouche's throat. Blood gouted on to the pale cobbles.

De Chargny wiped the blood from his blade and walked with his usual measured tread back to where Humbert and Guilbert stood, the former staring at him in horror, the latter stone-faced. De Chargny slotted his sword back into its scabbard. 'Arrange our passage on the next ship to Venice or Marseilles,' he told Guilbert. 'We have a great many deaths to avenge.'

# CHAPTER TWO

'HOW MUCH LONGER do we get stuck with the night watch, serjeant?' asked John Conyers.

'End of the month, lad,' Preston told him. 'You know that. One month on, one month off.'

'What day is it?' Conyers asked his companions.

'Tuesday,' Brewster replied, talking around the stalk of marsh reed he habitually chewed in the corner of his mouth.

'The Feast of Saint Matthias,' added Inglewood.

It was a bright morning in the middle of May, eight and a half months since the siege of Calais had begun, and they still seemed no nearer taking the town. At first the slow tedium of life in camp had dragged by, but now they had been there so long it was difficult to remember another way of life. For many of them, the life of a peasant farmer trying to scrape a living from the soil had been far inferior to their current status as archers. Food was plentiful as long as the supply ships got through, and occasionally they were sent on foraging expeditions into the Calaisian hinterland.

The sun shone in an azure sky dotted with tufts of cloud. Preston and his men were off duty, roasting a haunch of beef over a camp-fire. Conyers turned the handle of the makeshift spit as Brewster caught the dripping fat with a ladle and spooned it back on top with loving care. Kemp, who had been lounging on his back on the sand with his 'kettle' helmet tipped forward over his eyes, sat up sharply, pushing the helmet back on to his head. 'What did you say?'

'It's the Feast of Saint Matthias,' replied Inglewood. 'Since when did you ever care about holy days?'

'I don't,' said Kemp. 'It's just that means I've been in the army over twelve months now.' Was it really only twelve months since he had been impressed into the king's army? So much had happened since then it seemed more like a lifetime. 'I thought when the end drew near I'd be counting the days, not letting them fly past without being aware of them.'

Preston looked up from where he was honing the blade of his sword with a whetstone. 'End of what, lad?' he asked.

Kemp glanced at him in surprise. 'End of my term of service, serjeant.' He pushed himself to his feet, stretching stiff and aching limbs. 'I've done my twelve months. That was the deal. Twelve months in the king's army, and then I get my pardon.'

'You sit down, lad,' Preston told him sternly. 'Your term of service ends when my lord of Warwick says it does.'

Elias Jarrom was also paying attention now. He too had enlisted for twelve months in return for a pardon. 'God's bones, you're pulling our legs, aren't you, serjeant?'

Preston shook his head. 'You're to stay in the army for as long as the king stays on this side of the sea.'

'And how much longer will that be?' Jarrom demanded.

Preston jerked his thumb over his shoulder, towards the Valois banner fluttering above the battlements of Calais. 'Until them fleur-de-lyses are replaced with the arms of Saint George.'

'Lord Christ! That could take for ever!' exclaimed Jarrom. He hawked noisily and spat on the ground at his feet. 'To hell with that. What's to stop me from jumping on the next ship bound for Sandwich?'

'Nothing at all,' admitted Preston. 'Of course, you'll become an outlaw again when you get back to England. You won't see a pardon before the king's done with you.'

'And how much longer until we do see a pardon, if we stay?' Kemp asked, sharing Jarrom's feeling of betrayal. He had been a villein before he was recruited in the king's service, and his enmity with the lord of his manor, Sir John Beaumont, meant that he did not relish the idea of returning to his former life of servitude. If he resided in a borough town for a year and a day he would be granted freeman status, but the thought that once he was finished in the army he would have to spend another year away before he could return to his village as a free man chafed him sorely. 'Another twelve months waiting in this pestilential marsh, with nothing better to do than watch the moon rise and fall each night?'

'I wouldn't say that,' Preston replied evenly, and after a moment's hesitation he put down the sword and whetstone. 'They say Valois has left Amiens with a fresh army.'

The archers around him leapt to their feet and stared at him, except for Brewster, who continued to baste the meat as calmly as if Preston had been commenting on the weather, and Oakley, who was getting too old to start leaping about at the least provocation.

'How large?' asked Conyers.

'Large enough, by all accounts,' said Preston. 'His Majesty is writing to Henry of Derby, asking him to raise an army of reinforcement in England.'

'And how long will that take?' demanded Jarrom.

Preston shrugged. 'Not long, if I know his lordship. Derby's not one for wasting time when a battle's in the offing.'

'And how soon until Valois gets here?' asked Kemp.

Once again Preston hesitated before replying. 'They say he could be here by Monday,' he admitted.

Just six days away.

The next few days saw a flurry of activity in and around the English lines before Calais. When building the camp, the king had realised that the advent of a relieving army would be a far greater threat than any sally the town's garrison could muster, and had made sure that the camp's defences against attack from such an army were even more extensive than the ring of earthworks and palisades that surrounded the town walls to the landward sides. Even so, he decided that the defences must be strengthened and improved. Everyone was put to work in one way or another, building new palisades and look-out towers, digging fresh trenches, throwing up new ramparts, all the way around the camp's perimeter. Siege engines that had been facing the town walls were now moved to protect the roads. Reveille was sounded an hour earlier, and every soldier in the camp started the day with an hour of drill before being allowed to grab a breakfast of bread and ale. When Valois arrived with his army, it was imperative the English be ready for him.

Patrols of mounted archers set out in the direction of Amiens each day, and each night they returned to report that there was still no sign of Valois. The men stationed in the watch towers were changed constantly so that they would not grow bored with their duty and fall asleep.

Monday finally arrived.

There was no sign of Valois or his army.

The next day brought fresh reports – Valois had reached Arras, and could be expected by the following Monday. Far from relieving the tension, this news dragged it out to the point where, for the vast majority of the men in the English camp, it was unbearable. When the day finally came, the sounding of reveille woke few men – most of them had been unable to sleep the night before anyway. Red-eyed and weary, Preston's platoon reported for drill only to be instructed to take up position by the Nieullay Bridge.

Two miles to the west of Calais, the broad, sluggish waters of the River Hem flowed through the marshes and across the beach into the sea, protecting the western approaches. The road from Calais south-west to Boulogne ran along a causeway between the marshes and the beach. Where the causeway crossed the river at the tiny hamlet of Nieullay, an old stone bridge had been built, the only bridge across the Hem for several miles. Since the French were expected to approach from the south-west, a considerable amount of effort had been put into reinforcing the bridge, where perhaps a few men could hold off an army.

Sir John Chandos commanded the bridge and it was to him that Preston reported.

'You're Holland's men?' Chandos demanded curtly. He was a huge, heavily built man whose rough-hewn, square-jawed face gave him a brutal look which belied the keen and cultured mind that lay behind it.

Preston nodded. 'Aye, Sir John.'

'You can take a turn up in the tower today,' said Chandos, pointing beyond the bridge and a little to the south of it where a tall wooden watch-tower had been built. 'I hope you and your men have sharp eyes.'

A troop of men-at-arms were digging a network of trenches around the base of the tower. Preston and his men marched across the bridge and climbed up the ladder to the tower's top floor. The Heights of Sangatte, a line of escarpments, rose up about two miles to the south-west, ending at Cap Gris-Nez where they met the sea.

Kemp remembered the day he first landed in France, when he had been assigned to picket duty on the dunes overlooking the beach at Saint-Vaast-la-Hougue, looking out for the French. It seemed like a thousand years ago, yet at the same time he could remember every detail of that day – the first time he had killed a man – as clearly as if it were yesterday. Looking back, it was not himself he remembered standing on that dune but another Martin Kemp, younger, more naïve.

'What do we do if we see Valois' army?' asked Tate.

'Run for our lives,' Conyers replied jocularly.

'We could hold them off,' suggested Inglewood.

'What, just the twelve of us?' sneered Jarrom.

'On the bridge, I mean. Like Horatio and his friends.'

'Who in Christ's name is Horatio?'

'He was a warrior in the olden days,' explained Inglewood. 'I read about him in a book.'

'Oh, *books*.' Jarrom sniffed.

'He's a regular fund of useless information, is this one,' said Conyers, jerking a thumb at Inglewood.

'There were just three of them, Horatio and two friends, and they held a bridge against an entire army,' Inglewood said enthusiastically. 'Three men could hold off an army until Judgement Day, if they were guarding a bridge or a pass or something like that.'

'Didn't they have any bows?' asked Tate.

'Who?'

'The men who were trying to get across the bridge. They could have shot the three men guarding the bridge.'

Inglewood frowned. He hadn't thought of that.

'Maybe they thought that would be unchivalrous,' suggested Brewster, chewing his customary marsh-reed as he gazed out across the dunes.

'Come again?' scoffed Jarrom.

'You know, like a passage-at-arms,' said Brewster. 'Like at a tournament, where a knight vows to hold some narrow place – such as a bridge, or a pass – against any challengers.'

'Why?' asked Jarrom.

Brewster shrugged. 'For honour, I suppose.'

Jarrom's reply, as usual, was to hawk noisily and spit over the parapet of the tower.

Tate straightened suddenly. 'Look!'

Such was the urgency in his voice that immediately everyone strained to peer down the road to the south-west in search of Valois' army approaching. 'I don't see owt,' grumbled Jarrom.

'Not there,' said Tate, and pointed to the north, out to sea. '*There.*'

They all turned.

'A sail,' observed Inglewood.

'Three sails,' corrected Conyers.

'A dozen . . . no, wait, dozens . . . *hundreds* of sails,' said Kemp.

As they watched, hundreds of sails indeed began to emerge through the early morning haze, the red and white striped sails of cogs and carracks, with wooden turrets built fore and aft, the cross of Saint George flying from the mastheads.

Henry of Derby, Earl of Lancaster and Leicester, had arrived with reinforcements.

'You're thinking of him, aren't you, my lady?'

Joan, Lady Montague, turned her face away from the thatched rooftops of Villeneuve-la-Hardie visible through the window of her chamber in her husband's mansion and smiled at her maid's impertinence. After her marriage to Sir William Montague she had been taken away from her friends at court, and now Maud Lacy was the only person she felt she could confide in.

Joan sat in the window seat, the embroidery on her lap forgotten. She was not yet twenty, slender and petite, with long blonde hair, eyes of cornflower blue, and sensuous lips that contrasted sharply with her lily-white complexion. 'Who?' she asked.

Changing the sheets on the bed, Maud blushed. Almost the same age as her mistress, she was a small woman with bright green eyes and dark, curly hair. 'You know very well who I mean.'

'Sir Thomas? Why should I care for him? It is clear he no longer cares for me. Why else should he have left the moment we arrived here before Calais?'

From the smile on Maud's lips it was clear she was not fooled by Joan's feigned indifference. 'Has it not occurred to you that the thought of seeing you married to another man might have driven him away?'

It had, but Joan had not dared to believe it. 'William is my husband now.'

'But not the one you chose,' Maud continued. 'There are plenty of women at court who take lovers outside the marital bed.'

‘I could not betray my husband.’

‘But if your marriage to Sir Thomas is valid, then surely he must be your true husband, not Sir William.’

Before Joan could reply, the door burst open and her mother barged in.

At twice her daughter’s age, the Dowager Countess of Kent remained handsome, full-figured without inclining to plumpness, with a mane of ash-blonde hair fading to white. Only closer inspection revealed the crows’ feet at the corners of her eyes, her wide mouth hard and uncompromising. The death of her husband and the scandal of her daughter’s clandestine marriage to Holland had soured her, and that sourness was taking its toll on her beauty.

She held up a particoloured gown of red and white silk with a large wine-stain down the front of it. ‘Look at this!’ she protested angrily. ‘It’s ruined!’

‘Can’t you have it laundered?’ asked Joan.

‘It has already been washed once!’ said the countess. ‘Damn your cousin the king for dragging us halfway across the world to this pestilential marsh! The laundresses in this pox-ridden town are nothing more than camp-followers, fit only to wash the bloodstains from common archers’ lousy tunics. And I’ll wager there isn’t a decent dressmaker on this side of the sea. Now I shall have to send to London for a replacement, and that will cost us a fortune!’

‘I could make you a new one, my lady,’ offered Maud. ‘There is silk to be had in the market on Fridays, and I can . . .’

‘Don’t be stupid, girl,’ interrupted the countess. ‘You’re as clumsy with a needle and thread as you are with a hairbrush. I should look an absolute fright in anything sewn by you . . .’

She broke off at the sound of a rising hubbub in the streets outside. ‘What in God’s name is that awful row?’ Maud started towards the window but the countess pushed past her, knocking her back on to her seat.

The street below was full of men and women running in the direction of the beach. She singled out a young page and hailed him. ‘You! Boy! What’s all the fuss about?’

The page slowed, bowing awkwardly when he recognised the countess. ‘There’s a fleet approaching, my lady!’ he said. ‘They say the banner of my lord of Derby has been seen on the flagship. He has come from England with fresh knights and men to aid us.’

She turned away from the window. Both Joan and Maud had risen to their feet with excitement. 'Leave us, Maud,' the countess said quietly. 'And no listening at the door!'

For Maud it was clearly the last straw. 'I would never do such a thing, my lady!' she protested.

The countess strode across the room and slapped her hard on the cheek. Joan flinched in sympathy. The stinging blow left a crimson welt. 'How many times must I tell you not to answer back? Get out!'

Bowing her head to hide the tears welling in her eyes, Maud curtseyed to both the countess and Joan and ran from the room. The countess closed the door behind her and turned to her daughter. 'Useless, idle girl! You should dismiss her, dear, and employ someone else.'

Joan trembled with rage. 'How dare you strike her, Mother? I have told you before: Maud is *my* maid, employed with my husband's money. She's a servant, not a villein. You should treat her with more respect. She's of good stock, too . . .'

'Good stock for a serving wench, perhaps,' sneered the countess. 'Better stock than Thomas Holland, certainly. I'm warning you, Joan: if Holland is with Henry of Derby, you are not to see him. You are not to speak to him, you are not even to acknowledge his presence . . .'

It was an irony that never ceased to fill Joan with dismay. She was one of the most high-born people in the land, and yet ever since the death of her father she had been forced to do other people's bidding; first her mother's, then Sir William's – she could not bring herself to think of him as her husband, for all that they lived as man and wife – and now both of them together. Only Sir Thomas had been different, treating her not with the lovesick adoration of a moonstruck squire, but with the respect any man would give to an equal, despite the disparity in their ages. 'I shall see whom I like!' she protested.

'Not while I still draw breath!' the countess told her sharply. 'You're not so grown up that I can't take a rod to your impertinent back.'

Joan drew herself up to her full height, fire in her eyes. 'Just you try it!' she hissed.

'Anyway, you spend far too much time with that girl.'

Joan's face twisted. 'And with whom else should I spend time, in this God-forsaken marshland? The common archers and their strumpets, perhaps?'

'You should spend more time with ladies of your own class,' insisted the countess. 'You might even think about spending more time with your husband.'

'That boor? I hate him!'

'Ungrateful child. Do you have any idea how much time I spent with the king, persuading him that Sir William would be a fitting bridegroom for his cousin?'

'You should have saved yourself the trouble,' said Joan. 'Sir Thomas is my husband . . .'

Crimson with rage, the countess raised her hand to strike her daughter, but Joan caught her by the wrist before the blow could land. Breathing hard, the countess's eyes brimmed with anger and despair, tinged with fear as she realised she could no longer control her daughter.

There was a knock at the door.

'Who is it?' asked Joan, releasing her grip on her mother's wrist.

'I, your husband,' Sir William Montague's voice replied.

'One moment!' The countess patted her hair back into place. 'Enter.'

Montague came into the chamber and bowed low. He too was in his late teens, his weak chin covered by a stubbly and patchy excuse for a beard. 'Is everything well? I thought I heard raised voices . . . ?'

The countess gestured to the window. 'Churls shouting in the street, nothing more,' she said smoothly.

'My lord of Derby is arrived from England with reinforcements,' Montague explained. 'His Majesty is going down to the beach to greet him. I thought it would be fitting for us to accompany him . . .'

The countess nodded. 'You are right, of course, William. Let us change into clothes more suited for such an occasion, and go to greet Henry.'

The beach was already crowded by the time the dowager countess, her daughter and son-in-law reached it. It seemed as if all the soldiers in Villeneuve not otherwise engaged had come down to witness the meeting between King Edward and his cousin, Henry of Derby, Earl of Lancaster. The men laughed and cheered, making it a joyous occasion: Derby's reinforcements would improve the odds when Valois finally arrived with his army.

The countess, Montague and Joan made their way on horseback through the crowds without difficulty. Even those who did not know them recognised them as nobility by their dress. Further down the beach, King Edward had dismounted and waited with Queen Philippa and two of his sons: Edward of Woodstock, Prince of Wales, and the seven-year-old John of Gaunt. They stood with the Earl of Northampton, Sir John Chandos and a few other noblemen close to where the flagship, a massive cog of three hundred tonnes, had nudged its prow against the sandy shore. The king employed a hand-picked bodyguard of archers from Cheshire, but they were not in evidence today: Edward was well loved, and there were few men on the beach who would not willingly have laid down their lives for him.

A gangplank was lowered from the cog's deck into the spume, and two seamen hurried down to hold it steady at the bottom. Then the earl himself stepped down, flanked by several knights, all dressed in hose, particoloured cote-hardies and mantles. Henry of Derby was a tall, fair-haired man in his middle years whose bluff, soldierly manner disguised a pious and cultured mind. He waded through the surf and up on to the beach, bending down on one knee before the king and kissing his signet ring. The king motioned for him to rise, and the two embraced warmly.

'I thank God for bringing you to me so swiftly, cousin,' said the king. 'And with many men, unless you have brought me a fleet of empty ships?' he added, with a smile.

'The best men left in your realm of England, your Majesty,' asserted Derby. 'And supplies, horses, fodder, and arrows for your archers.'

'And Sir Thomas Holland,' added the king, turning to one of the knights who flanked Derby.

Holland wore his customary robes of azure and white, his broadsword hanging in an ivory-covered scabbard at his left hip. He likewise knelt before his king, kissing his ring. 'Sire.'

'And Sir Hugh.' The king turned to Sir Hugh Despenser, who had returned to England early in the new year. Like Holland,

Despenser's clothes reflected only a passing interest in fashion. Neither came from the best of families, but the king had always preferred soldiers to courtiers.

As the men began to unload the ships, the king walked back up the beach, Derby and the Prince of Wales alongside him, Despenser and Holland just behind. 'It is good to see you, Henry,' said the king. 'At times it seemed that hardly a day could pass without news of another victory from Gascony.'

Derby inclined his head in acknowledgement. 'What few skirmishes I fought on your behalf pale into insignificance compared to your own victory at the field of Crécy, sir. I hear his Royal Highness acquitted himself most nobly at the battle,' he added, gesturing to the Prince of Wales.

'Aye, he won his spurs right enough,' agreed the king. 'Never was a father more proud of his eldest son than I was of mine that day.'

'Has Sir Walter arrived yet, your Majesty?' Derby had last seen Sir Walter Mauny many months ago in Gascony, although he knew that Mauny had likewise been summoned to join the king's camp before Calais.

The king's face grew dark. 'No. He was captured and imprisoned by the French in Paris while travelling overland, despite having a warrant of safe conduct from Valois himself.'

'I have written to London, ordering that my prisoner, the Count of Tancarville, be put in close custody at Wallingford Castle by way of retaliation,' the prince added.

Derby nodded approvingly, angered by this latest evidence of French perfidy. 'And Valois himself? What news of his army?'

The king gestured helplessly. 'Each hour seems to bring fresh reports, all of them conflicting. One day he is at Amiens, the day after at Abbeville, and the following day at Arras.'

Holland smiled thinly. 'Such reports cannot be true, unless the sluggard Valois has learned how to fly – as swiftly as he does from the field of battle.'

They all laughed at that. Then Despenser spoke: 'Allow me to take two platoons of mounted archers, sire,' he offered. 'I shall have positive news of the usurper before the Feast of Saint Clothilda.'

The king nodded his assent. 'Very well, Sir Hugh. But tarry until the morrow, I pray you. Life before these walls grows tedious, and I intend that I should entertain you all tonight in royal style. And see, here is our cousin Joan, with my lady of Kent and Sir William.'

The countess, Joan and Montague all dismounted to greet the king. If Joan saw Holland standing behind Derby and Despenser, she gave no indication of it. Holland likewise failed to glance in Joan's direction, although the countess was not fooled, not doubting for a moment that the upstart knight still lusted after her daughter; aye, and her daughter's riches as sister to the young Earl of Kent. The countess herself looked at Holland and then averted her gaze in a deliberate snub.

After many formalities, the king made his way back to Villeneuve with the queen and the two princes, and Derby and Holland. He insisted that his cousin Joan accompany them.

The countess nudged her son-in-law. 'Go with her, you fool,' she hissed. 'Keep her away from Holland.'

'Will you not also come?' asked Montague.

She shook her head. 'Give my apologies to his Majesty. This ride has fatigued me, and I fear the sun may ruin my complexion.' The truth was that the quarrel with her daughter had drained her, emotionally at least, and the strain of trying to maintain her smile in public was proving wearying. She took her leave of Montague and returned to her son's mansion. She handed the bridle of her jennet to a squire and walked upstairs, unfastening her girdle as she entered her bedchamber.

'Good afternoon.' Sir Hugh Despenser was lounging on the bed, his sand-covered boots dirtying the coverlet.

The countess froze with a gasp in the act of removing her gown. 'What the devil are you doing in here, you rogue?' she demanded, her heart pounding.

'Why, waiting to pay my respects to you, my lady,' he responded easily.

'How dare you sneak unannounced into my bedchamber! Get out!'

Despenser did not move, grinning self-confidently. 'Are you not pleased to see your old lover? It was unmannerly of you to snub me so at the beach.'

'It was Holland I snubbed, as you damned well know.'

'I sometimes think you hate Sir Thomas more than you love me,' observed Despenser, still smiling.

'I never claimed to love you.'

He pushed himself off the bed and closed the door before replying, suddenly clasping her around the waist. 'But you keep coming back, don't you?'

She made a pretence of struggling. 'May I remind you it was you who came to me? Unhand me, you coarse dog! You forget yourself.'

He laughed, pulling her closer. 'My poor, sweet countess. How difficult it must be for a woman as proud and haughty as you, to find herself attracted to a man whose family is as disreputable as mine. Is that why you hate Sir Thomas, I wonder? Perhaps it is him you love, and you envy the attention he paid your daughter.'

She slapped him, though she was too close to get a good enough swing to hurt him. 'Holland was never good enough for my daughter, just as you are not fit to touch me.'

'Your past actions belie your words, my lady.'

'That was in the past when I was young and foolish. I do not want my daughter to make the same mistakes I did. Let go of me. You forget you are married; aye, to my own son-in-law's sister.'

'That milksop? Aye, I married her, but only that I might be nearer you.'

He pulled her against him, looping one arm around her waist and kissing her roughly. When he placed a hand on one of her breasts she hit him so hard that the faintest trickle of blood appeared at the corner of his mouth. He seized her arm and threw her face-down across the bed. Lifting the hem of his tunic and tugging at the strings that fastened his breech cloth, he wrenched up the hem of her skirts so that they gathered around her waist. She sobbed as he thrust himself into her from behind, and he reached underneath her to maul her breasts. He used her roughly, with no thought for her pleasure, yet he knew from experience that the very violence of his passion excited her. She was so very different from his own wife who recoiled at his very touch; and yet that too gave him a kind of pleasure.

The moment of climax came swiftly for both of them, and he stayed slumped over her, panting for breath. 'Bastard,' she whispered.

He chuckled. 'Why must you insist on pretending to hate me? I was never fooled, as well you know.'

'I have no need of pretence,' she sneered.

'I think it is yourself you hate, for loving such as me.' He stood up and began to rearrange his clothing.

'Now you have had your pleasure of me, you must return the favour.'

He laughed. 'Well, what is it you want, you hellspite?'

She hesitated before answering. 'I want you to destroy Sir Thomas Holland.'

He stared at her in astounded admiration. 'Destroy Holland? Why, you . . . !' He broke off. 'What do you take me for, a hired murderer? I should hang for such a deed. Although perhaps if I engineered a quarrel, and challenged him to a duel . . .' He mused, then shook his head. 'No. I think not.'

'You fear him!'

'Aye. What wise man would not?'

She shrugged. 'It matters not. I did not say kill him, I said destroy him. Ever since he captured the Count of Eu at Caen, his worth in the king's eyes has waxed daily. Now his Majesty seems to value Holland more than he does my son-in-law, when William is heir to the County of Salisbury and Holland is no more than a younger son of the traitorous Lord Holland.'

Despenser laughed. 'You wonder at it? Sir Thomas is a better man than my worthless brother-in-law will ever be.'

'I want him disgraced!' snarled the countess. 'I never want to suffer the sight of his upstart face at court again. Send him skulking back to his eldest brother's Lancashire manor with his tail between his legs, so humiliated he will never think to pester my daughter again.'

'What you ask is no small thing,' he said, rubbing his jaw thoughtfully. 'Why should I do this for you?'

'Because you love me?' she suggested.

'No,' he decided at last. 'I'll do it, aye, but not because I love you, nor because I've any great enmity for Sir Thomas, for in truth I care little for the man. But perhaps it will be amusing to help you in this deed. How do you intend to achieve his humiliation? As you say, his worth increases daily in the eyes of the king.'

The countess gestured dismissively. 'The higher a man rises, the further he has to fall, for fall he surely must. His very lust for Joan shall be the snare wherein we'll trap him.'

With the arrival of Derby's reinforcements before Calais, fears of Valois' army melted away like snow in the springtime. The seasoned campaigners constantly reminded everyone to remain vigilant, but even they felt relief that Valois had been beaten in the race to raise more troops. Despenser took his two platoons of mounted archers and searched the Pas de Calais for Valois' army, but failed to find it, returning with nothing more than further conflicting reports from the Frenchmen his troops had tortured. Fear of Valois had been replaced by contempt: once again the French usurper was proving sluggish in marching to battle.

Derby's troops, meanwhile, were assigned to the defences along the River Hem. Preston's platoon withdrew from the watch-tower and returned to its duties in the lines before Calais, where Holland's banner was now added to those fluttering over the trenches and palisades in the marsh.

One evening late in June, Maud Lacy approached the lines along one of the causeways leading from Villeneuve, at the start of the night watch. She surveyed the banners in the light of the many torches and braziers that illuminated the scene and, recognising the white lion rampant on a blue field powdered with *fleur-de-lys* immediately, she advanced, leading a white jennet by its halter. A number of men lounged around in the vicinity of the banner, some of them standing around braziers, others crouched in a circle playing jacks and joking amongst themselves, but all of them keeping a watchful eye on the walls of Calais, a good four hundred yards away.

Even if Maud's mistress had not explicitly told her to be discreet, she would not have liked the idea of approaching a gang of such rough-looking men. She could see only one man who was alone, sitting with his back to a wooden tun as he bound fletchings to an ash shaft. A bundle of shafts lay nearby, and some feathers spilled from a folded cloth next to them. He was a broad-shouldered young man with a scar on the left side of his head, disappearing into his hairline just above his ear. In spite of the scar – or perhaps even because of it – she had to admit to herself that she found him attractive. She approached him uncertainly, but he did not look up even when she came to within a few feet of where he sat.

She coughed to attract his attention. He stopped what he was doing with careful deliberation and looked up at her coldly. Something in those flint-blue eyes sent a shiver of excitement down her spine.

'Are you one of Sir Thomas Holland's men?' she asked.

'Aye,' he replied curtly.

'Can you pass something on to him for me?'

'Depends what it is.' Kemp picked up the arrow he had been fletching and went back to his work.

She glanced about her to make sure that no one was paying her undue attention, then tossed something into the archer's lap. She had positioned herself between Kemp and his companions, so they could not see the movement. Kemp picked up the object – a lady's velvet glove – and glanced at it briefly, before thrusting it inside his jerkin.

'Tell no one but Sir Thomas of this,' she murmured. 'I'm sure he'll reward you generously for your discretion.'

Kemp regarded her contemptuously. Holland did not need gold to earn his men's loyalty.

'Stand up,' she commanded. She was a gentlewoman, if not a noblewoman, to judge by her accent and the fine cloth of her grey cloak, so Kemp obeyed instinctively. What happened next was so sudden that Kemp did not have time to prevent it.

She leaned forward and kissed him on the cheek.

He stared at her in bewildered astonishment.

'So no one will wonder why I was speaking to one of Sir Thomas Holland's men,' she explained, smiling archly.

'Except me,' he replied. But she had already turned her back on him, and was making her way back along the causeway to Villeneuve-la-Hardie.

The pale grey light of the false dawn had risen over Calais, silencing the nocturnal chorus of the frogs in the marsh, when Holland and his squire made their way to where Preston's platoon was stationed early in the following morning. He found the serjeant and his men huddled around a brazier, trying to squeeze the last heat out of its dying embers.

Kemp doused his head in a barrel of icy water. Experience had taught him that if anything was going to happen, it was most likely to happen shortly before dawn. It was the time when the unwary were at their lowest ebb, towards the end of the night watch, tired and inattentive.

Holland greeted them cheerfully. 'Good morning, men.'

'Good morning, Sir Thomas,' they responded.

'A cold night.'

'Aye, sir,' acknowledged Preston.

Holland produced a stone flask and proffered it to Preston, who took a swig. It contained warm mead. 'That should keep the chill from your bones.'

'Thank you, sir.' Preston passed the flask on to the next man.

Kemp glanced across to the walls of Calais, where he could hear voices. He knew that out there somewhere in no man's land were hundreds of 'useless mouths', starving to death. Jean de Vienne had expelled another five hundred since Derby arrived at Villeneuve, but this time King Edward had been less magnanimous, refusing to let them through the English lines. Kemp felt pity for them. He knew all about hunger; his family had gone hungry enough times after a poor harvest on his lord's manor. He had no desire to return to that way of living. Holland had offered him a job as an archer in his retinue, but Kemp was a villein, and could not leave his lord's manor without permission, permission which he knew Sir John Beaumont was sure to refuse. The only other way for a villein to win his freedom was to spend a year and a day living and working in a borough, and to that end Holland had offered to arrange for Kemp to get a place in some rich burgher's household.

He suddenly remembered the glove Maud Lacy had given him. 'Sir Thomas?'

'What is it, Kemp?'

'I was wondering if I could have a word in private, Sir Thomas? About that job you said you'd try to get me in London?'

Holland nodded, and the two of them walked a short distance away from the others. 'Well? What is it?'

Kemp said nothing, leading Holland behind a palisade which gave them some degree of privacy. He produced the glove. 'A lady asked me to give you this.'

For a brief moment, Kemp had the impression that Holland's face had lit up, but then the knight's customary impassive mask fell back into place. Kemp suddenly remembered that he had seen the woman before: she had been riding alongside Lady Joan of Kent when she and her husband accompanied the king on one of his hunting trips into the surrounding countryside.

Holland took the glove from him, thrusting it into his purse. 'Tell no one of this,' he muttered.

Kemp thought he detected a faint blush in his master's complexion. 'No, sir,' he responded, a little hurt that Holland should think he might do otherwise.

'Now, what was it you wanted?'

'Nothing, sir. I just thought I ought to use some other excuse for talking to you, so's to be discreet.'

Holland turned away. Then he paused again, and looked back. 'Kemp?'

'Sir Thomas?'

'Well done.'

The two skiffs moved silently through the night, relying on the wind in their sails rather than risk the plashing of their oars alerting anyone to their escape attempt. They sailed past the Rysbank, a narrow spit of land that formed a natural mole of sand enclosing Calais harbour. The English had built a wooden stockade on the tip of the Rysbank, from which they could shoot bows and siege engines at any ships that slipped past the blockade and tried to enter the harbour. The watchmen in the stockade were not looking for small vessels trying to slip *out* of the harbour. The two skiffs drifted past the stockade which loomed dark and threatening above them, and found themselves tossed violently by the rougher sea beyond the harbour.

Sir Amerigo de Pavia sat in the prow of one skiff, heavily muffled against the cold sea breezes, and reached inside his cloak for the umpteenth time to make sure he still had the letter for King Philip with which de Vienne had entrusted him. It was now nearly ten months since King Edward had begun the siege of Calais, and still there was no sign of any relieving force. Despite the occasional victualling fleets which had managed to reach the harbour before the stockade was built on the Rysbank, the garrison of Calais was now desperately short of food, and could not hold out much longer. The letter contained a final impassioned plea for help. De Vienne had tried smuggling out another message with the second batch of 'useless mouths' he had expelled a fortnight earlier but the message, like the messenger who bore it, was still trapped in no man's land with the rest starving to death there; not that they were much worse off than the people inside the walls.

It had been de Pavia's idea to try to slip out by sea. He had been elated when de Vienne agreed to his plan, but now the moment of danger approached he was wondering if he might not be safer inside the walls after all. He reminded himself he had been dining on horseflesh for the past two weeks, and that soon he would be feasting on venison.

The stockade remained dark and silent and de Pavia was beginning to think they might make it to safety when a single fire-arrow was launched from one of the cogs in the blockade; at least one of the English mariners had good eyes. At once the smaller vessels in the English flotilla slipped anchor and began to converge on the two skiffs, many of them putting out cock-boats which scudded quickly across the waves.

The two skiffs parted, heading in different directions, one back into the harbour, the one de Pavia rode in turning to the west. The Genoese mariners pulled on their oars, desperate to escape capture, the need for silence past.

The men on the shore were fully awake now, the archers in the fort on the Rysbank shooting volleys of arrows at the first skiff as it rowed back down the channel into the harbour. The channel was only two hundred yards across at its widest point, optimum range for a longbow, and the first volley straddled the skiff, killing some of the men on board. Turning to the west, the second skiff slipped past the wooden piers that had been built out from the shore to stop small boats from slipping past in the shallows where the deeper-draughted English cogs could not go.

But now the cock-boats were closing in on the second skiff, cutting off all hope of escape. They were close enough for the archers on board to get a clear shot at the men in the skiff, despite the rocking of the boats. Three arrows struck home, killing oarsmen. With half the rowers dead, the remaining men lost control of the skiff. De Pavia clung to the bulwarks, white-faced with fear and dizziness.

The tide was coming in, the currents driving the skiff towards the beach. De Pavia could see a dozen archers standing on the shore, the surf surging between their ankles as it rushed across the sand. They had arrows nocked to their bows, taking no chances in case the Genoese mariners tried to put up a fight, but were not aiming, confident that the flood tide would drag their quarry to them. Seeing that capture was imminent, de Pavia reached underneath his cloak and took out the letter de Vienne had given him, wrapped in waterproof oilskin. He searched about on the floor of the boat and found an old axe-head, tying the letter to it and flinging it as far out to sea as he could, to stop it from falling into the hands of the English. It landed in the water with an audible splash, sending a brief plume of water into the air.

The surviving oarsmen were still trying to row clear of the beach, but the massive breakers were against them. A huge wave drove them high on to the beach, and stranded them there. They tried to drag the boat back down towards the sea, but it was too heavy for them to make much progress. Then the archers surrounded them, swords drawn.

'Don't kill them!' ordered Preston. 'Their lordships will want to question them. Besides,' he added with a grin, 'one of them might be worth ransoming.' He turned to Kemp. 'Which one did you see throw something in the water?'

'This one.' Kemp's voice was positive as he indicated de Pavia.

'All right, Conyers, you speak French,' said Preston. 'Ask him who he is and what he thinks he's about.'

The Lombard spoke arrogantly in response to Conyer's question, turning up his nose at the English archers.

'What does he say?' demanded Preston.

'He says he doesn't have to answer any of our questions.'

'Tell him he does if he doesn't want me to cut off his bollocks, smother them in pig-shit and stick them up his nose,' Preston responded cheerfully. 'Ask him what it was he threw overboard.'

But de Pavia knew Preston did not have the authority to carry out his threat, and refused to say anything. The serjeant ordered him and the other prisoners to be taken back to the fort, where Holland could decide what was to be done with them. 'It's no matter,' Preston added to Kemp, as the rest of his men escorted the prisoners back up the beach. 'We'll soon find out what it was he ditched overboard.'

'How d'you mean?' asked Kemp.

Preston grinned. 'Low tide in a few hours, lad. He didn't throw it nearly far enough out to sea.'

## CHAPTER THREE

TO ADD SPICE to the search and to make sure his men's hearts were in it, Preston told them that if it was treasure, whoever found it could keep it. They swept the beach around the spot Kemp indicated, prodding the wet sand with the tips of their swords, but their initial search turned up nothing. 'Are you sure it was here?' asked Preston.

Kemp nodded, his brow creased in thought.

'The undertow could've dragged it further out to sea,' pointed out Jarrom. 'The currents could've carried it further up the beach. Lord Christ! It could be anywhere by now.'

'We're going about this the wrong way,' Kemp said suddenly. 'We want to be more orderly.'

'How do you mean?' demanded Preston.

'We should divide up the beach into parts and have one man search each part, marking off the parts that have already been searched.'

Using their arrows as markers, they began their search once again, more methodically this time. The tide started to turn and Preston was beginning to lose all hope of finding whatever it was that Kemp had seen thrown overboard, when suddenly Brewster shouted that he had found something and sank to his knees, clawing at the sand with his hands. The others abandoned the search and swarmed around him.

'What is it?' asked Tate, as he crowded with the others to see what was being unearthed.

Brewster had scooped away enough sand to reveal something that shone in the summer sunlight. 'An axe-head,' he announced, disappointed.

'Is that what you saw?' Preston asked Kemp.

'It could have been,' admitted Kemp. He thought he could remember something glinting in the pale light of dawn.

'Hold on a minute, there's something tied to it,' said Brewster, scraping away more sand to pull out an oilskin package. He ripped it open and took out a crumpled piece of parchment with a wax seal on it. The package had leaked, and the address on the front had been all but washed away by the sea, but it was obviously a message of some kind, and important enough for the man in the boat not to want it to fall into the hands of the English.

'We should take it to Sir Thomas,' said Tate, as Brewster handed the letter up to Preston.

'All in good time,' replied Preston, breaking open the seal. 'Let's see what it is first, shall we?'

'What does it say?' asked Conyers.

'Nails and blood!' Preston snapped irritably. 'Do I look like a tonsured scholar? Where's Pisspants? He can read. He's always got his nose stuck in some book or other.'

The men moved aside to let Inglewood through. He looked at the parchment. The sea water had made the ink run, but the neat script was still clearly legible. 'It's in French,' he observed.

'Well, of course it's in God-damned French,' grumbled Preston. 'You didn't think the governor of Calais would write it in English for your benefit, did you?'

'Listen to this,' said Inglewood. 'It says: "There is nothing in the town which has not been eaten, even cats and dogs and horses, so there is nothing else to live off unless we eat human flesh. Earlier you wrote to say I was to hold the town as long as there was food; now there is none. So we have agreed that if we do not receive aid soon, we shall make a sortie beyond the walls into the marshes, to fight for life or death. For we would rather die honourably in the field than eat one another".'

Jarrom shrugged. 'If that's the way they want it . . .'

'And it finishes: "Unless some other solution can be found, this is the last letter that you will receive from me, for the town will be lost and all of us that are within it." Then it's signed John of Vienne, Governor of Calais, and dated on the Feast of Saint Eligius at Calais. That's yesterday, I think.'

'What does it mean?' asked Tate, pushing back his arming cap to claw at his scalp.

Preston was grinning delightedly. 'It means, lads, that we'll be going home soon.'

While Valois' army was gathering at Hesdin, Valois himself was called north to Saint-Omer on urgent business. He took only one knight and three squires with him. The town lay thirty miles north of Hesdin, and they reached it easily in a day's ride. The sun was setting by the time they reached the walls of their destination. Guards were posted at the gates, the town lying less than two dozen miles from the English encampment at Calais, but they recognised Valois at once and admitted him and his party. They were challenged again at the gate of the castle which dominated Saint-Omer, and by the time the drawbridge had been lowered and the portcullises raised, Don Carlos de la Cerda awaited them in the courtyard.

Although a Castilian, de la Cerda was a close friend of Valois' eldest son, the Duke of Normandy, and a brother-in-law of Charles of Blois, the Valois-backed claimant to the independent Duchy of Brittany. Despite his youth, de la Cerda had already begun to make a name for himself as a warlord and he had been placed in command of the Flemish Marches in the absence of the governor of Saint-Omer, Sir Geoffroi de Chargny. Nor had de la Cerda disgraced himself, defending the town against attacks from Flemish and English troops alike. He greeted Valois and his companions warmly.

'De Renty is still here?' asked Valois.

De la Cerda nodded. 'In the dungeons, your Majesty. I thought that a man such as he . . .'

Valois nodded approvingly. The bastard son of a nobleman, Sir Oudard de Renty had been banished from France for raping a noblewoman. He had promptly travelled to the court of King Edward and fought for the English against his own countrymen. Since then, he had returned to France, seeking a reconciliation with Valois. De la Cerda had been so astonished by de Renty's audacity that he refrained from having the renegade hanged, drawn and quartered there and then. Instead he held him prisoner until de Renty had had a chance to explain himself to Valois in person, for he would explain his motives to no other.

'Would you like him brought up to the great hall?' asked de la Cerda.

'Not yet,' said Valois, rubbing the scar on his cheek he had received from an English arrow in the thick of the fighting at Crécy. 'He has waited this long. Let him stew in his own juice a little longer. First we must refresh ourselves after our journey.'

The guests were shown to their chambers by the castle's steward so that they could change out of their riding clothes and wash their hands and faces before supper. The food was the best the castle could offer, and Valois enjoyed himself, tasting a little of every one of the myriad delicacies without gorging himself. It was good to be able to take his mind off the troubles of the realm for a short while.

But he could not turn his back on affairs of state for too long. At last, when the pages were clearing away the empty dishes and trenchers, he turned to de la Cerda. 'Let us have de Renty brought up to account for himself. I confess a curiosity to know how he will try to talk his way out of treason.'

De la Cerda turned to one of the pages who was replenishing the goblets from a flagon. 'Have Arnault bring de Renty up from the dungeons.'

Sir Oudard de Renty was an impossibly handsome young man, with a lean-jawed face bronzed from a lifetime spent out in the open, either hunting or campaigning. Normally clean-shaven, his jaw now sported several weeks' growth of beard from his incarceration, and his fine clothes were tattered and grimy. But his smile was as wide as ever as he bowed before his king.

'You must forgive my appearance, your Majesty, but I fear this gentleman denied me the chance to make myself presentable before I was brought before you.'

'Well, Sir Oudard?' Valois demanded. 'You insisted on speaking to me, and Don Carlos here was kind enough to grant you a few more weeks of life to give you the opportunity to do so. What do you have to say for youself, before I have you hanged, drawn and quartered for treason? Do you deny that I was justified in banishing you from my realm for an abominable crime?'

'Indeed, no, sire.'

'Or that you then at once swore fealty to King Edward, and took up arms against me and my people?'

De Renty gestured helplessly. 'So it might appear, to those who did not know me well enough to know I could never bear ill will to my one true kind.'

Valois frowned. 'You speak in riddles. Did you not lead the Flemings in an attack on this very town less than three months ago?'

De Renty smiled broadly. 'And did not that attack fail

miserably, when the Flemings came here a week too early, when they were supposed to attack in conjunction with the English under the command of the Earl of Warwick, who attacked a week later?'

Valois nodded; he had been wondering why the joint attack had been so badly concerted.

'And did not the young Count of Flanders escape to your court while I was there, away from the Flemish noblemen and burghers who so foolishly support King Edward and his cause?' continued de Renty. 'Do you really think so callow a youth could have achieved so daring an escape without the guiding hand of one so much more experienced in such matters than he?'

Valois rubbed his temples with his knuckles. He had always judged men by their actions, unable to comprehend that there might be deeper motives behind the more obvious ones.

De Renty could see Valois was reluctant to believe his explanation. 'You have only to ask Sir Geoffroi,' he persisted. 'He knows me well. If he were here, he would tell you . . .'

'Tell us what?' The knight who had accompanied Valois to Saint-Omer came down the steps from the minstrels' gallery where he had been sitting concealed in the shadows, listening to all that was said. Until that moment he had worn a cloak with a deep cowl to keep his face hidden, but now he threw back the cowl to reveal de Chargny's aquiline features.

Recognising him, de Renty stumbled over his words. A shiver of nervousness seemed to slice through his nonchalance, but only for a moment. 'Tell you that I am no lover of King Edward, but am, have been, and always will be a loyal servant of my true king,' he continued smoothly. 'You know me well, Sir Geoffroi; will you not vouch for my good faith?'

'Aye, I know you well,' hissed de Chargny. 'I know you for a rogue and a varlet.' Walking across to where de Renty stood, he embraced him. 'But I also know you for the loyal vassal of King Philip that you claim to be.'

The relief on de Renty's face was evident as de Chargny turned to Valois. 'You may trust Sir Oudard, sire, if only because you may rely on the fact he is too cunning to trust his fortunes to a cause so hopeless as King Edward's.'

Valois smiled. If de Chargny believed de Renty, then he could not doubt the renegade's loyalty.

'Does it please your Majesty to accept me back into your grace and favour?' asked de Renty, the easy smile back on his face.

Valois glanced at de Chargny, who nodded discreetly. 'Aye,' said Valois. 'And right glad we are to have a knight of your courage in our ranks once more . . .'

There was a knock on the door. 'See who that is,' de Chargny told Arnault, irritated by the interruption. The man-at-arms nodded, and hurried to answer. A stilted silence fell over in the great hall while Arnault slipped outside and talked with whoever had knocked. Presently he returned holding a letter and de Chargny crossed to speak with him. After a brief exchange he took the letter from Arnault and turned to Valois.

'Your pardon, sire, but this has arrived for you. The messenger says it comes from the English.'

Valois took the parchment from him, looking at it curiously. It was warped and crinkled, as if it had been soaked in brine. 'King Edward's seal,' he observed, glancing at the back before breaking the seal open.

'Perhaps he wishes to discuss terms,' suggested de Renty.

Valois read the letter and his face grew crimson with anger. It was from de Vienne, the same letter that Kemp and his companions had found in the sand. King Edward had forwarded it, resealing it with his own seal to mock Valois and let him know what desperate straits the garrison of Calais was in. Valois crumpled the letter in his fist and tossed it on to the rush-strewn floor. 'We return to Hesdin in the morning,' he said curtly, sweeping out of the room and heading back upstairs.

'I understand your captive, the Count of Eu, is still a prisoner in the Tower of London,' remarked King Edward, pouring Sir Thomas Holland a goblet of Gascon wine.

Holland nodded. He had captured Raoul de Brienne, Count of Eu and Constable of France, at Caen nearly a year ago. 'Aye, your Majesty. The ransom I have demanded is not inconsiderable. It will take his family time to raise that much money.'

It was mid-July, three weeks since the king had forwarded de Vienne's letter to Valois. Still there was no sign of Valois' army. The king had summoned Holland to his mansion in Villeneuve and now the two of them spoke in one of the king's private chambers. The quarrel they had had before Holland returned to England was forgotten; the king was swift to anger, but his rages were like summer storms, soon blowing themselves out by their very fierceness.

'How much do you expect to raise in ransom from him?' the king asked.

'Perhaps as much as fifty thousand florins, sire.' Holland tried to appear nonchalant. To him – indeed, to most men – it was a princely sum, and he wondered if he would be asking too much.

The king laughed. 'A paltry fifty thousand for the Constable of France? Your demands are modest, Sir Thomas.'

'In my observation, sire, it is not so much a question of what a prisoner is worth as what his family is prepared to pay for him.' Holland smiled wanly. 'To be blunt, sire, I need the money.'

'I'll give you eighty thousand florins for him.'

Holland was stunned. There was nothing unusual in a liege-lord buying a noble prisoner from one of his vassals; in an age where even pardons for sin could be had at a price, everything was negotiable. But eighty thousand florins? Holland was not avaricious but, on the other hand, he was not stupid enough to turn down such an offer.

'I'll have to pay it in instalments,' admitted the king. 'Say, a thousand pounds of gold at Michaelmas, and another thousand next Easter. The rest I'll be able to pay out of the wool subsidies over the next two years in regular instalments at Michaelmas and Easter.'

Holland frowned. 'You really think the count will be able to pay back that much, sire?'

The king smiled slyly. 'Not in money, perhaps. But he is lord of the castle of Guînes, which defends the approaches to Calais. When the town falls – and it will fall, in that I am determined – that castle will be the key to the Pale of Calais. Worth far more to me than its value in gold.'

Holland nodded, understanding. He bowed low. 'Very well, sire. I accept.'

As he made his way downstairs, he almost bumped into the queen and Countess Margaret. He bowed low to the queen and, in the same movement, ignored the countess. The queen returned his bow with a curtsey but the countess stared at him, her emerald eyes brimming with malevolence. A lesser man might have quailed under such an imperious glare but Holland was feeling buoyed up by the king's promise of such a generous amount. Chuckling softly to himself, he left the mansion and walked back to his house.

His good mood did not last, however, when he saw the chess problem he had laid out on the table in the main room. He much preferred to play with other people, enjoying the contest between two minds. The chess pieces looked forlorn, reminding him how lonely he was. In the few short weeks he spent with Joan before he went to Flanders they had often played chess. She was a good player and he had enjoyed the way they had been able to play in silence without the need for conversation. He wondered if she ever played chess with Montague; the thought made him almost as jealous as the thought of Montague making love to her.

Holland sat down at the table and opened his writing case. He dipped a quill in the ink-horn and launched into a lengthy letter in his crabbed and awkward handwriting. He was halfway through before he realised he would not be able to deliver it. He could send a go-between, of course, but who? He thought about his chaplain, Brother Ambrose, but the friar had a tendency to naïvety that made him unsuitable for the commission which Holland had in mind. Preston? The serjeant could be depended upon in military matters, but an errand requiring such discretion? He needed someone who could be relied upon to keep his mouth shut, even at the risk of openly defying a nobleman or woman if necessary. Holland smiled: the perfect candidate for the task, a young man who had already proven his discretion, sprang to mind. He rose to his feet and climbed the narrow staircase to the top floor, knocking on the door.

'Come in?'

Brother Ambrose was stretched on his pallet, reading the same book he had been reading on the voyage from England. They said that monks shaved their heads to make it easier for God to see their thoughts. Holland often wondered if Ambrose genuinely believed that a full head of hair made it more difficult for the Almighty to read a man's mind.

'What are you reading?' Holland asked him curiously.

'A tract on chivalry, Sir Thomas.'

Holland arched his eyebrows. He had never guessed that the friar had any interest in such matters. 'By whom?'

'A French knight. Sir Geoffroi de Chargny. Would you like to see?' He held the book out to his master.

Holland shook his head. 'Perhaps another time. I need you to fetch Kemp for me.'

Brother Ambrose closed the book around a leather bookmark and rose to his feet. 'Of course, Sir Thomas.' The two of them made their way downstairs, Holland entering the withdrawing room while Brother Ambrose left the house and hurried to the barrack house next door. Holland was concluding the letter when he heard a knock on the door.

'Enter.'

The door opened, and Kemp stood there, looking slightly worried, evidently wondering what Holland could want with him so late at night.

'Come in, Kemp. Close the door behind you.'

Kemp complied, and stood before Holland uncertainly while the knight wrote the last words of the final sentence. He did not sign his name. He did not speak immediately, drying the ink with sand while he chose his next words with care.

'I need . . . a favour.'

Kemp creased his brow. 'Sir?'

'I want . . . I would like you to deliver a letter for me.'

'Of course, Sir Thomas,' Kemp responded unhesitatingly.

'It isn't that simple,' Holland cautioned him. 'You know Lady Joan of Kent?'

'Sir William Montague's wife?' asked Kemp, and immediately regretted his description of her when Holland scowled.

'Aye,' he said tightly. 'I want you to deliver it into her hands, and her hands alone. Do you understand me?'

Kemp kept his expression neutral, although he was thinking of what Brewster had told him of the disputed marriage. 'Aye, sir.'

'Sir William is not to know of it. Nor is the countess, her mother. Better that the letter should be destroyed than it should fall into anyone's hands but Lady Joan's.'

'I understand, sir,' Kemp responded stoutly.

Holland sealed the letter with wax – Kemp noticed that he did not use his signet ring as a seal. The knight put no address on the front. After hesitating with uncharacteristic indecision, as if he had just decided the sending of this letter was a foolish project that was better abandoned, he handed the parchment to Kemp hurriedly, fearful that he might change his mind again. Kemp tucked the letter inside his jerkin and left the room without another word. Experience had taught him that when Holland gave an order, it was to be carried out instantly and without question. He had almost reached the front door when the withdrawing room door opened behind him, and Holland thrust his head out.

'Remember, Kemp. Not a word of this to anyone.'

Kemp nodded, and ducked out into the street.

Villeneuve-la-Hardie never really slept. Even at night, guards were constantly going on or coming off watch, and with so many men moving around there was little point in trying to impose any kind of curfew. This made the town even busier at night, for those soldiers who were not on duty were able to spend the hours of darkness crawling from tavern to brothel and back again. As a consequence, Kemp was able to make his way through the streets without having to worry about attracting undue attention.

Montague's modest mansion was considerably larger than the house Holland occupied. Kemp paused in front of it to drink from a wooden horse-trough that stood nearby while he considered his next move. There were no guards on duty at the entrance – with the mansion located close to the heart of the great English camp, there was no need – but Kemp could hardly march boldly through the front door. Light showed behind one of the shuttered windows on the ground floor, but Kemp could not peer through the cracks in the shutter without risking being noticed.

He wandered around to the back of the house and slipped into the dark stables. The horse in the first stall whinnied at the entrance of a stranger but Kemp stroked its nose to reassure it, listening carefully to make sure the whinny had not alerted the household. He could hear voices from the house; the loud and jovial tones of men who had had a little too much to drink.

The door opened behind him and he whirled around, reaching for the hilt of his broadsword. A petite, cloaked figure drew back with a woman's gasp. He froze in panic, but she did not cry out.

'Who are you?' she whispered. 'What are you doing here?'

'Sir John Chandos asked me to fetch his horse,' Kemp lied.

'There is no horse of Sir John's stabled here.'

'Isn't this Sir Reginald Cobham's stable?'

She shook her head. 'I know you. You're one of Sir Thomas Holland's men, aren't you?'

Kemp recognised her as Maud Lacy. If the Lady Joan trusted her to act as a go-between, perhaps he could do likewise. Perhaps.

He nodded.

'You have a message for my mistress?' guessed Maud.

He nodded again and, after a moment's hesitation, he reached inside his jerkin and gave her a folded piece of parchment. She hid it in the depths of her cloak, and then leaned forward to give him another peck on the cheek. He pulled back hurriedly, rubbing his cheek. 'There's no one watching this time,' he protested.

'You're right,' she agreed, and suddenly seized his head in her hands, pressing her lips against his. He felt her mouth open into his, her tongue flickering between his teeth. He drew back sharply.

'I've already got a girl,' he said, although he knew deep within his heart that was just an excuse.

She shrugged, smiling and unperturbed, then left the stable without another word.

He watched her disappear through the back door of the wooden mansion and then turned his attention to the wall above the stable. A light flickered behind a shutter and after a few moments he heard a door open and close, followed by the sound of women's voices.

He glanced up and down the alley behind the mansion. It was deserted. He climbed on to a water-barrel, then on to the roof of the stable, crouching just below the window so that he could listen.

'... Give it to me quickly,' he heard a noblewoman's voice say, a little impatiently. There was a rustle of parchment. 'What's this?'

'My lady?'

'"Pardon, in consideration of his good service in the War of France, to Martin Kemp of the County of Leicester, late villein of Sir John Beaumont, for the murder and rape of Kathryn Seagrave of Mountsorrel, and of any consequent outlawry; on condition that he do not withdraw from the King's service without licence so long as the King remain on this side of the seas."'

In the darkness outside, Kemp grinned.

'Oh, the jackass! He must have given me the wrong parchment.'

'Go after him, Maud. See if you can catch him.'

'Yes, my lady.' The door opened and closed again, and there was the faint noise of footsteps on wooden stairs.

Kemp knocked softly on the shutters.

Silence. Then: 'Who is it?'

'Martin Kemp of the County of Leicester,' he responded, still grinning. 'I've a message from Sir Thomas.'

The light inside was snuffed out, and the shutter opened. Kemp found himself face to face with Lady Joan of Kent herself. Close to, she was even more beautiful than she appeared from afar. Kemp caught his breath.

'Well?' she demanded boldly. She did not appear over-concerned to have a man convicted of murder and rape immediately below her window. 'I believe this is yours.' She showed him the copy of his pardon he had given to her chambermaid.

'I didn't know if she could be trusted, so I gave her that to see if she would take it straight to your husband.'

Joan smiled. 'Maud is totally loyal to me.'

'Sir Thomas said I should hand this to no one but yourself, my lady.' He gave her the letter Holland had asked him to deliver. 'I . . . I couldn't have my pardon back now, could I?'

She handed him the parchment. 'Did you really rape and kill that poor girl?'

'Would you believe me if I said I never even heard of her before the trial?'

But Joan was no longer listening. She had broken the seal on the letter and was studying its contents. She smiled at something Holland had written, and finally folded the letter, opening a casket and placing the letter within before locking it once more. Then she took a purse from the chest at the end of the drawer and held out a shilling. 'Thank you.'

Kemp shook his head. 'That's not necessary.'

Before Joan could reply, the door opened behind her and Kemp hurriedly ducked out of sight.

'Joan?' A man's voice. 'What are you doing?'

'Just enjoying the night air.'

'In the dark?'

'I can see the stars better this way.'

'Come to bed, my love,' said the man's voice and Joan pulled the shutters to. Kemp eased himself off the roof of the stable and returned to Holland's house, feeling sick with empathy on his master's behalf at the thought of his love sleeping with another man each night.

He thought of Lady Beatrice waiting for him back in the County of Leicester, and wondered if she had found another man in his absence; was he fooling himself by thinking that such a fine lady would really wait for a churl such as himself? But the thought of her was sometimes the only thing that kept him going through the horrors of war and he could not afford even to think that her love for him might be false. She loved him: had she not proved it by giving him her coverchief to wear into battle as a token of her favour, just as Queen Guinevere had given Sir Lancelot hers? He had worn that coverchief around his neck as a muffler ever since the day he left home, taking it off only to launder it with more care than he lavished on any of his own clothes. On one memorable occasion he had even been called upon to lend it to his king. Toying with the coverchief now, he remembered that day in Caen when he had sullied his love for Beatrice. He wondered if he could ever face her again with such a sin weighing on his conscience.

Entering Holland's house, he saw a light shining below the withdrawing room door, and knocked.

'Enter.'

Holland was sitting at the table where Kemp had left him, staring at the chess set. Kemp hesitated uncertainly on the threshold. 'I delivered the letter, sir.'

'Any problems?'

'None worth mentioning.'

'Well done. And . . . thank you.'

'It's an honour to be of service, sir.' Kemp was about to turn away, but Holland gestured for him to sit in the chair opposite. 'Come in, Kemp. Close the door behind you. Do you play chess?'

Kemp scratched his head. 'I've played chequers.'

Holland smiled. 'Chess is a little more complex.' He started to rearrange the pieces. 'Every piece has its allotted place on the board to start with, just as every man has his station in life: the king, the vizier, the knight . . .'

'Vizier, sir?'

'King's counsellor. Like the chancellor. Or rather, like Henry of Derby. The chess set is a battlefield, and the object is to capture your opponent's king . . .'

Holland explained the rudiments of the game to Kemp, and then they played a couple of short-lived games. Short-lived, because as Kemp observed to Holland, chess was obviously a game where beginner's luck was not a factor.

'A man must make his own luck in life, Kemp.'

'Yes, sir. I still don't understand how a peasant can . . .'

'Pawn, Kemp. In chess it's called a pawn.'

'Yes, sir. I still don't see how a pawn can suddenly become a . . . like Henry of Derby.'

'A vizier?' Holland smiled. 'Even a pawn can go a long way in life.'

'I hope so, sir.'

Holland chuckled, and then his face grew dark as his mind turned to other matters. 'Was she well?'

'She seemed well enough, sir.' He did not think it would be diplomatic to mention the circumstances of his departure from Joan's window.

Holland nodded thoughtfully, then yawned. 'Thank you, Kemp. I think we'd best get some sleep. Valois' army is expected to arrive any day now.'

Kemp rose with a grimace. 'Begging your pardon, sir, but Valois' army has been expected to arrive any day now for two months.'

Holland chuckled. 'Aye, well. Tomorrow, perhaps.'

Ten days later, the Oriflamme – the sacred banner of Saint Denys, patron saint of France, carried only when the King of France was present to indicate that no quarter was to be given – was seen raised on the Heights of Sangatte, five miles to the west of Calais and Villeneuve. Finally, after a siege lasting nearly eleven months, Valois and his army had arrived to relieve Calais.

# CHAPTER FOUR

THE LOOK-OUT TOWER guarding the road to the bridge at Nieullay was attacked by over a thousand men almost at once. The assault was undisciplined and the two platoons of archers guarding the tower held their ground bravely. But they were soon overwhelmed by the sheer weight of numbers and slain to a man.

The rest of Valois' army did not make the same mistake it had made at Crécy and rush immediately into battle. Instead it pitched its tents and made camp on the Heights of Sangatte while Valois himself sent forward two of his marshals, the Lords of Beaujeu and Saint-Venant, to scout along the English lines. When they reported back, he was less than overjoyed by the news. From the Heights of Sangatte, there were only two possible approaches to the English positions: along the beach, where the River Hem spread out to form a shallow ford as it trickled over the sand, or across the bridge at Nieullay. As soon as news of Valois' approach had reached the English camp, the king had brought in all the ships in his fleet bearing siege engines close to the shore to cover the beach and prevent the French from advancing across the sand, reinforcing them with several companies of archers. The bridge at Nieullay, meanwhile, was still heavily guarded by the Earl of Derby's troops.

Several of the younger blades in Valois' army rode down to the English lines and issued challenges to their English counterparts, many of which were taken up, enabling French and English foot-soldiers alike to watch as the knights engaged in single combat, tilting at one another across the sand. This diverting sport was cut short when heralds from both sides ordered the young knights to withdraw behind the lines. Both kings wanted every knight available fit to fight when battle was finally joined.

The beleaguered garrison of Calais could see the banners of Valois' army beyond the English lines, and that night they displayed the same banners on the highest tower of Calais castle, illuminating them with a great fire, to the noise of cheers and trumpets.

Like most of the men in the English army, Kemp was not frightened by the proximity of Valois' troops. At the battle of Crécy he had seen a far larger French Force routed by an army far smaller than the one in which he was currently serving. Then the English had had only the advantage of terrain over the enemy, but they had made it tell. Here at Calais, in addition to an army as large as, if not slightly larger than, the one fielded by the French, they had also had months in which to prepare a defensive position in anticipation of this confrontation, and they had used that time wisely. After sneering at the display atop the walls of Calais castle, he went to bed and slept as soundly as ever.

The following morning, the sound of reveille roused the camp at dawn. Trumpets could likewise be heard from the direction of the French camp, but as yet there was no indication they intended to attack. Holland's men formed up in platoons to be drilled by their serjeants, as they did every morning before breakfast. The only difference was that this morning, one of the king's heralds rode by to summon Holland to the king's presence.

When Holland returned from the palace he found that his men had finished their breakfast and were checking their equipment. 'Where's Kemp?' he demanded brusquely.

Preston pointed silently to where the young archer was lovingly honing the edge of the blade of his great broadsword to a razor's sharpness with a whetstone. Kemp glanced up and, realising he was wanted, pushed himself to his feet. He strode briskly towards Holland, knowing that while some knights liked their men to do everything at the double, Holland preferred a quality of calm, unhurried purposefulness; something which Kemp possessed in abundance.

Holland was holding a long, black garment folded over one arm, and he thrust it at Kemp. 'Put this on.'

Kemp glanced at the garment: a woollen travelling cloak, with long sleeves and a loose cowl, it was a simple, unostentatious piece of clothing which he had often seen Holland wearing on the march. Not being one to question orders, Kemp shrugged himself into it. It fitted well, Kemp and Holland having similar builds despite the fact the knight had a score of years on the youthful archer.

'I need a squire,' Holland explained. 'You don't exactly look the part, even dressed in that, but I need someone to tend the horses, and you can do that well enough.'

'Aye, Sir Thomas.'

'Well, go and fetch them, then,' snapped Holland. 'Bring me Ferraunt and fetch the piebald rouncy for yourself.' Ferraunt was Holland's name for his palfrey, as unimaginative an appellation for a blue-roan horse as Snowball for a white cat. To Holland, names for horses were merely labels, a convenient way of distinguishing one from another; he had lost too many in battle to allow himself to become attached to them. The piebald rouncy had belonged to the squire who died at Crécy.

Holland and Kemp rode through Villeneuve to the western gate, where they met Derby himself, along with the Earl of Northampton, Lord Burghersh, Sir Reginald Cobham, and Sir Walter Mauny, who had reluctantly been freed by the French and allowed to join the English before Calais. Mauny was a Hainault knight who had arrived in England in the queen's retinue and become a naturalised Englishman and a loyal servant of King Edward. The Margrave of Juliers, who had recently arrived with reinforcements from Flanders, was also there.

The whole party – fourteen in total – rode away from Villeneuve towards Nieullay, where two large pavilions were being erected at the edge of the marsh and only just inside the English lines. There they were greeted by Cardinal Ravaillac, one of the cardinals attempting to negotiate a peace between the rival claimants for the French throne. The English had not trusted the cardinals twelve months ago and they did not intend to trust them now. They were emissaries of Pope Clement, a Frenchman whose residence at Avignon would have forced him to defer to Valois had not the two of them already been implicit allies against the English.

The English noblemen dismounted, handing the bridles of their horses to their squires or – in Holland's case – acting squire. Then each in turn went down on one knee before Ravaillac, kissing his signet ring.

'Greetings, my son,' the cardinal said, as Derby kissed his ring. 'I crave your forgiveness for the delay. The delegates from King Philip of Fra . . .'

'Philip of Valois,' Derby corrected with a growl. It seemed the cardinal had to be reminded of one of the root causes of the war: the legality of Valois' claim on the French throne.

Ravaillac smiled thinly. It was obvious that Derby was the leader of the English delegation to these peace talks, and equally obvious that he was determined to be quite intractable. During the English delegates' earlier meeting with the king, when he had appointed them as his emissaries, he had made it clear that they were to remember at all times they were negotiating from a position of strength.

They did not have to wait long before Valois' emissaries arrived. Led by the Duke of Bourbon, they included the titular Duke of Athens – Gautier de Brienne, the son-in-law of Holland's prisoner the Count of Eu – the Lord of Beaujeu, Guillaume Flote and Sir Eustache de Ribeaumont. The sixth was a hawk-faced man with russet hair, dressed in fine robes of red and white. Northampton nudged Derby and nodded surreptitiously at the last.

'Sir Geoffroi de Chargny,' he murmured out of the corner of his mouth as the French delegates dismounted and handed their bridles to their squires. 'If you recall, I once had the honour of taking him prisoner.'

'The Sir Geoffroi de Chargny who is so wise in the laws of chivalry?' Derby murmured back.

Northampton nodded while he and his companions smiled welcomingly at their opposite numbers. 'The same. Let not that aspect of him fool you. He's as subtle as a fox and as ruthless as a serpent.'

Formal introductions were performed with the usual gallantry, on this occasion largely forced, and the delegates of the opposing sides followed Cardinal Ravaillac into one of the pavilions. The squires waited outside, talking amongst themselves. Both sets of squires spoke French and were happy to talk to the other side, the clever ones pumping their counterparts for information.

In the months he had been stationed at Villeneuve, Kemp had dealt with the locals on a day-to-day basis and had picked up a smattering of heavily accented French; enough to get his meaning across and to understand what others were saying. But on this occasion he was ignored, his peasant status obvious to all. He sneered to see the arrogant young English squires talking with Frenchmen in preference to a churl, but did not let their snub bother him. He might have high ambitions but he had no illusions about his origins, and did not care for those members of the aristocracy who could not treat the lower orders with at least some modicum of respect.

The conference was a long one. Occasionally Kemp heard voices raised in heated argument and strained to hear the words, but they were too indistinct for him to understand. Despite their conversation, the squires became bored with the wait long before Kemp, who had learned to keep his own company during countless nights of sentry duty. From where he stood, he could see just about the entire landscape between the opposing armies and he whiled away the time by imagining what tactics Valois might use to try to relieve the siege and how the English might counter the French. Whichever way he looked at it, the English defences seemed impregnable. The fact the French had chosen to negotiate rather than attack seemed to indicate they thought so too . . . or were they merely biding time until more reinforcements could be brought up to swell the ranks of their army?

He was broken from his reverie by the sudden realisation that one of the French squires was talking about him. Something about '. . . a hackney harnessed for the joust', clearly a jest about his ignoble origins.

Kemp grinned. 'Or a wolf in sheep's clothing,' he responded in his halting French.

The French squire crossed to where Kemp stood, regarding him with an expression of disdain. The squire was in his early thirties, the oldest one there, of a type instantly recognisable even to Kemp: the younger son of a knight, too impoverished to maintain the duties of a knight himself. He was a huge man: Kemp was tall and well-built, but this man towered over him.

'I do not recall giving you permission to speak, villein.'

Kemp shrugged. 'I do not recall being told that I needed your permission,' he replied.

At that moment Sir Geoffroi de Chargny emerged from the pavilion behind him, his crimson cloak billowing out behind him like a hawk spreading its wings to fly. 'Come away, Guilbert,' he called briskly, hardly bothering to glance in Kemp's direction. 'You might catch something.'

'Aye,' said Kemp, fingering the hilt of his broadsword. 'A bad case of death, most likely.'

That brought de Chargny to a sharp halt. 'So, it speaks French, does it?' he drawled, walking slowly to where Kemp and Guilbert stood. 'Badly, but it speaks it.' He stared at Kemp as he might at a particularly poor example of horse-flesh. 'So, this is one of the stout English yeomen who vanquished my kinsmen at Crécy.' He turned to address the squires, pointing to the longbow slung across Kemp's back in its bow-bag. 'You will note its weapon, gentlemen. Lacking the courage to meet steel with steel, it kills from a distance, with a poacher's weapon.'

Kemp threw a fold of his cloak back over his shoulder to reveal the broadsword hanging at his hip. 'If you wish to meet steel with steel, I'll gladly oblige you. Then we'll see who lacks courage.'

De Chargny chuckled dryly at the young man's bravado. 'Usually I prefer not to cross swords with my inferiors, but in your case I'm tempted to teach you a lesson for your insolence. Most fortunately for you, however, I was forbidden to wear a sword when entering this nest of vipers, otherwise I might have found myself forced to perform the work of a butcher – and that is hardly suitable employment for one of my blood.'

'The only nest of vipers I see lies yonder,' responded Kemp, nodding towards the French encampment on the Heights of Sangatte.

De Chargny slapped him across the face. 'That's for your insolence, churl. In future you must learn to treat your superiors with more respect.'

The Frenchman's blow merely stung Kemp, but it brought all his resentment of the nobility boiling up within him. He hated their arrogance, but he hated the haughtiness of the French nobility even more, having seen it routed before the arrows of himself and his lowly companions. He had thrown his fist at the knight even before he realised it.

De Chargny did not flinch, for Guilbert caught Kemp by the wrist before the blow could land. As the younger man whirled to face him, Guilbert let go of his wrist and rammed a fist into Kemp's jaw. Kemp did not see the blow coming until it was too late, and even then its power caught him off-guard, sending him flying so that when he finally landed on the damp greensward he slithered for several more feet. He could feel warm blood gushing from his nostrils, but he had learned to ignore the loss of his own blood when there was a battle to be won.

Guilbert moved in for another blow, aiming a vicious kick at Kemp's ribs. Kemp rolled swiftly out of the way, rose on one knee and drew his broadsword from its scabbard. He levelled it at Guilbert's chest, and the sight of that razor-edged blade brought the squire up short.

'Kemp! Put up your sword!' It was Holland's voice, curt and angry. Kemp had not seen his master emerge from the pavilion, but he was standing there now, with the other members of the English embassy. Glowering at Guilbert, Kemp replaced his sword in its scabbard and wiped the blood from his chin with his sleeve.

'I must apologise, Sir Geoffroi,' Henry of Derby was saying. 'That such a thing should befall you and your squire when you enter our camp under a flag of truce is inexcusable. You may rest assured the churl will be punished severely for his crime,' he added, indicating Kemp.

De Chargny made a dismissive gesture. 'It is of no consequence. I would rather you did not punish the peasant; that is a task I would prefer to reserve for myself, in the hope that God will one day grant me a small mercy in allowing me to encounter him when we are not under a flag of truce.'

'Yet I fear your opinion of English hospitality may be permanently damaged by this,' persisted Derby.

De Chargny smiled thinly. 'You may rest assured that this encounter has not changed my opinion of English hospitality one iota.'

Then, as the other members of the French embassy emerged from the pavilion, he mounted his steed, and rode back towards the bridge at Nieullay.

Remembering too late that de Chargny had once been a prisoner of the English, Derby rounded on Holland, his voice icy with rage. 'I could turn a blind eye to the fact that you chose a churl to act as a squire in the light of the fact you have not yet found a replacement for the man you lost at Crécy, Sir Thomas. However, I find it incredible you should choose one so hot-headed as to risk upsetting the most delicate negotiations by striking one of the French delegates.'

Holland seemed unperturbed by Derby's reproach. 'I greatly regret the scene we have just witnessed as much as any of us, my lord,' he replied. 'However, I ask only that you mark this: I ask not my yeoman if he was provoked beyond all toleration for the simple reason that I know the answer to my question can only be "yes".'

Northampton came to Holland's defence. 'It would not be out of character for one of de Chargny's overweening arrogance, Henry. Forget not that I warned you of his subtlety. See how he turns a blow received into a cause for dissent amongst his enemies.'

Derby frowned, his brows knitted in thought, and then his face cleared and he laughed out loud. 'By my truth, William, you are right. My apologies, Sir Thomas, both to yourself and to your yeoman. But mark I promised that vulture de Chargny your man would be suitably punished? I cannot go back on my word.'

Holland smiled. 'Leave the matter in my hands, my lord. I'm certain I can come up with a punishment to fit the crime.'

Derby returned his smile. 'Then so be it.'

They mounted their horses and headed back to Villeneuve. Riding at the rear of the cavalcade, Kemp could not resist listening with interest to the conversation of the noblemen; now he had a smattering of French, he could understand most that was said in the Anglo-Norman tongue of the nobility.

Their conversation was a discussion of the day's negotiations, and from what Kemp could understand it would take several more days before anything could be agreed. Valois' ambassadors had said he was keen for an end to the war and was thus prepared to make certain concessions to the English, practically an acknowledgement that the English had the upper hand, provided the negotiations were not part of some monstrous bluff to lull the English into a false sense of security. The question was, would the concessions be sufficient to justify everything the English had gone through to reach this position of strength, and to what extent would it be worth sacrificing that position to achieve an equitable peace? The terms they were discussing seemed no better than those that had been offered under the auspices of the same cardinals twelve months earlier, three weeks before Valois' last army was massacred at Crécy.

When Holland and Kemp arrived back at the barrack house where Preston's platoon was lodged, the knight ordered Kemp to stand to attention in the street outside while Preston was summoned from within. 'A grave crime has been committed by one of the men under your command, serjeant,' said Holland, when Preston emerged.

'Sir Thomas?' Preston looked bewildered, shifting his gaze from Holland to Kemp and then back.

Holland nodded, his face deadpan. 'Kemp struck one of the Frenchmen at the negotiations today.'

'Did he indeed, sir?' Preston regarded Kemp in wonderment.

'Aye, serjeant, and because of it, my lord of Derby has decreed that he must be punished. From now on Kemp is to be relieved of his usual duties and assigned to my stables . . . stop grinning, Kemp . . . and if his new duties should keep him from the usual round of sentry-go, then that is regrettable but, under the circumstances, unavoidable.'

Kemp could not help grinning. He loved horses, and he knew that Holland knew it.

That night, the Valois *fleurs-de-lys* were once more flown from the highest tower of Calais castle. This time, however, the bonfire illuminating them was markedly smaller.

'What know you of Sir Geoffroi de Chargny?' Holland asked his chaplain over dinner that night, recalling that lately the friar had been reading a book by the French knight.

'He is one of France's leading experts on chivalry and all that pertains to it,' replied Brother Ambrose. 'Why do you ask?'

'He was one of Valois' ambassadors at today's negotaitions.'

Brother Ambrose looked up from his trencher in some surprise. 'De Chargny is here?'

Holland nodded. 'That surprises you?'

Ambrose shrugged. 'The last I heard, he was heading for the east to crusade against the Turks.' He smiled. 'But that was a couple of years ago.'

'Would you say he is a man of honour?'

Ambrose thought carefully before replying. 'He would say he is a man of honour. He *is* a man of honour – by his own terms. But from what I have heard of Sir Geoffroi, I would not as an Englishman be too swift to trust him.'

The negotiations dragged on for the next few days and at the end of each day the bonfire atop Calais castle grew smaller until its significance became clear to all: it represented the waning strength of the garrison, symbolising that while they would do all they could to keep the Valois *fleurs-de-lys* shining over Calais, their ability to do so declined with each passing day. It must have been torture for the garrison to see that Valois had finally arrived with his army to raise the siege, and yet his army showed no inclination to tackle that of King Edward and his allies in battle.

For the rest of the negotiations, Holland chose a squire from Sir Reginald Cobham's retinue to serve him and Kemp, sweating in the summer heat as he mucked out Holland's stables and groomed his horses, could only pick up what news of the talks filtered down to his companions. The only concessions that Valois seemed prepared to make were the Duchy of Gascony – rightfully a fief of King Edward's anyway – and the town of Calais which, as the evidence of the bonfires testified, was as good as in the hands of the English already. The discussions were dragged out by the fact that at the end of each day the ambassadors had to report their opposite numbers' proposals to their respective monarchs, and at the start of each day they had to return to the negotiating table with fresh counter-proposals.

On the fourth day of negotiations – the last day of July – the French ambassadors came up with an entirely new proposal: that the English should come out of the marsh and fight a battle in 'a fitting place', to be chosen by a joint commission of eight knights, four from each side. When the English ambassadors reported this proposal to their king that night, he laughed out loud. This, he explained, was a bluff, a face-saving manoeuvre typical of the slippery Valois: a challenge made safe in the knowledge that he, King Edward, would never abandon his position of strength in the marshes to meet the French on more or less equal terms. Two could play at that game, he told his courtiers; he knew Valois better than Valois knew him, and with this in mind came up with a simple counter-bluff. The next day, the English ambassadors told their French couinterparts that King Edward would be more than happy to take Valois up on his offer. Valois had no choice but to accept. That night, however, the bonfire atop Calais castle was reduced to a flicker and all the banners were taken in except for the flag of Calais. The garrison could hold out no longer.

The following morning – the day appointed for the battle – Kemp was awoken before dawn by the sound of trumpets. Not the usual blare of reveille, but the call to arms. He jumped up from his pallet, hurrying to pull on his boots and buckle on his sword belt. He might be assigned to Holland's stables, he told himself as he reached for his longbow and his quiver, but he was damned if he was going to miss out on this battle, the long-awaited climax to this seemingly interminable siege. There was no fear in his heart, only excitement. Here at last was his chance to win glory and return home a hero, to capture some noble prisoner as Holland had done and return home fabulously wealthy. Kemp was the first one out of the door of the barrack-house by a long way. Without waiting for orders from Preston or Holland, he hurried through the streets of Villeneuve, still relatively empty in the dingy light of dawn as people only just began to stumble out of the buildings, sleepy-eyed, to find out what all the noise was about.

He ran all the way to the bridge at Nieullay and was gasping for breath by the time he reached it, his lungs aflame. He arrived in time to see Derby's men-at-arms in their full coats of mail mount their horses and form into troops, riding across the narrow bridge and setting out towards the Heights of Sangatte. He saw a man-at-arms he knew vaguely there, carrying a long lance upright. Seeing Kemp, the man-at-arms gestured helplessly, and then turned his attention back to the direction in which he was riding.

Kemp too looked in that direction, towards the French encampment, and his heart sank with despair.

Valois' mighty army was fleeing.

The king's bluff had worked. Valois had never had any intention of meeting the English on equal terms, and once Calais had signalled its intention to surrender, there seemed no point in lingering any longer. To de Chargny's dismay, Valois had ordered that camp be struck, that they should slip off during the night, getting as far away as possible before the English realised they were leaving – 'slinking away with our tails between our legs,' as de Chargny put it to Sir Oudard de Renty.

The last units to leave the encampment were ordered to put to the torch the tents and anything else they could not carry, and it was those fires that had alerted Derby's men to the flight of the enemy. Derby had ordered that his men hurry to arm themselves, furious that the French should seek to give up before the English had had a chance to defeat them.

Kemp watched as the men-at-arms rode up the escarpments of the Heights of Sangatte and turned the enemy's flight into a rout, riding down the fleeing Frenchmen with their lances. He was too exhausted by his run to find a horse, and anyway there would have been precious little a lone mounted archer could have done. Archers came into their own when a position needed defending. Once the enemy had been put to flight, it was the turn of the men-at-arms.

When the full light of dawn fell upon the countryside around Calais, Jean de Vienne made his way to the uppermost tower of Calais castle, using a crutch for support, his leg having been broken in a sally from the city walls a few weeks earlier. His subordinates had reported the flight of Valois' army, but he refused to believe it until he had seen it with his own eyes. Tears filled those eyes as they beheld the smoking waste where only a few hours earlier Valois' army had been encamped. For eleven months he and the townsfolk had held out against all the odds, remaining loyal to Valois, believing that sooner or later he would come to raise the siege. When he finally arrived, just as it seemed they could not hold out another day, it had seemed too good to be true. And now Valois had fled, abandoning his loyal subjects in the town of Calais. Everything they had suffered – the assaults, the bombardments, the hunger and privation – had been for nothing.

Holding on to the parapet for support, de Vienne picked up the pole from which the flag of Calais fluttered, tugged it from its socket and tossed it over the battlements. His last hope was gone, fled in the night like an impossible dream. It was time to surrender.

Sir Walter Mauny spent the rest of that day riding to and fro between his adopted king in his mansion at Villeneuve-la-Hardie, and Sir Jean de Vienne who stood on the battlements of Calais, parleying for the surrender of the town. When de Vienne had heard the terms under which the English king would accept the surrender, the parleying ended, and later that afternoon the church bells of the town pealed for the first time since the siege had begun, summoning the townsfolk to the market-place to discuss the terms.

King Edward was furious with the people of Calais for their lengthy resistance and was reluctant to grant them the honours of war, arguing that they had only offered to surrender when they had no choice. He wanted the whole city to be put to the sack, and the lives of the townsfolk to be forfeit. De Vienne had threatened to continue with the siege but the king knew there was so little food left in the town that the garrison could not even last another day. The town was his to do with as he pleased, the king argued, won by right of conquest. If he chose to put the townsfolk to death, there was nothing they could do to stop him.

Despite the king's evident determination to carry out his revenge on the people of Calais, Sir Walter Mauny courageously spoke out against such inclemency. He argued that if one day their positions were reversed and the English found themselves besieged by the French, then the French might exact vengeance by killing them in turn. The other noblemen who were with the king at the time backed Mauny, and the king reluctantly consented to spare the lives of the townsfolk, provided that six of the leading burghers of the town were handed over to him, with their heads and feet bare, halters around their necks, and the keys to the town and castle in their hands. Those six would be sacrificial lambs, to be dispensed with as he saw fit.

De Vienne rode out of the main gate the following noon, on a nag so emaciated that each of its ribs was clearly outlined through its taut skin. He was followed by six men – once plump, their skin now hanging loosely from their bones – stripped to their shirtsleeves, bare-headed and bare-footed, wearing halters around their necks, exactly as the king had demanded. Their faces were pale with fear, but nonetheless they followed de Vienne willingly.

Surrounded by scores of platoons of soldiers, drawn up in ranks to witness the formal surrender, the king awaited them with the queen and his noblemen. De Vienne handed over the keys of the town and castle to Sir Walter Mauny.

The king ordered that the burghers should be beheaded. Again Mauny boldly pleaded for their lives, arguing a second time that if they showed such cruelty to the French now, in future sieges when their positions were reversed the French would be unlikely to show mercy. But the king would have none of it, until Queen Philippa, now in an advanced state of pregnancy, added her pleas to Mauny's.

Finally the king relented, allowing the queen to see to it the burghers were spared and looked after. He then ordered Mauny and the earls of Warwick and Northampton to take possession of the town and castle of Calais.

Holland's company was one of the first to occupy the newly won town, and Preston and his men took up positions on the battlements while others were put to work rounding up prisoners or herding the townsfolk out through the gates. It was the king's intention to turn Calais into an English colony, repopulating it with true-blooded Englishmen, so he could be sure of its loyalty and rely on it as a base for future campaigns in the north of France.

Relenting even further, the king ordered the army's cooks to provide a dole of a sop of bread and some watered-down wine to the townsfolk before driving them out into the marsh and the countryside beyond. Some of the Calaisians gorged themselves so excessively after the months of hunger that they died from overeating.

Kemp watched the long queues of starving people that formed at each of the king's field kitchens. He was stationed with Conyers, Brewster and Inglewood on one of the turrets that buttressed the town wall. It was strange to be on the battlements at last, as a defender rather than an attacker, looking across towards the wooden buildings of Villeneuve-la-Hardie, a town that had outlived its purpose and was destined to be put to the torch in a few days' time. Turning his gaze to the streets of Calais below, he saw other troops carrying everything that could be moved – furniture, kitchen utensils, clothing, bedding, tapestries, books and caskets of jewellery – to the market-place for distribution by the marshals.

Calais was about the same size as Leicester, but before the siege it had clearly had a greater population. While the houses in Leicester were well spread out, with many gardens and open spaces, the houses in Calais were tightly packed and taller, with overhanging upper storeys built to gain space without incurring additional ground rent. When the Romans built the town they had tried to impose an orderly grid pattern on the streets, and traces of it remained, but they were hard to find as successive generations had crammed more and more houses into the confined space between the walls, creating a maze of higgledy-piggledy streets and alleyways. Calais had been a richer town, too, for there were more stone houses, but the high, overhanging buildings made it harder for the sunlight to reach ground level, and the streets below were dark and shadowy even at noon.

'Look yonder,' Conyers said suddenly, pointing towards the castle. Kemp turned his gaze in time to see the king's standard – the arms of England quartered with the arms of France – being raised on the tower of the castle where, until the previous morning, Valois' standard had fluttered in the breeze. It was not until that moment that the full significance of the past two days struck him.

After eleven months, the siege of Calais was ended. King Edward was the victor, the English in possession of the town. It was the climax of the whole campaign in which he had fought, from the beach near Saint-Vaast-la-Hougue in Normandy, where they had first landed, to the town of Calais itself, by way of the assault of Caen and the field of Crécy. It was over, and now Kemp could return home.

Or so he thought.

That night, the king held a victory ball in the great hall of Calais castle. It was a sumptuous gathering. All of the senior noblemen of the king's army were present, and many of his most senior knights, all dressed in their finest robes.

The Dowager Countess of Kent sat at the high table on a dais at the end of the hall with the king, the queen and the Prince of Wales. She watched the younger couples dancing to the stately *almain* played by the minstrels on psaltery, lute, rebec, pipe and finger cymbals, and admired the fine gowns on display. There was no denying that Joan was the fairest of all the women present, and watching Montague lead her daughter in the dance filled the countess with pride. Joan wore a close-fitting gown of crimson velvet and white crêpe shot through with silver thread, low-cut with an oval neckline. The countess remembered other balls, when she was younger and she had been fairest. Her husband had not enjoyed dancing, but it had not troubled her; she had never lacked for partners.

She found herself looking for Sir Hugh Despenser and saw him talking to one of the queen's ladies-in-waiting; a pretty woman, the countess thought, but perhaps not as pretty as she herself had been at that age. Casting her eyes across the room, she saw Holland seated in one corner between Sir Walter Mauny and Sir John Chandos. Mauny was dressed in the most fashionable clothes, the hem of his cloak dagged in a leaf-pattern, but neither Chandos nor Holland ever seemed to make much of an effort when it came to fashion. Holland was dressed in the same particoloured tunic of blue and white he always wore to court functions, and by now it was starting to look faded and threadbare. And he thought himself a suitable match for the countess's daughter? The very thought was ludicrous!

When the dance ended, Montague led an unresisting Lady Joan back to where the countess sat. The prince fiddled with his goblet as if wrestling with some inner indecision and then put it down, drumming with his fingertips on the table top. Finally, his mind made up, he pushed himself to his feet. 'By your leave, Father?'

The king made a magnanimous gesture, his beaming countenance in sharp contrast to the wrath he had shown earlier that day when dealing with the burghers of Calais. The prince bowed low and then made his way around the table to where Joan sat between her husband and her mother. 'My lady?' he asked, offering her his hand.

Montague was caught off-guard. 'Your Royal Highness! Your offer is most gracious, but you must forgive my wife if she declines, for we have just this moment quit the dance.'

Joan frowned at her husband, before turning her fair face on the handsome young man. 'I would be most honoured, your Royal Highness,' she said, taking his hand and rising to her feet.

Countess Margaret smiled approvingly, glad to see her daughter moving in the exalted circles that befitted one of her royal blood. Perhaps if Joan had not been married to Montague, she thought, she would have made a good bride for the prince. She looked briefly at her oblivious son-in-law, despising him as a soft-hearted weakling who might have abandoned Joan to Holland had it not been for her determination. Then she glanced across to Holland at the far side of the hall, apparently lost in his own thoughts, and consoled herself with the thought that at least Montague was the son of the dead Earl of Salisbury, and likely to become the earl himself one day.

Turning to her left, she saw the king smiling benevolently as he watched his eldest son lead Montague's wife in the next dance. It was a long-established chivalric tradition that every man of gentle birth should have a lady-love, preferably one who was someone else's wife.

'It seems Edward has an eye for the ladies,' the countess heard the king remark to the queen.

'He takes after his father, then,' Queen Philippa responded tartly. 'He will be in his nineteenth year come next summer. Do you not think it time he was married off?'

The king smiled. 'There will be time enough for that later. I am waiting for a suitable alliance to present itself.'

'Marriage alliance, or political alliance?'

The king chuckled. 'I was unaware there was any difference between the two. But we can worry about that at a later date. Tonight let there be naught but celebration!' He pushed himself to his feet, swaying only slightly. 'More wine! More women! Enough of this damned *almain*!' he boomed, snapping his fingers in the direction of the minstrels' gallery. 'Play me an *estampie*!'

The minstrels were swift to oblige, quickly winding up the stately German dance and pausing only long enough for the king to leave his table and cross to where Lady Alice Montague sat next to her husband, Sir Edward Montague, a cousin of Sir William's, before launching into a lively *estampie*. He offered her his arm, and she accepted it with a graceful smile.

It was well-known in court circles that Lady Alice was only the latest in the king's long line of mistresses. The queen bore it well, as always, but Sir Edward Montague's discomfiture was plain to see, his face the very picture of frustration, humiliation, and utter powerlessness as the king led the Lady Alice across the floor in the dance. The king was, after all, the king, and as such beyond reproach.

The *estampie* proved too lively for the prince, however, who was more noted for his skill with the lance than his gracefulness in dancing, and he took his leave of Joan with a bow. The countess saw her daughter turn back towards the high tables, only to be confronted by Holland, who had risen to address her and now seemed inadvertently to block her path. The tall knight towered over her and she started with fright, her normal composure momentarily lost. The countess hoped her daughter would have sense enough to come away quickly.

Holland bowed low, and exchanged a few words with Joan, making her smile. Then he offered her his arm and, to the countess's horror, Joan accepted it and allowed the knight to lead her back on to the dance floor. The countess rose to call her daughter away, and then realised that this would draw attention to the encounter.

Sir Hugh Despenser sat down beside Sir William Montague and gave him a nudge. 'It seems even the gruff Sir Thomas can find a troubadour's tongue where your wife is concerned,' he said, nodding towards Holland and the Lady Joan who were surreptitiously murmuring into one another's ears. 'Are you sure it is you she loves? Even now they may be arranging some assignation . . .'

Red-faced with wine and anger, Montague stumbled over to where Holland danced with Joan. He seized his rival by the shoulder and roughly pulled him away. Caught off-guard, Holland was spun around so that he came face to face with Montague. 'Unhand my wife, damn you!'

An uneasy hush fell over the hall as everyone stopped what they were doing to watch.

Holland regarded Montague with a mixture of amusement and contempt. He could defeat the younger man with sword, lance or fists, and everyone at the ball knew it, including Montague. 'Come now, Sir William, there is no sin in dancing.' In the shocked silence, his soft voice carried clearly to all corners of the room. 'You raised no such objections when his Royal Highness saw fit to choose your wife as his partner for the dance.'

Montague reached for the hilt of his sword with a snarl. Holland instinctively felt for his own in self defence, and the two of them would have come to blows there and then had not the king swiftly interposed himself before either man could draw his blade.

'Sir Thomas! Sir William! This is supposed to be a ball, not a tourney field. Keep your swords sheathed, I tell you, unless you both desire to rouse my wrath.'

Both knights moved their hands away from their sword hilts;

to draw one's sword in anger in the presence of the king was an insult to the royal dignity.

The king turned first to face Montague. 'Sir William, I loved your father as a brother, and because of that I saw fit to promote your marriage to my ward, Lady Joan. Yet as surely as you may count yourself blessed in having the fairest woman in my realm for your wife, you must remember that such a blessing can also be a burden. Youy must learn not to be so hot-tempered when other men look at your wife, and remember that at the end of the day she is yours, and yours alone.'

Montague nodded, and bowed humbly.

The king turned next to Holland. 'Sir Thomas. No one doubts your loyalty to me; nor would they dare to suggest that you have not performed great deeds in my service. Yet I must crave one more favour of you: that you accept that your clandestine marriage to Joan is invalid, and that her marriage to Sir William, blessed in the eyes of God and the Church, is sacrosanct.'

Holland bowed low. 'I have served your Majesty in your claim to the throne of France, by God and your right; if I should seek to establish my own rights, it is only to emulate yourself.'

It was an uncharacteristic and adroit compliment for Holland, but the king frowned, only too well aware that the knight had not agreed outright. 'Enough of this,' he said, with a dismissive wave. 'Let us return to the festivities.' And with that he turned back to Lady Alice and winked at her, bellowing his favourite festive chant in a voice slurred with drink:

*Hey, hey! The White Swan!*
*By God's soul, I am thy man!*

The countess became aware of Despenser and the Bishop of Durham nearby, joking with one another as they pointed to Lady Alice's blue satin garter which, having come adrift during the dancing, now lay on the floor near her feet. 'What's the difference between a woman's garter and her reputation?' riddled Despenser. The bishop shrugged. 'A woman's reputation, once it has slipped, may not be replaced,' explained Despenser, and they both laughed.

Hearing the joke, Lady Alice blushed bright crimson. As if to save her from further embarrassment, the king bent over and snatched the garter from the floor, tying it to his own leg just above the knee, as if it had been his garter rather than hers that had come adrift. No one was fooled, however, and the queen, who had moved on to the floor to join her husband, glared at him reproachfully.

'My lord!' she protested, in a low tone audible only to the king, Holland, Montague, Lady Alice and Lady Joan. 'What will people think?' It was true that everyone was staring at the scene. The nature of the king's court permitted a certain amount of licence, but from the gazes being levelled at them now it was clear that perhaps this time Edward's impropriety had stretched a little too far.

The king shook his head, smiling. 'Evil to him who evil thinks,' he said defiantly, loudly enough for all to hear. He indicated the garter he had tied above his knee. 'I see you all hold this garter a thing of no account,' he continued, still smiling. 'Yet I tell you that within the year you will see it revered before all else.' A blasphemy, to suggest that a garter might be more worthy of reverence than sacred relics, but no one paid heed to such niceties, not even the Bishop of Durham, who would only ever think evil of any man who tried to stand in the way of his liege.

Holland left early, apparently in poor humour after the confrontation, and the countess frowned as she watched him leave. 'Thank heavens he's gone,' she remarked to her daughter. 'Will that rogue never let the scandal die down? I thought I would die of shame.'

'Oh, be silent, Mother, I pray you!' Joan snapped. 'I've had enough. I'm going back to the house.' The king had already allocated the greater houses in Calais to his knights and noblemen, and one of these was now occupied by Montague and his household.

'Alone? At least wait for William to escort you . . .'

'I doubt anyone in this town would be foolish enough to harm a cousin of the king.' Joan slipped out of the great hall. A page retrieved her cloak from the garderobe and she left the castle, heading back to Montague's mansion.

The countess crossed to where Despenser was trying to cheer up Montague by telling him a lewd story. The young man sat with a face full of bitterness, not listening. He looked up at his mother-in-law's approach, and then remembered his wife, glancing around in search of her. 'Where's Joan?' he demanded sharply.

'Aye, now you wonder, after you have neglected her!' sneered the countess. 'She went back to the mansion.'

Despenser arched an eyebrow. 'So soon after Sir Thomas?' he asked provocatively.

'You had better go after her,' the countess said curtly, glaring at Despenser. Montague rose to his feet once more and hurried from the hall. 'Go with him, Sir Hugh,' she added. 'If she has not gone to our house, as she said she would . . .'

Despenser nodded, understanding, and rose with a grin. 'It is always a pleasure to serve you, my lady.'

The Lady Joan and Maud Lacy hurried through the dark streets, dressed in voluminous cloaks, their faces muffled and hidden by the loose-fitting cowls they wore. It would not do for a married lady to be seen alone and abroad at night, even with one of her ladies-in-waiting to chaperone her.

They reached their destination, a moderately sized house in the merchants' quarter. 'Here our ways must part,' Joan said, with a smile. She had chosen Maud as a chaperone because she knew she could rely on her discretion; besides which, the maid had already expressed an interest in one of Joan's paramour's archers, and could be relied upon to keep herself busy for the next hour or two.

Joan made her way around to the wooden stables at the back of the house. The door opened at her touch and she slipped inside. It was dark within and she felt her way hesitantly. She could hear nothing but the snores of a few horses, sleeping on their feet in their stalls. 'Thomas?' she whispered uncertainly. There was no reply. Her eyes growing more accustomed to the gloom of the stables, she moved further in.

Suddenly she was seized from behind, one arm catching her about the waist. She tried to cry out, but a hand was clamped over her mouth, stifling her. She felt herself spun around, pushed back against the stable wall. She was aware of the bulk of the man as he pressed himself against her trembling body. Then the hand was taken away from her mouth and almost immediately she felt his lips against her own. She struggled for a moment, and then she opened her mouth, her tongue flickering against his. They kissed hungrily, holding one another tightly, and then without a word they parted long enough to remove their undergarments before sinking into the straw that had been piled in one of the empty stalls.

After their stint on the walls of Calais, Preston's platoon had barely had time to grab a bite of supper before Holland, dressing for the ball, ordered them to move his possessions into the house allocated to him in the town. Kemp had been busiest of them all, now that he was fulfilling the functions of a squire as well as those of a humble archer. Holland's arms and armour had to be shifted, as well as his dappled-grey courser, Peledargent; his blue-roan palfry, Ferraunt; his pack-horse; and the piebald rouncy.

He left Peledargent until last. As much as he liked horses, the courser was huge, a powerfully muscled beast bred for war and a little too highly strung for Kemp's liking. It was long past midnight before he finally got around to moving it. All day and most of the night the causeway leading through the marsh between Villeneuve and Calais had been chock-a-block with traffic, the people of Calais leaving, and the men of the king's army moving in, so that each trip between Holland's old house and the new had entailed an hour of queuing simply to get into the town. The fact the sentries at the gates were under strict instructions to question closely any man who sought to enter the town did not speed up the process.

By the small hours of the morning the streets of Calais were relatively empty, the silence of the night broken only by the singing and shouting of drunken revellers. Carousing had taken place not only in the castle but also in the town's many inns, already restocked with wine and ale from the English camp. Kemp was in a foul mood, for while his companions had finished their duties earlier and joined in the celebrations, his own work was still not finished.

Approaching Holland's house, leading the courser by its halter, he became aware of a figure muffled in a dark cloak waiting in the shadows by the door. He could not see its face, but he knew instinctively from her stance that it could only be Maud, and realised she was probably waiting for him. His heart sank. When he forced himself to regard her with detachment he had to admit she was attractive. But the prospect of carnal intercourse had filled him with horror ever since he committed rape and he had no wish to be tempted to repeat such brutality with Maud.

She threw back her cowl to reveal her face and smiled at him. Her dark, curly hair shone in the moonlight. Aye, she was pretty enough, Kemp had to admit, but somehow she failed to stir any passions within his breast, or within any other part of his anatomy for that matter. Nowadays when his dreams were filled with lascivious thoughts, he woke up in a cold sweat.

'Good morning, Martin.'

He made a non-committal grunt by way of reply and led the horse past her without pausing.

'What are you doing?'

'Milking an oliphaunt,' he told her, and immediately regretted his curtness. He knew he should be flattered rather than irritated by her attentions.

She grabbed his arm and caught him off-guard. 'Don't you find me attractive?'

'I've already told you,' he explained patiently. 'It's not that. It's just that I love another.'

Maud grinned. 'She need never know.'

'*I* would.' He spoke with the force of one who knew all there was to know about guilt.

She moved closer to him. 'And what makes you so certain she is not betraying you with another man?'

'Beatrice isn't like that,' he insisted.

'Can you really be sure?' She tried to slip her arms around his waist, standing on tip-toe to kiss him, but he pushed her away. There was something akin to horror in his eyes.

'Please, Maud, stay away from me,' he pleaded. 'I'm not a good person to be with.'

'What is it you're afraid of?'

He stared at her with dark, hollow eyes, his face pale in the moonlight. 'Only myself,' he croaked hoarsely. He turned away abruptly and began to lead the courser down the alley at the side of the house.

'Where are you going?' she asked, in sudden alarm.

'Where do you think I'm going, leading this beast?' he asked, nodding towards the stables.

'But you can't go in there!'

'Why not?'

'Because . . . because you just can't, that's all! Please, Martin, trust me in this matter.'

'Sir Thomas told me to put all his horses in the stable. He'd be furious if I failed in such a simple task.'

Maud ran her fingers through her dark curls in agitation. 'Surely it can wait until the morn?'

Kemp shook his head incredulously. 'I've just led this animal all the way from Villeneuve. You can't expect me to turn around and head back now we're only a few yards from our destination?'

She grabbed his arm again, tried to hold him. 'Please, Martin, it can wait. Stay with me tonight . . . let's take the horse and go for a ride on the beach . . .'

He shook her off, his arm coming free more easily than he expected so that he struck her in the face with his hand, knocking her to the ground. He was filled with horror when he realised what he had done and crouched beside her.

'God in heaven! I'm sorry, I didn't mean to hurt you . . . forgive me . . .'

She was dazed by the blow, but otherwise unhurt. 'You churl! You damned, brutish churl!' she snapped, and struck him in the face, open-handed. 'Upon my life, I hate you!' She scrambled to her feet and fled into the night, sobbing.

Kemp remained where he was. She was right: he was nothing but a damned, brutish churl . . . but had he not tried to warn her it was so?

He rose and turned to Peledargent. Even the horse seemed to stare reproachfully at him with its huge, dark eyes. 'I know, I know,' he sighed, ruffling its mane. 'I don't deserve her. I don't deserve either of them.'

He picked up the halter and led the horse to the stable door. He frowned; he was certain he had left the door bolted. As he stepped inside, he thought he heard a noise – a whispering, rustling noise, suddenly silence. Rats? Rats did not whisper. Kemp knew instinctively that, apart from himself and the horses, there was someone else in the stable.

He looped Peledargent's halter to the nearest wooden post and reached for his broadsword. He grasped the hilt, and then realised the massive blade would be more of a hindrance than a help in the close confines of the stable. He transferred his grip to the round haft of his dagger, easing the long, triangular blade from its sheath. He realised that he too had caught his breath. Dagger in hand, he waited in deathly silence until his eyes became accustomed to the darkness – the first light of dawn was in the sky, and filtered through the gaps between the planks of the walls and roof – breathing shallowly through his mouth. Ever so slowly, he moved deeper into the stables, putting each foot down with infinitesimal care, so that his steps made not a sound. If whoever was in there was fool enough to think the silence meant he had left, then they might be tricked into making some sound that would give away their position. But the silence continued.

By now his eyes had grown used to the darkness and he could see that if there was anyone else in the stable, they were hidden. He asked himself where he would hide, if he was in the other man's position. The rafters, of course: people rarely looked up, even when they were searching for someone, and as a boy playing hide-and-seek he had always been the last found by hiding in plain view, high in the branches of a sturdy tree or on the roof of a cottage or barn. He slowly tilted his head back, his imagination populating the rafters with all manner of murderers, demons and monsters waiting to pounce down on him, but his gaze revealed no one.

That left only the stalls.

He continued to move cat-footed along the length of the stables, keeping his back to the wall opposite the stalls, dagger poised, his eyes searching each stall in turn as he drew level with it.

He came to the last empty stall, and froze.

Two eyes stared back at him, glistening in the darkness. He could see only the top half of a woman's face, peering at him over a man's shoulder, but even if he lived for a thousand years he would never forget a single feature on the face of the Fair Maid of Kent. And though the man had his face buried in the crook of the woman's neck and shoulder, the strip of white cloth that ran around the back of his head marked out his identity clearly enough.

Kemp was filled with the most acute embarrassment as he realised he had discovered not malefactors up to no good, but two lovers locked in carnal embrace. Instead of relief, he felt himself shaking with guilt at having interrupted them. His mind froze as he tried to think what he should do next. The obvious solution was to get out of there, but the woman had seen him, and she knew he had recognised her.

Recovering his presence of mind, he replaced his dagger in its sheath and turned to where he had left the courser tied up. 'No one here, Peledargent,' he said loudly. No longer making any attempt at silence, he crossed back to the far end of the stable, put the courser in an empty stall, and left, clattering the latch but leaving the door unbolted.

After all the tension, Joan giggled with relief, and Holland found himself laughing too. 'Did he not see us?' he asked at last.

Joan shook her head. 'He must have. It was one of your men: the young blond one you used to send me your letter.'

Holland nodded. He had realised it must be Kemp even before he recognised the archer's voice.

'Will he gossip about us?' asked Joan.

Holland shook his head. 'Kemp never speaks unless directly addressed and almost never volunteers information unless directly asked.'

'And if he's directly asked?'

'He's loyal to me. Besides, I promised him a position in some merchant's house in London for a year and a day so he can win his freedom from his own lord. I think we can rely on his discretion.'

'My lady-in-waiting finds him very handsome.'

'Kemp? Handsome?' Holland sounded unconvinced.

'You have not a woman's eye, my lord. I think she is right – he *is* handsome, in a rather brutish way.'

'You stay away from him!' snapped Holland.

'My lord! I do believe you are jealous.'

'It's not that. There's something about that lad . . . I am glad he serves the king and not Valois. I would hate to have such a man against me. There is something . . .' He shook his head. He could not articulate the sense of unease the young archer sometimes gave him, and he was not in the mood to try. 'Besides,' he continued, smiling as he lowered his head to brush her nipples with his lips, 'what man would not be jealous, when the woman he loves is married to another?'

She ran pale, slender fingers through his dark hair. 'How much longer, Thomas? How much longer must we put up with this charade?'

'You have heard that I sold the Count of Eu to his Majesty?'

She nodded.

'Your royal cousin has unwittingly given me the means to challenge his match between you and Montague. Now I can afford the legal costs of a protracted court case . . .'

'How protracted?' she asked.

He smiled down at her. 'The sooner it is begun, the sooner it will be ended.'

'There is a man who has been in the queen's service for nearly ten years now; a serjeant-at-law named Master Robert Sigglesthorne of Beverley. Her Majesty speaks highly of him as an attorney.'

Holland frowned. 'He sounds expensive.'

'But you can afford it now, can you not?'

'Aye . . .'

'And will it not be worth it to have me as your lawful wedded wife?'

He grinned. 'Worth every last farthing,' he assured her, and bent his head to kiss her again.

She pushed him away. 'I must get back, before William misses me.'

The two of them began to dress. Holland pulled his breechcloth back on, adjusting it around his hips below the hem of his tunic before fastening it to the laces of his hose. Joan was still sorting out her own undergarments as Holland buckled his sword belt around his waist. 'You wait here,' he told her. 'I'll make sure the coast is clear.'

She nodded and he lifted the latch before slipping outside.

The coast was not clear. Despenser and Montague stood there, dressed in cloaks and cowls. Montague looked nervous, his pale young face whiter in the moonlight, but Despenser was smiling, full of his usual self-assurance, and clearly in control of the situation. Both of them clasped the hilts of their scabbarded swords, blocking Holland's path.

# CHAPTER FIVE

HOLLAND'S MIND RACED. How long had they been waiting there? Did they know that Joan was in the stable? Had Kemp deliberately brought them there, so that they might catch him *in flagrante delicto*? No; Kemp would not betray him like that . . . or would he?

It was Despenser who brought the uncomfortable silence to an end. 'You are abroad late, Sir Thomas.'

Holland tried to look nonchalant. He did not fear Montague, but Despenser was another kettle of fish, a fighting man like himself. 'It seems I am not the only one, Sir Hugh,' he remarked.

'We are in pursuit of a fugitive,' explained Despenser.

'Oh?' said Holland. 'What was his crime?'

'Abduction and rape,' said Despenser, with a grin. 'We thought he might be hiding in your stables.'

Holland shook his head, hooking his right thumb over the buckle of his sword belt in a casual, relaxed pose which had the advantage of placing his hand inches from the hilt of his sword. 'There is no one in there.'

'But surely you can have no objection if we prefer to see for ourselves?' persisted Despenser.

'I object to being called a liar,' Holland replied evenly. 'Tell me, who was the victim of this rape and abduction?'

'Better for the lady's honour if her name is not brought into this,' Montague said.

Holland smiled. 'Then perhaps it might also be better for her honour if you do not insist on entering these stables.' The battle-lines were drawn now; they knew Joan was in the stables, and they also knew that Holland knew they knew it. 'If it is the honour of the victim and her husband you care to protect, then perhaps you should return in the morning to give the victim a chance to return home without any public humiliation.'

'And what would I find if I were to return in the morning, apart from the stable door bolted and the horse gone?' Montague asked coldly.

'You would find me ready to wash any slur on my honour in your blood.' The challenge was easily made, because Montague would never accept it: Holland was too good a swordsman.

Despenser shook his head. 'We settle this now, Holland,' he snarled, drawing his sword.

Holland and Montague did likewise. 'Two against one?' challenged Holland. 'Your sense of chivalry has abandoned you, Sir Hugh.'

'Two against two, Sir Thomas,' said a familiar voice, and they turned to see a fourth figure standing there, dressed in a black cloak with a loose-fitting cowl that concealed his face.

'And who are you?' demanded Despenser. 'A churl, by your accent.'

'Who I am does not concern you,' growled the newcomer.

'It concerns me greatly, if I am to cross swords with a churl . . .' began Despenser, breaking off in mid-sentence to lunge with his sword at Holland, judging the knight to be the greater threat of his two opponents. Holland knew Despenser of old, however, and had been awaiting such a tactic. He parried the thrust with ease, before swinging his sword at Despenser's head.

Taking his lead from Despenser, Montague joined the attack, charging at the other man, who seemed to be unarmed. Before he could cover even half the distance between them, however, the cowled figure reached inside his cloak and produced a broadsword, swinging it above his head to bring it crashing down against the up-raised blade of Montague's weapon. Montague stumbled under the force of the blow, and the cowled figure dashed in close, jabbing at his opponent's shoulder with the point of his sword. Montague fell back with a cry, clutching at a dark stain which spread across the rent in his tunic.

'Sir Hugh! I am wounded!'

Despenser was only too well aware of the fact because it meant he now faced both Holland and the newcomer alone. He hoped he could hold his own against Holland in single combat; but the peasant had proved to be surprisingly skilled with the broadsword and even Despenser knew when he was outnumbered. He levelled his blade at Holland's face. 'I'll not forget this, Holland!' he growled.

Holland smiled. 'I should hope not, Sir Hugh.'

Despenser returned his sword to his scabbard, and turned to help Montague. The two of them backed away, the younger man leaning on Despenser for support. The wound he had received was not serious but it would certainly provide him with some discomfort for the next month or two.

When they had disappeared from sight, Holland sheathed his own blade. 'Well done, Kem . . .' he began, turning, only to find that the archer had slipped away as silently as he had arrived. Holland shuddered with cold, only to realise that it was a warm midsummer's night, and any chill he felt must come from within.

Robert Sigglesthorne of Beverley was a portly middle-aged man with long, wavy iron-grey hair, a heavily jowled face dominated by a strawberry nose, and a pair of rheumy, bloodshot eyes. He was dressed in particoloured robes of brown and green, and a white silk coif, the uniform of a serjeant-at-law in court; the fact he was dressed so out of court suggested that he was at pains to present himself in a professional light. He allowed the page to take his cloak before following him into the main room of the house in Calais where Holland had just finished his supper. The page announced him in formal fashion and Holland rose to his feet to greet his guest.

'Sir Thomas Holland? It is a great honour, sir.' Sigglesthorne had a deep and fruity voice. 'Your reputation precedes you,' he said, bowing low.

'And yours you,' returned Holland. 'You were recommended to me by a lady of the queen's household . . .'

'Ah, yes. Lady Joan, I presume,' Sigglesthorne guessed shrewdly.

'Indeed,' Holland admitted, a little thrown by Sigglesthorne's presumption. He supposed that a serjeant-at-law of Sigglesthorne's reputation was permitted a certain degree of latitude in his behaviour towards his betters. 'You came swiftly in answer to my summons.'

Sigglesthorne nodded. 'I am already locked in a number of other cases of litigation back in London, but I confess that your particular case intrigues me. I would be most honoured to have the privilege of acting as your attorney in this matter. Is that claret in yon flagon?'

Holland hesitated. 'Would you care to help yourself?' he suggested at last.

'I'd be delighted to,' said Sigglesthorne, crossing to the table and filling a goblet. He took a deep draught of the red Gascon wine, licking his lips in satisfaction. 'Mmm! Magnificent. Your taste in wine is to be commended, Sir Thomas.'

'I did not invite you to Calais to discuss wine, Master Sigglesthorne,' Holland pointed out in irritation.

'Indeed not, Sir Thomas,' acknowledged Sigglesthorne.

'I should like you to tell me your especial qualifications for handling this case.'

'Indeed. It is quite right you should, Sir Thomas. Erm... would you mind if we sat?' Sigglesthorne gestured to the benches on either side of the table.

Holland made a gesture signifying assent and they sat down facing one another across the table.

'To start with, my qualifications. I am a bachelor of canon law, and I have served before the King's Bench for more years than I care to recall. Furthermore, I acted as the king's envoy to the Pope nearly four years ago and I spent a good deal of time representing a number of clients in litigation before the Papal Court last summer.'

'The Papal Court?' echoed Holland.

Sigglesthorne nodded. 'From what I understand of your case – and you'll have to forgive me if I'm labouring under any misapprehensions on that score – it will best be served if we take it directly to the Papal Court in Avignon. But first, it will be best if you tell me in your own words your side of the case.'

Holland shrugged. 'I met Lady Joan in the autumn of the thirteenth year of the king's reign, and we were married the following spring...'

'A clandestine marriage, without the publication of the banns and the blessing of a priest?' asked Sigglesthorne.

Holland nodded. 'But I thought a marriage contract between man and woman was valid in the eyes of the Church, to the exclusion of subsequent marriages?'

Sigglesthorne nodded. 'Provided there were no impediments such as consanguinity, conpaternity or previous espousals. I take it your union had no such impediments?'

'None.'

'The validity of marriages not made *in facie ecclesiae* – that is, without the publication of banns and the blessing of a priest – is somewhat of a grey area in law,' explained Sigglesthorne. 'In fact, it very much depends on what kind of law one chooses to consult, which is why I recommend that we petition the Papal Court. The Church distinguishes between espousals *per verba de praesenti* – by words of the present tense – and *per verba de futuro* – in effect, a betrothal, in which a couple express their intention to become man and wife at a later date. Now, according to canon law, a *de futuro* espousal is automatically transformed into an espousal *de praesenti* if the *de futuro* contract is followed by carnal intercourse prior to the public solemnisation of the marriage. I . . . ah . . . am I to take it that your marriage to the Lady Joan comes into the latter category?'

Holland shook his head. 'Our marriage was *per verba pre . . . prea . . .* in words of the present tense.'

'Then I do not see that we are likely to face any major impediments to the satisfactory resolution of this case, if we petition the Papal Court. Now, pray continue your tale.'

'After my marriage to the Lady Joan, I was called upon to go to Flanders in the service of his Majesty, after which I went on to crusade against the heathens in Lithuania,' said Holland.

'Splendid!' said Sigglesthorne. 'We can use that in our petition. His Holiness is a keen supporter of crusading. I am sure he would look favourably on any man who had proved his devotion to the Christian faith in such a manner. Pray continue.'

'By the time I returned, I found that his Majesty, as the guardian of the Lady Joan, had given her in marriage to Sir William Montague.'

Sigglesthorne nodded. Holland's account fitted in with what he himself had heard. 'That is the other reason for petitioning the Papal Court, of course. I'm certain I have no need to tell you there is no love lost between his Holiness Pope Clement and his Majesty King Edward on account of his Holiness's background as a notary at the French court. If the petition were to be presented before an English court, the court would be more likely to give a verdict favouring the marriage blessed by the king. His Majesty might even put pressure on the court to ensure the marriage backed by him was recognised as the legal one. His Holiness, on the other hand, is unlikely to be – how can I put this? – hampered by qualms about giving a verdict contrary to his Majesty's wishes.'

Holland frowned. He might win his case at the Papal Court, but in so doing there was a grave danger he might earn the king's displeasure, a risk not to be taken lightly. Did he love Joan enough to take that risk? To jeopardise his whole career?

He silently cursed himself for even having to think about it. 'Very well.'

'I take it you can produce witnesses to your marriage?' asked Sigglesthorne.

'To the marriage? Aye. As to the . . . consummation . . .'

'If, as you say, the marriage was made *per verba de praesenti*, that should not be necessary,' Sigglesthorne said hurriedly. 'Now we must consider the arguments likely to be put forward by Montague and his family . . . by the way, where do the Lady Joan and her family stand on this matter?'

'Her Ladyship will back me up,' Holland averred. 'Her father is dead, but her mother . . .'

'The Lady Margaret, Dowager Countess of Kent?'

'The same.'

'Dreadful woman,' sniffed Sigglesthorne. 'I presume she supports the Montague marriage?'

'Aye.'

'Hm – that could make things awkward. Since canon law is clearly on our side as far as the facts of the case are concerned, Montague's attorneys are most likely to call the reliability of your witnesses into question. I take it they are gentlemen of good character?'

'Naturally.'

'You must forgive me for asking such a question, but if any problems are likely to come up it is best I am prepared for them.'

'You are willing to take on the case?'

'If you are willing to pay for my services, yes. I am afraid my learning and rhetoric do not come cheaply.'

'So I had gathered,' Holland said dryly.

'Very well, then. Our first step will be for the two of us to travel to Avignon so you may present your petition to the Curia . . .'

'I'd like to say how much I'm going to miss this place after we've left,' said Conyers, gazing around at the marshes about Calais and the smoking ruins of Villeneuve, put to the torch a few days after the fall of Calais. 'But that would be lying,' he added. Like most of his companions, he had suffered several bouts of dysentery during their sojourn in the marshes, and they would all be glad to escape the unhealthy atmosphere of that place.

Preston's men were standing on the deck of a cog tied up alongside the quay in Calais harbour, waiting for the tide to turn so they could sail back to England. It was thirteen months since they landed in France, far longer than any of them had anticipated the campaign would last. Yet now they were only days from returning to their homes, they felt only gladness that it was over, rather than resentment at having been kept overseas for so long. Those who worked on the land – the majority of them – had missed the previous harvest, but they might yet be home in time for the next one.

Holland rode up on his blue-roan palfrey, followed by Preston on a bay rouncy. The two of them reined in on the quayside and dismounted, Holland handing his bridle to Preston before striding up the gangplank on to the deck of the cog. 'Kemp!'

Kemp took his leave of his friends, unconsciously adjusting his kit as he crossed the deck to where Holland stood at the top of the gangplank. 'Sir Thomas?'

'I have not yet had a chance to thank you for your assistance the other night.'

Kemp was embarrassed. 'You saved my life at Blanchetaque last year, sir. I was just returning the favour. There, er . . . there aren't likely to be any . . .' he struggled to recall the word he wanted, '. . . repercussions, are there?'

Holland smiled. 'For you? No. Speaking of Blanchetaque, Kemp, I recall striking a bargain with you that day.' He handed Kemp a parchment envelope sealed with wax. 'There is a wealthy vintner who lives in the Vintry Ward of London. Give him this letter.'

'Yes, sir.' Kemp hesitated, staring at what to him was a meaningless jumble of letters.

'It is a letter of recommendation,' explained Holland. 'Recommending you. The vintner is a wealthy man who I understand desires to hire a bodyguard. The letter explains that you would be ideal for the job, but you only want to take up the position for a year and a day, so you can qualify for freeman status. I am certain he will understand, and be sympathetic to your situation.'

'I . . . I don't know how to thank you, sir . . .'

'Once you are a freeman, you will be able to come to work for me at my manor at Broughton in the County of Buckingham. See that you do so. I should be back from Avignon by then, although with these legal wrangles one can never be certain.'

'You're not sailing back to England with us, then, sir?'

Holland shook his head. 'I have certain matters in Avignon that must be taken care of.'

He turned away without another word, and was halfway down the gangplank before a thought occurred to Kemp. 'Sir Thomas! Begging your pardon, Sir Thomas, but how am I to find this vintner?' he asked, indicating the address on the envelope which he could not read.

'He lives in a fine house on Thames Street in London,' Holland called back. 'Ask for him by name. Most people in the Vintry Ward will have heard of Master John Chaucer.'

'John Chaucer,' Kemp muttered to himself, to impress the name in his memory. 'Aye, sir!' he called after Holland, who reclaimed his bridle from Preston and swung himself up into the saddle.

Preston was climbing into the saddle of his rouncy when Conyers shouted down to him. 'Hey, Preston, you old whoreson!' He unfastened his breech-cloth and bared his buttocks over the ship's bulwark at the serjeant. 'Kiss my arse!'

Preston grinned, and raised two fingers. 'I may not be your serjeant any more, lad, but I've still got fingers enough to plant an arrow between your scabby cheeks!' Digging his heels into his rouncy's flanks, he rode off after Holland.

Kemp rejoined his companions. 'What was all that about?' asked Brewster, idly chewing the ever-present piece of marsh-reed.

'I'm not going back to my lord's manor when I get back to England,' Kemp said with determination. 'Sir Thomas has arranged for me to work as a bodyguard to some rich vintner in London for a year and a day, so I can become a freeman.' He turned to Conyers. 'What are you going to do when we get back to England, John?'

'When I get back to England,' mused Conyers, 'I'm going to take all the gold I won in booty, and open a brothel in Doncaster. The finest brothel in the town, with the most beautiful women that can be bought in England. And I'm going to fuck every one of them every night while I'm still young enough to enjoy it.' He turned to Inglewood. 'What about you, Pisspants? What are you going to do? Return to your father's farm?'

Inglewood shook his head. 'That old whoreson can go to the devil!' he sneered. Of all the men who had joined Preston's platoon, few had been more affected by their experiences than the once-sensitive franklin's son. 'I'm going to enter holy orders, and my father's farm can go to wrack and ruin for all I care.'

Conyers chuckled, and turned to Brewster. 'What about you, David?'

Brewster took the marsh-reed from his mouth and stared at it thoughtfully. 'I'm not going back.'

'Not going back!' exclaimed Inglewood. 'Why not?'

'Sir Thomas has asked me to keep his inn here in Calais,' explained Brewster. Like the houses of many rich men, the one granted to Holland had an inn attached, and it already bore his coat of arms. Brewster's parents owned an inn in Leicestershire so it was only natural Holland should turn to him to run the White Lion inn in Calais. For Brewster, who had always longed for an inn of his own, it was an opportunity he could not afford to miss. He turned to Tate. 'How about you, Limkin?'

Tate shrugged. 'I don't really know,' he admitted.

Conyers threw up his hands in despair. 'I don't know! Haven't you got any imagination? When I get back, I'm not going to do anything until I've found out where Wat Preston lives. And while I'm looking, I'm going to hire the biggest cart I can find and pile it high with manure, so that when I've found his house I can fill it from floor to eaves. I reckon I've taken so much shit from that God-damned old whoreson it's only fair I repay him in kind . . .' He broke off, suddenly realising he was no longer the focus of everyone's attention. Seeing they were all staring past his left shoulder, he twisted to see Serjeant Preston standing there, smiling evilly. Conyers blanched. 'You can't do owt to me now. My term of service is over,' he protested.

Preston's grin did not flicker for an instant. 'If I might remind you – all of you – that you're to serve the king for as long as he remains overseas . . .'

'But he's sailing back to England today!' protested Conyers. 'I heard Sir Thomas say so.'

'There's been what you might call a slight change of plan,'

explained Preston, obviously relishing every moment of this situation. He had been sullen for the past few days, haunted by the prospect of peace. 'It seems that on hearing of the fall of Calais, Valois made exactly the same mistake that you boys have made and assumed the war was over for this year. Seems he's gone and disbanded his army. Now wouldn't you say that gives us a perfect opportunity to wreak havoc on the French countryside?'

'But we're supposed to be sailing back to England as soon as the tide turns,' protested Inglewood, still the barrack-room serjeant-at-law at heart.

'No, you *were* supposed to be sailing back to England as soon as the tide turns. Like I said, there's been a change of plan. You're to disembark with your horses and await further orders.'

They stared at him in disbelief, wondering if this were just some witless practical joke. Most of them reached the same conclusion independently: it could not be, as Preston did not have that much imagination.

'Well? What are you waiting for, you God-damned miserable bunch of whoresons?' roared Preston. 'Shift your idle arses! Not you, Conyers. I want a word with you . . .'

'*Merci beaucoup*,' said Conyers, licking his lips as he gazed at the impressive cleavage of the serving wench who placed three cups of wine on the table in front of the tavern. He gave her his most disarming smile, and she smiled back. Kemp felt a twinge of jealousy, and tried to tell himself she probably flirted with all the customers. But he was not convinced; there could be no denying that Conyers had a way with women.

'*C'est trois sous, s'il vous plaît*,' said the wench, and Conyers gave her four.

'*Guardez la monnaie, mademoiselle*.'

'*Merci beaucoup, maître. Vous n'êtes pas d'ici?*'

'*Non. Nous sommes Bretons*.'

'*Ah! Les Bretons!*' The wench rolled her eyes, and went back inside.

'What were all that about?' asked Preston. Although the serjeant had spent more time in France than Kemp and Conyers put together, he had never made any effort to learn the native tongue. 'Learn French?' he had exploded one night in an inn in Calais, when his ignorance of the language had first been exposed.

'What's the point of fighting the French if I'm going to have to learn their foreign blabbing? Might as well surrender now and be done with it!'

'She wanted to know where we were from,' explained Conyers. 'I told her we were from Brittany.' There were many men from the independent duchy of Brittany fighting in the ranks of Valois' forces, although they spoke Breton rather than French. 'Most Frenchmen can't tell a Breton accent from an English one. In fact, most Frenchmen I've spoken to seem to think that Bretons are a bit peculiar all round.' He shrugged, leaning sideways against the table, and took a sip of his wine. 'This is the life, eh? Good weather, good food, good drink, and a pretty girl. What more can a man ask for?'

'I don't reckon much to the company,' muttered Kemp, glancing across to the market square of Saint-Omer where several hundred of the townsfolk were being drilled in spear-fighting.

'All right, enough chit-chat,' growled Preston. 'We're here to do a job, remember? And keep your voices down. If anyone suspects we're English . . .'

The troops were part of a citizens' militia being formed to defend the town against the Earl of Warwick, who was said to be raiding with a large joint Anglo-Flemish force in the vicinity. None of them suspected that the three soldiers who sat quaffing wine outside the tavern on the opposite side of the square were English mounted archers from that force, masquerading as French men-at-arms in order to assess the strength of the town's garrison.

When the three of them were ordered to scout the town's defences, it had been Conyers' idea to march through the gates and pass themselves off as Frenchmen. Both Preston and Kemp had liked the idea; despite his constant joking, Conyers occasionally managed to surprise everyone by proving himself a brave and cunning soldier who would doubtless make a good serjeant-at-arms one day.

'How many do you reckon, John?' asked Preston.

Conyers pursed his lips. 'No more than four hundred, serjeant.'

'Plus a garrison of twenty-two hundred makes twenty-six hundred,' mused Preston.

'That's a power of men,' observed Conyers.

'It is that, lad,' acknowledged the serjeant.

'That's that, then,' Kemp said nervously. What had seemed a good idea to him an hour earlier had lost its shine now he found himself in the midst of the enemy. 'Can we get out of here now?'

'Take it easy, lad. We'll go in our own good time, walking to our horses nice and casually, as if we didn't have a care in the world. No point in arousing anyone's suspicions with undue haste.'

'Hey, serjeant – some of them are coming over here.' Conyers nodded towards two French knights and their squires striding in their direction, with half a dozen retainers in attendance.

'Christ's pain!' hissed Kemp.

'What is it?' asked Preston.

'I know him,' explained Kemp. 'More to the point,' he continued, tipping his 'kettle' helmet forward so that the brim hid his face, 'he knows me.'

'How so?'

'You remember Sir Thomas told you how I struck that French squire?'

'Aye?'

'That's the one I struck,' Kemp said.

'Nails and blood! It's a pity you didn't strike him more forcefully, Kemp; he might not be here to trouble us now. All right, lads, stay calm,' he murmured out of the corner of his mouth. 'You let me do all the talking.'

Sir Geoffroi de Chargny halted before the table, flanked by Guilbert, and Sir Oudard de Renty and his squire. Arms akimbo, his fists balled on his hips, de Chargny regarded the three archers with contempt. 'With the Earl of Warwick and his Flemish mercenaries ravaging the countryside hereabouts, it is a matter of great wonder to me that you three fellows have time to sit about quaffing wine,' he remarked. 'You look to me like professional troops, rather than peasant levies. In whose retinue do you serve?'

'The Duke of Brittany, my lord,' muttered Conyers.

'I was unaware any of the duke's troops were in this region,' de Chargny said suspiciously.

'We left his retinue when Va . . . when the king disbanded his army,' said Conyers.

De Chargny slapped him across the face with the back of a gauntleted hand, scoring three threads of blood on his cheek. 'You address me as "my lord", filth!'

For a moment Kemp thought that Conyers would strike back, but the Yorkshireman had a tight and careful grip on his temper. 'Yes, my lord,' he apologised.

'There is something strange about your accents,' observed de Renty. 'They are not Breton. Are you certain you are not *routiers*, mere brigands with loyalty to none, seeking plunder and booty in the wake of war's path?'

'No, my lord.'

'What about you two?' demanded de Chargny, regarding Preston and Kemp in turn. 'Do you not have tongues of your own?'

'Yes, my lord,' mumbled Kemp. Preston merely imitated the Gallic shrug he had often seen French prisoners perform, drawing down his head as he raised his shoulders.

'Doff your helm when you address your betters!' snapped de Chargny, drawing his sword and flicking its point against the underside of the brim of Kemp's helmet, so that it fell from his head. Kemp caught the helmet before it hit the ground, and hurriedly placed it back on his head, but the damage was already done. His sword still levelled at Kemp, de Chargny stared at him incredulously. 'I know you, do I not?'

'I think not, my lord,' mumbled Kemp.

'Look me in the eye, damn you!' With the point of his sword against the underside of Kemp's jaw, de Chargny tilted back his head. 'I know you indeed! You are Sir Thomas Holland's churlish squire!'

'Aye, Sir Geoffroi. It is he,' growled Guilbert.

'I know this churl. He is an Englishman!' de Chargny told de Renty. He looked wolfishly at Kemp. 'We are no longer under a flag of truce. It is time for your lesson in manners, dog.' He turned to the two squires. 'These men are enemy spies. Seize them!'

Conyers snatched the flagon off the table and hurled it at de Renty's squire. It bounced off the man's helmet and he staggered, dazed. At the same moment, de Chargny raised his sword above his head to strike at Kemp. Kemp sharply tipped up the table, ducking down at the same moment, so that his opponent's blade bit deep into the wood. Then the edge of the table came down against de Chargny's shins and he over-balanced, sprawling on the cobbles.

De Renty's squire drew his sword and lunged at Kemp. The young archer drew his own sword almost as swiftly, parrying the blow. Guilbert engaged Preston, his superior strength and swordsmanship steadily driving the serjeant back; while Conyers found himself facing de Renty, desperately trying to parry the huge knight's unending succession of blows with no chance to make a thrust in retaliation. The tip of de Renty's arcing blade scored a line of blood across Conyers' brow, and he had to blink repeatedly as his own blood threatened to blind him.

Seeing de Chargny and de Renty assailed, some men-at-arms rushed to their assistance, swords drawn. Outnumbered and outclassed, the three archers found themselves surrounded. Slowly but surely they were herded back against the wall of the tavern.

# CHAPTER SIX

KEMP KILLED HIS opponent with a thrust to the throat, earning himself the briefest moment to look around. A man-at-arms had gone to de Renty's assistance, the two of them competing to slay Conyers. Kemp stepped up behind the man-at-arms and brought his blade down without warning. It glanced off the man's helmet and bit through the chain-mail links of his hauberk to rest on his left shoulder, slicing deep through bone and muscle. Wiping his own blood from his eyes with his sleeve, Conyers flashed a quick grin of gratitude at Kemp, then at once had to parry de Renty's next blow.

Kemp turned to Preston, who faced both de Chargny and Guilbert. Even as he moved to help, the point of the knight's sword entered Preston's side and blood splashed on to the cobbles. Kemp was about to stab the Frenchman from behind when it occurred to him that their best chance of escaping lay in keeping de Chargny alive. He grabbed a fistful of de Chargny's russet locks in his left hand, and with his right he pressed the flat of his blade against the knight's throat.

'Drop your sword,' he snarled and then repeated himself in French. The translation was unnecessary, however; even if de Chargny had not understood English, Kemp's meaning was painfully clear. De Chargny froze, holding his sword away from his body before allowing it to clatter against the cobbles. 'Order your men to do the same.'

'Enough, men,' barked de Chargny. 'Drop your weapons and do as he says . . . for now.' He seemed as cool and calm as ever, which made Kemp feel more nervous than he already was. Even with the blade of his sword at de Chargny's throat, it seemed to Kemp as if it was the Frenchman who was in control of the situation.

De Renty hesitated, reluctant to relinquish his blade.

'Drop it, I said!' snapped Kemp.

De Chargny nodded. 'Do as he says, Sir Oudard. They cannot escape.'

De Renty tossed his sword to the cobbles with a shrug.

Kemp glanced towards Preston, who was leaning against the wall of the tavern, his face pale, his bloody hand pressed hard against a dark stain on his brigandine. 'Are you all right, serjeant?' he asked, his voice sounding frightened and high-pitched to his own ears.

'Your friend is obviously badly injured,' de Chargny hissed in English. 'If he does not receive treatment from a surgeon quickly, he will certainly die.'

'Don't listen to him, Kemp,' growled Preston. 'I'll live.' But the wince of pain that stole across his features belied his words.

'Now what?' demanded de Chargny. 'You are fooling yourself if you think you will escape this town alive. If you surrender now, I may yet be merciful.'

'He's right, Martin,' said Conyers, wiping the blood out of his eyes. 'No one will think ill of us if we surrender now . . .'

'Pay no heed to him, Kemp!' snapped Preston. 'Throw down your weapons and you're as good as dead! They've nothing to gain by taking us prisoner . . .'

'Listen to your friend, Martin,' de Chargny said silkily. 'I promise you all your lives, if you will but lay down your arms. You have my word of honour on it as a gentleman . . .'

If there had been any doubt in Kemp's mind about the wisdom of his present course of action, de Chargny's ill-judged words swept it away. 'A gentleman?' he sneered. 'I piss on gentlemen! One more God-damned word out of you, *mon sieur*, and I'll carve you a second mouth below your chin! All right, John, we're moving across to the horses. If anyone else raises so much as an eyebrow, then it's your lord's widow you'll be making your apologies to,' he added in French.

Conyers held his sword in his right hand, ready to strike, still wiping blood from his eyes every few seconds, as he covered Kemp's back. Kemp forced de Chargny to follow the wounded serjeant, keeping the blade of his sword hard against the knight's throat.

A dozen rouncies were tied up on the other side of the street. Conyers swung himself up into the saddle of the nearest. 'Can you ride?' Kemp asked Preston.

'I don't see that I've got a lot of choice.' Preston put his foot into his stirrup and clambered up into the saddle.

Conyers rode round to where Kemp and de Chargny stood, laying the blade of his own sword against the Frenchman's throat so Kemp could sheath his weapon and vault into the saddle of the next rouncy. 'Ready?' Conyers asked his companions. They all nodded. 'Let's go!' He kicked de Chargny in the face, sending him sprawling on the cobbles once more, and the three of them dug their heels into their horses' flanks, drawing their swords again as they galloped through the town. The French militiamen who crowded in the street parted as the armed horsemen charged through.

Preston was half out of his saddle from loss of blood by the time he and his men met the Earl of Warwick's column about two miles from the walls of Saint-Omer, on the road to Calais. There were perhaps two and a half thousand men in the column: roughly seven hundred and fifty archers, five hundred men-at-arms, and twelve thousand and fifty Flemish foot-soldiers. The three archers reined in at the head of the column, where they were greeted by Warwick and Holland. 'Well?' demanded Warwick.

Preston tried to speak but he was weak from loss of blood and out of breath after the hard ride. He shook his head helplessly, gasping air into his lungs in huge sobs.

'Twenty-two hundred professional soldiers, my lord, and a citizens' militia maybe four hundred strong, all armed and ready for battle,' panted Kemp.

'You're sure, boy?' demanded Warwick.

Kemp nodded.

'What happened?' asked Holland.

Kemp gestured at the bloody stain that continued to spread around Preston's side. 'The serjeant's wounded, Sir Thomas.'

Holland nodded and turned to Conyers. 'Help the serjeant find someone who can tend to his hurt.' He turned back to Kemp. 'What happened?' he repeated.

'You know that French squire I had a scrap with during the negotiations at Villeneuve-la-Hardie, sir?'

'Sir Geoffroi de Chargny's squire, aye.'

'Him and his master – de Chargny – were there. De Chargny recognised me.'

Holland clenched one fist and beat it against his armoured thigh in frustration; he should never have allowed them to go on the reconnaissance mission.

'My lord!' A page pointed to where a large body of mounted troops was riding out of Saint-Omer, the banners of de Chargny and de Renty at their head.

'Too many for pursuing these men, Sir Thomas,' observed Warwick. 'I believe they mean to take us on!' He glanced over his shoulder, back at the column that straggled along the road behind him. The men were in good marching order, but it would take them several minutes to manoeuvre into a defensive position, and it would hardly take that much time for the advancing French to reach them.

Warwick searched the terrain for a suitable hill on which they could take a stand, but there was nothing they could reach and still have time to manoeuvre to meet the French. They would be as well to form up on the road where they stood. He began to bark out orders at his marshals, and the column slowly folded out into two battalions, one Flemish, the other the standard combination of English archers and men-at-arms.

'What about me, Sir Thomas?' asked Kemp.

Holland wheeled his horse amidst the confusion to glare momentarily at the archer. 'Rejoin your platoon. You're twentieth man now, Kemp.'

Kemp was deep in his own thoughts by the time he reached the other men of his platoon, who were tying up their rouncies to a nearby fence. Twentieth man – platoon commander – a great responsibility. Preston had been twentieth man up until now, doing all the thinking while Kemp and the others merely obeyed his orders. Kemp was not sure he was up to the task. When Preston had been wounded in the market-place of Saint-Omer he had taken charge of the situation but that was instinctive, when an obvious solution to their predicament presented itself to his mind.

'Where's the serjeant?' demanded Jarrom, as Kemp took his longbow back from Brewster.

'He's wounded,' Kemp told him tightly. 'John's taking him back to the baggage train. I'm twentieth man now.'

'You!' Jarrom exclaimed incredulously 'Says who?'

'Says Sir Thomas,' Kemp snapped.

'I've had much more experience than you!' protested Jarrom. 'Why, this is only your first campaign.'

'We'd better take up position over there, between those two units of men-at-arms,' decided Kemp, ignoring Jarrom.

Most of the others were happy so long as they were taking orders off anyone other than themselves, but Jarrom was feeling quarrelsome. 'What the devil would you know about it?' he demanded.

At that moment a herald rode up. 'Which one of you is in command here?' he asked the archers.

'I am,' Kemp told him.

'That's debatable,' muttered Jarrom.

The herald shot a glance of irritation in Jarrom's direction before turning his attention back to Kemp. 'You're to plug yonder gap,' he ordered, indicating the space between the two units of men-at-arms that Kemp had noticed earlier. Then he rode on, without another word.

Kemp did not even bother to smile victoriously, merely leading the way across to the designated position.

'Well, of course we're to plug the gap,' muttered Jarrom. 'It's God-damn obvious to anyone with any campaigning experience. I don't need no God-damned herald to tell me that. All I'm saying is, I don't see what right Kemp's got to go giving the rest of us orders.'

'Shut your God-damned mouth before I put one of my boots in it, Elias,' snapped Kemp. 'Is that a good enough right for you?'

They formed a line on the right flank of the battle-line drawn up by the earl. Kemp glanced towards the French, still advancing and now less than half a mile away. Behind the archers, Holland sat astride his palfrey. Aware that the knight's eyes were upon him, Kemp cast an anxious glance at the men temporarily under his command, lest their line be crooked or uneven; but they had all done this so many times that it was second nature. Holland fixed his single eye on Kemp and nodded, but Kemp did not dare to presume that it might be an indication of approval.

Kemp planted a sheaf of arrows in the ground at his feet, as did the other men of the platoon. Battles were decided by how quickly a large number of the enemy could be killed, and each arrow fired could mean one French knight or man-at-arms dead, wounded or unhorsed. Kemp might now be twentieth man but he was damned if he would use that as an excuse not to do his duty. He glanced over his shoulder every few moments to check what signals Holland and the earl were giving out. Holland had drawn his sword, and held it pointing straight down at the ground.

'Nock!' Along with his companions, Kemp plucked an arrow from the ground and nocked it to his bow. He felt the ground beneath his feet tremble as the French knights and men-at-arms accelerated into a lumbering canter, thundering towards them. The horses did not move swiftly – they and their riders were too heavily armoured to permit that – but their inexorable momentum, rather than their speed, did the damage. They couched their lances, their sharp tips coming down almost as one, reaching out towards the ranks of English yeomen who stood before them.

Kemp's hand was sweaty where it gripped the stave of his longbow. There was a tightness in his chest and stomach, that old, familiar feeling of fear. Normally he found the experience comforting, but it had a new element now, something less familiar. Kemp had faced death in battle before and knew he did not fear it. A greater danger lay in the fear of fear itself, the fear that would shame a man by driving him to flight, his own cowardice unmanning him. That fear, too, he had overcome.

But this time it was different. This time he was responsible not only for himself, but also the seventeen men who stood with him. His appointment as twentieth man might only be temporary; even if Preston died, Kemp knew he was too inexperienced to replace him. But if he did well, it would increase his chances of one day becoming a serjeant-at-arms. If he failed, he would have failed himself, failed the men he temporarily commanded, and failed Holland. It was fear of failure that gripped him now.

Holland raised his sword above his head, pointing the blade straight up into the sky. 'Mark! Draw!' Kemp forced himself to get a grip. If he wanted to be a serjeant-at-arms, why should he now fear the chance to prove he could do it?

He pushed the stave of his longbow away from his body, his powerful shoulder muscles holding string and stave apart, but he did not yet take aim, watching Holland rather than the approaching French, confident the knight was able to judge the right moment for the opening volley to perfection.

Holland brought the blade of his sword sharply down in a broad arc so that it glittered in the bright September sun. 'Loose!' ordered Kemp. Seventeen arrows arced away from his platoon, to merge with the hundreds loosed by the English archers. Kemp's arrow followed a moment later, as he paused to take careful aim before shooting. The horse he had aimed at went down, along with a hundred others, spilling its rider on to the ground.

The column of charging knights seemed to shudder as the first volley of arrows rained down on it. Then it split into two, de Chargny's banner leading the half that peeled to the right, where the Flemish foot-soldiers were still trying to manoeuvre into position, while de Renty's banner led the other half of the column round to the left, riding in front of Kemp's platoon. Kemp and his men kept on shooting, as quickly as they could nock arrows to their bows and let fly, but it was not fast enough. De Renty's knights wheeled in a tightly executed circle, and suddenly smashed into the end of the line, ploughing through the English ranks.

Five months earlier Kemp had been part of the Earl of Warwick's force that had tried to take Saint-Omer, and he had seen how a similar manoeuvre routed the English. He could see how the same success might be repeated now. 'Wheel right!' he snapped. The fear was gone now. There was no time to think of death, humiliation or failure.

'What?' Jarrom demanded incredulously.

'You heard me! Wheel right, damn you!'

There was enough urgency in Kemp's voice to ensure that he was obeyed, and the platoon turned to face the men-at-arms to their left, just as de Ribeaumont and his men-at-arms bore down on them. The English men-at-arms struggled to face the enemy, but they had no room to turn their spears in the close-packed crush. Men died screaming with lances thrust through their bodies, or disappeared beneath the hooves of horses to be trampled into the ground.

'Nock! Mark! Aim high!' Kemp did not want any of the men under his command shooting the men-at-arms on their own side.

The first of the French mounted men-at-arms were bursting through the English ranks, their lances levelled now at the archers.

'To hell with this!' screamed Jarrom, throwing down his bow and turning to flee. Two of his friends followed his lead.

'Stand fast!' ordered Kemp. 'Loose!'

Fifteen arrows flew forwards with unerring accuracy, but they were pitifully few. The French horsemen came on. They were too close for another volley.

'Side-arms!' Kemp drew his massive broadsword and raised it above his head. As a horseman tried to run him through with his lance, he swung the sword in a great circle, first slicing off the tip of the lance, knocking it aside, then burying his blade in the horse's skull. The beast went down, spattering Kemp with blood and brains. As the rider sprawled at Kemp's feet, the archer reversed his grip on the hilt of his sword and rammed the point straight down, plunging it cleanly through the horseman's chain-mail habergeon and into his chest. The rider coughed blood, and died.

Kemp tugged his sword free with a grunt, gazing about in search of his next victim. Horsemen were thundering past, paying little heed to him or any of the others, riding them down only when they got in the way. There was no point in Kemp giving orders: there was no one to give orders to. His first command, such as it had been, was part of a rout. He felt sick with failure and humiliation. He knew he could be a good soldier, given half a chance, but here he was being given no chance at all! The Flemish ranks had broken and were fleeing, the English lines similarly beginning to waver. Warwick's trumpeter sounded the retreat.

Holland was crossing swords with a French horseman. 'Fall back!' he shouted, even as he managed to thrust his blade under his opponent's guard and into his stomach.

A mounted man-at-arms headed straight for Ivo Attercross, one of Kemp's companions. The archer threw down his longbow and turned to flee, but the man-at-arms soon rode him down, spitting him on the tip of his lance. Attercross screamed horribly as the lance-tip emerged from his chest.

Kemp had to duck to avoid a sword stroke aimed at his head by a passing rider. Then he waited until there was a gap in the surge of warhorses and made a dash for it, sprinting after the others. He heard hoofbeats, and turned in time to see a French man-at-arms bearing down on him, swinging a battleaxe. Kemp flung up his arms instinctively, freezing in momentary panic, and then an arrow whistled over his head and embedded itself in the man-at-arm's shoulder. The stroke went wide, and the wounded man almost fell out of his saddle. Kemp reached up and pulled his opponent to the ground with a crash, stamping on his neck to finish him off, while at the same time boosting himself up into his saddle.

From the vantage point of the warhorse, he glanced about, taking stock of the situation. There was Brewster, coolly unstringing his bow and replacing it in its bag to carry it across his back, apparently heedless of the French men-at-arms who were advancing everywhere. Kemp did not doubt it had been Brewster who shot the arrow which saved him; the innkeeper's son had saved his life so many times now he had lost count, but Brewster never acknowledged the fact, expecting nothing in return.

Like Kemp, Brewster managed to pull a man-at-arms from his saddle, finishing him off with a blow from his maul which punctured the man's bascinet, before climbing astride the horse himself. He galloped off after the rest of the retreating force, and Kemp was about to follow him when he saw a page carrying Holland's banner run through by a lone French knight, who had broken from his own ranks to win the banner.

Kemp hauled on the courser's reins. It occurred to him that if he could get his hands on that banner he might yet rally Holland's company. As the Frenchman tried to ride back towards his own ranks, Kemp chased after him, drawing his sword once more. He swung his blade, aiming at the man's neck, but he was unused to fighting on horseback, and struck the knight across the back, failing to pierce his chain-mail. The knight reeled from the force of the blow, and tried to wheel his horse to face his assailant, reaching for his sword. Kemp struck again, this time piercing the knight's chain-mail sleeve and cutting down to the bone. The knight screamed, and the blue and white striped lance to which Holland's banner was tied went down, landing point-first in the earth, where it quivered.

The knight was too busy clutching his wounded arm to present any threat. Kemp sheathed his sword and wheeled his mount again, snatching the lance from the ground as he rode past and twisting his wrist badly in the process. Clutching the banner-bedecked lance awkwardly to his chest, he began to ride after the retreating English column. The French were rallying, regrouping, preparing for a rout.

Kemp galloped through the fields alongside the road, clinging for dear life to the reins as the courser leapt over the hedges. He passed most of the fleeing column, which was bogged down in the narrow, muddy lane, and did not stop until he saw one of the wagons of the baggage train abandoned by the side of the road. There he reined in, planting the lance in the ground so that the mud-stained banner hung limply in the still air. Then he jumped down from his horse, tethering it to the wagon, and began to pull away the horse-hair canvas that protected the wagon's cargo from the elements.

Recognising their master's banner, Brewster and Inglewood reined in to find Kemp opening one of the wicker baskets stacked in the wagon. 'What are you doing?' Inglewood asked curiously.

'Making a stand,' said Kemp. 'The French haven't finished for today. If we keep running, the French will just ride us down and wipe us out.'

'He's right,' admitted Brewster.

'Then don't just stand there – help me with these baskets,' snapped Kemp.

They opened a few more of the arrow-packed baskets, hurriedly thrusting the arrows beneath their belts. As they were doing so, other members of the platoon reached them. Jarrom and his two friends simply rode past, but Conyers, Oakley, Tate, and four more reined in to lend a hand. Conyers had tied a rag around his head to staunch the flow of blood from his wound. Just ten of them, thought Kemp – was this really all that was left of the forty men who had sailed from Portsmouth all those months ago?

Holland rode past with two platoons of archers and a troop of men-at-arms he had taken under his command. Seeing a ready supply of arrows, he decided that he too would make his stand here, and took charge of the situation. 'Clear the road! Push that damned plunder wagon into the ditch there – gold's no use to you in the grave!'

Enough space was cleared to form a line across the road, forcing the last of the retreating English to squeeze past in the ditch. Behind them came the French, formed up into close order once more, thundering down the road towards them.

Inglewood and Tate hurriedly passed out fresh sheaves of arrows from the wagon.

'Ready!' Kemp found himself shouting, as he nocked an arrow to his bow. 'Stand fast, lads . . . mark . . . loose!'

Closely bunched in the middle of the lane, the charging French found that the volley of arrows wrought havoc amongst their ranks, as the bodies of men and horses piled up in the road preventing those behind from getting through.

Kemp nocked another arrow and took aim. 'Loose!'

More death, and yet more, turning the narrow lane into a killing ground, and the French advance became an even more confused mess than the English retreat. Finally realising they could not break through, a French trumpeter blew the retreat, and they withdrew beyond bowshot to regroup. The English archers and men-at-arms used the lull in the fighting as an opportunity to mount up, galloping back down the lane after the rest of the earl's column.

Less than a mile further on, the earl had finally halted the flight, imposing a semblance of order on his men with little more at his disposal than sheer will-power. Now the men formed another defensive position across the path. They parted to allow the men under Holland's command to pass through, and then quickly closed ranks, ready to meet the next French attack.

Leap-frogging in this manner, the earl's column retreated to within ten miles of Calais, harassed every step of the way by de Chargny and de Renty as they fought their rearguard action. It was a miracle of belated discipline that the Flemish and English lost less than two hundred men in total.

Dusk was falling by the time the battered column limped back into the safety of Calais' walls. After a quiet, dispirited supper, Kemp walked the short distance to Holland's house, and the two of them played chess in the withdrawing room as usual, sharing a flagon or two of wine. Practice had made Kemp a competent player, although he had yet to beat Holland. They played in silence, as was their custom. Both were taciturn by temperament, and they had little to say to one another. Kemp felt guilty that he had let Holland down in the withdrawal from Saint-Omer, but was not sure how to apologise.

Only fourteen men were left in the platoon now, including Preston, who was expected to recover from his wound; and Jarrom and his two friends, Simon Elliott and Baldwin Gower: the three cowards, as Kemp thought of them. He had not reported their cowardice to Holland who, in his current mood, would almost certainly have them hanged for it. Instead he made sure that everyone else in the platoon knew of it, so that the three were snubbed and shunned at every opportunity by men who had been their closest friends only a few hours earlier. They had broken the first rule of soldiering, that of sticking by their companions, and now no one would care to rely on them, or to serve in the same unit.

With his mind not on the game, the standard of Kemp's play was poorer than usual but Holland too seemed preoccupied. Kemp noticed he was drinking more heavily than normal. He wondered if Holland also felt as if he had somehow failed in the skirmish.

The silence of the room where the two men stared at the pieces on the chessboard was matched by the silence of the streets of Calais, a silence broken only by the melodic sound of a minstrel singing a ballad, while plucking the hopeful tune on a gittern.

*Lady, from whom all my joy comes,*
*I can't love or cherish you to excess,*
*Nor praise you enough as becomes,*
*Nor serve, honour nor obey you no less;*
*For the gracious expectancy,*
*Sweet love, I have of seeing thee,*
*Gives me a hundred times more happiness and cheer*
*Than I could deserve in a hundred thousand years.*

*This sweet hope, with loving desire,*
*Which nourishes me and keepeth me whole,*
*Gives me ev'rything I require*
*To hearten, comfort and gladden my soul;*
*Nor does it depart, morn or eve,*
*But gently maketh me receive*
*Even more of the sweet pleasures that Love rears*
*Than I could deserve in a hundred thousand years.*

*And when Hope, which stays in my heart,*
*My lady, bears such happiness to me*
*When we two are so far apart*
*If I, as I wish, could see your beauty,*
*My joy, as I truly believe,*
*Could not be thought of or conceived*
*By anyone, for I would have more of it, dear,*
*Than I could deserve in a hundred thousand years.*

Kemp was so busy trying to decide what his next move should be that he paid little attention to the words of the song, and he was caught off-guard by Holland's question in the silence that followed.

'Have you ever been in love, Kemp?'

The young archer looked up sharply. 'N . . . no, sir,' he stammered. 'At least, not that I'm aware of. I mean, I thought I was in love, once, but looking back, I don't think I was, if you see what I mean.' Realising that he was gabbling, he fell silent.

Holland chuckled. 'Is there a difference between being in love and believing yourself to be in love?'

Kemp shrugged. 'I couldn't really say, sir. I'm not really sure what love means any more.'

'What about that girl of yours in Leicester County? The noblewoman who gave you that coverchief you hold so precious. Don't you love her?'

'Lady Beatrice?' Kemp hung his head. He did love her but was ashamed to admit it: ashamed of himself. 'She's too good for the likes of me.'

'By birth, you mean? Perhaps.'

'By everything,' Kemp said miserably, thinking of the woman he had raped in Caen.

'I see. And what about Maud Lacy?'

Blushing, Kemp shook his head.

'When I was your age,' said Holland, his words slightly slurred by the wine, 'I was in love with a very beautiful girl. She was very kind and understanding but she said she did not love me and, that being the case, it could not be true love that *I* felt for *her*.' Raising his cup to his lips, he chuckled into it. 'It was of little comfort to me at the time.'

'Do you believe it now, sir?' Kemp asked curiously, moving his vizier.

Holland shook his head. 'No,' he said firmly. 'Love is like . . . like a fever. You cannot eat, you cannot sleep, you cannot think of anything but the object of your affections,' he added. 'And when you see her in another man's arms, it is like being kicked in the stomach.' He picked up a pawn and toyed with it thoughtfully. 'They say I only love her for her money, Kemp.'

Kemp shook his head. 'I don't believe that sir.'

'Why not?' asked Holland, putting down the pawn from where he had taken it and picking up a rook.

'I've seen her. She's very beautiful, if you'll forgive me for saying so.'

'I'll not condemn a man for speaking the truth,' said Holland smiling. 'But Maud Lacy is also very beautiful, and yet you say you don't love her.'

Kemp shrugged awkwardly, and then grinned. 'She's not very rich, though.'

Holland chuckled. 'I don't believe you have been in love, Kemp.'

'Aye and like, sir. And from the sound of it, I'm not sure I want to be.'

'Checkmate,' said Holland, putting down the rook and reaching for his cup to drain it to the dregs.

Kemp stared at the board for a moment, and then shook his head. He rose to his feet. The end of the game usually signalled time for him to return to the inn next door, but his defeat on the chessboard reminded him of the defeat outside Saint-Omer, and his part in it. He knew he could not put off his apology any longer.

'Sir Thomas?'

Holland glanced up.

'I just wanted to apologise,' explained Kemp.

'Apologise?' Holland was bewildered. 'What for?'

'For letting you down, sir. Outside Saint-Omer, I mean, when you made me twentieth man . . .'

'Oh, for heaven's sake!' Holland exclaimed. 'We were defeated, aye. It happens sometimes,' he added, with an ironic smile. 'Surely you don't expect me to blame you, simply because I gave you command of a dozen men? If any one man is to blame it should be me. However, I think if we are to blame anyone, it should be de Chargny. The man's no fool, and bears watching.'

'Aye, Sir Thomas.'

'And as for your performance today, know you the difference between a retreat and a rout?'

'No, sir,' said Kemp. He thought he might understand the difference but did not want to have to try to explain it.

'Sometimes it's as little as one man, Kemp. Just one man.'

There was great excitement in the Sicilian port of Messina when the Genoese fleet entered the harbour. The lateen-rigged galleys were not men-of-war but trading vessels returning from the East, doubtless packed with silks and spices. There were many merchants in the town who would now realise the profit of an investment made several months previously and many women who would buy the luxury goods for their household.

One of the richest of the town's burghers made his way directly to the harbour as soon as the fleet was sighted, and waited on a stone pier as the lead galley approached the quayside. As it neared the pier, the oarsmen shipped their oars, allowing the galley's own momentum to carry it in. Genoese mariners jumped down from the galley's side to tie the mooring ropes to stone bollards and iron rings set in the masonry, helped by dockers waiting on the pier. The gangplank was lowered and the burgher waited at the foot, while the shipmaster appeared above him. The burgher beamed up at him, but the pale-faced shipmaster seemed distracted, descending as if in a daze.

The burgher, who had opened his arms to embrace his friend, now lowered them. 'Matteo? Are you all right?'

The shipmaster seemed to notice him for the first time. 'Eh?' He shook his head. 'Aye. Aye, I'm fine.' He wiped sweat from his brow, although the October sun was temperate.

'You seem distracted. Are you ill?'

'Ill?' The shipmaster grimaced. 'Aye, sick at heart, as any man would be after seeing the things I have seen.'

'There were difficulties in the venture?'

The shipmaster shook his head. 'No. No, the trading went well.' He forced himself to smile, putting an arm around the burgher's shoulders. 'Come. Let me show you what I have brought you from the East.' The two of them ascended the gangplank to the galley's deck.

'So, if the trading went well, what is it that troubles you, Matteo?'

'We lost many men, Signor Villani. Constantinople is cursed. The Lord has seen fit to visit a pestilence upon its people, the foulest I have ever seen. Many of our men succumbed.'

The burgher shrugged, unconcerned. 'God disposes, my friend. The people of Constantinople are schismatics, little better than heathens. If a pestilence troubles them, then it is no more than God's judgement. Besides, Constantinople's loss is our gain, eh? They brought such a punishment upon themselves, with their attempts to restrict the trade in silk.'

The shipmaster nodded, smiling, and led the burgher down to the hold, where bundles of silk were tightly stacked. As they descended the steep companionway, they could hear rats scuttling into the safety of the shadows.

The burgher reached out to test the quality of the silk between his fingers, and a grin slowly spread across his face. 'It's good – very good!'

'Aye. And it came at three-quarters of the usual price. With so many of the people of Constantinople dead, the silk merchants must sell it to whom they can.'

'Has the pestilence affected so many?' the burgher asked in wonderment.

'Aye. A vile death, too. I blanch just to think on it . . .' He grimaced, and pinched at the bare skin on his arms. 'God damn it!'

'What's wrong?'

'Nothing.' The shipmaster held up the forefinger and thumb of his right hand, a flea pinched between them. He cracked its shell between his fingernails, and wiped them on his tunic. 'Just a flea bite.'

Three days later he was dead. The burgher died a day after that. And within a matter of months, a third of the population of Sicily had been wiped out.

The pestilence had arrived in Europe.

# CHAPTER SEVEN

A WEEK BEFORE Martinmas – the anniversary of his birth, if his mother's account of how he had come to be named Martin were true – Kemp came to London.

He approached from the south, walking up the insalubrious high street of the Borough of Southwark with its inns and stewhouses, overhung with the combined stink of the nearby tannery and lime-kilns. He passed the priory of Saint Mary Overie on his left and then the River Thames came into view, and beyond it the skyline of London itself.

Here was a city of about forty-five thousand souls crammed into the square mile of land enclosed within the ancient, crumbling city walls. To the left he could see turreted battlements of Baynard's Castle – now part of a Dominican convent – glowering over the river. Behind it, the spire of Saint Paul's Cathedral on Ludgate Hill rose over five hundred feet into the sky, one of the eighty or so spires that filled the city's skyline. To the right the view was dominated by the ninety-foot high whitewashed keep of the Tower of London, where King David of Scotland was said to be imprisoned following his defeat and capture at the battle of Neville's Cross the previous year. Below the Tower, the king's ships were anchored on the river.

As he approached the bridge, he had first to cross a drawbridge before he came to a fortified gatehouse where two guards were on duty; but this was a city far from the threat of war, and their only tasks were to collect tolls from those who brought goods into the city by packhorse or cart, or to turn away lepers. Kemp was made to relinquish his broadsword, for the carrying of swords within the city itself was illegal. He surrendered it reluctantly, feeling naked without it. The chit the guards gave him would be little protection against a surprise attack by French men-at-arms . . . he caught himself: the war was over and he was back in the safety of England.

Then Kemp was on the bridge. Three hundred yards long, almost a hundred shops and houses were built on it so that, as he crossed, he caught only occasional glimpses of the river. There were glovers' shops, pouch-makers', goldsmiths' and bowyers'. Kemp had seen enough plundered treasure in France for the sight of jewellery to leave him cold. He fancied that many of the treasures on display had been taken from France anyway; but then perhaps they had been stolen by Norman pirates from Englishmen before that.

He emerged from the bridge on to the north bank of the river by the Fishmongers' Hall. Now he was in the City of London itself. A few houses were built of stone, with tiled roofs, like some he had seen in Caen, but most were made of wattle and wood, lath and plaster. Many of the houses were as tall as three or four storeys, and like the buildings on the bridge, the upper floors had overhangs to create more floor space without increasing the ground rent. In many of the narrower streets, the overhang was so pronounced that the streets were more like tunnels, with barely a glimmer of sky visible between the roofs of opposing buildings.

He walked five hundred yards up one street until he came to a busy corn-market, and found himself turning left because that was the way that most of the people who pressed around him seemed to be going. He had never seen so many people all crammed into one place: finely dressed young noblemen, rich burghers in gowns of costly cloth, artisans, farmers, labourers, housewives, people of every imaginable degree and station, all rubbing shoulders together. At first he was convinced that he must have entered London on the day of some local fair or festival, but slowly it dawned on him that the city was like this every day of the year.

A truce had been signed between King Edward and Philip of Valois a few weeks after the fall of Calais. The truce was for nine months, well into the following summer; the English would remain in possession of all the territorial gains they had acquired up to that point, including not only Gascony and Calais, but also land in Brittany and Poitou; and the independence of Flanders was to be preserved.

Like many of the men in the king's army, Kemp had received the news of the truce with mixed feelings. Despite Warwick's defeat near Saint-Omer, many men felt the English were poised to win the war outright, at least to the extent that they could dictate their own terms to Valois, perhaps even demanding their king be granted the throne of France. Many of the professional troops felt deflated by the anti-climax of it all: Calais was won, the French nobility on its knees, and suddenly there was no more fighting to be done, no more booty to be taken. Only the older, wiser heads smiled to themselves and pointed out that nine months was not such a long time, and that if the king ever did decide to renew the war, then his possession of Calais would make it easier for him to land troops in northern France.

Kemp at least had the advantage of knowing how he was to earn a living for the next twelve months, and the offer of a more long-term post in Holland's retinue after that. He had looked forward to the end of his term of service for so long, and knew now that within a little over a year he would be a freeman, and able to return to Knighton and Lady Beatrice. Yet at the same time he too felt disappointed. Serving as an archer in the king's army overseas was more interesting than the monotony of working in the fields, and at least in the army his social superiors treated him with respect; not the respect accorded to an equal, perhaps, but at least an acknowledgement that his services were valued. He had found more companionship than he ever had at home. For the first time in his life, he had felt as if he *belonged*.

The king and the Prince of Wales had sailed for England two weeks after the Truce of Calais, and from that day Kemp's pardon came into effect. He had fulfilled his duty to his king. His ship had landed at Dover in the middle of October, and there he took his leave of those amongst his companions who had likewise settled for returning to England. Many did not. Holland and Preston had taken advantage of the truce to head south for Avignon, accompanied by a portly serjeant-at-law, leaving Brewster in charge of Holland's inn in Calais, which was already starting to fill with English colonists.

Kemp passed a butchers' market on his left, where stray cats, dogs and pigs scavenged amongst the offal. A man was imprisoned in a set of stocks, a loaf of bread hung around his neck to indicate his crime: selling bread in short measures. A few children paused in their game of leap-frog to jeer at him and scrape dung out of the gutter at the centre of the cobbled street to fling in his face, but most people walked past heedless. They had had stocks in Knighton where Kemp grew up. He considered it a good punishment, for if the man placed in them was thought to have been ill-served by justice, then people would bring him food and drink, rather than throw rotten food at him, and chat to him to keep him company.

Kemp walked on, through a market where hens and fish were on sale and market-traders' wives sat in blizzards of their own making as they plucked dextrously at the white feathers of capons and pullets. He passed a church – Saint Thomas of Acon – and a side-street, Ironmonger Lane, which rang deafeningly with the dinning of hammers against anvils. Almost immediately there was another church on his left, Saint Mary le Bow. A gaggle of geese being driven before a young poultry-herder overtook him, on their way to be slaughtered at market. He noticed a stone edifice, where the nets of Thames fishermen, confiscated for having too small a mesh, were being burned.

He was on West Cheap now, a broad thoroughfare lined with merchants' two-storey storehouses, and countless stalls laden with country produce, the traders crying their wares. In the centre of the street stood the Great Cross, one of the marble edifices erected in honour of Queen Eleanor, the king's grandmother, to mark her death fifty-seven years earlier. The cross was surrounded by stalls selling quill pens, ink, parchment and sealing wax. There were chapmen and hawkers everywhere, selling ale and wine, cherries and strawberries, peascods, pepper and saffron, hot sheep's feet, cod and mackerel, pies and pasties.

'Buy! Buy! Buy!'

'What d'you lack? What d'you lack?'

'What'll you buy? What'll you buy?'

Well might they ask. It seemed to Kemp that everything he could possibly imagine was for sale in London, as well as many things he could never have imagined.

He slipped into the precincts of Saint Paul's Cathedral in search of respite from the crowds, but even here there was nothing but bustle. In addition to the priests and prelates hurrying to and fro, gardeners sold fruit and vegetables, cutlers sold knives from sheds built against the side of the chapter house, serjeants-at-law wearing red caps over their white silk coifs touted for clients in the cathedral porch and from the pulpit below the lead-plated wooden cross known as Paul's Cross a friar preached a sermon to a crowd consisting of the devout and the curious, as well as unashamed hecklers.

Everywhere Kemp turned there were beggars in filthy rags. He saw one seated on a small wooden trolley, pulling himself about using the wooden blocks he gripped in hands at the end of muscular arms; his legs ended just above where the knee should have been. He wore a wooden placard on a string about his neck, and although Kemp could not read the crudely daubed words thereon, he could guess at them from the beggar's cry for alms:

'Alms for a veteran of Crécy! Please give generously. Won't you spare a few farthings for a man who lost both legs at Crécy?'

Kemp felt sick. There but for the grace of God go I, he thought to himself, and was about to hurry past when something made him take a second glance at the beggar's filthy, scabrous, unshaven face with its matted and tangled beard. The face seemed to have aged twenty years since he last saw it, yet that had been just over a year ago.

'Hick?' he asked incredulously.

The beggar looked up at him, and his seamed face cracked into a crooked grin, revealing blackened teeth. 'Why, it's Master Kemp, isn't it?' Hick Lowesby had always addressed Kemp as 'Martin' when they were companions-in-arms, but now that Kemp was walking around in a fine black cloak with a bulging purse at his hip and Lowesby was a filthy, stinking, crippled beggar dressed in foul and lousy rags, any other form of address would have seemed ludicrous. 'I hardly recognised you in your fine clothes. How are you?'

'Well enough,' replied Kemp. 'And you?' he asked, not realising what a stupid question it was until the words were past his lips.

'As well as can be expected,' Lowesby replied with a cheeriness that seemed quite sincere. 'I seem to manage. You know how it is.'

Kemp did not know how it was, nor had he any wish to find out. 'I thought you were going back to . . .' He struggled to recall whichever part of Leicester County it was that Lowesby had hailed from. '. . . Harborough?'

Lowesby shrugged. 'So I once thought, too. But I can't very well ride there, and I don't intend to try dragging myself the whole way.'

'But I thought you had a wife and family?'

‘Aye. But I heard tell as how they think me dead. I reckon it’s just as well.’

Kemp’s expression was one of undisguised horror. If it had been his legs that were crushed instead of Lowesby’s, he could not with confidence have said he would return to Knighton to see if Beatrice still loved him.

‘Anyway, it’s all for the best,’ Lowesby continued. ‘I’d like as not just be a burden on them. At least in London there’s enough money around for folks like me to scrape a living from begging. But you look well enough. What brings you to London?’

‘I’ve only just got back from France.’

Lowesby nodded. ‘All the talk has been of the fall of Calais these past few weeks. Is there any fresh news of the war? I’d heard a rumour it was ended.’

‘There’s a truce,’ admitted Kemp. ‘How long it will last, I don’t know.’

‘Are you headed back to Leicester, then?’

Kemp shook his head. ‘I’ve engaged to work here in London for a year and a day, to earn my freedom. Perhaps you can help me,’ he added. ‘I’m looking for John Chaucer’s house, in Thames Street. In the Vintry Ward.’

‘I don’t know of any John Chaucer, but Thames Street is easy enough. You leave the cathedral precincts by that gate there and turn right. Keep walking until you come to a junction like this – ’ he made a T-shape with both arms – ‘and you’re there. Turn left, and eventually you’ll be in the Vintry Ward. Chances are someone around there will have heard of him.’

‘Thank you.’ Kemp fumbled for his purse, found a penny, and then rejected it in favour of a shilling; extravagance, but with a purse bulging with the proceeds of French plunder he could well afford it.

‘Thank *you*, master!’

Kemp hurried away, his heart heavy with guilt, his stomach churning with revulsion. It had been sheer luck that the dying warhorse had fallen across Lowesby’s legs rather than Kemp’s in the thick of the fray at Crécy. Lowesby had always been one of the quieter members of the platoon, never getting into trouble, never wishing anyone any harm; not even the French, much to Preston’s annoyance. That he should be cast so prematurely into such a living purgatory while Kemp, whose sins weighed so heavily on his conscience, continued to enjoy rude health and a moderate degree of financial comfort, seemed like a mockery of any concepts of natural justice. *It should have been me*, Kemp found himself thinking over and over again: *it should have been me*.

He was so lost in his thoughts that he did not notice the ragged street-urchin until the two of them bumped into one another. 'Watch where you're going, damn you!' growled Kemp.

'Sorry, master.' The boy grinned at him, making it clear that he was not sorry at all. Kemp aimed a cuff at the boy's head, but the urchin dodged nimbly out of his way and ran off. Scowling, Kemp continued on his way down Thames Street until he was passing the fortified enclosure called the Steelyard, the enclave of the Easterling merchants of the Hanseatic League, where ships from Bremen, Hamburg and Lübeck unloaded their cargoes of wheat, flax, hemp, timber, ropes and cables, and the steel that gave it its name.

A hand grasped his shoulder. 'Pardon me . . .'

Kemp whirled around to face the man, his hand reaching under his cloak for the hilt of his sword only to find it was no longer there, of course. The motion was not lost on the man, however, who backed away, holding his hands up to show that they were empty, except for the leather purse he held in the right one. 'I think you dropped this.'

Kemp reached for his purse. It was gone, the thongs that had attached it to his belt neatly severed. He remembered the boy who had bumped into him, and cursed his own carelessness. 'Dropped it?' he echoed scathingly.

The man shrugged apologetically. He was probably around ten years older than Kemp, a tall, lean man of athletic build. His eyes twinkled with mischievous intelligence and his hair was pulled back in a short pony-tail, an outlandish fashion that Kemp had not encountered before. He wore charcoal-grey breeches, tall leather boots with the tops folded down, and a soft leather jerkin over a white silk chemise. A cloak of grey worsted was wrapped around his shoulders and pinned in place with a metal brooch. On his head was a broad-brimmed pilgrim's hat of brown felt, tilted at a rakish angle. Kemp tried to guess what manner of man he was, and eventually had to give up.

'I fear the young cut-purse I saw stealing this from you was too nimble for my clumsy feet, but when I called out after him he dropped this in his flight.' The man handed the purse back to Kemp.

'Thank you,' Kemp responded grudgingly.

'Perhaps it is just as well,' continued the man. 'There's more than a shilling in there, and it would be a tragedy for one so young to be hanged for a youthful indiscretion.'

'Maybe,' allowed Kemp, who had come too close to being hanged for a crime of which he had been innocent to have much sympathy for those who were guilty.

'You've come to London to seek work?' asked the man.

'What makes you think that?'

The man laughed at the suspicion in Kemp's voice. 'You're not from London – your Midlander accent makes that much plain. And London is full of archers disbanded from the king's service these days. Your broad shoulders and callused fingers betray your craft. You'll be lucky to find work, unless you have some particular skill other than the ability to use a bow – a commonplace skill, I fear, and one little demanded in England these days.'

'I already have a position,' grunted Kemp; and then it occurred to him that since he had to ask directions, he might as well ask this man. 'Do you know where I can find the house of John Chaucer?'

'Do I know . . .?' the man exclaimed. 'Well now, here's a fine coincidence. I was heading that way myself when I saw the cutpurse trying to rob you. You must have passed it already: it's back this way.' The man set off and Kemp followed him, heading back the way he had come down Thames Street, passing Three Cranes Wharf in Dowgate, where square-rigged cogs from Bordeaux and Antwerp unloaded barrels of Gascon and Rhenish wine.

'What's your name?'

'Kemp. Martin Kemp.'

'I'm John Curtis,' said the man, extending one hand as the two of them walked side by side.

Kemp ignored the proffered hand. He had already taken a dislike to the man, with his outlandish style of dress and rather effete manner. Curtis seemed momentarily put out by Kemp's lack of manners, but then shrugged.

They did not have far to walk. The house was a large one in the more fashionable west end of the city, abutting the culvert where the Walbrook carried a foul variety of effluvium down to the Thames. Three storeys high, it had a steeply pitched roof of tiles and bay windows of leaded glass: an unmistakable display of wealth that could not fail to impress Kemp. Curtis seized the brass door-knocker and rapped it boldly.

The door was opened after a few moments by a bearded man, dressed in robes that were sober of hue but of costly cloth. He stared at Kemp's companion for a moment, and then rushed forward. For a moment Kemp thought the man was about to attack Curtis, but instead he seized the younger man in a huge bear-hug, lifting him clean off the ground and squeezing all the breath from his body, before depositing him back on the cobbles.

'Jack Curtis! You God-damned rogue, I'd heard you were killed!'

Curtis was grinning. 'Which just goes to show you shouldn't believe all you hear.'

'I never said I believed it, you dog! Well, don't just stand there,' chided the bearded man. 'Come in, come on in. I'll let you try some of that claret you brought me last time.'

'I told you it was good, didn't I?'

'Aye, but I never know whether it's the truth you're telling me, or if you're just giving me the hard sell.'

'Have you ever known me to give you the hard sell?' protested Curtis.

'When have I ever known you *not* give me the hard sell?' chuckled the older man, and indicated Kemp. 'Who's this?'

Curtis turned to glance at Kemp as if he had forgotten all about the archer. 'By God that sits above, how remiss of me! I thought you two were already acquainted.'

'Not that I am aware of,' said the man, peering at Kemp from beneath bushy eyebrows.

'Perhaps I misunderstood. The young man gave me the impression that he was already in your employ . . .'

'I am seeking work, Master Chaucer. Sir Thomas Holland said you were thinking of hiring a bodyguard. I have a letter of recommendation.' Kemp took out the letter and handed it to Chaucer.

Chaucer and Curtis exchanged glances as the former broke open the seal before perusing the letter's contents. While he read, Curtis produced an apple from somewhere beneath his cloak, polished it on the sleeve of his chemise and munched it noisily.

'Have you read this?' Chaucer asked at last, wagging the letter at Kemp.

'I don't read,' Kemp replied boldly, as if challenging either of the two men to pass comment on his peasant education.

'Good for you,' said Chaucer. 'Agnes insisted that I pay for our Geoffrey to attend Saint Paul's school, and now I never see the lad but he's got his head stuck in his primer. Well, I'll tell you, Sir Thomas speaks very highly of you; and I've no cause to misdoubt him. So, you want to live in London for a year and a day? Get away from your lord's manor and become a freeman?'

Kemp nodded.

'I've no quarrel with that,' said Chaucer. 'I'll pay you tuppence a day until such time as I find your conduct unsatisfactory, though if what Sir Thomas says is true, I doubt it will come to that. You'll get board and bed and a roof over your head as well.'

It was a generous offer – less than he could earn as an archer, but with the Truce of Calais in force there was little call for archers, and it was the year's residence in London he was truly interested in.

'You're agreeable?' asked Chaucer.

Kemp nodded again. 'Aye.'

'Then we'll shake on it,' said Chaucer, and they clasped hands. 'Wat will show you to your garret,' he added, and turned away to call for his apprentice. 'Wat? Wat! Damn the lad, where is he? Well, never mind; you have no baggage?'

'No, Master Chaucer.'

'Then take off your cloak and join me in the hall. It will be time for supper shortly. If I know Master Curtis here at all, I dare say he has a few tales of his adventures with which to regale us; and if you're just back from the war in France, I'll wager you can likewise keep us entertained.'

During the course of that evening it quickly dawned on Kemp that there were none of the master-servant attitudes in the Chaucer household that he had known on Stone Gate Manor. John Chaucer was a self-made man, easy-going enough not to have been made proud by the wealth he had gained in life. It was true he had married into most of it; but that which he had married he had invested wisely and, from the friendly relationship between Master Chaucer and Mistress Agnes, it was quite clear he had married for love before money.

The servants dined with the family in the hall, treating their employers with respect but without subservience. The family was a small one: Master John; Mistress Agnes; young master Jankin, Agnes' son by her first marriage; Geoffrey, the first child they had had together, now somewhere in the vicinity of his eighth year; little Kate, Geoffrey's younger sister; and Chaucer's apprentice, Wat, only a little younger than Kemp himself.

They sat down to eat, and Kemp tucked in, biting off a mouthful from a hunk of bread and chewing it for some time before becoming aware that everyone was staring at him. Realising that they all had their hands clasped to say grace, he blushed and swallowed the bread as discreetly as possible, clasping his own hands while little Geoffrey said grace, a Latin prayer recited by rote out of his primer. It was strange to be back in the bosom of a God-fearing family, albeit one other than his own, after so many months in the king's service.

The food likewise caught Kemp off-guard. It was richly spiced, either to hide the fact the meat was past its prime or to advertise the fact the Chaucers were wealthy enough to afford such spices. Either way, Kemp was used to eating his meat unspiced and, in chewing his first mouthful, he almost choked, forcing Curtis to cover for him by remarking that perhaps Chaucer's cook had over-done it with the pepper – whatever that was – and obliging Chaucer himself to agree out of politeness.

Curtis dominated all the conversation during supper with outrageous tales, not only of his own escapes and escapades, but also of thunder below the ground in far-off Cathay, of purple clouds that struck down the heathens in the east by the thousand, of mermaids and witches, oliphaunts and pirates. Kemp was sceptical of many of Curtis's stories, not least the ones wherein Curtis himself was the hero, and when Chaucer pressed him to tell some of his own experiences at Crécy, Calais and Saint-Omer, he made light of his own deeds, not wanting to seem boastful.

After supper, while Curtis and Chaucer retired to the withdrawing room to talk business – Curtis wanted to borrow money from a number of wealthy merchants to finance his next voyage, and Chaucer was high on his list – Wat showed Kemp up to the garret at the top of the house where the servants slept. Kemp was not entirely happy about the arrangement. Not because he would have to share a bed with four other people; there was nothing unusual in that, his entire family had shared a single – albeit large – bed in the bower of their two-roomed cottage in Knighton. But Kemp intended to take his duties as Chaucer's bodyguard seriously, and he felt he should sleep immediately outside his new master's bedchamber on a straw-stuffed pallet stretched across the threshold so that no one could enter without waking him. It took the combined efforts of Wat and the servants to convince him that Chaucer's life was in no way under threat. He was a member of the Guild of Vintners, and popular and respected enough to have no real enemies. Kemp had been employed because all merchants of any standing employed bodyguards to protect themselves against thieves and brigands, although such attacks were rare enough; it was just another way for merchants to display their wealth. Only the richest merchants could afford to employ bodyguards in addition to all the other servants necessary for the smooth running of a large and wealthy household.

Too tired to give proper answers to the hundred and one questions the other servants had to ask about the war in France, Kemp turned away and closed his eyes to sleep, reflecting he would rather be a bodyguard in the Chaucer household than a villein slaving in the fields of Stone Gate Manor. In a year and a day's time he would be a freeman, free to do as he pleased, free to return to Knighton to be reunited with Beatrice.

He smiled to himself. He was convinced that everything was going to work out just fine.

The walls of the hall of Stone Gate Manor House were decked with wreaths of holly at the approach of Yuletide, but there was nothing festive about the gaze that Sir John Beaumont turned upon the dark-haired villein who stood cowering before him, twisting his cloth cap in his hands.

'You sent for me, Sir John?' stammered the villein.

'You are Michael Kemp?' asked Beaumont. Unlike his youngest brother, Michael Kemp had always made a habit of keeping his head down whenever the lord of the manor was present, and thus his face was less familiar to the knight.

'Aye, Sir John.'

'Master Croft informs me that your brother Martin has not yet returned from France,' Beaumont said neutrally.

'That is so, sir, aye,' Michael replied uncertainly.

'Yet all the other men from the county who went to fight for the king in France have returned. I myself have been back for two months now. Martin has had ample time to return, has he not?'

'Aye, sir.'

'Have you any thoughts as to what may have delayed his return?'

'Nay, sir.'

'He has not tried to get word to you? And I suggest you think very carefully before answering.'

Michael shrugged helplessly. 'I've heard nowt, sir.'

Beaumont essayed a benevolent smile, but it was so out of place on his harsh features that it only made Michael shudder. 'You do not think, then, that he may be staying in some borough town for a year and a day, in order to win his freedom?'

'He might be, sir, aye.'

'And he has made no attempt to let his family know? You expect me to believe that?'

'It's the truth, Sir John; I swear it, as God's my life.'

Beaumont leaned back in his chair. 'Of course, if Martin were seeking to gain his freedom, I would expect his eldest brother to lie for him anyway.'

'Not me, sir,' Michael said hurriedly. 'If Martin's getting ideas above his station, he'll get no help from me.'

'Well said; but no more than you would say if you were trying to protect him. Are you certain you do not seek to deceive me?'

'I wouldn't dare, sir,' Michael said truthfully.

'No, you would not,' agreed Beaumont. 'I am certain you are mindful of the fact the cottage you inhabit is my property, and you only live there on my sufferance.'

'Aye, sir.'

'How is your mother, Michael? She must be advanced in years by now. I understand that the exposure of Martin's crime hit her badly.'

'She's never recovered, sir, and that's a fact,' said Michael. 'Me, I blame Martin. He may be my brother, but he's a bad one, sir, and I'll be the first to admit it.'

'I do hope so. Winter is drawing on, the weather growing cold. I would hate to be forced to evict you and your mother with the snows of January just around the corner.'

Michael nodded miserably. 'Aye, Sir John.'

'If you hear anything from your youngest brother – anything at all – you will let me know, won't you?'

'Aye, Sir John.'

Beaumont made a dismissive gesture, and Michael allowed himself to be escorted from the hall by his master's steward. Once Michael was seen on his way back to the village, the steward returned to the hall where he found Beaumont pouring himself another cup of mead spiced with ginger and nutmeg.

'I cannot allow anyone from this manor to gain the status of a freeman, Treroose,' said Beaumont. 'It sets an unfortunate precedent. A bad example, you understand.'

The steward inclined his head. 'Aye, Sir John.'

'Martin Kemp must be made an example of. A painful example. He has escaped my vengeance too many times for my honour to permit his life to continue.' The case of a villein running from his lord's manor was one that could be dealt with in the manorial court, where Beaumont had the power of life and death over his villeins. 'I want him found, Treroose, no matter what the cost. Send out men to seek for him; you can start with London.'

'London is a big city, Sir John,' Treroose pointed out. 'A very big city.'

'Exactly,' agreed Beaumont. 'A man can lose himself in London, and that's precisely what Kemp will be seeking to do. I want him found. Discreetly, mind. When you have found out where he is hiding, I want you to send word back to me. I shall come in person to see him dragged back to the manor in chains.' Under the level of the table at which he sat, Beaumont clenched his fists so tightly that his nails drew blood from his palms. 'And when that has been done, I shall personally mete out the punishment he has avoided for so long.'

# CHAPTER EIGHT

SIR THOMAS HOLLAND removed his robes, stripping down to his chemise, and then allowed his squire to help him don his armour. First he pulled on a pair of leggings, over which he fastened cuisses of brigandine construction – gilt-headed rivets securing small metal plates between a fabric cover and a leather foundation – to protect his thighs. Then he clipped a pair of steel greaves over his calves, before pulling on a pair of leather shoes. Next came his gambeson, a quilted undercoat worn under his armour to prevent chafing and to act as a shock-absorber against any blows he might receive.

Over this he pulled a chain-mail habergeon, with sleeves long enough to protect the backs of his hands, leaving only his palms free so that he could be sure of getting a good grip on whichever weapon he wielded, and a chain-mail coif. Plate-steel rerebraces and vambraces were clipped around his arms. Then the squire helped him buckle a breastplate of *cuir bouilli* – hardened leather – over his torso. He ducked his head so the squire could put his jupon of azure silk, patterned with *fleurs-de-lys* and emblazoned with a white lion, over his armour.

The squire buckled Holland's jewelled sword-belt around his hips, the broadsword hanging in its ivory-covered scabbard. Next he fastened Holland's articulated sabatons over his shoes, and then gauntlets made of latoun, an alloy of bronze and tin resembling brass. Finally the squire handed his master his bucket-shaped great helm, with its ornate crest in the shape of a white lion rampant, which Holland lowered over his head until it rested on his shoulders. Despite the pattern of tiny holes in the lower half of the front of the helm, his breath was thrown back against his face, warming it in the cold air of a grim April afternoon. He could hear his breath rasping noisily within the close confines of the helmet. All he could see through the eye-slit was a wide but narrow strip but he knew from experience that this would be enough for his purposes.

Both knight and squire left the blue and white striped, bell-shaped tent, walking across to where another squire nervously held the halter of a white Percheron destrier, a massive eighteen hands in height, caparisoned in azure and white cloth, its harness covered in jingling bells. Holland put one foot into the stirrup – his armour, made specifically for him by a skilled craftsman, was light and easy to move in – and swung himself up into the high-seated saddle with its pommel and cantle raised so that there was less chance of him losing his seat if he should receive a powerful blow.

The squire handed him his heater-shaped shield, made of stout wooden boards nailed together and bound with casein glue, covered with a heavy hide surrounded by a metal rim. A metal boss in the centre protected the knight's hand. He gripped the shield in his left hand along with the destrier's reins, holding out his right hand. The squire handed him his steel-tipped fourteen-foot lance, carved from cypress wood and painted in blue and white spirals. Holland carried it upright, resting it on the felt butt on his saddle bow as he urged his horse into a gentle trot.

His opponent already awaited him, similarly armed and armoured, his white surcoat emblazoned with a crimson wyvern, the same wyvern represented by the crest on his great helm, his bay destrier caparisoned in crimson and white. The two of them faced one another on horseback, separated by about ninety yards of open ground strewn with sand and sawdust.

A herald sat astride a black palfrey to one side, dressed in a tabard decorated with the king's livery – not the quartered arms of England and France that the king wore into battle, but the dragon of Uther Pendragon and the great King Arthur. He raised the jewelled gilt baton in his right hand. Holland watched him out of the corner of his eye-slit. The herald brought down the baton with a sharp motion, at the same time shouting: '*Laissez aller!*'

Both knights dug their rowel spurs into their horses' flanks and the two destriers launched themselves forward. The horses' powerful haunches accelerated them at once into a gallop, their iron-shod hooves thundering against the packed earth, throwing up clumps of soil in their wake. Holland pressed his feet down against the stirrups, squeezing his legs tight and allowing his body to go with the rhythm of the steed's movement. He couched his lance, levelling it at his opponent, the weight of it resting on his palm. carefully balanced to ensure that it remained parallel with the ground. He kept his eyes and attention focused on his opponent, allowing his destrier – a veteran of almost as many courses as he was himself – to worry about following a path just to the left of the oncoming horse.

His whole attention stayed on his opponent right up to the moment when the tip of his lance struck his opponent's shield, brought in the way at the last possible moment so that the lance glanced off to the right, twisting Holland's arm painfully. At the same time he felt his opponent's lance strike him in the shoulder, the powerful buffet making him reel in the saddle, so that he would have been unhorsed had the lance not broken. A great roar went up from the watching crowd: one *atteint* to the knight in crimson and white.

Cursing his own over-confidence for losing him the first point, he rode to the far end of the tilting-field and wheeled his horse swiftly. His opponent had already collected a fresh lance from a waiting squire and turned, his destrier powering across the field towards him. Holland dug in his spurs once more, vanquishing all chargrin at his earlier mistake, chagrin that might cloud his judgement and lead him into another error.

The two horsemen passed again, both lances striking home and breaking with a loud, splintering snap. Reeling once again from the strength of the blow, Holland dropped his broken lance, using both hands to steady himself in the saddle. Reaching the far end of the field, he motioned for a fresh lance, but the squire shook his head, gesturing back towards the centre of the field. Holland had to turn his horse to look, and through his eye-slit he just made out his opponent's black destrier, cantering away riderless, pursued by a couple of squires. Unfastening his helm and pulling it off, Holland saw that his opponent was lying flat on his back in the middle of the field, motionless. Holland immediately rode across to where he lay, reining in his destrier a few feet away and jumping down to offer assistance. There was no wound visible, but it was not rare for an unhorsed knight to strike his head in such a way that he might be badly stunned.

But then the other knight raised his hands to remove his helmet, his gauntleted fingers struggling with the laces that held it in place. Finally he succeeded, to reveal a face streaked with sweat and rust. Holland offered a hand to help him to his feet, but the other knight knocked it away and pushed himself up unaided.

'Well played, Sir John,' said Holland. He was not diplomatic by nature, least of all in the presence of unchivalrous behaviour, but on this occasion he thought it necessary to make an effort. It was the Feast of Saint George – the saint chosen by the king to be the patron saint of England – the twenty-third day of April, and the fourth day of the tournament that the king had called at his castle at Windsor. Knights had come from all over Christendom, from as far south as Castile and as far east as the kingdom of Cyprus.

The tournament was being held in the castle's upper ward, in the shadow of the round stone keep that stood on a mound at its centre. The tourney-field had been fenced off, and around it crowded men and women of every degree, from the highest magnates in the land to the lowliest beggars, all of them claiming – most without justification – to be veterans of Crécy. Many people stood or sat on the cat-walk of the castle's curtain wall, from where they had a splendid view of the tournament. In addition to the tournament itself there were various side-shows. Mummers performed a play about Saint George and the dragon on a wooden stage, while the younger members of the crowd were entertained by the antics of a puppet show. There were barber-surgeons drawing teeth and selling miraculous remedies, pardoners selling holy relics and pardons for sins, fortune-tellers and conjurors, jesters reciting verses, friars preaching sermons, pie-vendors and ale-sellers; and a troupe of female tumblers, a fair but wanton collection of young women who had arrived at the castle dressed as noblemen, to the scandal of the ladies and the amusement of the men. Bear-baiting and cock-fighting competed for an audience with wrestling and boxing and all comers could display their skill with the longbow at the archery butts.

A wooden grandstand had been built for courtly spectators: amongst them were prisoners such as King David of Scotland, Duke Charles de Blois of Brittany, and Holland's own prisoner, Raoul de Brienne, Count of Eu and Constable of France, now a prisoner of the king himself. Quite at ease with these noble prisoners were the ladies of the court: Queen Philippa, Alice Montague, Countess Margaret, and others. All around the grandstand, on both sides of the tilting field, stood the bell-shaped tents of the knights who were taking part in the tournament, and their coats of arms were hung on the outside wall of the great hall. Each time a knight was defeated, his arms were removed, so that now only twenty-four arms were displayed there, after Sir John Beaumont's had been taken down.

The tournament was *à plaisance* rather than *à outrance* – for amusement rather than to the death – and the jousters used arms of courtesy, weapons not intended to inflict serious damage, their lances tipped with coronels: heart-shaped iron heads with several blunt points rather than one that was sharp.

'My arms and steed are yours,' Beaumont acknowledged; even he had to admit that it was no great dishonour to be vanquished by Sir Thomas Holland, a knight whose prowess was growing in renown seemingly with each passing day. The two of them walked away from the tilting field, Holland leading his destrier. 'You recall the day we met?' Beaumont continued.

Holland was puzzled. 'We have met before?'

'Aye – I served in your company,' growled Beaumont.

Suddenly Holland was able to put a name to the coat of arms emblazoned on Beaumont's surcoat. 'Sir John Beaumont, of Stone Gate Manor,' he said, and realised that this was the very man whose lordship Kemp was trying to escape. Then he remembered the day they first met, and his overwhelming contempt for any man who would wage a private war against a mere villein. Beaumont had tried to murder Kemp in the confusion of the skirmish at the ford of Blanchetaque, and would have succeeded had Holland not stepped in, initially thinking that the blow aimed at Kemp was a genuine error.

The scowl appeared to clear from Beaumont's face when Holland recalled not only his name but the name of his manor. 'Aye, Sir Thomas. I am glad we meet now, even under circumstances such as these.'

'I also,' agreed Holland. 'I have no need for a second suit of jousting armour, but I dare say that nag of yours will fetch a pretty price at Smithfield horse fair.'

Beaumont visibly suppressed a snarl of anger. 'You recall there was a villein from my manor serving in one of your platoons of archers? A boy named Martin Kemp?'

'Kemp, Kemp . . .' Holland shook his head, as if trying to recollect. 'So many villeins have served under my command, it is difficult to put names to their unwashed faces . . . wait a moment, now I remember. Was it not Kemp you wanted to see hanged, the day you joined my company?'

Beaumont ground his teeth. 'Aye.'

'I understand he was accused of the rape and murder of Kathryn Seagrave?'

'He was convicted and duly sentenced to death,' asserted Beaumont.

'Although according to one rumour I heard, he was falsely convicted by a justice of the peace who had the jurors bribed, because he was becoming over-familiar with a certain knight's daughter.'

Beaumont's hand flew to the hilt of his sword and he pulled it from his scabbard, quite forgetting that both he and Holland carried arms of courtesy. The blade he now levelled at Holland was made of whalebone rather than steel; hard enough to deliver a powerful knock, but of limited use in delivering a fatal blow against a man in armour.

Holland had not forgotten, however, and his hand did not even flinch in the direction of his sword-hilt. He smiled. 'It is as well your blade is not dangerous. I might have been forced to interpret your actions as a threat and then I should have to slay you.'

'Kemp is my villein and his place is on my manor. If you have any idea where he may be found I suggest you tell me.'

'If you have mislaid one of your villeins, it is no concern of mine,' Holland replied. 'Do you think I keep track of every man who passes under my command? Good day to you, Sir John. You may send your squire to me with your arms, armour and horse as soon as it pleases you.' Without another word, Holland strode into his tent, leaving Beaumont fuming.

Dressed in his master's azure and white livery, Preston waited for Holland inside. He rose to his feet. 'Sir Thomas, can I have a word with you?'

Holland nodded. 'Leave us,' he told his squire. The lad nodded nervously, ducking out of the tent.

'That was Sir John Beaumont,' said Preston, when they were alone. 'The lord of the manor that Kemp hails from.'

'You remember him?'

'I remember you asking Kemp to leave his manor and come and work for you, if you'll pardon me saying so.'

Holland made a dismissive gesture. 'He certainly remembers Kemp,' he observed.

'Kemp's here,' said Preston.

'At Windsor?'

'Aye. At the tournament.

Holland's face registered surprise. 'I had thought he would be working for Master Chaucer by now.'

'He is. Master Chaucer is here too, with his family.'

'Then someone had better warn the lad, before Beaumont sees him first. Which reminds me, Wat; I shall not be needing your services again today.'

Preston grinned. 'Aye, Sir Thomas.' He ducked out of the tent and hurried off in search of Kemp.

Kemp had already seen Beaumont. On the whole he now found jousting boring: it was too regulated, too far removed from the reality of battle for his liking. Yet he could not resist making a point of watching first Sir John Chandos defeat Sir Walter Mauny – two of the finest knights in Christendom, a spectacle that any man would count himself lucky to witness – and then Holland's turn. He had immediately recognised Beaumont's coat of arms, and raised the cowl of his cloak to hide his face. Chaucer turned to regard him with bemusement.

'Expecting rain, Martin?'

'Someone I know,' replied Kemp. 'Sir John Beaumont, the man whose manor I should have returned to.'

'We can leave, if you think . . .' offered Chaucer, to the horror of the rest of his family, who were having a splendid day out.

Kemp shook his head. 'He will not see me amongst these crowds, if I keep my face hidden.' He grinned. 'Besides, I want to see him knocked off his horse.'

Three minutes later his wish was fulfilled.

Kemp had been in Chaucer's service for nearly six months now. The time had flown by; it was amazing to think that in a little over another six months he would be a freeman. So far they had been happy months, too. Chaucer's servants had been right about there being no need to protect their master from assassins. The only time Kemp had suffered any injury in a fight had been when Chaucer got into a tavern brawl with a Flemish merchant who insulted the king, and Kemp had to try to break it up. He received a black eye on that occasion – meting out several more to the Fleming and his compatriots – and when the two of them returned to the house that night, Mistress Agnes ministered to his swollen face as tenderly as his own mother might have done, chastising her husband for putting his bodyguard in the way of such blows.

In that short space of time, the Chaucers had become almost as much of a family to Kemp as the one he had left behind in Knighton, and he suspected that in years to come he would remember these days as among the happiest of his life. Unlike his own family, the Chaucers were wealthy and, as long as he lived with them, he never lacked for anything.

Except perhaps for two things: Beatrice Beaumont and, strangely, the war against the French.

At times the war had seemed nightmarish and the most painful memories refused to die, so that he would wake up in a cold sweat in the small hours of the morning. But he missed it. He missed the companionship. The Chaucers might treat him as one of their own, but he knew he was not of their class, did not fit in, and never would. He knew now that fate had not intended him for a life of peace. It was insane, he knew, but he missed the tight feeling of fear and excitement in the pit of his stomach before a battle. He missed the time that had been ended by the Truce of Calais, a time when even the thorniest problem could be solved with a sword or burning brand, and the application of a little lateral thinking, perhaps. He missed the danger, he missed the lifestyle, he missed the challenge.

'Martin?' Chaucer was speaking. 'We're off to the archery butts. Are you coming?' Chaucer was a competent archer with the longbow and after mass on Sunday mornings he would often join Kemp at the butts at Smithfield.

Before Kemp could reply, Chaucer's step-son Jankin tugged at his step-father's sleeve. 'Wait a moment, Father. What's this?'

They all turned their attention in the direction in which the youth pointed, where a knight was marching across the tilting field towards a small but sturdy wooden bridge, built across the ditch at the foot of the mound on which the circular keep stood. He was clad in 'all-white' armour, without jupon, surcoat or crest bearing a coat of arms which might give away his identity, except for a silken azure ribbon tied about his left leg, just below the knee; some lady's favour, perhaps. He stood at the end of the bridge facing across the ward with his legs apart, drew a whalebone broadsword from his scabbard and planted its tip in the soil at his feet, resting his gauntleted hands on the curved crossguard.

'The unknown declares a passage-at-arms, challenging all who may to try to pass him if they dare,' a herald announced loudly, in a manner not unlike that of a fairground barker, to Kemp's mind. 'Is there any knight bold enough to face him?'

Chaucer nudged Kemp. 'Go on, Martin! Here's a chance to make a name for yourself. Why don't you see if Sir Thomas Holland will let you borrow his suit of armour? One unknown against another!' He chuckled at the idea.

Kemp smiled thinly. The unknown was a tall, well-built man, and he moved in his armour with the practised ease of one used to fighting in it. 'I think not.'

'I wonder who it can be?' mused little Geoffrey.

'Someone famous, I'll be bound,' said Mistress Agnes. 'Why else would he keep his face hidden behind that visor?'

'Perhaps he doesn't want to get a sword-thrust into his eyes,' Kemp said cynically.

'Fie, Martin!' protested Mistress Agnes. 'What chivalrous knight would deal such a blow?'

'One who was fighting for his life, dear, rather than playing games at a tournament,' chuckled Chaucer.

'That'll be the king,' sniffed a familiar voice with a Lancastrian accent, and Kemp turned to see Preston standing there, smiling.

'Good day, serjeant.'

'I'm here as a friend now, lad, not your serjeant,' said Preston. 'You can call me Wat.'

'Aye, serjeant . . . Wat.'

'Sir John Beaumont is here. Sir Thomas thought you might like to be warned.'

Kemp nodded. 'I saw him fighting Sir Thomas earlier. But thank you.'

They stood watching as the twenty-four knights and noblemen present stood in a huddle on the far side of the tilting field, doubtless arguing which of them should be the first to have the honour of facing the unknown.

'What makes you think it's the king?' asked Kemp.

'I can't see him anywhere else, and this is exactly the kind of thing he loves to do. His head's full of the tales of the Knights of the Round Table; something the two of you have in common, Lancelot,' Preston added with a chuckle. 'But he knows how to beat the French, I'll say that much for him, and what more can a man ask of his king? You'll see, Kemp: if he seems to beat every man who dares to fight him, you'll know it's the king.'

One of the twenty-four knights and noblemen strode across the ward, to the end of the bridge where the unknown stood. Kemp recognised the arms of Sir John Chandos. 'Does he know he's going to fight his own king?' wondered Kemp.

'Chandos is no fool,' said Preston. 'He'll have guessed.'

'The challenge has been taken up by Sir John Chandos!' announced a herald, and the crowd cheered.

Chandos halted a few feet from the unknown and the two of them bowed to one another courteously. Then they unslung the shields they wore across their backs and held them in their left hands, gripping their whalebone blades in their right hands as they circled one another, each seeking an opening. Chandos lunged forward suddenly but the unknown caught the thrust on his shield, riposting with a stroke aimed at Chandos' head that the knight only just managed to duck.

The two men fought on, backwards and forwards, exchanging blow for blow. Kemp could see that it was all expert stuff, nobleman's fighting, with none of the low blows and dirty tricks they would use in war if they wanted to stay alive. Finally the unknown gained the upper hand, driving Chandos to his knees, and the knight yielded, acknowledging the unknown as the victor.

While the remaining twenty-three knights discussed who should be next, a page crossed the ward and handed the unknown a cup of watered-down wine. He accepted it, raising his visor just enough to drink without revealing his face. Kemp thought he caught a glimpse of a golden-brown beard.

The Earl of Warwick was the next up and, although he fought just as well as Chandos, he too was eventually defeated. Next Sir Thomas Holland volunteered. Kemp and Preston exchanged glances.

Holland and the unknown fenced up and down before the bridge. The unknown was showing signs of wearying by now, and Holland was rested after his joust with Beaumont. Kemp realised that Holland had not guessed who his opponent was: his blows were too hard-struck, the blows of a man intent on winning, oblivious to the fact that no matter how honourable his victory might be, it would not be appreciated by a king who only enjoyed a good jest if he were not the butt of it. If Holland were foolish enough to humiliate the king – albeit without knowing what he was doing – it would end any hopes he might have of advancement, either at court or in the field.

'There must be some way we can warn him!' Kemp said to Preston.

The serjeant turned to regard him with amusement. 'Let's bide a while and see, shall we?'

Then Holland's sword flew from his grasp and he sprawled on his back, at the mercy of the unknown. Kemp had seen him fighting for real enough times to know that he would not normally make such a careless error. Holland, he realised, not only knew who his opponent was but had played along, pretending to be intent on winning the fight only to throw victory away at the last moment. Despite his earlier concern for his former master, Kemp felt disappointed that Holland should choose to be party to such a charade and deliberately lose a fight he could have won.

The unknown helped Holland to his feet and handed him his sword, clapping him on the back. Henry of Derby was next up and he fenced with the unknown just as ferociously as Holland had done, until the unknown's whalebone blade snapped off near the hilt, leaving him unarmed and helpless. The crowd roared; lacking the expert eyes of experienced campaigners like Preston, Chaucer and Kemp, they did not realise it was mere mummery. Derby should have carried the day, and taken the unknown's place to defend the passage-at-arms, but instead he went down on one knee before his opponent, and offered his own sword as a replacement. The crowd went wild, and even Kemp could not help but be impressed by such a chivalrous gesture.

The unknown accepted the sword with a bow, gesturing to Derby to rise, before removing his helmet. To Kemp's complete lack of surprise, it was indeed the king. The crowd cheered and clapped ecstatically. There were few there who did not know the face of their king, the victor of Crécy and Calais, for it had been much in evidence during the past four days.

'Today I have seen much evidence of the valour of my companions,' said the king, his strong voice carrying clearly across the ward so that all could hear. 'But I have witnessed nothing that I have not seen before, in countless campaigns against the Scots and the French, and other enemies of this realm. To honour these men, my companions-in-arms, I declare the foundation of a new order of chivalry. Its members shall be the twenty-four knights and noblemen you see standing before you here today, men who have gone unvanquished this week, in addition to myself and my eldest son, Prince Edward of Woodstock. Twenty-six shall be the total number of its members, and not one more member shall be admitted before the death of a member, the new member to be elected by the existing ones. The patron saint of this most holy and chivalrous order will be the patron saint I have chosen for my realm, the saint who has brought us victories on land and sea. The order shall be called the Most Chivalrous Companionship of the Knights of Saint George and its emblem shall be this garter.' He untied the azure ribbon from his arm, and held it above his head, displaying it to the crowd. 'And the motto of the companionship shall be this: "*Honi soit qui mal y pense*" – "Evil to him who evil thinks".'

The Knights of Saint George dined in the great hall at Windsor Castle that night, before undertaking a night-long vigil in the castle's impressive chapel, rededicated by the king to Saint George earlier that year. Each member was given a stall and the twenty-six men were divided into two teams, led by the king and the Prince of Wales respectively. It was not a specifically English order of chivalry: its members included the Hainaulter Sir Sanchet d'Aubercicourt, the Gascon Jean de Grailly, Captal de Buch, and the Flemish Sir Henri d'Eam. Nor was its membership exclusive to the higher nobility, for Sir John Chandos was a member, while the earls of Arundel, Huntingdon, Northampton and Suffolk were amongst those excluded by their defeats at the tournament. The captive Constable of France, Raoul de Brienne, Count of Eu, had been allowed to take part in the tournament, but he had been beaten by one of Holland's younger brothers, Sir Otho, earning the latter not only a place in the companionship but also custody of the count until his ransom was paid, on condition that the count was not seen armed in public, or allowed to leave England. While the members of the order might range from the highest in the land down to some of the realm's humbler knights, they were all to be equal, brothers-in-arms, and to be honoured before all others.

Next day – the morrow of the Feast of Saint George and the last day of the tournament – the two teams fought one another in a mêlée in an enclosed area in the middle of the tilting field, using their whalebone swords. The two Hollands found themselves in opposing teams: Sir Thomas in the Prince's team, with the Earl of Warwick, Sir Bartholomew Burghersh and the young Sir James Audley; and Sir Otho in the king's team, with Derby, de Grailly, Chandos and Sir John Beauchamp, the younger brother of the Earl of Warwick, who had borne the king's banner at Crécy. Each of them wore an azure garter embroidered with the words "*Honi soit qui mal y pense*" in gold thread, as well as whatever lady's favour they saw fit. The two teams fought long and hard, occasionally breaking off to seek a short respite in one of the enclosures roped off for that purpose. Heralds stood by attentively with kerchiefs known as *couvre-chefs de mercy* tied to the ends of lances with which they touched knights who were seen to be in serious difficulties to signal that no further attack was to be made on them.

Perhaps inevitably, Holland found himself facing Montague. The two of them had not exchanged a single word since the night of the ball at Calais castle. Even so, Montague had not even suspected Holland's intention to petition the Papal Court until a summoner arrived from Avignon, ordering that both he and Joan must either appear before a tribunal of the Papal Court or appoint attorneys to do so on their behalf. Joan's mother, the Dowager Countess of Kent, had responded to this by insisting that her son-in-law keep his wife in seclusion, so that she would learn nothing of these proceedings.

Holland could not resist taunting Montague. 'Where is Lady Joan, Sir William? I have not seen her once at this tournament, so far.'

'She is not well enough to travel,' muttered Montague as he tried to parry Holland's thrust.

'That is not what I have heard. Rumour has it that you are keeping her locked up in the Castle of Mold so she cannot appoint a proctor to act on her behalf in our dispute. What are you afraid of, Montague? That she may not love you?' Holland was by far the superior swordsman and he played with

Montague, dictating the younger man's every move by keeping him on the defensive.

'She loves me well enough,' asserted Montague. 'What concerns me is that, despite your fraudulent claim to be her lawful wedded husband, you wear the favour of another lady on your crest.'

'Another lady?' Holland threw back his head and laughed, without letting down his guard for one moment. 'Do you not recognise the coverchief? It was given to me by your wife, after all.'

'You God-damned whoreson!' Montague roared. And he launched himself at Holland with such fury that even the older knight was caught off-guard and was hard-pressed to defend himself against a rapid succession of blows which had all the savagery of Montague's uncontrolled wrath behind them. Then Holland's superior skill and control began to tell once more. He regained the initiative, driving Montague back with a succession of forceful strokes until finally Montague's sword flew from his hand, leaving him unarmed.

Suddenly Montague whipped a dagger from his belt, and thrust it at the eye-slit in Holland's visor. Holland jerked his head aside and the razor-sharp blade of the dagger glanced off his helmet. He drove his gauntleted fist into Montague's stomach. Despite his mail habergeon, Montague was winded by the blow, giving Holland the chance to raise his opponent's visor and punch him on the nose. Knocked out cold, Montague went down, blood splashing on his upper lip where Holland's gauntlet had broken his nose. A herald rushed forward to touch Montague with his *couvre-chef de mercy*, and Sir Otho and Sir James Audley hurried to restrain Holland before he could deliver further blows in anger. But Holland was in control of his temper, and he allowed his fellow knights to hold him without struggling in their grip.

As the knights stopped fighting to see what was going on, the two sides parted, and the king made his way between them to where Montague lay. Chandos was already crouching over the unconscious young man. 'He'll live, sire,' he remarked.

'What befell here?' demanded the king, gazing at them each in turn.

'I saw it, your Majesty.' Sir Hugh Despenser, excluded from Companionship of Saint George by his defeat at Sir John

Beauchamp's hands in the lists, climbed over the barrier at the edge of the enclosure in his red and white robes. 'Sir Thomas raised my noble brother-in-law's visor and struck him in the fae. A villainous blow if ever I saw one.'

'If ever you saw a villainous blow, Sir Hugh, it was one you struck yourself,' retorted Holland.

'Hold your tongues, the pair of you!' snapped the king, and turned to Holland. 'Well, Sir Thomas? Is there any truth in Sir Hugh's accusation?'

Holland, who did not doubt that Despenser had seen the whole incident, bowed low before replying. 'Sir Hugh speaks the truth, your Majesty, as he saw it; but I do not believe he saw it all. I acted only in self-defence. Sir William grew over-excited in the heat of the mêlée, and such was the fire in his veins that when I successfully deprived him of his sword, he drew his dagger on me.'

'Sir Thomas speaks faithfully, your Majesty,' said Chandos, removing Montague's dagger from his gauntleted hand. 'Here is the proof.'

'Enough,' said the king. 'I did not form the Companionship of Saint George so the best knights in my service might fight one another with such hostility, when Valois openly seeks to renew the war. Sir Hugh, you and Sir Otho shall take Sir William and see to it his injuries are attended to. The rest of you will return to your quarters and prepare for supper. We dine at the Round Table in Saint George's Hall tonight. No, not you, Sir Thomas. I would have words with you.'

Holland nodded and marched alongside his king across the upper ward towards the keep. 'Sir William acted wrongly, that I will accept,' said the king. 'He is young, and his spirit is fiery. Are you certain you did not say something to provoke that temper of his, Sir Thomas?'

Holland said nothing.

'You are so much older than Sir William,' continued the king. 'You should know better. You made reference to my cousin Joan, I presume? Aye, I know all about your petition to the Pope, and I cannot say I am pleased you have gone behind my back to see that which I have decreed overturned by a foreign pope.'

'Forgive me, your Majesty. If I could have found an English Pope . . .'

The king began to scowl, but then laughed instead. 'An English pope! Now, that's not such a bad idea . . . but in all seriousness, Sir Thomas, I beg you: end your persecution of Sir William, out of love for me if for no other reason.'

'That I cannot do, sire. Call it treason if you will, but my love for the Lady Joan is greater.'

'I do not call it treason, Sir Thomas, for I have been in love myself and have acted as foolishly as you are doing now. But there are those who say your claim on the Lady Joan is false; that you had never met her before you returned from Prussia and were given an appointment as steward of her household; that the two of you became lovers, and cooked up this scheme whereby her marriage to Montague could be annulled, and she could have you in his place, and you could have access to her legacy.' He shrugged. 'Such is what they say, at least.'

Holland looked his king boldly in the eye. 'Evil to him who evil thinks, sire,' he said coolly.

As the time left until the end of the truce grew short, messengers came to England from the Papal Court. A little over a month after the tournament at Windsor, the Archbishops of Canterbury and York, and the Bishops of London and Norwich, received letters from the Pope demanding that the Lady Joan of Kent be set free, so that she could appoint a proctor to act on her behalf in the dispute between Holland and Montague. Shortly after that, the Pope wrote to both the English king and Philip of Valois, exhorting them to prolong the truce a little longer, until a more long-term peace between their countries could be arranged. Plantagenet and Valois reluctantly agreed, and the truce was extended until September.

Summer came and went, and it was the most miserable one Kemp had ever known. Rain fell continuously, turning roads into rivers and fields into lakes. Kemp's thoughts turned to the fields of Knighton and he wondered if the weather was as bad there as it was in London. If so, then the harvest would be poor, the crops drowned before they could ripen. He thought of his mother and his eldest brother, and old Simkin Sewell, and he wondered how much would be left for them once Beaumont had taken his share of the harvest.

September finally came, and the truce was extended for another two months, until the end of October. There was no let-up in the weather, however. It was raining one day early in October, when Kemp accompanied Chaucer down to Three Cranes Wharf, both wearing their hoods pulled up against the constant deluge. There they found Curtis's ship, the *Magdalen*, tied up. At a hundred and fifty tonnes, the *Magdalen* was a relatively small cog. Curtis was overseeing the unloading of her cargo of Gascon wine, the first press of that year's harvest. He was in a grim mood. His debts still hung over him like the sword of Damocles, and the profits from his next trading venture in the *Magdalen* would do little to pay them off.

'So what are you worried about?' demanded Chaucer, who seemed cheerful in spite of the weather. 'You weren't expecting to be able to pay off your debts after a single trading voyage, were you?'

Curtis shook his head, the water running off the brim of his hat in torrents. 'No, but I was hoping I might be allowed to use the *Magdalen* for a second trading voyage. The king's ordered that she be discharged of her cargo so that she can be employed in his service again. A team of his carpenters is coming by next week to convert her for war.'

Chaucer shrugged. 'Look on the bright side. The turrets they will build on her will prove useful next time you encounter those French pirates you're always crossing swords with.'

'Aye, unless the *Magdalen* is sunk in service against the French before then,' Curtis replied bitterly.

'The war is to be renewed, then?'

'So it seems.'

Chaucer looked grave. War was bad for trade, and Curtis's ill-humour was infectious. 'I hear of dark portents. They say the bells of Saint Mark's in Venice were set ringing, yet when the priest went to investigate, there was no one in the bell tower.'

'If it's portents you seek, then look closer to home,' replied Curtis, who was normally dismissive of such omens. 'They say a pillar of fire was seen over the Pope's palace at Avignon one dawn, and the market place at Villach burst open in the shape of a crucifix, and vomited blood. In the Bay of Biscay I came across a ship without a living soul left aboard her.'

'Did you bring her in for salvage?'

Curtis shook his head. 'The stink of death was upon her – a pestilential vessel if ever I saw one, the steersman dead with his hands still on the tiller, steering a course for hell I've no doubt. I for one would not step aboard her, and could hardly order my mariners to do that which I feared to. There is a pestilence sweeping across Christendom from the east, a foul disease that slays all who are infected by it.'

Chaucer crossed himself. 'Saints preserve us!'

'Aye,' agreed Curtis, and managed a dry, humourless laugh. 'It's enough to make even a heretic like me seek absolution!'

They heard a cry and turned in time to see one of the mariners slip from the rain-slick gangplank as he carried a cask of wine down on to the quayside. He fell into the dock and the cask bounced off the gangplank before splashing down on the patch of water where he had gone under.

They waited for an instant that seemed like a century before the mariner finally appeared, surfacing just to one side of the floating cask. He was face-down in the water.

Curtis whipped off his hat and handed it to Kemp with his right hand, at the same time using his left hand to unclasp the brooch which held his cloak in place. Even as the cloak fell to the ground, Curtis was diving off the quayside into the dock, cleaving the water like a dagger. Surfacing, he swam across to the unconscious mariner and rolled him over so that he floated on his back, before dragging him across to some stone steps cut into the quayside.

Several of the marines were waiting for him on the steps, and they lifted their companion's body out of the water, laying it on the quayside. Curtis sloshed out after them, water streaming from his sodden clothes.

One of the mariners crouched over his companion's body and searched for a pulse in his neck, before slumping down beside him. 'He's dead.'

Curtis looked at him in surprise and then his face became grim. 'He's not been paid off yet,' he growled. 'No one in my employ dies before I say they can.'

The assembled mariners laughed uncertainly. In such violent times, death was an every day occurrence, but not one for jesting about.

Curtis sat astride the dead man's hips, put his hands on the man's stomach and pushed up, towards his ribs, expelling water from his lifeless lips. Then he bent over him, putting his mouth over the dead man's, and breathed air into it.

'You cannot restore the dead to life, Master Curtis,' Chaucer told him gently, while Kemp watched, fascinated, wondering what the shipmaster was trying to achieve. 'The gift of life belongs to God alone . . .'

And then the dead mariner coughed and spluttered, his eyes blinking open. The watching mariners crossed themselves in awe; Curtis merely smiled with relief.

'You would cheat Death?' one of the more superstitious mariners asked incredulously.

Curtis shook his head. 'Merely a postponement. Death gets us all in the end.'

The gravedigger pushed the handcart right up to the rim of the pit and lifted the handles above his head so the pestilence-blackened bodies tumbled out to land in the bottom in a tangle of limbs. One of the corpses ruptured, its corrupted entrails spilling out with a cloud of noxious fumes that made the onlookers retch through their tears. Grotesquely, one of the corpses in the cart had become wedged, and would not drop. The gravedigger called to his apprentice, who took the spade and used it to dislodge the body.

The on-lookers – the kin of those in the grave-pit – wept loudly, beating their breasts and tearing at their hair in an agony of grief and incomprehension. The pestilence seemed to have come from nowhere, slaying the just and unjust indiscriminately. They were pious people, believing that God rewarded the good and punished the bad. Now God had chosen to visit the town of Saint-Omer with the kind of punishment unknown since the destruction of Sodom and Gomorrah, or when Egypt had been visited with plagues in the days of Moses. Was Saint-Omer a den of vice and heresy comparable with those of the Biblical pagans?

Typhaine Agache, her full lips and dark brown eyes making her seem older than her seventeen years, stared down into the pit, trying to distinguish her husband's corpse from the others. On top of the horror of death by the pestilence, this was the final indignity. The pestilence was so virulent that its victims were too many to be given the luxury of individual graves; instead they were tipped by the dozen into the fresh pits that were dug each day.

Typhaine asked herself the same question the other mourners

were asking: why? What had Pierre Agache done to deserve such an early and horrible death? He had killed, it was true, but Pierre had been a soldier, fighting to protect his country against the English invaders. Was that a sin? Typhaine knew her husband had taken no pleasure in the killing. He had been a good man and she had loved him dearly. She had lost count of the nights she lay awake when he was away from her, dreading the news of his death at the hands of the feared English 'God-damns' with their crooked sticks. But always he had returned, each time more appreciative of life, and of a wife who loved him so much.

And now he was dead. Killed not by an arrow, but by a strange pestilence. What had he done to deserve this fate? She feared she knew the answer. Perhaps his death was as much a punishment for her as for him. It was too cruel that she should be subjected to such grief twice in one lifetime.

The first time had been after the battle of la-Roche-Derrien, a year ago. Pierre's serjeant had returned from the battle with news of his death. Typhaine was grief-stricken, but the serjeant was on hand to comfort her. She resisted his advances at first, still mourning her husband, but the serjeant was handsome, and seemed kindly. Finally when the days had turned into weeks, she succumbed, seeking solace in the serjeant's arms.

Pierre had returned the next day, sufficiently recovered from his wounds to ride.

The serjeant had left the house by the time Pierre arrived, but Typhaine at once broke down and told him the whole story without hesitation. He listened in silence, then kissed her forgivingly, and went out. For the next few days he was taciturn but just when life had begun to return to normal, she learned the serjeant had been murdered, stabbed through the heart.

She had never mentioned the serjeant's death to Pierre, for fear that her worst suspicions might be confirmed. But they were never again as happy as they had been before. From that day on Typhaine had been racked with guilt: guilt at her adultery, guilt at perhaps having driven her husband to murder.

Now Pierre was paying for his sin; the pestilence was killing so many that there were not enough priests to ensure that all its victims were shriven before they breathed their last. She feared her husband's soul would burn for eternity in the fires of hell.

And she too was paying. It was as if God was punishing her by taking away the man she had loved.

'Why?' Typhaine's mother-in-law turned that single word into a long, drawn-out, keening wail. 'Why? Why did they take my Pierrot?'

'It was the Jews,' asserted someone. 'Everyone knows this pestilence is their doing. They've been poisoning the wells.'

'It's not the Jews!' Pierre's sister pointed at Typhaine. 'It's her! She seduced Pierre to the worship of the Devil and now God has punished him. I curse the day Pierre chose that Breton witch in preference to an Artoisian girl. I pray that she be the next victim!'

Typhaine shook her head, too numbed by the shock of Pierre's death to take in the sense of her sister-in-law's words.

'Aye!' said someone else. 'She's right. It's the Breton witch!'

'Kill the witch! Burn her!'

Many in the crowd believed it, those whom grief had robbed of their senses; then there were others, men whose advances had been spurned by the beautiful young Breton woman, and the wives of those men, who knew their husbands committed adultery with Typhaine in their minds, and often wondered if they were not equally guilty in the flesh.

Despair easily turned to anger once an object was found, and suddenly the crowd seemed to surge towards her. She felt herself seized, and cried out in panic. The crowd was deaf to her entreaties, hoisting her aloft.

'Burn her!'

'No!' screamed Typhaine's sister-in-law. 'Cast her into the pit! Let her be buried alive with her victims!'

This suggestion was greeted with general acclamation and Typhaine was carried to the edge of the pit, struggling and screaming. Two of the women seized her by the wrists and ankles and swung her between them.

Typhaine screamed in desperation, and then felt her body slam against something hard. Strong arms encircled her waist, dragging her from the grip of the two women. Men-at-arms moved through the crowd, roughly pushing the townsfolk away.

'What in the Devil's name is going on here?' Sir Geoffroi de Chargny demanded, his voice carrying clearly through the crowd in the sudden silence.

'This woman's a witch!' spat Pierre's sister, indicating her sister-in-law. 'It was she who brought about the pestilence. She's poisoned the wells. She's in league with the Devil!'

De Chargny did not glance in the direction of the woman standing trembling between two of his men-at-arms, who flanked her protectively. 'Don't be stupid,' he said. 'The pestilence has struck at towns and cities as far afield as Castile and the Empire. Do you suggest she has been responsible for poisoning so many wells?'

'Anything's possible when the Devil helps!' shouted someone. 'She travels abroad at night on the back of a monstrous goat which can leap a thousand leagues in a single bound.'

'A thousand leagues in a single bound,' de Chargny echoed, a hint of amusement in his expression. 'Tell me, has anyone seen this monstrous goat?

'My brother-in-law has!' shouted someone.

'Everyone knows your brother-in-law drinks too much!' called one of the more level-headed members of the crowd. Several people laughed at this.

'Who is the gravedigger?' demanded de Chargny.

The gravedigger stepped forward, clutching his cap. 'I am, my lord.'

'Then finish your work. The rest of you go back to your homes, and pray that this pestilence will swiftly pass. And no more talk of witchcraft! I had thought the people of this town rational; now you betray yourselves as ignorant and superstitious, no better than country peasants. Go back to your homes, I say!'

The crowd hesitated, but there was little it could do in the face of de Chargny and his men-at-arms. People began to wander truculently away from the side of the grave-pit.

'What about her, Sir Geoffroi?' The serjeant in command of the men-at-arms indicated Typhaine. 'We can't leave her here. They may yet come back for her.'

De Chargny glanced at her with a flicker of irritation. 'Can you scrub linen, make a bed, sweep a floor, girl?'

Typhaine curtseyed. 'Aye, my lord. I kept my husband's house . . .'

'Then you may work at the castle,' de Chargny interrupted. 'The pestilence has killed one of my chambermaids. You will replace her. You will be safe inside the castle precincts until the pestilence has passed and this hysteria has died down.'

Shc curtseyed again. 'Thank you, my lord . . .'

But de Chargny was already on his way to the castle that loomed over the town.

'You're Pierre Agache's wife, aren't you?' said the serjeant, walking with Typhaine towards the castle. 'The one he married in Brittany.'

She nodded, wiping tears from her eyes.

'How is he?'

'Dead.'

'I'm sorry to hear that.' He put a comforting hand on her arm but she shook it off, thinking of another serjeant who had once sought to console her.

A month later Chaucer made his way across the bridge to the Tabard Inn in Southwark with his son and step-son, accompanied by Kemp. They were all soaked to the skin by the time they arrived and Chaucer and his step-son sat by the log fire roaring in the hearth, supping pots of ale as they tried to get warm and dry, while little Geoffrey played noisily with Mistress Bailly's little son Harry.

'John Comyns is dead,' Chaucer announced gloomily, staring into the flames. 'Killed by some strange pestilence, they say. I was speaking to him only a few hours before. He seemed fine just before vespers, yet come prime the following morning . . .' He shook his head. 'What illness could kill a man so swiftly?'

Kemp was lost in his own thoughts. In a week's time he would have been resident in London for a year and a day. Chaucer was already making arrangements with a notary so that the Lord Mayor and the Alderman of the Vintry Ward could confirm him as a freeman. It was hard to believe the year had passed so quickly. Soon he would be able to return to Knighton. Yet he could feel his instincts pulling him in another direction.

For the past few weeks, the king's preparations for his next campaign overseas had been evident, with archers mustering at Smithfield, ships being converted for war before being sailed down the Thames to Sandwich, and victuallers busy purveying food supplies for the troops. Even the Chaucer household had been affected, for Chaucer himself was the deputy to the king's butler for the port of Southampton and he had been called upon to provide a vast amount of low-quality wine for the embarking soldiers.

Kemp envied those soldiers; not because of the wine, but because of the opportunities for booty they would find on campaign. Now that freedom was almost his, it did not seem enough. He wanted more, something physical he could show to Beatrice when he returned to Knighton, to prove that in his absence he had made something of himself. He wanted to ride back into the village on a fine black courser, dressed in elegant robes, rather than skulk back on a hackney cob, dressed in his plain and simple cloak. The king's departure for France might yet be held up a few more days; until he could join the army, perhaps. If Beatrice had indeed waited for him all this time, of course she would not mind waiting a few months more, while he . . .

He shook his head, dismissing the thought. At the end of the week he would set out for Knighton, just as he had been planning for the past two years. There would be other campaigns, other chances to win glory and booty.

Or so he hoped.

His reverie was broken by the sound of the door banging open with a gust of wind and rain, and the entrance of a dozen archers dressed in green and white particoloured livery. As they began to gather around the fire, dripping and shivering, their serjeant walked to the counter and waved Mistress Bailly across.

'We need lodgings for the night, and a warm cup of mead apiece would not go amiss either,' he told her. He had the sing-song voice of a Welshman, though his English was fluent enough. She nodded, and went to prepare their drinks.

The Welsh serjeant glanced across to his men, who were settling by the fire. Seeing Kemp, he smiled and leaned back against the counter, his hands clasped across his chest. 'Well now, if that's the best archer the English can muster then it's small wonder King Edward needs must employ good Welshmen for his retinue.'

Hearing the word 'archer' Kemp looked up, realising that he carried no longbow and was too far away for the man to be able to see the calluses on his fingertips. He scowled to hear English archery belittled by a Welshman, but his anger melted away when he recognised the serjeant.

'Ieuan!' He leapt to his feet, and then swayed suddenly, as if drunk.

'Are you ill?' asked Chaucer.

'Aye, the kind of malady caused by too much strong ale, I'll warrant!' chuckled one of the Welshmen.

Kemp felt a wave of cold dizziness sweep through him and he shivered. Wiping his brow with his sleeve, he found it damp with sweat. 'A chill, that is all. This damned weather . . .' He crossed to the counter and clasped Ieuan by the hand. 'Ieuan, you old dog! How are you? I've not seen you since Crécy.'

Ieuan nodded, grimacing. 'Aye, that was a black day, that one,' he mused, and then smiled. 'But we beat them, eh? And said we'd laugh about it over a pot of ale.'

'No time like the present,' said Kemp. 'Can I get you one?'

Ieuan shook his head firmly. 'This one's on me.' He paid for the drinks, directing one of the wenches to carry the tray over to where his men sat. He remained standing at the counter with Kemp. 'I hear Master Richard Stamford was slain that day, though they found his body far from the fighting,' he murmured as he raised his pot to his lips. He took a deep draught and lowered his pot, wiping ale from his moustache with his sleeve. 'Not that you'd know aught of that,' he added sardonically.

'It was self-defence,' Kemp assured him, his thoughts turning once again to Knighton where Lady Beatrice awaited him. She had been betrothed to Stamford, although Kemp felt sure it was himself she loved. Would she love him if she knew he had slain Stamford?

Ieuan was talking. 'You remember Madog, don't you? Madog Fychan?'

Kemp looked around in search of the big Welshman Ieuan referred to. 'Madog? Aye, of course. How could I forget? Where is he?'

'Saints preserve us, you've not been listening to a word I've said. Madog's dead.'

Kemp stared at him in astonishment. 'How?'

'Killed by the pestilence. It did not take long, God be praised, though the end was bad. Him and thirty others it took in our village alone. And Dafydd too; he would go to tend to the sick, though he knew no cure for it. There is none, they say: 'tis the wrath of God, sent to purge the sinful from amongst us.' He smiled. 'Why you and I have lived for so long is but a mystery.'

Kemp grinned. 'What brings you to London?'

'We're on our way to Sandwich. Most of us have relatives to visit in the Welsh quarter.'

'You're off to fight in France?'

Ieuan nodded. 'And not before time, too, I might add. I feared I might die of boredom.'

The strange thing was, Kemp knew exactly what he meant.

'How about you?' asked Ieuan. 'Aren't you coming?'

Kemp shook his head. 'Not this time. I've another week before I've earned my freedom; and then I must return to Knighton to take care of some personal business.'

'Can it not wait?'

'No.' Kemp smiled wryly. 'I have put it off too long . . .' He winced as a spasm of pain racked his chest.

'Are you all right?' Ieuan asked with concern. 'Your hue is pale . . .'

'I'm fine,' insisted Kemp, and frowned. Suddenly he could only see Ieuan through a purple mist. Then the whole room seemed to spin around him, and he found himself staring up at the ceiling.

'Is he drunk?' asked Mistress Bailly. Her voice seemed to come from a long way away.

Ieuan crouched over the younger man, fastidiously pulling back his cloak to expose the dark buboes swelling at the base of Kemp's neck. He recoiled in horror.

'By the Trinity! The pestilence!' He rose to his feet, backing away hurriedly. 'Come on, men. We're leaving.'

'But what about your drinks?' demanded Mistress Bailly.

Ieuan tossed some coins on to the counter: enough to buy his men a dozen rounds of drinks. It was clear he had no intention of tarrying for his change.

Chaucer crossed to where Kemp lay on his back, hardly conscious of what was going on around him. 'What's wrong with him?'

'It's the pestilence, no doubt about it,' Ieuan replied grimly.

'Someone fetch a physician!' Chaucer snapped.

'Save your gold.' The Welshman was hurrying towards the door. 'He's dead already.'

# CHAPTER NINE

SIR JOHN BEAUMONT entered the Tabard Inn at Southwark that evening, on his way to join the fleet mustering at Sandwich. He had arrived in London a few days ahead of schedule to join the king's army so that he would have time to search for Kemp, his man Treroose having failed to trace the villein. He knew that if the churl were living in London to gain his freedom, then he could not be far short of the prescribed year and a day. But London was a large city – by English standards, at least – and one he little knew. He had reluctantly abandoned his search, knowing that if he tarried any longer he might miss the sailing of the fleet. He consoled himself with the knowledge that Kemp did not have to be a villein for him to exact his vengeance upon him.

Mistress Bailly served him truculently, slamming the flagon of ale down on the table in front of him, and reminding him why he hated London so much. At home the lesser orders treated him with the respect due to a man of his status, but here in London the wealth of the burghers made the people arrogant. It amazed Beaumont that men who had had to earn their wealth should have the gall to show contempt to men who had inherited it. Not that Beaumont was rich; countless campaigns had taken their toll and he had not had the good fortune to capture anyone so noble that their ransom would fill his empty coffers.

He glanced contemptuously at the other patrons of the inn: craftsmen and merchants for the most part, low-born men whose aspirations to belong to the nobility were exposed by their pathetic attempts to match the grandeur of noblemen's dress. His eyes fell upon the man seated alone at the next table. Unlike the other customers he was soberly dressed, a dark grey fustian cloak wrapped around his shoulders. The pilgrim's hat he wore lent an incongruous touch to his appearance, his head bowed so that the hat's broad brim cast his face into deep shadow. Even though the man's expression was hidden, there was something lugubrious about him, an air of melancholy in his stooped shoulders and his bowed head.

Mistress Bailly came by the man's table and refilled his cup from a flagon of claret. Then she waited while he downed it in a single draught and filled it again.

'I heard about Mistress Curtis,' she told him. 'I'm truly sorry. She was a fine young woman.'

'Aye.' The man's voice was cracked with grief.

'They say the pestilence is a punishment for our sins, but if it can carry off one such as Mistress Curtis, then I for one cannot accept that. A more blameless woman has not trod the earth since the Assumption of the Lady Mary.'

The man managed a wan smile. '*Quem di diligunt adolescens moritur*,' he said.

Mistress Bailly nodded sagely. She was used to Curtis spouting Latin. 'John Chaucer's bodyguard has got it now, too. I saw him fall right before my very eyes, even as he was talking to another one of my customers.' She sighed again and crossed herself.

Curtis looked up sharply. 'Martin Kemp has caught the pestilence?'

'Aye. Though at the speed at which it works, I dare say he is dead already . . .' She broke off and turned to stare at Beaumont, who had leapt to his feet as if his stool had suddenly become red-hot.

'You know Martin Kemp? Martin Kemp of Knighton?' the knight asked.

'And if I do, what of it?' snapped Curtis. 'My remarks were not addressed to you, sir.'

Beaumont grabbed Curtis by the collar of his chemise and hauled him roughly from his stool, dragging him halfway across the table and upsetting the flagon so the wine splashed across the table and dripped on to the floor to stain the pale rushes red. 'Where can I find him?' he demanded.

'Unhand me! You may be a nobleman, sir, but that does not give you the right to assault me so!'

'I asked you a question, damn you!'

'Damn *you*!' retorted Curtis, catching Beaumont on the underside of his jaw with a right uppercut. Caught off-guard, the knight released Curtis and staggered back. Curtis straightened, and began to dust himself down. 'Count yourself lucky, sir knight,' he sneered. 'I'll not report this to the constable, but in future I advise you to bear in mind that the people of this city are not your villeins, who may be used and abused at your will. We are free citizens . . .'

Beaumont seized Curtis by the scruff of the neck and slammed him against a wall with all his might. 'Where can I find Martin Kemp?' His voice was a menacing growl.

'Go to hell.' Curtis's voice was slurred with pain, but still full of defiance.

Beaumont clenched his fist, and drove it into one of Curtis's kidneys. As his opponent doubled up, Beaumont lifted his knee into his face. Curtis sprawled on his back amongst the rushes, his face covered in his own blood. Beaumont grabbed a fistful of the front of his chemise, and pulled him a few feet off the ground. 'I'll ask you one last time, scum: where can I find Martin Kemp?'

'Let him alone!' screamed Mistress Bailly. 'Can't you see he's had enough?'

Beaumont shook his head. 'There's plenty of fight left in this one, unless I'm very much mistaken.'

'Go . . . to . . . hell,' Curtis repeated thickly.

Beaumont raised his left fist to smash it into Curtis's face, but Mistress Bailly grabbed him by the wrist, hanging from it in her effort to hold back the blow. 'For Saint Paul's love, Jack, tell him. Kemp's no doubt beyond any harm this whoreson can do him,' she sobbed.

Beaumont dropped Curtis to the flagstone floor and turned his attention to the landlady. 'What do you mean?'

'He doesn't know where Martin is; I do. He was taken to the hospital attached to the Priory of Saint Bartholomew in Smithfield.'

Beaumont shook his head. 'If only you had told me that sooner, you could have saved your friend a great deal of unpleasantness,' he said, as he turned towards the door.

'If you're going to see Kemp, I should hurry,' Mistress Bailly called after him. 'By now he's probably already beyond your reach.'

'I doubt it. My reach is long.'

'Does it reach as far as heaven?'

Beaumont laughed harshly. 'If Kemp is dead, that would be the last place I should seek him.'

*

The knight crossed the bridge and made him way through London, asking the way to Saint Bartholomew's Priory. He was directed through Newgate to Smithfield, where he found the hospital attached to the priory. As he approached the door, he encountered a physician, recognisable from the red gown and furred hood he wore.

The man moved to block Beaumont's path. 'Are you ill?'

'No.'

'Then I should not enter this house of death, unless you wish to be.'

'I'm looking for Martin Kemp of Knighton.'

'Are you a relative?'

'I'm his master!' protested Beaumont, growing impatient at being questioned like this.

'Then he can serve you no longer. Master Kemp is yet another victim of the pestilence.'

'What is this pestilence of which everyone talks?'

The physician stared at him incredulously. 'Are you a hermit, that your life is so secluded you have not yet encountered its horror? The black swellings which indicate that death can be no more than days away at most, perhaps even hours?'

'It is fatal?'

'It is beyond the power of my art to cure it.'

'And you say Kemp suffers from this malady?'

The physician nodded. 'There is naught you can do for him. Only a priest can save him now, and then only his soul. His body is corrupted beyond all hope of redemption.'

'I must see for myself,' said Beaumont. He pushed past the physician and entered the hospital.

The foetid stench hit him at once, a smell foul beyond description, the stink of death intensified a thousand times. Beaumont found himself retching instantly, uncontrollably. It took all of his concentration to keep his supper down, so he was only dimly aware of the Austin monks in their brown habits who moved amongst the beds of the dead and dying. He glanced at the huddled form on the nearest bed, and saw a face that was riddled with livid carbuncles and blood-black blisters that wept pus in sluggish streams across the cheeks. Huge black-swellings distorted the man's neck.

One of the monks suddenly collapsed. Two of his brothers

hurriedly crossed to where he lay and examined him, presently announcing that the pestilence had claimed another victim.

Meanwhile one of the patients levered himself off his bed, and began fumbling his way towards the door. He was naked except for a foully soiled breech-cloth, and his whole emaciated white body was covered with carbuncles. Dark swellings glistened in his armpits and on his thighs close to his groin.

'Air! Air! For the love of God, I must have more air!' he screamed in a despairing and high-pitched voice.

Two of the monks seized him by the arms and wrestled the man back to his bed. As they did so, one of the swellings in his armpits burst, splashing black pus on to the already soiled bed-linen.

Beaumont could take no more of this vision of hell. Feeling the bile rise to his gorge, he rushed out of the hospital, vomiting uncontrollably even as he stumbled over the threshold. Outside, he pressed his forehead against the cold stonework of the hospital wall and gasped for breath. After a few moments, the cold night air began to revive him. He smiled. Such a death was far worse than anything he could wish on Kemp.

Lying on a pallet in one corner of the main room, Kemp had been too far gone even to be aware of Beaumont's visit. He was hardly aware of anything any more. Only the occasional moment of lucidity, in which he was conscious of little more than the fiery pain of the swellings on his neck and under his arms, would sweep over him, quickly to be replaced with yet another bout of fever. Those moments of his life he would most like to have forgotten were replayed before his eyes in a series of visions that were neither nightmares nor hallucinations, but something in between. He was in the cells at Leicester gaol again, lying in complete darkness in a pool of his own vomit, awaiting execution. Then the dim light of a torch appeared, revealing a black-clad priest holding a small, leather-bound Bible. With his pale, cadaverous features in the shadow of his cowl, he looked like the Angel of Death.

'I have come to hear your confession,' said the priest.

'Go to hell,' Kemp told him bitterly. 'I've not done owt wrong.'

'Would you go to your grave with your sins unpurged?'

'I've not committed any sins, yet I'm to die for a crime which I didn't do. I've prayed to God for salvation, but he has forsaken me. Now I'd make a pact with the Devil himself, if it would free me from this unjust fate,' spat Kemp.

'Blasphemous wretch! Would you burn in the fires of hell for eternity?'

'For a full span of life? Aye.'

The priest snapped his Bible shut. 'There is nothing I can do for this one,' he announced. 'He has chosen his path.'

Then the darkness of the gaol melted away, leaving bright sunlight, and Kemp was standing on a road somewhere in Normandy. He saw an armoured figure riding a courser, wearing the arms of Sir John Beaumont. A young man who had once been in Kemp's platoon, Piers Edritch, was also standing on the road, seemingly oblivious to Kemp's presence, even though he was staring straight at him. Standing stock still as if frozen in time, Edritch had his back to the rider, and the courser's hooves were eerily silent on the road. The rider removed his helmet and revealed not Beaumont's face, but the face of his daughter, Beatrice. Laughing, she swung at Edritch's neck with a broadsword. Edritch's head was lopped from his shoulders, and rolled down the road until it came to rest at Kemp's feet. He glanced down at the disembodied head, but instead of seeing Edritch's face he saw his own, laughing up at him. He tried to scream, but no sound would come out.

The countryside seemed to boil away, and he found himself floating in a purple haze. Faces swum out of the mist at him: his brother Nicholas, Sir Thomas Holland, Wat Preston, John Chaucer. He saw de Chargny staring at him with those gimlet eyes, like a hawk studying some kind of insect it had not encountered before and wondering if it were good to eat. Then the French knight's features melted into those of a priest, and Kemp could hear a distant voice droning the last rites. He watched his own hand reach up and grab a fistful of the priest's black robes, pulling him down so that his ear was close to Kemp's mouth.

'No, priest!' he snarled. 'I'm not dead yet!'

Then the priest was gone, to be replaced by more faces: John Conyers, Jack Curtis, Hodge Rudcock wide-eyed with surprise as he stared down at the haft of the dagger that had been thrust into his chest.

There were voices, too. 'What do you think you're doing?' A woman's voice, terse and angry.

'The swellings must be lanced! It's his only chance for survival!' The voice was vaguely familiar, but Kemp could not place it.

'And who are you?'

'A friend.'

'A physician?'

There was a pause. 'Not exactly. But I did train briefly as a barber-surgeon . . .'

'Get away from him! Master Aderne, do something to stop this man. He's interfering with one of the patients.'

'Are you bleeding him?'

'I'm lancing the swellings prior to applying an ointment made from Armenian clay. It's a technique described to me by a Saracen physician . . .'

'Get away! I'll have no paynim magic here!' the woman's voice screeched. 'This is supposed to be a house of God!'

'It's not magic, you stupid old . . . It's medicine. It hardly ever works, I'll admit, but at least it works sometimes, which is more often than anything else anyone has tried . . .'

'You'll kill him!'

'So what? He's going to die anyway . . .'

Sheets of fire exploded through Kemp's torso, burning the voices away. Darkness settled over him, but its coolness was refreshing after the flames. He felt himself floating.

He was standing in a room that was strangely familiar but distorted, the posts of the four-poster bed defying all the laws of perspective, as did the walls and the ceiling. A sword was in his hand and it felt comfortable there.

Two large blue eyes peered at him over the edge of the bed.

'Come out from behind there,' he heard a voice order. It was his own. 'Show yourself.'

She rose trembling to her feet: a young woman, with a pale face and red hair. He walked around to the other side of the bed to face her. She shrank away from him, but he caught her around the waist, pulling her against him. She cried out, but he pressed his lips against hers, forcing his tongue between her clenched teeth. She tried to push him away. Laughing, he grabbed the front of her dress and ripped it open. She gasped in horror and tried to break away from him, but he grabbed her by the arm and hauled her back, throwing her against the wall. He slapped her back-handed across the face, drawing blood from the corner of her mouth, then tore the rest of her clothes from her body and held her: one hand on her throat, the other fumbling with the hem of his tunic. He pushed his breech-cloth down over his hips, and forced himself into her.

Suddenly her arms were enfolding him, her moans no longer of pain but of pleasure. Her embrace grew tight around his body, squeezing the breath from his lungs. He looked at her, and his stomach churned with revulsion and terror. Her skin had grown leathery and turned as dark as clotted blood. Filled with horror, he tried to pull away. Even as he watched, her features changed, forming into a grotesque snout, with tusks protruding from the corners of a mouth full of jagged teeth. The thing threw back its head and laughed, and Kemp found himself falling. He landed in a sea of fire, and then the thing was standing over him, its forked tail twitching with pleasure, its goat-legs bestriding Kemp, as tall as the steeple of Saint Paul's Cathedral. Gnarled horns twisted out of its head, and a white eye patch incongruously covered one eye. The Devil pointed one of its talons down at Kemp.

'Your soul is mine! Your soul is mine!'

'Yes!' Kemp was sobbing now. 'Yes! I never denied it! You can have it, and you're welcome to it! Only release me from this pain! I can't take any more of this pain . . .!'

A great gout of fire exploded upwards, engulfing Kemp, the Devil, everything, leaving only blackness in its wake. Blackness, and a strange kind of peace. The peace of oblivion.

'Jacques! Fetch two casks of wine from the buttery. Sir Geoffroi's finest Burgundy, mark you! Jeanne, take down Sir Geoffroi's finest plate and make sure it is properly polished. Henri – are the rushes in the great hall clean? Good – then get the fire going here, and then see to the one in the hall. Robert – fetch the biggest pig from the sty and start roasting it, quickly!'

'Not the fat sow!' protested Robert, the cook. 'We were saving that for Christmas.'

'We'll have to find another one for Christmas, Robert,' replied the steward. 'Today we must prepare a feast fit for a king – for it is the king we serve! Where is Typhaine?'

Typhaine stepped forward and curtseyed. Below stairs, the

steward was a king in his own domain, and to be obeyed without question. De Chargny's steward could be sharp-tongued when he was impatient, but he was a fair man, and had been patient with Typhaine from the first day she started working at the castle.

'Here, *maître*.'

'Did you make up the guest bedchamber?'

'Yes, *maître*.'

'Can you pour wine, girl?'

'Of course!'

'Good. Louis is ill, so you'll have to do it.'

'Me? Pour wine for the king?' she stammered.

'Jacques will decant it, so you don't have to worry about that. Fetch Sir Geoffroi's best goblets from the garret.'

Typhaine made her way to fetch the goblets in a daze. In the few weeks she had been at the castle, she had quickly grown used to her new life. At first everything seemed to happen in a whirl, and it was as if she were sleep-walking. When she woke up, she found herself so used to the strictly regulated daily routine that the chaos and uncertainty of her previous life already seemed like a dim and distant memory.

News of de Chargny's unexpected return from Paris – with the king and several senior knights of his court – had already spread through the castle at Saint-Omer, and now everyone was in a panic to make sure a proper feast was prepared. If the king was not pleased by the banquet, de Chargny would see to it his staff suffered for their incompetence.

Typhaine was carrying the salver of gem-encrusted goblets along the gallery leading to the main bechambers when she met one of de Chargny's men-at-arms coming in the opposite direction.

Arnault was a squat, broad-shouldered man with a face that must have been ugly even before it was grotesquely disfigured by a multitude of scars. Seeing her, he grinned and, as he passed, knocked the salver from her hands, sending the goblets clattering noisily to the floor.

'Now look what you've done, you clumsy oaf!' she snapped. As she bent down to retrieve the goblets, he slapped her on the rump. She straightened at once to strike him across the cheek, but he caught her by the wrist, twisting her arm.

'Come on, then!' he jeered. 'How's about a kiss?'

'Let go of me, you pig!' she hissed, struggling to keep herself from crying out in pain.

A hand tapped Arnault on the shoulder, and he released her at once, turning. A massive fist slammed into his face, hurling him against the wall. He glanced up to find Sir Eustache de Ribeaumont, one of the knights Valois had brought with him, standing over him. De Ribeaumont was a massively built man, and not all of it muscle. His lank blond hair fell to his shoulders, and his nose was over-large, but there was something handsome about him nonetheless. He glared down at Arnault.

'The lady is right, my friend,' de Ribeaumont said pleasantly. 'You *are* a pig.'

'She's no lady!' sneered Arnault, forgetting himself. 'She's a whore!'

It was a mistake. De Ribeaumont had no qualms about driving a booted foot into Arnault's side. 'When next I see Sir Geoffroi, I shall advise him against employing worthless filth such as yourself,' he said. 'Get out of my sight, you excrement.'

Arnault clutched his side in agony and stumbled away. De Ribeaumont turned to Typhaine. 'Are you all right, mademoiselle?'

She nodded, curtseying. 'Yes, thank you, my lord. But I'm not a demoiselle, I'm a chambermaid.'

He smiled disarmingly. 'One so beautiful as yourself?' he asked. 'I cannot believe it. Surely no one as fair as you could have sprung from anything other than the bluest blood.' She giggled, and he bowed. 'And now I must take my leave of you; and may it flatter you to know that nothing short of the express command of my king, on whom I now must attend, could drag me away from your presence.'

She continued down to the kitchens, where the steward set her to work polishing the salver and the goblets while the final touches were put to the banquet. One of the goblets had a scratch where it had fallen on the floor. She prayed no one would notice.

'Remember, serve the guests in order of precedence,' the steward told her when she had finished. 'First the king, then his son the Duke of Normandy, then Sir Eustache, Sir Oudard, and leave Sir Geoffroi and Geoffroi le fitz until last.'

'But how will I know which is which?'

'The king will be sitting at the head of the table; the others will be seated around the table in order of precedence. Just work your way around the table from left to right.' The steward placed a large flagon of wine on the salver with the goblets. 'As soon as the flagon is empty, come straight down and fetch some more. And don't meet anyone's gaze.'

She climbed the spiral staircase and paused behind the arras to take a deep breath before entering the great hall.

Soft music filtered down from the minstrels' gallery above her head. Most of the hall was in darkness, apart from pools of light in front of the log fire blazing in the hearth and the wrought-iron candle-stands which were placed around the high table on the dais at the far end. She had to walk the full length of the hall to reach the table. The thudding of her heart, as she did so, seemed almost as loud as the rattle of the goblets against the salver she carried. It was too much to grasp: a few weeks ago she had been the wife of a simple man-at-arms; now she was waiting upon the king himself! She had been vaguely aware that de Chargny was a great lord in Artois, but it had never occurred to her that he might be on speaking terms with King Philip himself.

As she approached, a tall, handsome young man with red hair and a beard was speaking. He sat to the left of the man at the centre of the table, who she realised with a shock must be the king, even though he wore no crown. Even in his rich robes, she was surprised that he looked so – well, so *ordinary*. She realised the red-headed man on his left must be his eldest son, Duke Jean of Normandy.

'To defeat the English, one must fight like the English,' said one of the other men.

'The English depend upon their churls for victory,' snorted Duke Jean. 'Where is the glory in that?'

'The English win,' pointed out the man. 'Where is the glory in defeat?'

As she mounted the short flight of steps on to the dais the nightmare that had haunted her as she crossed the room came true, and she slipped. The goblets rattled loudly on the salver, but she caught herself in time and avoided dropping any. She blushed, convinced they must all be laughing at her, although only de Chargny spared her a glance.

As Typhaine balanced the salver on one hand and put a goblet at the king's right hand, he turned to de Chargny. 'You are acclaimed above all others when it comes to an appreciation of chivalric code, Sir Geoffroi. What say you?' He made no attempt to acknowledge Typhaine as she poured wine into the goblet.

'I wish there were a simple answer, sire, but there is none that I know of,' replied de Chargny, as Typhaine poured out wine for Duke Jean. 'The codes of chivalry were drawn up in earlier times, when honour was less rare than it is today.'

'When the English stayed at home, you mean,' said Duke Jean, and they all laughed. Even de Chargny smiled thinly at the jest.

Next Typhaine came to the knight who had come to her rescue earlier. He smiled at her as she poured out his wine. She blushed again and, feeling her face grow hot, blushed all the more.

De Ribeaumont gave her a wink and supped his wine, smacking his lips in satisfaction. 'Excellent. Your taste in wine remains as good as ever, Sir Geoffroi. Burgundian, unless I am mistaken. From your vineyards?'

De Chargny nodded curtly, and Typhaine felt his eyes on her as she served Sir Oudard de Renty.

'Will the English stay at home now, do you think, Sir Geoffroi?' asked the king.

'My spies inform me that their preparations for war are nearing completion. They are in earnest, sire.'

The king sighed, rubbing the scar on his cheek. 'What would you have me do, gentlemen? Yield to their demands?'

'The English are mustering at Sandwich, a port on the south-east coast of England, just across the sea from Calais,' mused de Chargny. 'Obviously they intend to use Calais as their base-camp for their next invasion. If we seize Calais before it can be reinforced, then their plans will be ruined.'

De Ribeaumont shook his head. 'It took the English eleven months to take Calais, with an army far greater than any we can muster now. We could not hope to take Calais by storm, and a siege would take too long.'

'Then we take it not be siege or by storm, but by stealth,' said de Chargny.

De Renty smiled. 'Fight like the English, you mean?'

'Aye, if necessary,' de Chargny agreed. 'There can be no peace until Calais is restored to France.'

'And how would you take Calais by stealth, Sir Geoffroi?' the king asked.

'The governor of Calais, Sir John Montgomery, is dead, killed by the pestilence,' said de Chargny, and the whole company crossed itself at the mention of the plague which had already swept through France. 'My informants tell me that the captain of the Calais galleys – a Lombard knight named Sir Amerigo de Pavia – is acting in his stead.'

'He has no loyalty to the English king?' asked de Ribeaumont.

'Before Calais fell, he served in the French garrison with Jean de Vienne,' de Chargny shrugged. 'De Pavia is a Lombard. Doubtless like all his folk, he has a greater loyalty to gold. I think he could be bribed into betraying Calais to us.'

'You would *buy* Calais?' de Ribeaumont asked. 'I see no honour in such an adventure, Sir Geoffroi.'

'No honour for the men who did so; but the honour of France and her king demands that Calais be restored,' said de Chargny. 'And what greater glory could there be, than to sacrifice one's own honour for a higher purpose?'

The king considered the proposition for a moment, but then shook his head. 'I could not countenance such an inglorious conquest; not while the truce remains in force.'

'The truce will remain in force until the English break it; and they will break it when it pleases them to do so, with the sword and the lance,' protested de Chargny.

'Then let the dishonour go to them for their deceit, for I shall not be party to such a plan.'

De Chargny shrugged. His counsel had been sought, given, and was now to be ignored. 'As your Majesty decrees,' he said, glancing at Typhaine as she poured the last of the wine into his goblet.

The flagon empty, she was glad to be able to return to the more comfortable surroundings of the kitchens to refill it. As she made the long walk back across the great hall, she heard the king speaking.

'Have one of my clerks write to Cardinal Ravaillac. Tell him that I agree to an extension of the truce for another two years, on the terms of the English. Time is what we need, gentlemen. Time to rebuild our army. We are weak now, but it will not always be so. One day we will have recovered sufficiently to meet the

English on the field and we will be in a position to defeat them chivalrously, without resorting to underhand methods.'

She made several more trips between the great hall and the kitchens before the banquet ended, but spent most of the evening standing in the shadows, waiting for one of them to wave her across when his goblet needed refilling.

It was late before de Chargny and his guests retired for the night, and she was glad to return to the room in one of the outhouses in the courtyard where she slept with the rest of the castle's domestic staff. Most of them were already asleep, at least as exhausted by the night's work as she was. She sat down on the edge of her pallet and took off her shoes, rubbing her aching feet. She was about to start undressing when the door opened, and the steward thrust his head through.

'Typhaine?' He beckoned her with one finger, and she hurriedly pulled her shoes back on.

'What is it, *maître*?' she asked, as she followed him back across the courtyard. But the steward would not say anything until they had reached the kitchens. He pointed to where the salver stood on one of the tables, bearing the flagon and a single goblet. At first she thought someone had noticed the scratched goblet, and she was in for a beating.

'Sir Geoffroi wants wine taken up to his chamber,' the steward told her. Typhaine wondered why the steward himself could not perform such a simple task, but he continued. 'He specifically asked for you.'

She had got as far as the door when he called after her. 'You . . . you are not a maiden, are you?'

She blushed. 'No, *maître*. I was married for . . . oh!' She broke off as the full import of his words hit her.

He nodded apologetically. 'It is just as well. Sir Geoffroi . . . well, just do as you are told, and you will be all right.'

'Do I have any choice?'

He pursed his lips. 'Typhaine . . . you are a good girl. If you want to leave the castle now, I will help you. But you will have to leave Artois if you do.'

She hesitated. De Chargny was not an unattractive man and, because he had saved her life and taken her in, she felt as if she were in his debt. 'Thank you, *maître*, that will not be necessary.'

The steward nodded, evidently relieved, and she carried the

salver up to the gallery, her heart pounding. She found herself thinking of Sir Eustache de Ribeaumont; he was not as handsome as de Chargny, but there was a warmth and a kindliness to him that her master lacked.

But it had not been de Ribeaumont who had summoned her, so it was useless to think such thoughts.

She reached the door to the smaller bedchamber de Chargny was using while the king was a guest at the castle. Swallowing hard, she knocked.

De Chargny sat at the desk in front of the window, working by the light of a candle, his quill scratching on a piece of parchment. She knew that when he was at the castle he spent much of his time working alone in his room, and she wondered what he was writing.

He did not glance over his shoulder at her, but continued to scratch away. 'Put the wine down on the chest.'

There was a chest at the end of the bed, with two heavy, silver-plated candlesticks on it. She put the salver down between them and hesitated. Had the steward misinterpreted de Chargny's intention in asking specifically for her?

De Chargny drained the excess ink from the nib of his quill and laid it across the top of the desk, before turning to regard her thoughtfully. 'Close the door. Bolt it.'

She did as he bade her.

He sat with his legs crossed, his elbows resting on the arms of his X-pattern chair, fingers steepled. 'Take your clothes off,' he ordered her, as if it were the most natural thing in the world.

She hesitated only briefly before stripping off her clothes, trying to seem neither demure nor teasingly coy. She stood on the hearth rug, her arms straight down by her sides, consciously stopping herself from trying to hide her nipples. She was grateful for the warmth of the embers in the grate.

De Chargny rose and walked around her as if he were examining a piece of horseflesh that was up for sale. She remembered the steward's earlier injunction not to meet a nobleman's gaze and stared straight ahead, keeping her eyes fixed on the candles flickering on the desk until de Chargny moved into her line of vision once again, standing facing her.

'Damn you,' he muttered, and she gasped as he clasped her around the waist, pulling her forcefully against him. She stood on tip-toe to kiss him, and pressed herself against his hips.

He pulled away from her, as if he had betrayed a weakness, but he recovered quickly, sinking to his knees before her and nuzzling her breasts while she ran her fingers through his locks, clenching her fists in his hair as she pulled him against her.

Then he was on his feet again, whirling her around and seizing her by the arms as he marched her across to the bed. Before she realised what he intended, he had pushed her to her knees at the side of the bed and bent her over the mattress.

'No,' she panted. 'Not like this . . .'

He did not seem to hear her, quickly entering her from behind. He thrust himself rapidly in and out of her, his hands gripping her hips, pulling her buttocks back against him. It hurt, but she did not dare protest; after all, was this not what she had wanted?

But somehow it wasn't. She wanted to look into his eyes as they made love, to feel his lips upon hers. This was not lovemaking, merely carnal intercourse, and she realised she had mistaken her simple lust for some deeper longing.

De Chargny's breathing came in ragged gasps now, as rapid as his almost frantic thrusts, then suddenly he groaned and slumped over her, still. She realised his pleasure had had nothing to do with her, she had merely been a vessel into which he could empty his urges. She felt used, cheapened.

After a few moments he pulled out of her, straightened his clothing and returned to the desk, sitting with his back to her. She remained where she was, listening in shocked disbelief to the scratching of his quill on the parchment. 'You can go now,' he said, when she did not move.

Blinking, she stood up and got dressed. She stumbled out of the chamber, fighting back the tears until she could reach the sanctuary of her garret, where she threw herself on the bed and wept.

The master of Saint Bartholomew's Hospital was roused before dawn by the sound of the priory's bells tolling, calling the brethren to lauds. He dressed in his habit and sandals and made his way to the cloister, washing his hands and face in the lavabo with the other monks before attending the early morning service of prayers and hymns.

He visited the hospital before breakfast, knowing that he could not face the stench of the pestilence victims on a full stomach. The main room was dimly illuminated by a number of rush candles, their weak flames guttering as they neared their end. The pestilence had filled every bed in the hospital and brought more victims besides, so he had had to arrange for straw-stuffed pallets to be laid on the floor wherever there was space, to accommodate the additional patients. Most of the patients were asleep, some of them twitching feverishly, others snoring peacefully, while others lay absolutely still, having found a deeper peace: nothing short of a release, after the suffering the pestilence inflicted. The master wondered how many more of their patients would have to be carted to the burial ground. The death toll was growing so rapidly that the gravediggers could no longer cope, and there was already talk of building communal pits for the victims. At least any deaths which had occurred in the course of the night would make more places available, but the master did not doubt that those places would be quickly filled as fresh victims were brought in.

The plump Austin nun who had watched over the patients during the course of the night sat in a chair in one corner, a psalter open on her lap, her head bowed, her ample chest rising and falling rhythmically with her snores. The master felt no anger that she had fallen asleep while on duty; if any one had needed help in the course of the night their groans would have roused her in time to fetch a priest, for their was little else to be done for these poor souls. Some of them even refused the last rites, like the young man who slept . . .

Glancing across, the master noticed that one of the beds was empty, the soiled sheets tossed back. He crossed quickly and seized the nun by the shoulder, shaking her to rouse her. She snorted and opened her eyes, blinking owlishly at him.

The master pointed across to the empty bed. 'The young man who slept there. What happened to him?'

Still half asleep, she shrugged helplessly. 'I . . . I don't know. All the beds were full when last I looked.'

The master hurried out of the building. The false dawn had turned the sky a pale grey, and the city was only just beginning to stir. Smithfield was empty as yet, with none of the market stalls set up for the day's trading. A figure stood stock-still in the middle of the market place, dressed in a black cloak with a loose-fitting cowl. The master crossed to where he stood, and was about to touch the man on the shoulder when something about his stance made him think better of it. He moved round to stand in front of him.

It was the young man who had refused the last rites; the same man whose swellings the stranger had insisted on lancing. It was common enough for victims of the pestilence to rise from their beds as the end drew near, and sometimes they even enjoyed moments of lucidity, but although the young man's complexion was as pale as the sky overhead, the spots on his face seemed to have faded from their earlier lividity, and his eyes lacked the bright shine of those close to death.

'You're . . . alive,' the master said helplessly.

Gazing north up Saint John's Street towards the village of Islington and beyond, the man's eyes did not even flicker in the master's direction. 'Aye.'

'You feel . . . well?'

'Well enough,' allowed the young man. The quality of his voice had changed, the pestilence leaving it slightly hoarse.

It was the first time the master had ever seen a victim of the plague recover and he could not quite believe that it was possible. 'It's a miracle! God be praised!'

The young man turned his dark blue-grey eyes on the master for the first time. 'God had nothing to do with it,' he said. Something in his voice sent a shudder down the older man's spine.

The young man began to walk away slowly, almost hobbling, his limbs emaciated by his illness. But there was a kind of determination in his step, something that convinced the master that he would live.

'*Panem caelestem accipiam, et nomen Domini invocabo*.' The chaplain took the two pieces of the sacred host in his left hand. '*Domine, nom sum dignus ut intres sub tectum meum: sed tantum dic verbo, et sanabitur anima mea*.' He repeated these words three times, striking his breast with his right hand as he did so.

The bell was rung, and Sir John Beaumont and his daughter Beatrice rose and crossed to the altar rail in the small chapel attached to his house on Stone Gate Manor, kneeling down once more.

'*Corpus Domini nostri Jesu Christi custodiat animam meam in vitam aeternam*.' The chaplain made the sign of the cross. '*Amen*.'

It was two weeks since Beaumont had returned to Stone Gate

Manor. The day after visiting Saint Bartholomew's hospital, he had bought a fine new courser at Smithfield Market for the forthcoming campaign against the French. It cost him the best part of a hundred pounds, but it had been worth every penny: a thoroughbred animal, an Old English Black like his destrier, a fine steed for a knight to ride into battle on. Then he had ridden directly to Sandwich, only to find that the campaign was cancelled, the truce with France extended for another two years. Bitter with disappointment, he had headed for his home in the County of Leicester.

An even greater horror had greeted him on his return. A band of outlaws led by the notorious Folvilles had attacked the village of Knighton in his absence, murdering and raping, stealing the animals and what little grain had been produced by the year's poor harvest. The under-sheriff of Leicester had persuaded the king to appoint a commission of *oyer* and *terminer* to catch and try the outlaws, but they had escaped justice as usual, riding back into their fastness in the Forest of Leicester. The next time the king campaigned overseas, the Folvilles would agree to serve him in return for pardons for their crimes, and would then return to Leicester County to live in peace, untroubled by the law, until such time as they chose to defy it afresh.

As he waited to receive the sacraments, Beaumont turned his thoughts to the future. Since the death of his son-in-law at Crécy, only the war against the French and his hatred of Martin Kemp had kept him going. Now Kemp was dead, and the latest campaign against the French was cancelled. The realisation struck him like a physical blow. Suddenly, he had nothing left to live for. Nothing, except for his daughter and his two-year-old grandson.

The chaplain was picking the crumbs off the sacramental cloth and putting them into the chalice. '*Quid retribuam Domino pro omnibus quae retribuit mihi . . .*?'

The door burst open, and Beaumont twisted round to see a tall figure in a voluminous black cloak with a large, loose-fitting cowl. The man strode in, sweeping his cloak back across his left shoulder to reveal a large broadsword hanging in a leather-bound scabbard at his hip.

'How dare you barge into this house of God bearing that tool of Satan?' the chaplain demanded. 'Do you want to burn in hell for eternity?'

'Hell holds no terrors for me,' replied the stranger. His voice had a sepulchral tone, as if it had come from the depths of a tomb. 'I was at Crécy.'

Beatrice stared at him in astonishment. 'Martin?'

Looking at her for the first time in over two years, Kemp felt a lump choking his throat. The thought of her had sustained him through the horror of the campaigning in France, and now he found that she was even more beautiful than he remembered. 'Hello, Beatrice,' he said hoarsely.

Both Beaumont and Beatrice were on their feet now. 'You!' exclaimed Beaumont.

Turning his attention back to Beaumont, Kemp bared his teeth in a cruel sneer. 'Aye.'

'I'd heard you were dead! Killed by the pestilence . . .'

'It takes more than the pestilence to kill me,' Kemp responded.

'How dare you burst in here unannounced?' Beaumont struggled to regain his composure. 'You should have returned to Knighton over a year ago. You owe me fifteen months' labour, churl. I shall have you flogged, by God's flesh.'

Kemp reached inside his cloak and produced a scroll of parchment that he unrolled to show Beaumont. 'Do you see that seal? That is the seal of the Lord Mayor of London. It testifies that I, Martin Kemp of Knighton, having resided in the Borough of London for a year and a day, have been granted the status of freeman in accordance with the laws of this realm. I don't owe you a God-damned thing!' he spat.

Beaumont trembled with rage. 'Get out of here!' he snarled. 'Get out of here at once!'

Kemp shook his head. 'I've come for Beatrice.'

Beatrice blanched. 'What the devil are you talking about?'

'Come on. We're leaving.'

She stared at him in astonishment. 'Has the moon touched your wits? I'm not going anywhere with you!'

Kemp was confused. Suddenly, the dreams he had treasured for so long seemed to come crashing down around him. 'But . . . I thought you loved me!' he protested petulantly.

She stared at him in mute horror for a moment, and then her face softened and she threw back her head with a peal of laughter. 'Oh, you poor, sweet, naïve churl. How ridiculous you are.'

He frowned. 'How so, my lady?'

'Jackass! Surely you don't believe that I could ever love you?'

'But I thought . . .'

'It's not your place to think.' She looked scornful. 'Besides, what can a churl like you understand of the nobility of true and genteel love?'

'I'm as good a man as any noble. A better man than Richard Stamford ever was, aye and like.'

Suddenly Beaumont understood. 'It was you who slew Richard, wasn't it?'

'Aye,' Kemp admitted absently.

'God's love, I ought to . . .' He broke off abruptly and moved closer to Kemp, fists clenched to strike him. But Kemp was faster, driving a powerful punch into Beaumont's stomach. The knight doubled up, gasping in pain and clutching his midriff.

The chaplain moved to intervene. 'How dare you fight in a house of God . . .?'

Kemp levelled his sword at the chaplain's chest. 'I've never killed a holy man, father,' he said coldly. 'Do you wish to be the first?'

Ashen-faced, the chaplain backed away. At that moment the door opened and Beatrice's maid walked in, leading a small, blond-haired, blue-eyed toddler by the hand.

'No!' Beatrice screamed a warning to the maid. 'Don't bring him in here!'

'Bring him in, Edith!' wheezed Beaumont, rising to his feet. 'Let him see the man who slew his father.'

Kemp stared first at the toddler, and then at Beatrice. 'Your child?'

'Aye, mine and Dickon's, she said coldly. Then she turned her back on him, scooping the child up in her arms, and walked out of the chapel, followed by the maid.

The scales fell from Kemp's eyes. She had betrayed him all along, telling him she loved him while giving herself equally to him and to Stamford. 'You talk of noble love?' he snarled after her, seething with rage and humiliation. 'You're nothing more than a whore! One day I'll be a greater man than your father. When that day comes you'll beg to be my wife. And beg in vain!'

Beatrice's laughter echoed outside.

'You can leave now,' Beaumont told him icily.

Kemp shook his head and seized Beaumont by the mantle,

dragging him outside. 'Don't you believe it. I've a score to settle with you.' He was thinking of a day three years earlier when Beaumont had had him flogged for striking Richard Stamford.

'Unhand me, you dog!' protested Beaumont, struggling.

There was no sign of Beatrice, Edith or the child, but the steward was still standing there, unsure of what to do. 'Treroose!' shouted Beaumont. 'For the love of God, aid me!'

'Get the whip, Treroose,' Kemp ordered.

The steward hesitated.

'The whip,' insisted Kemp. He still had his sword in his free hand, and he held the blade against Beaumont's throat. 'Or your master dies.'

The steward nodded, and hurried into the stable.

Beaumont continued to struggle, so Kemp sheathed his sword and punched him in the stomach. Winded, Beaumont was unable to resist as Kemp tied his wrists to the tailboard of the cart that stood there. Then he tore open Beaumont's robes to bare his back. The steward emerged from the stables and, as soon as Kemp had taken the whip from him, he fled into the manor house.

'I'll see you burn in hell for this, Kemp!' screamed Beaumont.

'Your squire once said exactly the same thing to me,' Kemp replied. 'I dare say his soul awaits mine there even now.' He lashed the whip across Beaumont's back, and as the first bloody weal was raised, the knight howled in agony.

On the seventh lash, Beaumont fainted.

'Stop it!' Beatrice had emerged from the house and was running down the wooden steps into the courtyard. 'For pity's sake, stop it! Can't you see he's suffered enough?'

'No,' Kemp said tightly, lashing Beaumont's back once more. The fact that Beaumont could no longer feel it only angered Kemp further and he lashed even harder.

Beatrice tried to grab him by the arm but he pulled free and struck her in the face with his other hand, knocking her to the ground. She lay there, sobbing, as Kemp delivered the last four lashes. Then he coiled up the whip and tossed it down beside Beatrice. He turned away, and paused, unlooping the coverchief she had given him all those months ago from around his neck. Screwing it up into a tight wad, he dropped it on top of her before swinging himself back into the saddle of his horse and riding out of the courtyard, back in the direction of Knighton.

Kemp's mother was buried in the graveyard of the church of Saint Mary Magdalen in Knighton. The markers at nearby plots showed the last resting places of other villagers. 'It were a band of brigands,' Kemp's eldest brother, Michael, explained grimly. 'They rampaged through the village, stealing everything they could find of value, raping the women . . .'

'What about Beaumont? Didn't he try to protect you?'

'He were away at the time. Looking for you,' Michael added, looking significantly at his brother. 'Not that he could have done much if he had been here. They took us by surprise. Simkin, Croft and some of the others tried to put up a defence with their bows, but they were no match for these men. They tortured Hayward Forester to death – they were convinced he must have had a cache of gold somewheres, and nowt anyone could say would convince them otherwise. A few were spared. I only escaped by hiding down by the river . . .'

'I can well imagine,' Kemp snorted.

'What would you have had me do? I'm a farmer, not a warrior. These were hard men, Martin, veterans of Crécy. Trained killers . . .'

'Men like me, you mean,' Kemp observed.

'I didn't say that.'

'You didn't have to.'

The two of them stared at the grave markers in hostile silence for a few moments.

What about Nicholay?' Kemp asked finally. Nicholas Kemp was the middle brother, who had gone to study at Oxford.

'He's well – at least, he were the last time I saw him. He visited the village during the summer. He came top of his class at college and won a bursary to study at the Sorbonne College in Paris. He seemed pleased at the prospect.' Michael tried to put warmth into his voice.

Kemp said nothing.

'I know the future looks bleak, but things will be different now that you're back,' Michael continued. 'We can start afresh . . .'

Kemp was not listening. He stared down at his mother's grave. He should be feeling something more than this . . . this *emptiness*, he thought to himself. 'I'd like to be alone for a little while,' he told his brother.

'Of course.' Michael moved away, walking to the lych gate where Kemp had tied his horse. He watched as his brother stared at the various grave markers. Then, after a pause, he saw Kemp rise to his feet and tilt his face to the heavens.

'Why not me?' he roared in anguish.

Michael shuddered. This was not the little brother who had left Knighton so long ago.

Martin Kemp was still standing with his back towards the lych gate. Michael could not see what he was doing, but his shoulders shook as if he were sobbing. Then he walked back to the gate, unfastening the hackney's halter.

Michael looked at him uncertainly. 'Things will be better now, you'll see,' he persisted. 'We must be strong. We have our whole lives ahead of us.'

'Aye,' Kemp agreed grimly. 'That's what I'm afraid of.' He swung himself up into the saddle.

'What are you doing?'

'I'm not staying, Michael. There's nothing for me here now.'

'But where will you go? What will you do?'

Kemp shrugged. 'I'll follow the trade I've learned.' He patted the hilt of his broadsword.

'Fighting?' Michael looked disgusted. 'What kind of a life will that be?'

'Life is for the living,' Kemp told him softly. 'And I died a long time ago. Maybe it was on a beach in Normandy, maybe it was in a city called Caen, or maybe it was in a field in Picardy. But my last rites are long overdue.'

Michael furrowed his brow. 'What are you talking about? I don't understand.'

'Goodbye, Michael.' Kemp dug his heels into his hackney's flanks, chucked the reins, and rode out of the village heading south, towards Broughton Manor in the County of Buckingham and a knight who wore a white silk patch over one eye.

A few weeks after Valois' visit to the castle at Saint-Omer, Sir Geoffroi de Chargny sat at the table in his chamber, scratching away at a roll of parchment with a practised hand as he wrote another of his treatises on chivalry. Periodically he would dip the nib of his quill into the ink-horn, and sometimes he paused to lean back in his chair, staring through the narrow lancet window at the fields of Artois beyond the town walls. He did not see the countryside, however, but another walled town twenty-five miles to the north-west, a town that was a slur on French honour for as long as it was allowed to remain in the hands of the English.

He stared at the last words he had written:

*If a man lays claim to a town, does he earn the greatest dishonour in failing to win it, or is there a greater dishonour in declining a challenge to battle in the field during the siege?*

He dipped his quill in the ink-horn, drained off the excess ink, and held the nib poised above the next line. There was a knock on the door: Guilbert's familiar, heavy rap. 'Enter.' De Chargny did not turn, nor even pause in his writing.

'There's a messenger arrived, Sir Geoffroi.'

'Where from?' de Chargny asked evenly.

'From the king, sir. He brings a gift for you.'

The nib of de Chargny's quill halted in mid-word. After the briefest pause, he finished the sentence he had been writing and laid his quill aside. Rising to his feet, he turned to face Guilbert. 'What manner of gift?' he asked, his curiosity piqued.

'I don't know, sir. The messenger brought it in a chest on the back of a packhorse.'

De Chargny stood contemplating Guilbert for a moment, and then gave the tiniest shrug. 'Let us find out, then.' He led the way downstairs, to where the messenger was unfastening a large coffer tied to the back of his packhorse. A troop of men-at-arms sat astride their horses nearby. They were obviously an escort for the gift, indicating that it must be something of great value. Seeing de Chargny approach, the messenger stopped what he was doing to turn and bow obsequiously, before handing the knight a sealed envelope. De Chargny checked the wax seal, and saw the familiar mark of Philip of Valois. Without further ado, he broke it open and read the letter within.

*My dear Sir Geoffroi,*

*Please receive my gift as a reward for the good service you have done me in the past, and in anticipation of greater service in future. To what use you see fit to put my gift I leave entirely to your discretion, for I know you will use it wisely.*

*Valois*

'What is it, Father?' De Chargny's son descended the wooden steps leading from the main entrance of the keep.

'Let us see, shall we?' De Chargny turned to the messenger. 'Have it carried inside.'

The messenger grimaced. 'Begging your pardon, your lordship, but it's a bit heavy . . . If I could have a little assistance, the job would be done the sooner, I reckon.'

De Chargny sighed. 'Guilbert!'

The squire bent, seized one of the handles on the side of the coffer, and with a single movement hefted it on to one shoulder as if it were empty, carrying it unaided up the stairs. The messenger stared at Guilbert in outright disbelief.

De Chargny and his son followed Guilbert into the keep, where the squire was waiting for them in the great hall. 'Do you want me to put it down here?' he asked, nodding to the table.

'No. Bring it up to my chamber.'

The three of them made their way up to the chamber, where Guilbert put the coffer down on the oak chest at the foot of the massive four-poster bed. De Chargny inserted the small brass key the messenger had given him into the lock and turned it, pushing back the lid.

Twenty thousand gold coins glinted back at them, glistering in the flickering light of the brand which burned in a nearby wall-bracket.

'By God and Saint Denys!' exclaimed de Chargny's son.

Rendered speechless, Guilbert could only make the sign of the cross in awe.

'A generous gift,' observed de Chargny.

'A king's ransom, Father!'

'Aye,' agreed de Chargny. 'Or the price of a town.'

# CHAPTER TEN

THE SNOWS OF winter lay thick upon the ground when Kemp came to Broughton. Clouds of condensed breath billowed from the depths of his deep, dark cowl and from the nostrils of his pale grey hackney. He reined in his horse in the middle of the village and stopped a fearful peasant who was carrying a bundle of twigs back to his hovel.

'Is this Broughton?' Kemp asked peremptorily.

'Aye, master.' The peasant nodded, knuckling his brow.

'Which way to Sir Thomas Holland's house?'

'Straight up the lane, master, at the far end of the village.'

Kemp chucked the hackney's reins, and followed the peasant's directions until he came to the manor house. It was built along similar lines to Beaumont's. A main building with a chapel attached and a number of outlying buildings, including stables, kitchens, and kennels, were surrounded by a high stone wall. In addition, a small moat lay outside.

Kemp dismounted and crossed the wooden bridge across the moat, drawing his sword and using the wheel-shaped pommel to hammer loudly on the great oaken gates three times. After a moment, a grille opened in one of the gates and Conyers' face peered out at him.

'What do you want?' he demanded. It was evident that he did not recognise Kemp.

'Hello, John,' Kemp said softly. 'I've come to see Sir Thomas.'

Conyers stared at him. 'Martin? By the Holy Cross of Bromholm, you've changed since we all parted at Dover! Wait a moment,' he added, his face disappearing as he opened the gate sufficiently to admit Kemp and his horse. 'Come in, come in.' Conyers wore a chain-mail habergeon and a visorless steel bascinet, a broadsword at his hip and a longbow slung across his back in a woollen bow-bag.

‘Expecting trouble?’ asked Kemp, as Conyers closed the gate behind him.

‘Nothing but,’ admitted Conyers. ‘These are troubled times, Martin. Nothing but thieves, brigands and murderers abroad these days.’

Kemp nodded. ‘I’ve come to join Sir Thomas’s retinue.’

‘You too, eh?’

‘Meaning?’

‘Nearly all the old platoon’s here. Hamo, Simkin, Baldwin, Elias . . . and Preston, of course.’

‘And you,’ observed Kemp. ‘I thought you were going to open the biggest stewhouse in Doncaster?’

Conyers grimaced. ‘Remember all that booty I won? Lost it all, didn’t I?’

‘How?’

Conyers shurgged. ‘Wine. Women. Dice. You know how it is.’

Kemp did not, but he could imagine. He thought of the others: Hamo Newton, Simon Elliott, Baldwin Gower and Elias Jarrom; they had all had plans when the truce started, and none of them included working for Holland. Did they all have tales similar to Conyers’? ‘What about the others? Daw, Pisspants, Limkin and that lot?’ he asked.

‘Daw and Perkin are dead.’

‘Christ’s blood!’ The grizzled ancient had always seemed invincible to Kemp. ‘What happened to them?’

‘The pestilence, of course. What else?’

Kemp nodded grimly. Perkin Inglewood had been a franklin’s son, a mother’s boy, always whingeing and whining, and yet suddenly Kemp knew he would miss him.

‘John Horton died of it, too,’ Conyers continued relentlessly. ‘And Jankin Launde and Tom Wistow.’

‘And Limkin?’

Conyers shook his head. ‘He was hale and hearty the last time I saw him. We travelled north together as far as Leicester. He got a job there working for the under-sheriff. How about you, Martin?’ added Conyers, smiling. ‘What have you been up to? Did you get your girl?’

Kemp’s face twisted with bitterness. ‘That bitch? She can burn in hell for eternity, for all I care.’

Conyers chuckled. ‘How was your family?’

'My mother's dead,' Kemp said flatly.

Conyers' face fell once more. 'By Christ's sweet tree, I'm sorry. Was it the pestilence?'

'Brigands.'

'God damn it!' Conyers exclaimed. 'The whole world is going to hell, Martin.'

Kemp grinned savagely. 'Didn't they tell you? This *is* hell.'

'Aye, right enough.' Conyers turned and Kemp followed his gaze to see Holland crossing the courtyard to where they stood, dressed in dark blue robes of thick wool and a fur-lined cloak.

'Who's this, Conyers?' he called.

'It's Martin Kemp, Sir Thomas,' replied Conyers, and Kemp pulled back the cowl of his cloak to reveal his face.

'So it is,' Holland agreed. 'You've lost weight, Kemp.'

'Aye, Sir Thomas. I've had a touch of the pestilence,' he explained.

Holland threw back his head and laughed. 'No one gets a "touch" of the pestilence, Kemp; or if they do, they certainly do not live to tell the tale. Have you come to join my retinue?'

'If it still pleases you, sir.'

'It does indeed, Kemp, it does indeed. Have you eaten?'

'Not since breakfast, sir.'

Holland pointed out the kitchens. 'Have my cook give you a bite to eat and something warm to drink. While you're doing that, I'll ask Brother Ambrose to draw up a contract of indenture.'

Holland's cook was an elderly but kindly woman who bade Kemp sit by the cooking hearth to warm himself with a cup of mead while she warmed up some leftover oatmeal pottage for him. 'So, you're another one of the men who served under Sir Thomas in the last campaign?' she asked.

'Aye.'

'What's your name?'

'Martin Kemp.'

'I'm Mary Cook, although everyone here calls me Malkin, so you might as well do so too. Whereabouts do you hail from, Master Kemp?'

'Knighton.'

'In Wales?'

'In Leicester.'

'Oh.' Malkin was usually quite chatty with Holland's men, but Kemp's curt responses made it clear that he was not in the mood for small talk.

Kemp had almost finished eating when Preston stuck his head through the kitchen door. 'Hullo, Kemp.'

Kemp rose instinctively to his feet. 'Master Preston,' he said, acknowledging the serjeant with a nod.

'Come on, lad. Sir Thomas says I'm to get you kitted out.'

Kemp mopped up the last of his pottage with a sop of rye bread which he chewed as he followed Preston across the courtyard to the armoury. There they found a habergeon, coif and bascinet, like the ones Conyers had been wearing. 'I see you've still got your sword; and a new bow, too, by the looks of it,' said Preston. 'Are you happy with those?'

Kemp nodded.

'Fine. The armour belongs to Sir Thomas, so if you leave his service you'll have to return it.' He chuckled. 'It's just like old times, isn't it? I can remember that day at Bosworth when you and the other wet-behind-the-ears recruits stood there like a flock of lost sheep. You in your girl's coverchief, dreaming of chivalry and glory. How is she, by the way?'

'Well enough, I suppose. She's a mother now.'

'Nails and blood! You didn't waste any time, did you?'

'I'm not the father,' Kemp said bitterly, and suddenly Preston understood.

'Ah. So it were like that, were it?'

Preston led Kemp to the great hall where Holland waited with Brother Ambrose. The friar greeted Kemp warmly. 'Conyers told me about your mother, Martin. I'm truly sorry.'

Kemp shrugged. 'These things happen.'

The indenture sheet was couched in legalistic terms that went over the top of Kemp's head, and he was glad when the friar explained the details to him in plain English. 'You're to serve Sir Thomas as a mounted archer in his retinue for thruppence a day, to be increased to sixpence if Sir Thomas indents to fight for the king in future campaigns, as I'm sure he will.' Holland nodded. 'The terms of the indenture are for life, or until such time as Sir Thomas decides to terminate the contract. You'll also get bed and board provided – subject to availability on campaign, as I'm certain you'll appreciate by now – as well as any arms, armour and equipment you may need.' He laid the sheet of parchment back on the table and dipped a quill pen in an ink-horn, handing it to Kemp. 'Sign here and here.'

'Sign?' Kemp echoed uncertainly.

'He means put your mark, lad,' explained Preston.

Kemp wondered if he were signing his life away. Probably, he reflected, but since he learned of Beatrice's falseness it had become something which he valued little anyway. Bending over the table, he handled the quill awkwardly. He had seen other people use quills before, but had never been called upon to use one himself. He scrawled a crude cross, breaking the nib and blotting the parchment; but the ink did not spill across the writing, so Ambrose let it pass. Then Holland countersigned both halves of the indenture sheet with a fresh quill, while Preston and Ambrose witnessed it. Ambrose added the words, 'Martyn Kempe de Knighton, his mark' under both of Kemp's crosses, and 'Walter de Presstone, his mark' under the serjeant's. Finally he produced a pair of scissors and used them to cut the indenture sheet in half in a random, jagged line which would mean that the two could later be matched up, preventing forgery. He kept the upper half to go with the rest of Holland's documents, giving the lower half to Kemp.

'Of course, the best part of this job is you get paid each week in advance,' said Preston, as Ambrose unlocked a small, iron-bound coffer and counted out one and a half shillings, handing them to Kemp, who slipped them into his purse.

Martin Kemp had become a professional soldier.

There was no sign of spring's thaw when Sir Hugh Despenser reached the castle of Mold in Flintshire. Identifying himself to the man-at-arms on duty at the gatehouse, he rode into the courtyard. A squire emerged to take his palfrey's bridle as he dismounted.

Sir William Montague came down the wooden steps from the entrance of the keep. 'Sir Hugh! What brings you to Wales?'

'A letter,' explained Despenser, handing him a parchment envelope.

Montague glanced at the seal. 'From the king!'

Despenser nodded. 'When I told him I would be passing this way, he asked me if I would bring it to you . . .' He broke off as a fit of coughing wracked his body.

'Are you all right?' asked Montague, concerned.

'A touch of ague, that is all. This damned weather . . .'

Montague gestured to the keep. 'Come inside, and warm yourself by the fire.'

'How is Lady Montague?' asked Despenser, following him up the stairs.

'Well enough,' said Montague, although there seemed to be a trace of doubt in his voice.

'And the Countess Margaret?' asked Despenser.

'She is well also.' Montague had broken the seal on the letter and was reading it as he led the way into the great hall. A log fire roared in the hearth and the countess sat in front of it, embroidering. She looked up as Montague and Despenser entered.

'See who has come to visit us, my lady,' said Montague, before turning his attention back to the king's letter.

'An unexpected pleasure,' the countess said drily.

Despenser bowed low. 'I am pleased to find you well, my lady, and to see your radiance undimmed.'

'By all that's wonderful!' Montague exclaimed. 'I am to inherit my father's title, and be created Earl of Salisbury!'

'Did you ever doubt it?' asked Despenser.

'It is not before time,' agreed the countess.

'We are to attend parliament at Westminster this year, for the ceremony of girding, and I am to renew my oath of fealty to his Majesty.'

'Once you are Earl of Salisbury, the king will never accept . . .' Despenser put a hand to his forehead. His face had grown pale.

'Sir Hugh! Are you certain you are not ill?' asked Montague.

Despenser nodded, and slumped into a chair. 'The heat in here, after the chill outside . . .' He gestured dismissively. 'What was I saying? Ah, yes: the king will never accept Holland's claim on Joan once you are Earl of Salisbury. The Earl of Kent's sister could not be married to an obscure knight in preference to a peer of the realm.'

'Not so obscure any more, now he is a knight of the Companionship of Saint George,' said the countess.

'As am I!' protested Montague, and then turned and ran for the stairs. 'I must tell Joan.'

'I'm certain she will be delighted by the news,' the countess said sardonically, but Montague had already gone.

'How is your daughter?' Despenser asked her.

'As troublesome as ever. We have to keep her all but locked up. When the summoner arrived from Avignon it was all we could do to prevent her from learning that Holland had taken his case to the Papal Court. We appointed an attorney on her behalf.'

'And does he represent her?'

The countess looked scornful. 'He represents her interests, as an attorney should.'

'How goes . . .?' Despenser broke off to clear his throat. 'Excuse me,' he said, coughing into his fist. 'This damned ague . . .' He tried to clear his throat, but a spasm of coughs racked his body so violently he fell forward on to his knees.

'Sir Hugh! You are gravely ill . . .'

A spasm shook Despenser and he retched horribly. A torrent of blood and bile gushed from his mouth, spattering on to the pale grey flagstones.

The countess leapt to her feet, upsetting the stool she had been seated on. 'God preserve us! The pestilence!'

Despenser stared down at the pool of blood he knelt in, and confronted what he had been trying to convince himself for the past two days could not be true: he had contracted the plague. He raised his head to stare at her beseechingly, tears of pain running down his blood-flecked cheeks. 'Help me!' he sobbed.

The countess's revulsion gave way to fury. 'You knew, didn't you? You knew you were carrying the plague when you came here!'

Despenser struggled to his feet. 'I thought it no more than an ague . . .'

'How dare you endanger us by bringing the pestilence into our home!'

'For the love of God, help me,' he pleaded. 'It's not too late . . . send for a physician, I pray you!' He staggered towards her, his arms stretched out imploringly.

Deaf to his entreaties, she retreated from him until she felt one of the huge stone pillars supporting the mantelpiece against her back. 'Get out! Get out of here at once, before you infect us all!'

'For the love of the Virgin, have I meant nothing to you?' he sobbed.

She snatched an iron poker from the fireplace and brandished it. 'Stay away from me! I'm warning you. One more step . . .'

'Please. Margaret. Don't let me die!'

She tried to slip past him but he lurched towards her, his face a mask of terror. She swung the poker at him with all the strength of her disgust and fear of the pestilence. It struck him on the side of the head and he fell prostrate in front of the fire.

The countess stared at his prone body, waiting for him to rise, but he was dead. She replaced the poker where she had found it, and wiped her sweaty palms on the front of her gown. He had been dead already, she told herself. The pestilence spared none. It had been a mercy killing, really.

She heard a sound from the minstrels' gallery and raised her head sharply, but her eyes could not penetrate the shadows. 'Who's there?' she demanded.

There was no reply. A chill ran down her spine.

'My lady?' Montague emerged at the foot of the spiral staircase at the far side of the hall. Then he saw Despenser's corpse. 'Sir Hugh!' he exclaimed, and started across the room.

'Stay away from him!' she shrieked. 'The pestilence . . . there is nothing you can do for him.'

'He seemed well enough a moment ago . . .'

She pointed to the pool of blood. 'He spewed up that gore, and then collapsed. I think he must have hit his head on the mantelpiece as he fell,' she added hurriedly. 'Fetch the servants at once. Send for a physician, lest we all contract it.'

On learning there was pestilence at the castle, the physician refused to come in person, but gave strict instructions to the servant sent to fetch him. He ordered that aromatic herbs be burned in every room to purify the air and keep out the miasma that caused the pestilence. He also advised that everyone avoid carnal intercourse and eating vegetables such as beetroot and lettuce, and then gave the servant a large bill.

'Is there nothing else we can do?' asked the servant.

'Aye,' the physician told him sternly. 'Pray!'

Back at the castle, the countess ordered Maud Lacy to fill a hot bath for her. Alone in the privacy of her room, she wiped sweat from her forehead with her sleeve. Had there been someone hiding in the gallery? Had anyone seen her kill Despenser? No one had said anything. No one would dare, she told herself. If it had been a servant, they would not be believed above a noblewoman.

Glancing at her dishevelled state in a mirror, to her horror she saw sooty marks down the front of her gown. She must have wiped her hands there after handling the poker. When Maud returned with the hot water, she would get the girl to launder it – no, that would never do. The girl would wonder how the marks had got there. She hurriedly stripped off the gown and tossed it on the fire that blazed in the hearth in her chamber.

She fell into a trance as she watched the expensive cloth burn to a crisp, the flames dancing before her eyes. Presently there was a knock on the door and she started guiltily. 'Who is it?'

'Maud, my lady.'

She glanced in the mirror to check her appearance. 'Come in.'

Maud filled the bath with steaming water. When the countess was satisfied with the temperature she dismissed the young woman, locking the door behind her, and lowered herself into the tub. The heat brought beads of sweat to her skin, and she scrubbed herself thoroughly with soap before lying back in the tub, allowing the water to wash away the strain of guilt and fear.

She was Countess of Kent still; no one could touch her.

It was a June afternoon as wet and miserable as any in the depths of winter when Master Robert Sigglesthorne of Beverley returned to Broughton after his fifth trip to Avignon on Holland's behalf. Reining in his palfrey at the entrance to the manor house, he dismounted and rapped loudly on the heavy wooden gates. After a brief pause, the grille set in the gate opened, and Wat Preston's face peered out.

'Good day to you, Master Preston,' Sigglesthorne said cheerfully.

Preston rolled his eyes heavenward to take in the relentless torrents of rain. 'I don't know about that,' he said, his voice becoming muffled as he moved away from the grille to remove the bar on the gate, swinging one half open to create a gap just wide enough for Sigglesthorne to lead his horse through. 'How was your journey this time?'

'Awful,' admitted Sigglesthorne, as Preston closed the gate behind him. 'These are ill times, Master Preston.'

'That they are,' the serjeant agreed dourly.

The pestilence had swept through the length and breadth of the land in the past few months, leaving no town or village untouched by its corruption, slaughtering one person in three without mercy. No one was immune; from the lowliest churl to the king's second eldest daughter, all were carried off regardless of their rank and station, even the new Archbishop of Canterbury, John Offord. It slew weak, new-born babes and it slew strong men. It had slain the heathen and now it slew the Christian; it took Frenchman and Englishman alike, without regard.

What had caused the pestilence no one knew, although the most learned men agreed that it had been brought about by a fatal conjunction of Saturn, Jupiter and Mars in the sign of Aquarius, and ordained by God in his wrath at the sinfulness of man.

What it had caused was plain to see. As fields and streets filled not only with dead people but also livestock, no one could deny that the pestilence was a disaster of Biblical proportions. The Four Horsemen of the Apocalypse were abroad, or so it seemed. Pestilence and Death cut down people in their thousands. The shadow of the war with France still hung over the realm despite the truce and a poor harvest was made poorer still by a shortage of labour to bring it in. The only thing that might yet keep famine at bay was the fact there were so many fewer mouths to feed.

But the widespread feeling that the world was coming to an end did little to mitigate behaviour; if anything, people began to act with abandon, as if, with the end of the world nigh, it no longer mattered what they did. Peasants could no longer be bothered to work so untended cattle died and fields of grain ripened and rotted with no one to harvest them. Labourers took advantage of the shortage of manpower to demand higher wages. Whole villages became deserted except for the dead. Manorial mills fell into disuse. Financially ruined, many landlords like Sir Edward Montague turned to crime and became outlaws, Sir Edward himself stealing horses and cows, and eventually battering his wife to death out of jealousy for her liaison with the king.

Many people turned to God, but more turned to drink or lost themselves in other carnal pleasures. Some who had lost loved ones went mad with grief, imagining themselves to have the symptoms of the pestilence even when they were perfectly healthy, throwing themselves into the common burial pits to die atop the putrid corpses of their friends and families. Merchants shut up shop. The parliament summoned for January had to be postponed, and then postponed again, until there was no meeting of the parliament that year. The law courts went into recess, giving men another excuse to resort to the violence they had practised in France to solve their problems in England.

Sigglesthorne was shown into Holland's chamber in the main house where the knight was studying a chess problem. The room was Spartan and furnished in accordance with the taste of an unmarried man more at home on campaign than in an English manor house.

Sigglesthorne was followed in by a servant carrying two cups and a large flagon of claret; Holland had soon learned how to make the serjeant-at-law feel at home during their association. They greeted one another cordially before getting down to what Sigglesthorne referred to as the serious business of the day, pouring himself a generous measure of wine.

'Tell me, Master Sigglesthorne: why have I the feeling that the case has not yet reached a resolution?' asked Holland.

Sigglesthorne grimaced. 'The attorney claiming to represent Lady Joan still had nothing to submit to the court. There is no longer any doubt in my mind: he does not act on her behalf at all, but on behalf of Montague. Montague's legal advisors know our case is strong and they are resorting to delaying tactics.'

Holland wearily ran his fingers through his hair. 'Is there anything I can do to spur things on?'

'Nothing can be resolved until her ladyship's side of the story has been heard. The Pope has already decreed she be freed to appoint her own proctor; I suggest you make sure she is given an opportunity to do exactly that.'

Holland smiled. 'I think I can manage that much.'

'Be careful, Sir Thomas,' warned Sigglesthorne. 'If you rescue Lady Joan from wherever it is that Montague has confined her, his attorneys will be able to claim that you have abducted her, and it is you who is imposing your will upon her, not Montague. Any action you take must be done in co-operation with the proper legal authorities. You cannot afford to put any arrows under the belts of Montague's attorneys at this delicate stage of the proceedings.'

Holland nodded. 'I think the perfect opportunity may be about to present itself.'

*

The king spent most of that year at his palace at Havering atte Bower in Essex to avoid the pestilence, but in June the court made its way to Westminster for Sir William Montague's investiture as Earl of Salisbury. Montague had reached his twenty-first year, and although ceremonies of investiture were usually carried out in the presence of the parliament, which did not meet that year, the king could not reasonably put off Montague's elevation to his father's earldom any longer.

A great banquet was held in Westminster Hall the night before the ceremony, but the mood of the guests was low. The king set the tone. He had recently been forced to make a proclamation to peg down wages and prices, which were increasing as the survivors of the pestilence sought to profit from the shortage of manpower. He sat at the centre of the royal table, truculent and ill-tempered, drinking aggressively and glowering all the while.

The days after Despenser's death had been days of terror for the countess. All in the castle had waited in trepidation for someone else to fall prey to the pestilence; for the countess there had been the added fear that someone might yet accuse her of murder. But as the days passed into weeks, it became clear she had escaped both pestilence and accusation. Then, two weeks before Montague's investiture, her brother had died of the pestilence at his estates in Wake. She had never cared for him, and his death meant that she inherited both his title and estates as Baroness Wake.

Now she forced herself to smile. Her daughter was about to become Countess of Salisbury, a destiny she had hoped for since she persuaded the king to arrange Joan's marriage to Montague. Holland's unexpected claim that he had already married Joan had almost upset the apple-cart, and the regular reports she received from the tribunal in Avignon worried her. Her one consolation was that now her son-in-law was about to become Earl of Salisbury, the king, who was known to have little time for the Papacy, would not accept any ruling by the Papal Court against the son of his old friend, the previous Earl.

Montague himself seemed equally glum, the wine making him maudlin. The countess leaned across to clasp her son-in-law by the shoulder. 'Why so gloomy, William? Have you forgotten that by sundown tomorrow you will finally be Earl of Salisbury, one of the senior peers of the realm? This is supposed to be a joyous occasion!' the countess told the company in general. 'Let there be more wine, more music. Minstrels! Play a lively tune there!'

After a few moments, the minstrels began to play an *estampie*. Montague turned to Joan. 'Will you accompany me on to the floor?' he asked, offering his arm.

She shook her head. 'I fear I must decline, my lord,' she responded distantly. 'I should like to retire, if it pleases you. I do not feel well.'

'Should I call for a physician?'

She shook her head again. 'I am tired, that is all. It is nothing that a good night's rest will not cure.' She bade him good night and, with a number of her husband's liveried retainers to accompany her as a bodyguard, she left Westminster Hall for the Bishop of Salisbury's inn where she, her mother and her husband were lodged. Montague slumped in his seat with a sigh, more depressed than ever despite the merry music of the minstrels.

The countess had caught the gist of their conversation, and she leaned across to address her son-in-law once more. 'My daughter has been your wife for eight years now and yet you continue to treat her as a lovelorn squire treats a lady from whom he seeks the gift of mercy.'

'Would you have me cease to love her because we are married?' asked Montague, signalling for one of the pages to refill his goblet with wine.

'If you wish to earn her love, first you must earn her respect. Why do you think she clings to this childish infatuation for Sir Thomas Holland? She needs a man who will dominate her, not one who lets her walk all over him.'

'Perhaps you are right.'

'Of course I am right. Do you not think I know my own daughter? Go to her. *Make* her respect you.'

But Montague could not leave the great hall until his liege had expressed the desire to turn in for the night, and that was not until the small hours of the morning, by which time he had consumed more wine than was good for him. He forced himself to be merry, and danced with the young ladies-in-waiting of the court, flirting with them, much to the king's approval. They seemed to find him attractive and he decided he could have slept with any one of them if he had so chosen.

He was swaying unsteadily when he made his way along the Strand. As he passed the House of the Carmelite Friars he felt a shudder run down his spine, as if someone had stepped on his grave. Finally he reached Salisbury House, close by the bridge leading across the River Fleet to the City of London. When he entered the main bedchamber, Joan was already in the huge four-poster bed, apparently asleep.

Montague bolted the door and began to undress, falling across the bed as he struggled to remove his hose. Then he blew out the candles he had used to light his way to his chamber and slipped under the covers beside his wife. Feeling her warmth beside him filled him with lust. He reached across to fondle her breasts.

She brushed his hand away. 'Not tonight, William,' she mumbled, still half asleep.

Montague decided that this was the perfect opportunity to assert himself as her husband. 'Aye, tonight, my love.' He began to fondle her once more.

She knocked his hand away. 'I told you, I'm not well.'

'There's nothing wrong with you,' he snapped.

'You're drunk,' she told him testily.

'What of it?'

'You should sleep it off.'

'There's plenty of time to sleep in the grave,' he said, trying to kiss her as he climbed astride her under the covers.

She struggled against him. 'Stop slobbering over me! I'm not in the mood.'

'But I am, my love,' he said, fumbling with the laces at the neck of her nightshirt.

She slapped him hard across the cheek.

'Damn you!' Losing his patience, he began to rip at her nightshirt, the delicate material tearing easily in his hands. 'You are my wife, and I shall have you as and when I please.'

'William! What's come over you? Stop it!' She tried to push him off. 'Get away from me, you filthy beast!'

He tried to thrust himself into her, but her legs were squeezed too tightly together. Losing his temper, he punched her on the cheek, just below her left eye. The sudden pain was such a shock that she did not even cry out, and merely stared at him in astonishment in the glow of the dying fire. Realising that he had struck her harder than he had intended, he felt a pang of guilt.

'Oh, God save me! I'm sorry.'

'Get out!' she hissed, backing away from him on her hands and knees.

He tried to grab her, but she dodged him easily, and he landed face-down on the bed. She sprang from the mattress and, crossing to the end of the bed, where her gown was folded on the chest, plucked her dainty dagger from the jewelled sheath attached to her girdle. She pointed it at him as he rose from the bed.

'Stay away from me!'

'Joan!' he protested, holding his arms wide as if to embrace her.

She waved the dagger under his nose. 'You heard me. Stay away!'

He beat his fist against one of the bedposts. 'Damn you, Joan. You are my wife, I will have my way with you. It is your duty!' He lunged, and she slashed at him with her dagger.

Backing away, he stared in disbelief at the blood coursing from the long but shallow cut on his forearm. 'You – you bitch! Damn you, Joan. Don't you see? If I am to be Earl of Salisbury, I must have an heir!'

'Not by me, you won't. You've had your way with me plenty of times before, and naught has come of it. Come near me again, and it won't be your arm I'll cut.'

Clutching his arm in an effort to stanch the flow of blood, he gazed at her in horror, unsure whether to believe her. The look in her eyes suggested he would be wise not to take any chances. He found a tippet and wrapped it around his arm as a makeshift bandage, then donned a robe.

'Damn you, you bitch,' he hissed, retreating to the door. 'Damn you to hell!'

The ladies and gentlemen of the court gathered in Westminster Hall for breakfast at dawn the following morning. Several members of the court remained in their beds, nursing sore heads after their night of revelry, but Montague and Joan were most notable by their absence. The king turned to the countess. 'Does Sir William sleep late on this morning of his investiture?' he asked her, with a smile.

'I know not, your Majesty,' she said, and waved a page across. 'Attend to Sir William, boy, and find out what delays him.' The page nodded and hurried out of the hall. He was back before the end of breakfast, still panting from the exertion of his ride back to Salisbury House. The countess's face grew dark as the page whispered in her ear, but she forced herself to smile as she turned back to the king. 'It seems Joan is ill, sire.'

A hint of fear entered the king's eyes. Even he had already lost a daughter to the pestilence. 'It is not . . .?'

The countess shook her head hurriedly. 'A little over-indulgence, sire. Joan is not used to strong wine.'

'And William?'

'He is attending her. I shall go in person to fetch him.' She rose to her feet and curtseyed out of the king's presence.

Once out of the hall, her face darkened again as she mounted her palfrey and rode back to Salisbury House. Inside, she rapped on the door of Montague's chamber.

'Who is it?' called Montague's voice.

'Margaret of Kent.'

The door opened. Montague was already dressed, in his finest robes of red and white silk. Joan, however, remained in a state of undress, sobbing silently as she sat on the edge of the bed. The bruise on her left cheekbone was so livid that no amount of face-paint could disguise it.

'A word, if you please, William,' said the countess, beckoning for Montague to join her in the corridor outside.

As he stepped outside and pulled the door to behind him, the countess rounded on her son-in-law with a snarl. 'You damned fool! She cannot attend your investiture looking like that.'

'Do you not think I realise that?' Montague snapped back. 'The ceremony will just have to be postponed, that is all.'

'Again? And disappoint all the good and noble people who have gathered here for this occasion? I think not. I have told his Majesty Joan is unwell; that explanation will have to suffice for her absence from the ceremony. It is a great shame, but the gossip will be the less than if she turns up looking as she does this day.'

'You would have me attend my investiture without my wife?'

'Rather than put off the ceremony again? Aye. You have brought this on yourself, Montague; do not blame me.'

Montague and the countess left Salisbury House with their combined retinues less than an hour later. As they rode past the stone cross erected at the hamlet of Charing in memory of the king's great-grandmother, they passed five beggars who sat by the roadside, their cowls perhaps hiding the faces of lepers. The countess tossed one of them a shilling.

'Thank you, your ladyship!' grunted the beggar. He waited until the tail of the cavalcade had passed by, and then flipped the shilling to the man sitting next to him, before pulling back his cowl to reveal a face with a white silk patch over one eye. 'She was not with them,' he said, his voice heavy with disappointment.

Sitting next to Holland, Brother Ambrose tossed the shilling to the third man. 'No, Sir Thomas,' he said sympathetically. Holland knew all about Montague's forthcoming investiture, even though he had not been invited. He had hoped to use the public ceremony as an opportunity to demand that Joan be allowed to appoint a proctor of her own choosing.

Wat Preston tossed the shilling to the fourth man, John Conyers, who slipped it into his purse. 'Perhaps they left her at Salisbury House, Sir Thomas?' Preston suggested.

'It's possible,' agreed Holland. 'But the inn will be guarded, and if the guards are under instructions to keep any one man away from Joan, that man will be me. I can hardly force my way into the Bishop of Salisbury's inn and break her out, can I? The scandal would destroy us all.'

'No, sir, you can't do that,' agreed Preston, and grinned. 'But we can,' he added, indicating himself, Conyers and Kemp.

Preston outlined his plan to Holland, who reluctantly gave his assent. 'Don't forget,' he called after them. 'You're not in France now, so for heaven's sake try not to kill anyone.'

Preston grinned, and the three archers made their way down the Strand, past Henry of Derby's mansion, the Savoy Palace, and the Temple Bar – where a chain between two posts symbolically delineated the western limits of the City of London – by the buildings that had once belonged to the Knights Templar, before the suppression of that order had led to all its properties being handed over to the Hospitallers. There the Strand became Fleet Street, and just beyond it stood the House of the Carmelite Friars. Between that and Saint Bride's Church stood Salisbury House.

Two men-at-arms stood guard outside the main entrance, and since Preston had no wish to be arrested for brawling in the street, he led Kemp and Conyers along Saint Bride's Passage, down the side of the inn towards the Thames. A stone wall about eight feet in height ran alongside the inn's extensive and well laid out gardens. Preston clasped his hands together with the palms upwards to make a step-up, boosting up first Kemp and then Conyers. The two men sat astride the wall, hauling Preston up between them. He was heavy even without his armour, and they grunted under the strain as his feet scrabbled against the brickwork. Finally the three of them dropped down into the garden, landing in a flower-bed, and crouched down behind some rose bushes that hid them from view of the inn.

'I'd much rather have done this at night,' grumbled Conyers, who had some experience of breaking and entering. 'Do you think anyone saw us?'

'So what if they did?' responded Preston. 'This is England. We're not at war. We can do what we like.'

'The word "trespass" springs to mind,' Kemp pointed out.

'We'll be all right. The Pope ordered that Lady Joan be set free, didn't he? We're only obeying the Pope's orders. No one can argue with that.'

'They'll try, though, I'll wager,' said Conyers.

'We'll cross that bridge when we come to it,' said Preston. 'Now let's stop wasting time and get on with it. You go first, Lancelot,' he added to Kemp. 'Rescuing a damsel in distress should be right up your alley.'

Kemp led the way, creeping between the bushes and flower-beds as stealthily as he had done on scouting missions in French-dominated territory. They managed to reach the back door without any shouts of alarm being raised. Preston tried the door. It was locked. 'We'll try round the side,' he suggested.

They made their way round to the far side of the house where some stables abutted on to an enclosed yard with a gateway opening out on to Fleet Street. Two more men-at-arms were on guard at the gate, but they had their backs turned to the yard. Another door was set in the side of the house, also locked, but hidden from the gateway by an outhouse. Kemp was about to kick it open, but Conyers hurriedly pushed him aside.

'Do you want to alert the whole household?' he whispered. 'Leave this to someone who knows what he's doing!' He took some small, curiously shaped tools from his purse, and inserted them in the lock, fiddling about for what seemed an inordinately long time.

'Hell's teeth!' muttered Kemp. 'At this rate the ceremony will be over by the time we get inside.'

'You obviously don't know how long these ceremonies take,' replied Conyers, the tip of his tongue protruding from the corner of his mouth as he concentrated on his work. 'A job like this requires a craftsman, and a craftsman requires . . .' the lock snapped open, and Conyers smiled '. . . a little time.'

'Which is something we've just run out of,' said Preston, as the two men-at-arms rounded the outhouse and marched purposefully towards them.

'Hey! What are you three doing? Don't you know you're trespassing?'

'Where can I find the captain of the guard?' Preston demanded, in his most commanding tones. His self-assurance was such that the two men-at-arms were momentarily thrown.

One of the men-at-arms removed his helmet and pushed back his mail coif to scratch his scalp. 'That's me, I suppose . . .'

'His right reverence has hired us to make sure that his guards were rigorous in their approach to their duties,' explained Preston and, as the two men frowned with worry, Kemp and Conyers each laid one of them out with a punch to the jaw. 'And I'm afraid you two fall woefully short of the mark.'

The three men slipped inside and found themselves in the kitchens. The house seemed deserted, most of the guards and servants having accompanied Montague and the countess to Westminster Palace as part of their retinue. As they entered the dining hall, they were challenged by two more men-at-arms.

'We've orders to fetch Lady Joan,' said Preston, with all the confidence of one who spoke the truth.

'From whom?'

'Sir William, of course.'

'Let's see them,' the guard suggested sceptically.

'Spoken orders,' explained Preston.

'Then you'll have to go back and get written ones, won't you?' said the guard. 'I'm under strict instructions from the countess. We're to let no one see her ladyship without written and sealed authorisation from the countess until she returns.'

Preston, Kemp and Conyers exchanged glances. 'Shall we show them our authorisation?' asked Kemp.

Preston nodded.

Once again Kemp and Conyers threw their punches simultaneously, and the two guards went down as one, sprawling on the polished wooden floor. Then Preston directed Conyers to go to the stables and saddle three horses, while he and Kemp searched the upper storeys. 'How will we find her?' asked Kemp, when they reached the first-floor landing. 'We don't even know if she's here at all.'

'If she's here, we'll find her,' said Preston. 'Search every chamber. These are the residential apartments. If she's not on this floor, she'll be on the next one up.'

Kemp nodded, and they headed off in different directions. Kemp had not gone far down one corridor when he encountered a chambermaid carrying a pile of neatly folded bed-linen. 'Can you direct me to the Lady Joan's chamber?' he asked her.

'Go to the end of the corridor, up the stairs, and it's the second door on your left.'

'Thank you.' Sometimes it was as easy as that.

Finding the door, he tried the handle. It was locked.

'Who's there?' a woman's voice called from within.

'Who's in there?' responded Kemp.

'Joan of Kent. Is that Will Falconer?'

'It's Kemp, my lady. Martin Kemp, of Sir Thomas Holland's retinue.'

'Martin! I remember you. Is Thomas here?'

'He's waiting not far from here. He sent me to fetch you. Can you let me in?'

'I fear not. The door is locked . . .'

Kemp raised one leg and smashed the sole of his foot against the door, close to the jamb and just below the handle. The heavy door sprang open under the force of the blow. 'Not any more, my lady,' he said, and then gasped in astonishment for several moments before averting his eyes. 'I beg your pardon, my lady. If I had known . . .'

Smiling, she wrapped a sheet about herself. 'My mother had the chambermaids take away all my gowns so that I could not go anywhere in her absence.'

Kemp hurriedly turned his back on the chamber. 'Have you any idea where they were taken?'

'To the garderobe, I expect, to be aired. You can turn around now, if you like.'

Kemp did so, and immediately wished he had not. At twenty, Joan was in the full bloom of her womanhood, a fact that was patently obvious even through the sheet enveloping her. He turned away again, flushing.

She chuckled at his embarrassment. 'Poor Martin. Do you recall the last time we met?'

'No, my lady,' he lied, although the image of her lying in Holland's arms in the stables at Calais flashed through his mind.

'You always seem to find me at embarrassing moments.' From the tone of her voice, it was obvious that these moments were more embarrassing to him than they were to her.

Summoned by the sound of the door being kicked open, Preston came hurrying up the stairs. 'What's going on?'

Kemp jerked his head towards the room behind him, at the same time spreading his arms to block the doorway as fully as possible. 'I've found her.'

'Well done, lad.' Frowning, Preston tried to peer past Kemp. A sudden widening of his eyes indicated that he had seen her. 'Nails and blood!'

'Her ladyship's mother took all her clothes away,' Kemp explained. 'She says they may be in the garderobe.'

Preston nodded. 'I passed it earlier. I'll go back and see what I can find.'

The serjeant-at-arms seemed to take for ever to return and Kemp, standing in the doorway, expected the alarm to be raised at any moment. He could hear voices downstairs. Then Preston reappeared, clutching a bundle of clothing which he hastily tossed through the door, his eyes closed. He pulled the broken door to.

The raised voices were coming closer. 'Has anyone searched upstairs?' called someone.

'Nails and blood!' Preston exclaimed again. 'How are we going to explain this one to the justices? I hope Sir Thomas is prepared to pay Master Sigglesthorne to get us out of it.'

Half a dozen guards emerged from the stairwell at a run. 'There they are!'

Kemp and Preston drew their daggers, bringing the six guards to a sharp halt. 'Drop your weapons!' the leader of the guards ordered nervously. 'I don't know who you are or what you hope to achieve but, if you surrender now, the countess may yet be merciful.'

'Kiss my arse,' sneered Kemp.

'Right, lads!' the leader told his men. 'On the count of three. One, two . . .'

At that moment, the door opened behind Preston and Kemp, and Joan appeared. 'What's going on, Rokeby?'

The leader bowed and, seeing the bruise on Joan's cheek, jumped to the obvious if incorrect conclusion. 'Have they harmed you, my lady?'

'Harmed me? No. Why should they have?'

'They knocked out three of my men . . .' Rokeby, the man who had admitted to being the captain of the guard, neglected to mention he had also been knocked out.

'Are you sure it was these men? These men are loyal servants of a close personal friend of mine.'

Rokeby removed his helmet and pulled back his coif so that he could scratch his scalp. 'Well, my lady, now that you mention it, I suppose it might have been two other men. But we saw the broken door . . .'

'Hadn't you better search for those two other men?' Joan dissembled magnificently. 'How do you know they are not loose in the bishop's vaults?'

A look of horror crossed Rokeby's face. 'Quick, men, to the vaults! No, wait, you two stay here and guard her ladyship . . .'

'That will not be necessary, Rokeby. I think Wat and Martin are perfectly capable of taking care of me. Have one of your men go to the stables to saddle my white jennet.'

Rokeby looked confused. 'Begging your pardon, my lady, but the countess said that I wasn't to let anyone out of or into the house until she got back. That's why I was so concerned about these two, you understand.'

Joan's amusement turned to anger. 'Which countess was that, Rokeby?'

'Why, my lady, the Dowager Countess of Kent.'

'You forget, Rokeby, that by the time my mother returns from Westminster Palace, there will be a new Countess of Salisbury.'

Rokeby hung his head. 'Yes, your ladyship.'

'Wat? Martin?'

Preston and Kemp stood to attention. 'My lady?' said Preston.

'Would you be so good as to escort me to the stables?'

Preston grinned. 'It'll be our pleasure, your ladyship.'

The king sat on his throne on the dais at one end of the White Chamber in Westminster Palace, dressed in his full robes of state and surrounded by the officers of state. Clad in a ceremonial vesture of honour of crimson velvet trimmed with ermine and miniver, the garter of the Companionship of Saint George tied just below his left knee, Montague approached the king, flanked by the earls of Northampton and Oxford who were acting as his sponsors. The Bishop of Salisbury read out the patent of creation and then Montague knelt before the king, who rose to place a sword in its scabbard around Montague's neck. Montague drew the sword, resting its point on the flagstones before him, his hands clasped around the hilt.

'Before God and the eyes of my peers and sponsors, by this sword I solemnly swear to hold the Earldom and County of Salisbury in fiefdom from my liege lord, his Royal Majesty King Edward, the third after the Conquest, and hereby renew my pledge of fealty.'

The king clasped his hands over Montague's to receive the oath of homage.

'I become your man of such tenement to be beholden of you, to bear to you faith of life and member and earthly worship against all men who live and can die, saving the faith of my lord Edward, King of England, and his heirs, and of . . . of my . . .'

Becoming aware of a commotion at the far end of the chamber, Montague stumbled over the words. Even the king had taken his eyes off Montague to stare over his head, and Montague could no longer resist glancing over his shoulder to see what all the fuss was about.

As he did so, his heart sank with despair.

Holland and Joan were marching up the aisle that ran down the centre of the chamber, the former now in his best azure and white robes. The two were surrounded by a cordon of seven archers who used strong arms to keep at bay any who sought to block their master's path.

His face turning puce with rage, the king rose to his feet once more. 'In the name of God and Saint George, Sir Thomas, how dare you barge in here like this?'

Countess Margaret stepped forward to stand by the king's side.

'See how the upstart bursts uninvited into this most solemn ceremony merely to press his own cause?'

'All I see now is my dear cousin, Joan of Kent, her face bruised and in Holland's custody, when I had thought her lying ill in her bed at Salisbury House,' growled the king. 'Have you dared to abduct her, Sir Thomas, and do you now bring her into my presence to boast of your audacity?'

Now that Holland had the king's attention, the archers relaxed their cordon, enabling Joan to hurry forward and kneel before the king. 'Please, your Majesty, if you have any love for me you will be merciful to Sir Thomas. He has not acted unlawfully, and has brought me here of my own free will.'

Holland also knelt before the king. 'I crave your forgiveness, your Majesty. I would not presume to thrust my own problems before you in such a manner, did I not feel that the course of justice were being perverted in such a way that I know you would find intolerable, and would seek to remedy.'

By now the king was prepared to give him a fair hearing. 'How so?'

'As your Majesty is well aware, I have petitioned the Papal Court about my claim to your fair cousin's hand, and I am sworn to abide by whatever decision that court may reach. The cardinal presiding over the tribunal has decreed the court cannot reach a decision until the Lady Joan's side of the case has been heard. But contrary to a Papal Bull insisting that Joan be allowed to select a proctor of her own choosing to represent her, she has been kept in seclusion and another man not representing her interests has been acting on her behalf. I ask only that the demands of that Papal Bull now be met in full.'

The king's face remained dark. 'You know I have little love for the court of his Holiness Pope Clement, Sir Thomas.'

'Aye, sire. But even you cannot deny the righteousness of that bull.'

The king turned his gaze on Joan. 'Is this true?' he asked, his voice gentler now. 'Speak freely, cousin – whatever your feelings, you know I am honour-bound to defend your interests.'

Joan nodded. 'It is true, sire.'

'Sir William?' The faintest of smiles tweaked the corners of the king's mouth upwards. 'Or perhaps now I should say, your lordship?'

Montague hung his head, and said nothing. The king's face grew dark again, and he turned back to Joan. 'How came you by that bruise on your cheek?'

She blushed. 'I would rather not say, sire.'

'Was it Sir Thomas's doing?'

'No, sire, it was not.'

The king looked thoughtful and turned back to Montague. 'Arise, William Montague, Earl of Salisbury, and follow me. Before we proceed any further in this matter, I would have words with you in private.'

A path was cleared through the noblemen and ladies who were clustered around as Montague followed the king into one of the adjoining rooms.

'Close the door behind you,' the king ordered curtly, and Montague did so.

'Please, sire, allow me to . . .'

Before Montague could say more, the king punched him on the left cheek. Montague found himself sprawling on the floor.

'Do I have to tell you what that blow was for?'

'No, sire,' whispered Montague.

'Do you question the justness of that blow?'

'No, sire.'

'As a Knight of the Companionship of Saint George, you are sworn to revere women, to treat them with honour and to defend them whenever the opportunity arises. Yet I see that you cannot even protect my cousin, your own wife! And in that I am being charitable in assuming it was not you who struck her. Do you deny it?'

'No, sire.'

'I am of a mind to strip you of your peerage even as I bestow it, but out of love for your dear departed father I shall hold back my wrath. You have been a grave disappointment to me, William. I had hoped you might be the new Galahad at my Round Table; instead I find another Sir Kay, full of jealousy and hatred. On this occasion I shall overlook the matter, but do not try my patience a second time. Now rise, and let us return to the White Chamber.'

A bruise was already rising on Montague's cheek as they re-emerged. The king turned to Holland.

'The matter is concluded, Sir Thomas. I must now ask you to

leave so that this ceremony may be concluded. I promise you only this: as you have done, so shall I undertake to abide by whatever decision is reached by the Papal Court.'

'And the appointment of Joan's proctor, sire?'

The king sighed, and turned to Joan. 'You are ready to choose a proctor?'

She nodded fervently, crossed to where a group of clergymen stood and picked out one of them, an elderly but sprightly little man with bright blue eyes and snow-white hair shorn in a tonsure. 'I choose my confessor: John Vise, sub-dean of the diocese of Salisbury and Bachelor of Arts and Canon Law.'

'Upon my faith, my lady, I wish you would choose some other,' stammered Vise. 'I have little experience at this kind of thing, and I am sure I would let you down.'

'You would never let me down, Dean Vise,' said Joan. 'Only tell them the truth, and I will be satisfied my best interests are represented.'

'I fear I no longer know what is truth and what is lies,' Vise said sadly. 'But if your wish is also your command, I can hardly reject the honour . . .'

'It is,' Joan told him gravely.

'Are you willing to shoulder the burden of this duty?' demanded the king.

Vise nodded. 'I am, your Majesty.'

'And you, Sir Thomas? Are you satisfied this man will represent Lady Joan both properly and fairly?'

'I am, sire.'

'We don't want there to be any further disputes about this later,' the king muttered in an aside to Henry of Derby, who struggled to stifle a chuckle. The king turned finally to Montague. 'And how about you, William Earl of Salisbury? Do you dispute the selection of this man to represent the interests of the woman you claim to be your wife?'

'No, sire,' Montague said miserably.

'Good,' the king concluded. 'The sooner we get on with the ceremony, the sooner we can get back for supper.'

After the celebratory feast – at which Holland was notable by his absence – the new Earl of Salisbury sat alone at the head table, long after the king and the other revellers had retired for the night. A few other revellers still remained in the great hall, snoring loudly as they sat with their faces on the tables or amongst the rushes strewn on the floor. Only Montague was awake. He had looked forward to this day for his whole life and, thanks to Holland, it had proved to be a disaster. He had lost the king's favour and been publicly humiliated. Before retiring, the king had even decreed that when he departed for Havering on the morrow, Joan would go with him to reside at his court as his ward once again until the Papal Court had reached its decision.

Montague refilled his goblet with wine but tonight, when he desperately needed to get drunk, oblivion eluded him. He gazed at the debris of the banquet, chicken, peacock and swan carcasses strewn across the tables or cast on to the floor for the dogs. His life seemed as empty as those picked-clean bones.

'Still abroad? I had thought you would have been long abed by now.'

Montague looked up to see Countess Margaret.

'Well, what's done is done,' she said. 'The question is, what do you intend to do next?'

He shrugged. 'What can I do? It is all in the hands of the Papal Court, and our respective attorneys.'

'Tcha! You talk of defeat when battle is only just joined! Well, you may yield to fate if you so choose, but if you think I'm going to stand back and allow my daughter to become the wife of that brutish little upstart Holland, then I can assure you that you are very much mistaken.'

'But what can we do?' pleaded Montague, wringing his hands.

'What we need is time to come up with proof that Holland's claim to have married Joan is false.'

'But our attorney has already been delaying the court for two years now. What else can he do?'

'He can absent himself. The court cannot proceed without him . . .'

'Yes it can,' Montague said gloomily. 'Sigglesthorne will accuse him of contumacy, and then the case will be forfeit in Holland's favour . . .'

'Not if Sigglesthorne and Vise are also absent.'

'But they won't be absent!' protested Montague.

'They will be . . . if we arrange for them to be. And I know of certain men well-versed in making people absent . . . permanently.'

# CHAPTER ELEVEN

'HOW ABOUT ANOTHER flagon of this splendid claret?' suggested Sigglesthorne, as he drained the dregs of the last flagon into his cup.

'I don't think I should,' Vise replied dubiously. They had already drunk three flagons of wine between them.

'Go on,' persisted Sigglesthorne. 'The case seems to be going well. I think we can treat ourselves with a clear conscience.'

Vise smiled. 'Well, if you insist . . .'

'Good man.' Sigglesthorne waved across to the innkeeper who stood at the counter, wiping spilled ale from its polished surface. 'Another flagon of your finest claret, if you please, Master Brewster!'

David Brewster stepped into the back room to refill another flagon from the barrels stored there, and then crossed the main room of the White Lion inn, attached to Holland's house in Calais. He had been given strict instructions to see that Sigglesthorne's every whim was catered for whenever he stayed there, so he did not ask for payment. Not that Sigglesthorne's whims extended much beyond generous helpings of good food, a comfortable bed at night, and heroic quantities of claret.

It was two months since Montague had been invested as Earl of Salisbury, and Sigglesthorne and Vise were returning from their second trip to Avignon in the intervening time. On their first trip they had fallen in with the retinue of Thomas Bradwardine, on his way to Avignon to be confirmed as the new Archbishop of Canterbury following his predecessor's death from the pestilence. Ironically, Bradwardine himself had died of the pestilence within a week of returning to England.

The case itself had actually progressed little but, as Sigglesthorne explained to Vise, there was nothing unusual in that, considering it had already dragged on for nearly two years now: a long time even by the standards of the cardinals' courts where attorneys often had to travel great distances just to consult their clients.

Since Sigglesthorne and Vise usually found themselves arguing along similar lines in the cardinal's court, they had become friends, and had begun to travel together, staying at the same inns along the way and lodging together in the same house in Avignon.

Sigglesthorne drank heavily because he enjoyed the taste of claret rather than because he sought oblivion, so it did not worry him over much that as the years went by his resistance to drunkenness had increased. Thus even as the comfortable glow of mild intoxication began to settle over him, he still had his wits about him. Nevertheless, when two burly, rough-looking men entered the inn, Sigglesthorne paid them little attention. They were clearly men who had fought in the king's service and would most likely do so again when the truce was ended. Such men were common enough in English-occupied Calais, and in the White Lion inn in particular.

The town had changed dramatically since Brewster had become the innkeeper at the White Lion nearly two years before. Then, with its native population expelled and with only soldiers to occupy it, Calais had been half-empty, and had had the aspect of a military camp rather than a town. Now the garrison had been joined by an increasing number of civilians, merchants and craftsmen, not to mention adventurers seeking to make a quick profit from booty in the occasional raids made into French-held territory in spite of the truce.

These men looked like two such adventurers. They crossed to the counter and ordered a pot of ale each. As Brewster turned away to the casks behind the counter, the men cast their eyes over the room. The place was empty except for the innkeeper and the two attorneys.

Brewster placed their pots on the counter. 'Two farthings, please, gentlemen.'

One of the men paid for both of them, and took a sip of his ale. Almost immediately he spat out his mouthful in disgust.

Brewster arched an eyebrow 'Not to your taste?'

'It's off,' asserted the first man, with a grimace.

'Let me see,' said the second, tasting his own ale. He too spat it out. 'Ugh! You're right.'

Frowning, Brewster reached across to take a sip from one of the pots. 'There must be something amiss with your palates. It tastes fine to me.'

'You would say that, wouldn't you?' sneered the first man. 'I'm not drinking that. It's foul.'

Brewster brewed his own ale according to a recipe which had been handed down in his family across generations, and he was proud of it. Forcing himself to smile, he waved across to where the two attorneys sat. 'Would you care to sit in judgement in a difference of opinion we have here, Master Sigglesthorne?' he asked with a smile.

Sigglesthorne shook his head. 'All ale tastes disgusting to me.'

'Never mind what they think,' growled the first man. 'They're probably friends of yours. I says it's not fit to drink, and if you think I'm paying for that, you've got another think coming. Either serve us with something drinkable, or give us our money back and we'll spend it somewhere where they serve *real* ale.'

Sighing, Brewster lifted the trap door behind the counter, and made his way down to the cellar to fetch another cask of ale.

As soon as Brewster's back was turned, the two men crossed to Sigglesthorne and Vise's table. 'Master Robert Sigglesthorne of Beverley?' asked the first.

Sigglesthorne frowned. 'Aye. What can I do for you?'

The first man ignored him, turning to Vise. 'Master John Vise?'

Vise nodded muzzily.

The first man gave a curt nod to his companion, and suddenly the two of them produced daggers.

'By the blood of Christ!' Sigglesthorne raised his arms to protect himself and, as the first man tried to plunge his dagger into his heart, caught him by the wrist. Despite his age and portly girth, the serjeant-at-law was a powerful man, and the assassin had underestimated his victim's strength. The two of them wrestled, Sigglesthorne trying to keep the dagger's razor-sharp tip at bay.

At the same moment, Vise turned to face the second man, who was also trying to stab his opponent. It was drunken luck that saved Vise, for as he twisted on his stool his buttocks slid from the seat, and he landed on his backside with a thump. With Vise no longer there to receive the dagger-thrust, the second man stumbled forward, burying his blade in the wooden table.

With a strength born of outrage and desperation, Sigglesthorne managed to struggle back to his feet with an apoplectic roar, wrestling the first man around until he had his back to the table, and then forcing his dagger-arm back against the table's edge. His attacker groped on the table behind him with his left hand until it found the flagon of wine, and then brought it up sharply, dashing it against Sigglesthorne's skull. The flagon remained intact, while Sigglesthorne's eyes rolled up in his head, and he began to slide towards the floor. His right arm free once more, the first man raised his dagger to plunge it into Sigglesthorne's exposed throat.

Emerging from the cellar, Brewster took one look at the scene that greeted his eyes, snatched another flagon from the counter and hurled it across the room with all his might. It bounced off the first man's head and he fell, joining Sigglesthorne on the rush-covered floor. Brewster vaulted over the counter. Seeing him approach, the second man abandoned his attempt to kill Vise and turned, hurling himself at the nearest window. The wooden shutters splintered under his weight, and he rolled on the cobbles outside before picking himself up and running away down the street.

Brewster crossed to the stone hearth in three long strides and took down the smoke-stained longbow that hung there, at the same time snatching a single arrow from the mantelpiece. He swiftly restrung the bow with a well-practised motion. Then he crossed to the door and stepped outside into the cold night air, nocking the arrow to the bow as he did so. The second man was already more than a hundred yards away, disappearing into the gloom as he fled. Brewster raised the bow, pushing out the bowstave and taking aim, all in one smooth movement. The only illumination was provided by the moon and stars, and the street was dark compared to the brightness inside the tavern, but Brewster had shot in the dark before. He let fly. The arrow's pale fletchings vanished into the night. The fleeing man threw out his arms and stumbled, falling.

Brewster strode briskly down the street to where the man lay, pulling his dagger from his belt as he did so. The man sprawled in the gutter running down the middle of the street, his arms outstretched on either side of him so that he lay in the shape of a crucifix. The arrow had taken him in the small of the back, penetrating his spine and killing him outright. Brewster left the body there for the night-watch to find and puzzle over, and hurried back to the inn.

The attempt on Vise's life had rapidly sobered him up, and he had helped Sigglesthorne back on to his seat. Brewster crouched over the first man's inert body. He was still alive, so Brewster removed the string from his bow and used it to tie the man's wrists tightly behind his back. Then he fetched a cloth and soaked it in cold, clean water, giving it to Vise to use as a compress on Sigglesthorne's temple.

Sigglesthorne moaned. 'It's been a long time since drinking wine has given me a headache such as this.'

'What the devil was all that about?' Brewster asked the two attorneys.

'I don't know,' Sigglesthorne said heavily. 'I've never seen either of these two men before in my life.'

'They knew us, though,' observed Vise. 'Or at least, they knew our names.'

'What happened to the other one?' asked Sigglesthorne. 'Did you raise the hue and cry against him?'

Brewster smiled faintly. 'No. I did not want to disturb the sleep of the good citizens of this town.'

Sigglesthorne was about to berate Brewster for allowing the other man to get away when the first man groaned, slowly beginning to regain consciousness. Brewster crouched over him, grabbing him by the front of his tunic and hoisting him on to his feet. Then he slammed him back against the wall forcefully. The man winced as the back of his head connected with the stonework.

'Why were you and your friend trying to kill these two?' demanded Brewster.

The man shook his head, and then met Brewster's gaze defiantly. 'The devil carry you to hell,' he sneered.

Brewster shrugged, made as if to turn away and then lifted his knee sharply into the man's groin. He doubled up with a strangled gasp, and Brewster kneed him in the face. The man was thrown against the wall and slid down on to the floor. Brewster seized him again and hurled him back again, even harder this time. The man's nose was broken and his upper lip and chin covered in the blood which ran steadily from his nostrils.

'Why were you and your friend trying to kill these two?'

'Kiss the devil's arse,' the man responded thickly.

Brewster dragged him across to the counter, slinging him over it like a sack of grain. 'So, you don't like my ale, eh?' he asked, lifting a barrel from its rest and sitting on its end before broaching it with a small axe. 'Maybe you'd like to try it again; we'll see if you'll change your mind.' He grabbed a fistful of the man's hair, and forced his head down into the ale. The man suffered it in stillness at first; but then his breath began to run out, and he struggled to break free from Brewster's hold. But Brewster was unrelenting, keeping his opponent's head submerged until bubbles began to rise around it as he gasped for fresh air and swallowed only ale.

'You'll kill him!' protested Vise.

Brewster shook his head. 'That's not what I have in mind.'

'But you can't do this. You can't just torture a man like this.'

'Torture?' asked Sigglesthorne. 'I don't see any torture taking place. Do you, Master Brewster?'

Grinning, Brewster shook his head again.

Sigglesthorne indicated the struggling man. 'Believe me, Master Vise, as far as the law is concerned it will be his word against all of ours, and who's going to believe a common assassin against those of a respected innkeeper, a sub-dean, and one of England's foremost serjeants-at-law?'

The assassin's struggles were beginning to subside. Brewster lifted his head from the barrel and he gasped air into his lungs in great, whooping gulps, coughing and spluttering. Then Brewster released his grip so that the man fell forward on to his face, and lay retching, his cheek pressed against the floorboards.

'Why were you and your friend trying to kill these two?' he asked.

This time, the man told him.

Kemp was off duty, and Preston found him fletching arrows in the barrack room they all shared at Holland's manor house. 'Sir Thomas wants to see you in the great hall at once,' the serjeant told the young archer.

Kemp knew better than to question Holland's orders and stopped what he was doing, briefly making sure he was reasonably presentable before leaving the wooden barrack house and crossing the courtyard to the main building. It was rare for Holland to ask to see one of his men other than Preston, and it usually meant he had received some complaint about misbehaviour in the village, for which the summoned man could expect to be upbraided. Trying to recall if he had done anything that might have aroused Holland's ire, Kemp climbed the wooden steps to the upper floor and rapped on the door to the hall.

'Enter!'

Kemp opened the door and marched in, standing to attention just inside the threshold. Holland sat at the high table with Brother Ambrose, Master Sigglesthorne and Master Vise. Kemp recognised the two attorneys; he had seen Vise on the day of Montague's investiture at Westminster, and this was Sigglesthorne's third visit to the manor house since that day.

'Ah, Kemp, good. Close the door behind you and come here. Take a seat.' There were no chairs left, so Holland pointed him towards the large oak chest that stood at the end of his four-poster bed.

Kemp did as he was bade.

'Can I offer you a cup of wine?' asked Holland, gesturing to a flagon of claret which stood on the table in honour of Sigglesthorne's presence.

Kemp had not been upbraided by Holland in the eight months he had been working for him so he did not know what the procedure was, but he was fairly sure it did not include offers of wine. 'No thank you, Sir Thomas,' he said.

Holland shrugged. 'You know Master Sigglesthorne?'

'We've met briefly, sir, aye.' Kemp had been on duty at the gate at the time of one of Sigglesthorne's visits.

'This is Master Vise, who is acting as the Lady Joan's proctor in the tribunal currently being conducted in at the Papal Court in Avignon,' said Holland, gesturing to the sub-dean.

Kemp nodded an acknowledgement at Vise, but his mind was racing. He had picked up a fairly good idea of how the court case was progressing thanks to scullery gossip, but he was not sure what any of it had to do with him.

'Wat tells me that you are growing bored with my service, Kemp.'

Kemp shook his head. 'Not I, sir.'

'Nevertheless, would you deny that you have become restless of late, chafing at the bit, longing for the end of the truce?' Holland asked with a smile.

'The war has started again, sir?' Kemp asked eagerly.

Holland laughed. 'Alas, no. But I have a task that will take you out of Broughton and keep you occupied. It may even provide you with some excitement. How do you feel about a trip to Avignon?'

'Avignon, sir?' Kemp had never been further afield than Normandy before. Avignon might as well have been at the farthest corner of the world.

Holland nodded. 'Master Sigglesthorne is of the opinion that one last trip to the Papal Court should clear up my dispute with Montague for good. However, on his way back from the last meeting of the tribunal, he and Master Vise were set upon by a couple of hired assassins: Montague's hirelings. If the men had not been foolish enough to attack Master Sigglesthorne and Master Vise in the White Lion inn, where your old companion-in-arms David Brewster keeps house, they might have succeeded in killing them. Brewster killed one of the men, and the other is in Calais gaol awaiting trial; but Montague must have learned by now what has happened and, if he can send two assassins one time, he may send four the next.'

'And you want me to act as bodyguard, sir,' guessed Kemp, both flattered and worried that his master should consider him the equal of four men.

Holland nodded. 'Exactly so. You are strong, skilled and courageous in a fight, you speak some French, you are good with horses, and you are capable of acting on your own initiative. In such troubled times as these, I wonder that I did not think of giving you this task before. All I ask is that you see to it that Master Sigglesthorne and Master Vise are allowed to travel to Avignon and back unharmed.'

'I'm sure there will not be any more trouble,' Sigglesthorne hastened to assure Kemp. 'His lordship the Earl of Salisbury has tried to have us killed, and it has failed. If he tries aught else, it will be something different. However, I think he is more likely to do nothing. We already have a prisoner who has admitted to being hired to kill myself and Master Vise by the Countess of Kent's serjeant-at-arms. We could make life extremely awkward for his lordship if we chose to, and he knows it.'

'Assassination is still an option that remains open to him, however, and even if he does not choose it, there are plenty of robbers and brigands on the road today,' Holland told Sigglesthorne. 'I think the company of an armed man will help to make your journey free of incident.'

Kemp remembered his year spent as a bodyguard for Master Chaucer: a pleasant time, but hardly one of excitement. But there was no sign of the truce with France coming to an end and a journey to Avignon would be more interesting than life on Holland's manor. 'When do we leave, sir?' he asked Holland.

The knight smiled. 'Tomorrow.'

Kemp was up at the crack of dawn next day, saddling the horses while Sigglesthorne and Vise finished a more leisurely breakfast. He was tightening the belly-strap on his own nag when Conyers sidled into the stable. 'Off to see the Pope, I hear tell,' he said.

'Aye, well, off to Avignon, at any rate. I don't suppose I'll be meeting his Holiness. I'm not sure that I care to, either.'

'I know this story about an English abbot who went to see the Pope.'

Kemp grimaced. 'Somehow I thought you might.' Conyers was an unquenchable fund of humorous tales, most of them lewd.

'One day he decides there's nowt for it but to go on a pilgrimage to Saint Peter's in Rome – this were back in the days when the Popes lived in Rome, you understand.'

Kemp nodded. 'Go on.'

'While he's staying at a tavern in Rome, he gets invited to go to the Vatican to meet the Pope, and of course he can hardly say no, can he? So that morning he rushes out and gets a new set of robes made up so's he can look his best for his meeting with the pontiff. Then he has a bath, brushes his hair and puts on his new robes, looking all spick and span. Only when he gets there, there's a dozen other bishops and priests waiting to meet the Pope. They're all made to stand in a line in a courtyard and wait for the Pope to emerge.

'While he's waiting, he notices this scruffy beggar standing there, with all these churchmen. Not being very charitable, he wonders what this beggar's doing, amongst all these rich prelates, but everyone else seems to be ignoring the beggar, so he decides to do likewise.

'Eventually the Pope emerges and starts to make his way along this great long line of people, with the English abbot standing at the very end of it. But the Pope doesn't actually seem to be saying anything to any of them, he just raises his hand in benediction to each of them. Well, the abbot says to himself, I don't reckon much to this. Here I am, I've come all the way to Rome to meet the Pope, I've bought some new robes especially for the occasion, and all he's going to do is give me his benison, without so much as a word?

'Then the Pope comes to this old beggar, and he puts his hand on the beggar's shoulder and leans forward to whisper something in the beggar's ear. A fine to-do, thinks the abbot, with all these rich priests standing here, and the only one the Pope speaks to is this filthy beggar. But not one to miss out on a good opportunity, he slips away from the end of the line and hurries after the beggar, who's wandering away. 'Let me swap clothes with you,' says the abbot. The beggar looks at the abbot's fine robes, and his own lousy rags, and quickly agrees, as you would. The two of them slips into an alcove and swaps clothes, and then, dressed in the beggar's rags, the abbot runs back to take his place at the end of the line, just in time to meet the Pope.

'The Pope looks the abbot up and down, taking in his scruffy rags, and the abbot's delighted when his holiness puts a hand on his shoulder and leans forward to whisper in his ear. And you know what the Pope says to him?'

Kemp shrugged.

'"You again? I thought I told you before: bugger off!"'

Sigglesthorne and Vise emerged from the manor house a few minutes later, talking to Holland. Kemp led the horses out into the courtyard: his own fleabitten grey hackney, Sigglesthorne's bay palfrey, and Vise's skewbald pony. Malkin Cook came out from the kitchens with a lunch of bread and cheese and a flask of ale so they would not have to stop before they reached Amersham. Dressed simply in his white chemise, jerkin of toughened leather and black cloak, Kemp swung himself up into the saddle of his hackney. Sigglesthorne and Vise also mounted their steeds.

Holland indicated the longbow that hung by the strap of its canvas case from the pommel of Kemp's saddle. 'Are you sure you want to take that? It'll mark you out as an Englishman and, truce or no truce, you'll not be welcomed as such in France these days.'

'Our accents will mark us out as English, Sir Thomas.' Kemp

patted the bow and the broadsword at his hip. 'I'd rather have these with me in case anyone wants to make something of it.'

Holland nodded, grinning. 'Very well. Good luck and God speed, all of you.'

Sitting unsteadily in the saddle of his palfrey, Sigglesthorne raised his hat to Holland. 'We'll be back by Yuletide, the case concluded, Sir Thomas,' he said cheerfully.

'In my favour, I hope,' Holland growled.

'Of course,' the serjeant-at-law assured him.

'We're wasting daylight,' said Kemp. Holland nodded in agreement, and Kemp, Sigglesthorne and Vise rode out of the courtyard without another word.

'Give the pontiff my regards!' Conyers, standing on guard by the gateway, called after them. Sigglesthorne and Vise chuckled, and Kemp touched the hem of his cowl in a gesture of farewell.

It was September, and there was already a chill nip in the air. The dark grey sky threatened rain. They headed south-east, crossing the Chiltern Hills, and reached London towards the end of the second day, entering the city at Newgate.

As they rode over the blood-soaked cobbles of the Butchery towards West Cheap they became aware of a murmur running through the crowded street around them, and suddenly everyone seemed to be hurrying in the direction of Saint Paul's Cathedral.

'They've come!' shouted a fishwife. 'They've come to save us!'

Leaning down from his palfrey, Sigglesthorne managed to stop her. 'Who's come to save us?' he demanded. He had to shout to make himself heard amongst the hubbub.

'The martyrs! They've come to wash away our sins in their blood!'

'Flagellants,' Sigglesthorne explained as the fishwife broke away, moving with the crowd towards Saint Paul's.

Vise's curiosity was piqued. 'I've heard much talk of these so-called martyrs, but I've yet to see them with my own eyes.'

Sigglesthorne made a dismissive gesture. He had already seen a band of the flagellants on one of his visits to Avignon earlier that year and had been unimpressed by their self-imposed martyrdom. However, if he had hoped to avoid this performance he was soon disappointed: so thick were the crowds surging down Ivy Lane that the three horsemen were swept along with them.

The flagellants had formed a circle around Paul's Cross, the crucifix-adorned pulpit immediately outside the cathedral. Although a large crowd of spectators had already gathered, Sigglesthorne, Vise and Kemp were able to see clearly from the backs of their horses. The flagellants numbered over a hundred, the women dressed in cowled white robes emblazoned with red crosses on the front and back, the men, with three weeks' growth of beard adorning their chins, stripped of their sombre robes and clad only in loose kilts that came down to their ankles. They sang hymns while the master of their band stood in the centre of the circle with two assistants, watching the rite with approval. Both assistants held aloft banners of purple velvet and cloth of gold. The dirty, naked torsos of the men revealed backs already scarred and scabrous from previous scourgings, many of them swollen and infected. Then, as one, the men prostrated themselves on the ground in a crucifix position while the master moved amongst them, lashing them with a leather-thonged scourge tipped with spikes of iron.

Next the flagellants rose to their feet. Each one of them had a scourge of his own, with three or four thongs and spikes of bone or iron, and they began to lash themselves. As they did so, the master moved amongst them, calling for God to have mercy on all sinners. At each lash of the scourges, blood would spurt out, running across the flagellants' pale flesh and collecting on the ground until the puddle of blood in which they stood matched that of the butchers' market a few hundred yards away. Sometimes one of the spikes became so deeply embedded that it could only be pulled out by a second wrench.

The sight of blood was nothing new to Kemp, but he winced to see men subject themselves gladly to such torture. 'Hell's teeth!' he hissed. 'Why do they do it?'

'They see the pestilence as God's punishment for the sins of mankind,' explained Vise. 'They hope to cleanse us all by washing our sins in their blood and suffering.'

'More fool them, if they think this nonsense will bring the pestilence to an end,' grunted Sigglesthorne.

Kemp forced himself to watch the grisly spectacle. A few of the flagellants winced at each lash of the scourge but most smiled in beatific ecstasy, their eyes shining with religious fervour. Some spectators were sobbing, wailing, and tearing at their hair, while one woman – the fishwife – darted forward to dab a rag in the blood which ran over the cobbles, treasuring it as if it were a holy relic. Someone broke into the cathedral and rang one of the bells, but only one. For as long as Kemp could remember, it had been a tradition that church bells were to be rung singly except in the event of an invasion, in which case the ringing of them all would pass news of the invasion throughout the length of the land. A young woman laid the body of a still-born child within the circle of discarded clothes that formed the arena in which the flagellants scourged themselves, as if its proximity to such piety might raise it from the dead. Like Sigglesthorne and Kemp, however, the vast majority of the spectators remained unimpressed by the antics.

The flagellants continued to scourge themselves rhythmically, slowly increasing the tempo as the rite progressed, until they had literally whipped themselves into a frenzy.

Kemp shook his head in disbelief. 'Jesus! The whole God-damned world's gone mad.' Without waiting to see if Sigglesthorne or Vise were ready to follow, he chucked the reins of his hackney and rode away from the cathedral, heading down Watling Street towards the bridge.

'Who are we supposed to be meeting?' The young squire's nervousness was betrayed by the tremor in his voice.

'That is no concern of yours,' hissed his master. 'Stay by me and say nothing, and you will be all right. You have my word of honour on it.'

It was a dark night late in October. The two men were mounted on fine palfreys, riding through the Calais Pale, the no man's land around the English-occupied town that was still disputed by the rival kings despite the truce. They were on the road between Calais and Saint-Omer, near the village of Ardres, halfway between the two towns.

A dozen horsemen, mounted on black horses and wearing dull brigandine armour that barely glinted in the moonlight, their surcoats and jupons unadorned with any coats of arms, appeared out of the darkness and surrounded the squire and his master. The squire's palfrey reared skittishly. Somebody struck tinder and flint, lighting a brand that flamed in the darkness. Sir Oudard de Renty took the brand from one of his men and guided his horse forwards a few steps, holding the torch up the better to see the two riders. 'Sir Amerigo de Pavia?'

The squire's master nodded and reached up with a hand encrusted with jewelled rings to pull back the deep cowl of his dark but costly robes.

De Renty indicated the squire with a curt nod. 'You were told to come alone.'

'There are just the two of us,' de Pavia protested, in a silky but rather nasal whine. 'You cannot expect me to ride out here at this time of night without at least one servant to protect me.'

'You were promised safe conduct,' said de Renty. 'Or are you suggesting that Sir Geoffroi is not to be trusted?'

'Far from it,' de Pavia replied hurriedly. 'But there are other dangers on this road; robbers and brigands.'

De Renty grunted. He and his men had been watching de Pavia and his squire ever since they left Calais; not to protect them but to make sure they were not followed. 'Come with us.'

De Pavia and his squire had no choice in the matter, for two of de Renty's men leaned from their saddles and took their bridles to lead the horses a little further down the road. A few hundred yards away they came to an inn that was so dark and quiet de Pavia thought it must be deserted; not an uncommon sight in those days of the pestilence when it seemed that a black flag flew from the steeple of every church in Normandy.

'Dismount,' ordered de Renty. De Pavia and his squire swung themselves down from their saddles. 'Inside.' He nodded towards the open door of the inn.

De Pavia had never seen a less inviting portal. He glanced up at de Renty but the Frenchman's handsome face was impassive in the torchlight, giving no indication of what might await him within. He moved towards the door and the squire began to follow him, but de Renty leaned forward and laid the flat of his broadsword across the young man's chest, blocking his path. 'Just you,' he told de Pavia.

Fear filled the squire's eyes as his master turned to face him but de Pavia gave what he imagined to be a reassuring nod and entered the inn alone.

Inside it was pitch black but for the splash of torchlight spilling through the open doorway. This, however, was cut off when the door closed behind him without warning.

'Hello?' he called. Edging deeper into the room, he barked his shin on the corner of a bench. 'San Cristoforo!' he hissed into the darkness.

Iron and flint sparked several times, and the glow of tinder was followed by the flare of guttering candle-light. The flame's yellow aureole widened to reveal a hawk-like face, its dark eyes fixed unblinkingly on de Pavia as a bird of prey watches a rabbit.

'Sir Geoffroi de Chargny?'

De Chargny nodded. 'And you are Sir Amerigo de Pavia, Captain of the Galleys of Calais, and the town's acting governor.' It was a statement rather than a question.

De Pavia nodded.

'Sit down.' De Chargny gestured to a flagon of wine on the table in front of him. 'Can I offer you a drink?'

De Pavia sat down opposite him. De Chargny snapped his fingers and the massive bulk of Guilbert loomed in the candle-light, startling de Pavia who had not suspected the presence of a third man. Guilbert picked up the flagon and poured the contents into a silver goblet, placing it in front of de Pavia. The Lombard lifted it to his lips and was about to sip when a thought occurred to him, and he turned fearful eyes on the flagon.

De Chargny leaned across the table to seize the goblet, lifting it to his own lips and drinking deeply before handing it back. Relieved, de Pavia drank.

The Lombard had come at de Chargny's invitation. A sealed letter bearing only de Pavia's name had mysteriously appeared in his chamber one morning. The letter had mentioned money, implying a substantial amount without saying how it might be earned; but de Pavia's avarice had been sufficiently piqued. Now he waited for de Chargny to speak, but the French knight did not seem to be in any hurry.

'You sent for me, Sir Geoffroi?' he asked at last, allowing the slightest hint of annoyance to enter his tone. 'My servants think I lie abed in my chamber at Calais castle. If I am not back by dawn, there will be questions asked.'

De Chargny shrugged. 'They will think you spent the night in a stewhouse. I gather it would not be the first time.'

'How did you . . . how dare you!' spluttered de Pavia.

'That is unimportant. What is important is what lies in yonder coffer.' De Chargny gestured to an iron-bound coffer standing on the next table.

De Pavia rose and crossed to the coffer. The clasp was unfastened. The Lombard put his hands on the lid to lift it and then hesitated, wondering what it contained. A poisonous snake? A severed head? With a man like de Chargny, it was impossible to guess. He threw open the lid and stepped back, just in case whatever lay within tried to jump out at him.

Thousands of golden coins glinted in the pale light of the single candle.

'Twenty thousand *écus d'or*,' de Chargny hissed persuasively. 'And they're all yours. At least, they will be soon enough. All I ask is one thing in return.'

De Pavia faced him with an expression of suspicion. 'Do not ask me to betray my king, de Chargny. That is the one thing I will not do for any amount of money.'

'I would think little of you if I thought you would,' de Chargny replied. 'But you were born a Lombard. Surely you cannot count King Edward your liege lord?'

'I have served him . . . taken his salt . . .'

'And I have served the Dauphin of Vienne, but I do not count him my lord. I was born in France, and my only loyalty is to Valois and his line.'

'You are known for your great knowledge of all that is chivalrous,' admitted de Pavia. 'You would not ask any man to do anything that contravened the code by which we live as brothers in knighthood.'

'No.'

'Then tell me what it is you want.'

'Calais,' de Chargny said simply.

De Pavia turned pale.

'It is a small matter, in terms of the great scheme of things,' de Chargny continued blandly. 'Compared to the vast area of Gascony, for example, what import can a small town like Calais have?'

'If the king learned I had betrayed the town he spent eleven months besieging . . .'

'With twenty thousand *écus d'or* in your coffers, would you really care what the king thought?'

De Pavia's brow glistened with beads of sweat. 'It's not what he thinks, it's how he would repay me . . .'

'You could return to your native Lombardy, far beyond King Edward's reach.'

'I could . . .' admitted de Pavia.

'Twenty thousand *écus*, Sir Amerigo. All yours. And no one need ever know. Why did you think I asked you to come here alone?'

'You could guarantee me immunity?'

'From everything but the pestilence.'

De Pavia's eyes flickered between de Chargny's smiling face and the open coffer. Finally he reached for the gold, but Guilbert slammed the lid down before his hand came close. 'The gold becomes yours, Sir Amerigo, on the day Calais becomes mine,' said de Chargny.

'And which day is that?'

'New Year's Day. I will bring men to regarrison the town and castle about two hours after midnight. All I ask is that there is no guard to stop us from entering that night, and no gate or door remains locked to bar our way. Sir Oudard will meet you at the postern gate of the castle with ten thousand *écus*. You will admit him and his men, and hand over a hostage – your son, I think – as surety. By dawn, when both town and castle are in my hands, you will have the remaining ten thousand, your son will be returned unharmed together with a letter of safe conduct to Lombardy.' He leaned forward suddenly and blew out the candle, plunging the room back into darkness.

'Supposing something goes wrong?'

'If anything goes wrong then it will mean you have betrayed me.' De Chargny's voice hissed eerily. 'And if you betray me, then no matter what happens, I will hunt you down and, when I find you, I will have you cut into very small pieces, starting from the toes up. Do I make myself plain?'

'Yes, Sir Geoffroi!' de Pavia stammered. 'But what if . . .'

A cold wind blew through the room, and de Pavia sensed that he was alone once more. He groped his way over to where the coffer of gold had stood but that too was gone. Shivering with fear, he moved slowly towards the door. He pawed at the latch, lifted it and stumbled outside. There was no sign of de Chargny, de Renty, or any of the others; just the two palfreys, and his squire, leaning against the wall by the door.

De Pavia put a hand on the squire's shoulder. 'Come on, boy, let's leave this place swiftly.'

The squire fell away from him, toppling over to land on his side at the foot of the wall. De Pavia crouched over him and found a gash in the boy's throat like a second mouth, grinning up at him in the darkness, the slick blood black in the moonlight. De Pavia vomited uncontrollably. When he had finally recovered, he swung himself into the saddle of his palfrey and dug his spurs into the horse's flanks, galloping north-west, back along the road to Calais.

De Chargny and de Renty watched de Pavia leave from an upper-storey window of the inn. De Renty smiled at the Lombard's evident discomfiture. 'A weak man,' he said, and frowned. 'You think we can rely on him?'

De Chargny nodded. 'I like weak men. They are easy to control. Controlling a man like de Pavia is like guiding an ass: one uses a carrot and a stick. The carrot is gold, the stick is fear. Tonight we gave him a taste of both.'

De Renty looked thoughtful. 'You will ride back to Saint-Omer with me?'

De Chargny shook his head. 'I head south. I hope to be in Avignon by the end of the month. I shall return to Saint-Omer in time for the Feast of the Conception.'

De Renty did not know what business de Chargny might have in Avignon but knew better than to ask. 'And then?'

De Chargny permitted himself a smile. 'And then we shall drive the English back into the sea.'

# CHAPTER TWELVE

RETURNING TO HIS castle at Mold, William Montague, Earl of Salisbury, found his mother-in-law at her usual place, embroidering by the hearth. 'Your damned assassins failed. Now everyone believes me guilty of ordering the deaths of Master Sigglesthorne and Master Vise!' he declared angrily.

'Be calm, William, I pray you,' she replied, without even looking up at him. 'They can prove nothing.'

'They don't have to prove anything. Their wagging tongues are enough to flay my reputation from my back. Why, only last week his Majesty himself snubbed me in public.'

'The humiliation will pass,' the countess assured him. 'Better that, than the humiliation of losing your bride to Holland.'

'I think not,' Montague said heavily.

At last the countess looked up at him. 'What mean you?' she whispered.

'Holland can have your bitch of a daughter. She's brought me enough misery already.' He turned his back on her and headed for the door. 'I've washed my hands of her.'

'The devil you have!' she snapped, rising. 'After all I've done, to win the king's consent for the marriage, to block Holland's attempts . . . listen to me when I speak to you!'

He paused, then turned back to face her. 'No, you listen to me, you evil old bitch. His Majesty entrusted me with his cousin, believing that I would protect her with all my honour. Well, you've robbed me of my honour by pouring poison in my ear and turning me into an accomplice to attempted murder. No more, damn you!'

'What will you do?'

'I've already done it. I've instructed Master Bugwell to contest the case no longer. He left for Avignon six days ago, so there's naught you can do to prevent it. Now I want you out of my castle before the week is out.' Without another word, he stormed upstairs.

The countess hurried up the spiral staircase after him, catching up with him in the gallery. 'You can't do this to me,' she protested, seizing him by the arm. 'I am the Countess of Kent.'

'You are the Dowager Countess of Kent and a murderous old bitch.' He broke free of her grip. 'Unhand me! Even your touch defiles.'

'You're just as guilty as I,' she hissed. 'I told you I was going to send men to kill the two attorneys, yet you did not attempt to warn anyone. Throw me out, and I'll tell everyone! They all know how much you hate Holland. Do you really think they'll believe it was I who ordered the attorneys' deaths?'

'They will when they learn she also killed Sir Hugh, my lord,' said Maud Lacy, emerging from the shadows.

The countess turned pale. 'Sir Hugh died of the pestilence. Everyone knows that.'

Maud shook her head. 'I saw you. I watched from the gallery, as you struck him with the poker.'

Montague stared at her in disbelief. 'If this is so, why did you not speak out before?'

'Who would believe the word of a common chambermaid over that of the Dowager Countess of Kent?'

Montague turned to the countess. 'Is this true?'

'Of course not! The spiteful little bitch is making this up. You know how much she hates me.'

'I know how much you have abused her, making her life a misery,' said Montague, nodding thoughtfully to himself. 'Aye, I believe it. There's murder in your blood and blood on your hands.' He turned to Maud. 'Fetch my cloak, girl.'

'Where are you going?' demanded the countess.

'To the county sheriff. It's time justice was done.'

'Stay where you are, girl! snapped the countess, and rounded on Montague. 'You'd see me hanged for murder?'

'Why not?' asked Montague. 'It's no more than you deserve . . .'

She lunged at him, her fingers reaching out to claw at his face. He managed to grab her wrists and the two of them grappled at the top of the spiral staircase. The countess struggled like an enraged cat, snarling and spitting. Montague was terrified, reluctant to hurt her, yet fearful she might scratch out his eyes. She raked her fingernails across his cheek, scoring four lines of blood, and he lost his temper, slapping her back-handed. Staggering back, she tripped over the top step and lost her balance.

Everything seemed to slow down. Realising what he had done, Montague tried to catch her before she fell, but it was like trying to move through water. All was silent as she toppled backwards, eyes and mouth wide in shock, her arms flailing wildly. Then the back of her head struck one of the stone steps, snapping her chin down against her chest.

Maud screamed.

Skirts and hair flying, the countess tumbled down the steps, bouncing off the masonry until she disappeared from sight.

For a few moments Montague stood frozen, staring after her. Then he rushed down the steps, almost losing his footing in his panic, closely followed by Maud. They found the countess lying at the bottom, in the great hall. There was little point in searching for a pulse. Her neck was twisted at an impossible angle.

'It was an accident!' stammered Montague. 'You saw, didn't you? I never meant for . . . sweet Jesu preserve me, it was an accident!'

Maud nodded. 'Aye,' she agreed softly. 'It was an accident.'

From his vantage point seated on a stool by the upper-storey window, Kemp could see the barges sailing down the Rhône. Many of them tied up at the quayside of Lyon, and he watched porters loading the vessels with barrels of wine, or unloading large terracotta jars of spices brought from the East via the Mediterranean. Rain fell heavily, but in spite of this there was considerable activity on the riverside; one thing that Kemp had learned while working for Chaucer was that trade, like war, was rarely stopped by inclement weather. Passengers, too, thronged on the quayside: messengers on their way to the Burgundian court, clergymen going to the Papal Court at Avignon, pilgrims heading for Rome.

It was over two weeks since they had left Broughton. From London they had followed the pilgrim trail to Canterbury, and from there on to Sandwich, taking passage on a ship across the Channel to Calais. It had seemed strange to Kemp to be back in France now that the war was over, although one would not have guessed it from the attitude of the local people they encountered.

But the sullen hostility of the French only served to remind him that he was on what effectively remained enemy territory, and that he must be on his best behaviour if he was to avoid trouble.

From Calais they travelled south, through a country depopulated by the ravages of the pestilence, by-passing Paris, whose crowded streets had been hit particularly badly. But on the whole it seemed in France as if the worst of the sickness were past. It filled Kemp with a sense of hope to think the deadly plague that had entered the world might in time pass on, leaving at least a few survivors behind.

South of Paris, in country as yet untouched by the ravages of the war between Plantagenet and Valois, the attitude of the local people had changed, becoming perceptibly more polite towards the English travellers. From the Île de France, they headed south-east through the Côte d'Or, down a route already familiar to Sigglesthorne and Vise. They lodged in the guest houses of priories whenever the opportunity presented itself, or in inns when it did not.

In the room behind Kemp, Sigglesthorne lay snoozing on his back on the bed, while Vise sat with his nose buried in his psalter. It was barely past noon. The barge on which they had arranged passage to Avignon would not be sailing until the following morning, and in the meantime there was nothing for them to do but while away the time in idleness.

It was then that Kemp saw the banner carried by a page at the end of a lance. He recognised it, and felt a shiver pass through his spine. Three white shields on a crimson background: the arms of Sir Geoffroi de Chargny.

Kemp stared at it in disbelief. De Chargny was the governor of Saint-Omer; what was he doing so far south? Even in the midst of the truce, the thought of de Chargny's proximity made him feel uneasy.

Ten men emerged from one of the other inns overlooking the riverside and Kemp recognised de Chargny amongst them, flanked by the ever-present Guilbert. After a split second's indecision he jumped to his feet, knocking over the stool on which he had been sitting.

Vise stared at him in astonishment. 'Master Kemp?'

But Kemp had already left the room. He ran down the stairs, vaulting over the bannister at the bottom, and hurried to the stables at the back of the inn. There he found his longbow and arrows hanging up with his horse's saddle and harness. Taking them down, he sprinted back up to the upstairs room, crossing to the window.

'Kemp? What are you doing?' asked Vise.

Kemp looked out. De Chargny and Guilbert were still standing on the wharf less than a hundred yards away, watching as the men-at-arms in de Chargny's retinue led their horses down the gangplank on to a sail-barge which already flew de Chargny's banner from the masthead.

Kemp began to remove his bow from its cover. 'It's Sir Geoffroi de Chargny,' he explained. 'The governor of Saint-Omer. He was one of the French knights at the negotiations at the siege of Calais.'

'So?'

'So I'm going to kill him.'

Vise leapt to his feet and even Sigglesthorne, who had only been dozing, sat up on the bed.

Kemp nocked an arrow to his bow and began to take careful aim. It was an easy shot, even at that angle, which was why he wanted to take extra care to ensure he did not miss with the first shot through over-confidence. De Chargny's men would get him afterwards – there were too many for him to be able to kill them all – but it would be worth it to rid the world of a man who was such a great enemy of King Edward.

'Kemp!' snapped Sigglesthorne.

Kemp lowered his aim fractionally. 'What?' he asked.

'Forgive me for saying so, but Sir Thomas ordered you to see that we get to Avignon and back safely. I fail to see how you can achieve that if you're languishing in a cell awaiting execution for murder.'

Vise placed a hand on Kemp's left arm. 'The war is over, Master Kemp,' he said softly.

Slowly Kemp let in his draw on the bow and took the arrow from the string. What had he been doing? Had he been out of his mind? He laughed nervously, and looked down at his hands. They were trembling. He realised he was fighting for breath.

De Chargny and Guilbert had followed the men-at-arms and horses on to the barge, and now the bargemen cast off, guiding the vessel into mid-stream and heading south with the current.

'Are you all right?' Vise asked him.

Kemp nodded. He felt very weak. 'I . . . I'm sorry. I don't know what came over me. I must have been thinking that . . .'

Sigglesthorne stared penetratingly into his eyes. 'You still have nightmares about the war, don't you?'

'Aye,' Kemp admitted. He jerked his head through the window to where the sail-barge was disappearing down the river. 'And he's in them.'

Sigglesthorne put an arm around his shoulder. 'Come on,' he said. 'A flagon or two of claret should restore your humour.'

Failing to kill de Chargy there and then was a decision Kemp would come to regret.

Avignon was the greatest city Kemp had ever seen. It frowned over the Rhône Valley, the close-packed huddle of houses of stone and wood dominated by the pinnacles and crenellated battlements of the vast Papal palace, built of pale grey stone on a great spur of rock overlooking the river. Disembarking from the barge in the shadow of the great Saint-Bénézet bridge, Sigglesthorne, Vise and Kemp did not make directly for the palace, however, heading instead for their lodgings.

Despite the pestilence, which had already ravaged Avignon, the streets remained crowded, for the city's population was constantly fluctuating. Pilgrims came from all over Christendom to receive the Papal blessing, petitioners and their attorneys came to plead at the Curial courts, penitents visited the city's numerous shrines, ambassadors from many princes and many lands came to do homage to the pontiff, Papal legates departed on or returned from missions with their great retinues, and clergymen came to consult the cardinals of the Sacred College.

The dung-filled streets were crowded with the same hawkers, pedlars and hucksters that had become so familiar to Kemp in London, but here there was so much more: fountains and statues; broad boulevards and terraces lined with vistas of mulberry trees; spacious squares where markets traded all manner of goods; noblemen and cardinals riding through the streets with clothes, jewellery and retinues so splendid it was impossible to tell the latter from the former. And there were whores everywhere, their dress so shameless they were instantly recognisable, plying their trade on street corners or leaning from the windows of stewhouses in their low-cut gowns, displaying their wares, calling out to plump, elderly cardinals who waved and called back unashamedly. Kemp saw all of this and he understood why his king had so little time for Christ's vicar on earth. Avignon had become the new Babylon, a city of whores and priests where there seemed little to choose between the two.

Sigglesthorne, Vise and Kemp did not lodge at any of the city's countless inns and taverns, but at a large house in the wealthier quarter, the home of an Italian nobleman called Count Niccolino del Fiesco, a hanger-on at the Papal Court. The count had been recommended to Holland by a canon of the King's Chamber, and it was at his house Sigglesthorne and Vise had stayed on their previous visits to the city. They had found a warm welcome there, for del Fiesco kept an open house, and was always glad to hear the latest news and gossip. He threw lavish balls on more nights than not, balls which were the toast of Avignon; the pontiff himself had been a guest under del Fiesco's roof on more than one occasion.

The three men stood under the impressive portico and Sigglesthorne pulled a handle that rang a bell deep within the house. Presently the door was opened by the count's major-domo who ushered them into a marble-floored entrance hall while a stableboy appeared to take care of their horses.

The house was like nothing Kemp had ever seen, with its exquisite architecture, marble floors and pillars and airy, high-ceilinged rooms. It put to shame any of the dark and dingy castles which King Edward inhabited; but somehow Kemp could not imagine his king amidst such finery, built to impress rather than protect. King Edward was a fighting man who revelled in hardship and Kemp knew just from the look of this house that whatever sort of man the count was, he was not a fighting man. The floors of the house were scattered with rose petals, and the air was scented with the sickly-sweet odour of burning incense to keep out the stench of the gutters outside and the poisonous air by which the pestilence was spread.

The count himself soon appeared to greet them, a handsome man with black, well-oiled hair, a neat, pointed beard, and dark eyes that twinkled with mischief. Something about him reminded Kemp of Jack Curtis. He was exquisitely dressed in sequined hose of orange and blue, and a tight-fitting doublet of green velvet decorated with gold brocade. His head was bare, and he carried a slender-bladed dagger in a matching sheath encrusted with jewels and gold filigree that looked as if it had been designed as an ornament rather than a weapon.

He clasped the serjeant-at-law by the hand. 'Master Sigglesthorne! How splendid to see you! It will be good to have an epicure with your appreciation for the finer things in life under my humble roof once more.' His English was perfect, if a little accented. 'And Master Vise back again! You are most welcome, sir, most welcome. And who is this?'

'Signor Conte Niccolino del Fiesco, may I present Master Martin Kemp of Knighton? Kemp is an archer in Sir Thomas Holland's retinue. He's been appointed to act as our bodyguard.'

The count smiled. 'A bodyguard? Has the legal business really become so dangerous since last you were here?'

'Well may you jest,' Sigglesthorne responded with a grimace. 'On our way back last time, while staying at an inn in Calais, we were set upon by a couple of assassins hired by the Countess of Kent.'

'Countess Margaret? Surely not!'

Vise nodded. 'I fear it's true. One of them admitted as much, albeit under a certain amount of duress.'

'I fear grave news precedes you, my friends. Or, since it seems that this great lady wishes you dead, perhaps it is good news to you. Her ladyship is dead.'

Sigglesthorne arched an eyebrow. 'Dead? I had thought her relatively young.'

'It was an accident, they say,' explained the count. 'She was killed in a fall of some kind.'

Vise crossed himself. 'I pray that God may have mercy on her soul,' he said.

'So it seems you have brought along this bodyguard needlessly,' the count continued with a smile.

'We did not know the countess was dead, my lord,' Kemp responded truculently. 'Perhaps there are yet assassins out there who are as ignorant of the death of their employer as we were.'

'By God, you are right!' acknowledged the count. 'And there was I thinking this man was employed purely for the breadth of his shoulders. But come, supper is almost served, and the three of you do not look as if you have eaten for a week.'

The fare on board the barge from Lyons had been lean, but not enough to justify the count's observation; Sigglesthorne would not have looked as if he had not eaten for a week had he fasted for seven years.

Despite the grandeur of the surroundings – a grandeur that only made Kemp feel ill at ease – there was no suggestion he should eat with the servants. He dined with the others in the atrium. Del Fiesco liked to dine in the fashion of the ancient Romans, reclining on a couch beside a fountain in a courtyard, with music played by his Provençal troubadour, who sang a ballad of love and war while strumming a gittern. Kemp did not feel comfortable trying to eat in a reclining position, so he insisted on sitting on the edge of his couch with his platter balanced awkwardly on his knees.

The food was both richer and more delicate than Kemp was used to, the spices designed to complement the flavour rather than to hide any rottenness as had been the case in the Chaucer household. Here they were waited on hand and foot by silent servants: a new experience for Kemp, along with the tiny roasted songbirds with almond-milk sauce that formed the first course. They ate with their fingers, washing their hands with ewers of water and drying them on fine linen cloths handed to them by pages between each course. The portions were tiny, but Kemp soon lost count of the number of courses, and each brought with it such a variety of dishes that he was just getting into his stride when he was astonished and embarrassed to find that he had eaten his fill. There were Lombard slices made from pounded pork, eggs, raisins, currants and minced dates, flavoured with rich spices and coloured with saffron; and a '*pomme d'orange*': spiced pork liver garnished with parsley, basted with egg-yolk and dyed with indigo. These were followed by roasted duck, pheasant, boar, venison and a tasty meat which Kemp found delicious until he was foolish enough to ask the count what it was, and found out it was hedgehog.

Kemp's contribution to the conversation over supper was minimal. Sigglesthorne listened attentively to the latest gossip of the Papal Court, in case there were any new developments at Avignon which would require alterations to his summing up of Holland's case at the final meeting of the tribunal; but little had changed in the court since his last visit to the city. The Pope himself still resided out of the city, in his mansion at Valence, to avoid the pestilence, and none of the more eminent cardinals seemed keen to replace him, following the pontiff's example by living as far from the common folk as possible. In return, however, Sigglesthorne felt obliged to relate the latest scandals from the English court, the depth of his knowledge and the enthusiasm in his telling betraying his genuine interest in such gossip.

They drank heavily and, even though the wine was watered down, Kemp found himself swaying as he made his way to bed. The large house chanced to be relatively empty, so for the first time in his life Kemp found he had not only a bed to himself – a great four-poster with silken sheets and an embroidered coverlet, such as he had only seen in houses he had pillaged – but even a whole room. He was too tired to appreciate this luxury, however, and he sprawled across the bed fully clothed to fall asleep the moment his head hit the feathered bolster.

'Supposing Calais were to be seized by a *coup de main*?' de Chargny asked Cardinal Ravaillac. 'How would his Holiness react?'

The cardinal raised an eyebrow. 'Just how hypothetical is this question, Sir Geoffroi?'

De Chargny smiled thinly. 'Let's keep this hypothetical for now, and see what fate has in store for the town.'

The cardinal shrugged. 'It would depend who seized it. King Philip agreed to a truce which stated that both sides would retain any land they had won. If he were behind such a *coup de main*, he would be greatly criticised for failing to honour his word.'

De Chargny nodded. 'And if King Philip were unaware such a move were planned until after it had happened? If the plan were laid and carried out by certain of his courtiers acting on their own initiative?'

'And how close to King Philip would these courtiers be, Sir Geoffroi? As close as you, perhaps?'

'Perhaps.'

The cardinal considered de Chargny's question for several moments. 'Despite his elevation to the See of Rome, his Holiness has not forgotten in which court it was he first cut his teeth in the world of diplomacy, as well you know,' he said at last. 'Naturally he could not condone such a move. Whoever carried it out would have to be publicly condemned, forced to carry out some kind of penance on pain of excommunication.'

'What sort of a penance?' de Chargny asked sharply.

The cardinal smiled. 'Oh, he would have to say a few *Ave Marias* at the very least.' He tilted back his head to kiss the bare breasts of the young woman who stood over him, soaping his naked body with practised hands as he sat in a tub of warm, perfumed water in a stewhouse in the more respectable quarter of Avignon.

Sitting in the other tub, de Chargny realised he had lost the cardinal's attention, so he grabbed the other naked wench and pulled her in with him. She turned to face him so that her thighs straddled his hips, but he pushed her around, the soapy water slopping from the tub as he entered her from behind. His moment of release came quickly and silently and the girl squealed with unconvincing delight. De Chargny ignored her; none of it had had anything to do with her, as far as he was concerned.

'Of course, it is not how his Holiness would react that should concern you,' the cardinal continued when the two of them were sated, the exhausted whores lying sprawled against them. 'Regardless of whoever was behind such a move, King Philip would be expected to return Calais to English control or else be in direct contravention of the truce. In that event, King Edward would be fully within his rights in declaring the truce null and void.'

'The truce cannot last either way,' de Chargny responded. 'At least this way the English would be deprived of their toe-hold in the Pas-de-Calais.' He rose to his feet and reached for a towel, drying himself vigorously.

The cardinal stared at him in open admiration. 'Are you really planning such a move?'

De Chargny glared at him. 'You grow indiscreet in your old age, your eminence. Know you not the old proverb which says: "Ask questions of none, and you shall be told no lies"?'

'But how can such a thing succeed? The English will have the town of Calais well-defended . . .'

'Even the strongest defences have their weak spots. It is simply a matter of finding one.'

'And you have found the weak spot in Calais' defences?'

De Chargny could not resist a smile. 'The acting governor. He is a Lombard and, like all of his race, his love of gold is great.'

'You have the governor of Calais in your purse?' The cardinal was impressed.

'The governor now; Calais itself before the coming year has seen its first dawn.'

'But is France ready for a renewal of the war?' the cardinal wondered out loud. 'The pestilence has left her woefully depopulated . . .'

'Aye,' admitted de Chargny. 'I had planned such a move earlier, but the pestilence deprived me of many of my best troops. But now England is stricken with the pestilence and she has fared just as badly as France, if not worse. Perhaps the English may no longer have the stomach for a continuation of the war.'

The cardinal shook his head with a wry grimace. 'That would be too much to hope for.'

Kemp accompanied the two attorneys to the Papal palace the following morning, crossing the Place du Palais and approaching the Porte des Champeaux, the main entrance beneath two towering pinnacles. The two guards on duty admitted Sigglesthorne and Vise but, when Kemp tried to follow them, they blocked his way with their halberds. He had left his longbow behind at del Fiesco's mansion, but one look at him was enough to convince the guards that they should check beneath his cloak where, to their complete lack of surprise, they found his broadsword and dagger hanging from his belt.

'No weapons in the palace,' growled one of the guards. 'This is a house of God.'

Kemp was tempted to take issue with that fact: the rule against weapons clearly did not encompass the guards, and this particular house of God had been constructed with battlements and walls twelve feet thick. He unbuckled his sword belt and handed it over reluctantly. 'I want those back when I leave,' he growled.

Making his way down a short tunnel, he emerged into a great courtyard where Sigglesthorne and Vise were waiting for him. 'What kept you?' asked Sigglesthorne.

'They would not let me in with my sword and dagger,' Kemp explained.

Sigglesthorne looked amused. 'Of course not. Will you be able to protect us, Master Kemp?'

'I still have my fists,' he replied. He took his duties rather more seriously than Sigglesthorne appeared to.

Vise glanced around at the courtyard. 'I'm certain you won't need them in here.'

Kemp was not so sure. All his life he had grown up with stories about how corrupt the Papacy had become since it had been forced out of Rome to settle in Avignon. From the day he landed in Normandy with the rest of King Edward's army to the day he sailed from Calais back to England, Kemp had seen Pope Clement's legates claiming time after time to be trying to negotiate truces, when in reality they were doing everything in their power to delay the march of the English army. Even as he stood in the great courtyard of the Papal palace he saw a cardinal descending a flight of stone steps, unrecognisable as such in his worldly clothes and priceless jewellery were it not for his red, broad-brimmed cardinal's hat. He glanced at Kemp and frowned at the sight of a commoner muddying the palace courtyard with his dirty boots. Kemp scowled back at him, and the cardinal's fat face blanched as he hurried away.

Presently they were summoned by an usher to a small audience chamber. A new attorney was now representing Montague. He introduced himself as Reginald Bugwell, a canon of Exeter and an expert in canon and civil law. He explained that he had been appointed to represent the earl following the death of Joan's mother, the Dowager Countess of Kent.

'Master Vise and I shall be formally requesting the tribunal to pronounce sentence,' Sigglesthorne told him. 'I trust you have no objections?'

Bugwell shook his head. 'I shall not oppose any such request. His lordship the Earl of Salisbury has decided that this case has dragged on far too long, and is as keen as the rest of us to see it concluded.'

The court rose to its feet as the presiding cardinal swept in, resplendent in crimson robes. Everyone remained standing until he had seated himself. He leaned forward to exchange a few words with the notary sitting just below and in front of him, and then declared the court in session.

Kemp had been admitted to the chamber and was allowed to sit on one of the benches immediately behind Sigglesthorne. The serjeant-at-law had given him strict instructions that as an observer he was to say nothing and hold his peace throughout the proceedings; but since the tribunal was conducted in Latin, Kemp soon lost interest. He pulled up his cowl and bowed his head as if lost in thought, but his snores soon betrayed him. At a command from the presiding cardinal, the usher tapped him on the shoulder and requested him to leave. Quite unabashed, Kemp walked out of the chamber, and sat down on a stone bench in the courtyard outside. Presently he was fast asleep once more.

Count Niccolino del Fiesco had not joined Kemp and the two attorneys for breakfast and was still asleep when his major-domo knocked on the door of his bedchamber at noon. 'Come in.'

The major-domo entered the room and crossed to the bed, holding out a sealed envelope. 'Forgive me for disturbing you, Signor il Conte, but a messenger just called at the servant's entrance and asked that this be delivered to you. I thought it unusual enough to bring it to your attention without delay.'

'You did right, Benedetto.' The count took the envelope and turned it over in his hands. The wax seal was plain, and the envelope bore no address. He shrugged, and broke open the seal, peering blearily at the brief note scrawled within.

'Shall I open the shutters, Signor?'

The count nodded, and immediately regretted it. He considered himself a hearty drinker, but even he had to acknowledge that he had been outclassed by Kemp and Sigglesthorne. He winced as the major-domo threw back the shutters, allowing harsh sunlight to invade his skull.

'Shall I have breakfast prepared, Signor?'

'Yes, please.' The count turned his attention to the note:

*Come immediately.*
*Bring money.*
*K.*

The handwriting was neat. Katerina might be illiterate, but thanks to her lucrative profession she could afford the services of a scribe. 'Stoke up the fire on your way out,' the count told his major-domo. 'I shall have breakfast in here.' The major-domo complied, closing the door behind him. As soon as he was gone, the count jumped out of bed and padded across to the fireplace, tossing the letter on the flames.

He ate a leisurely breakfast – what Katerina considered urgent might be anything but – and dressed in some of his more sober robes. Riding in a covered litter – one which did not display his coat of arms – he made his way to the nearby stewhouse where Katerina worked. As soon as they were alone together in one of the rooms on the upper floor, she started to undress him.

'You said it was urgent.'

'It is.' She pulled his unbuttoned doublet off his shoulders.

'Your note gave me the impression it was something important,' he said, as she unfastened the laces which tied his hose to his breech-cloth.

'You remember you said you would be willing to pay me for any interesting pieces of gossip I might pick up?' She held out her hand.

He reached across to where she had put his belt and purse on the chest at the end of her bed and took out a gold coin.

She shook her head. 'This could be very important.'

'It could be,' agreed the count. 'On the other hand, it might be quite insignificant.'

'You'll never know if you don't pay me.'

He sighed and gave her another coin. She closed her hand over them, and hurried across the room to put them in a coffer, which she locked.

'Cardinal Ravaillac was here last night with another man . . .'

'That's not the kind of gossip I had in mind.'

'I know what kind of gossip you had in mind. I overheard them talking. The other man spoke of taking Calais back from the English. He wanted to know how his Holiness would react.'

'With ill-concealed delight, I should imagine,' the count commented. 'I don't suppose you know the name of this other man?'

'I've never seen him before.'

'What did he look like?'

She knitted her brows in concentration. 'He was good-looking – in his late thirties, I think – with red hair. He was a French nobleman, I think.' She grinned lasciviously. 'He liked to fuck like a dog.'

The count grimaced. 'If I should happen to meet a red-haired

French nobleman who likes to fuck like a dog, I'll know it was the one you speak of.'

She pouted. 'Next time I shall not trouble to tell you such things.' She frowned as she remembered something. 'Wait a moment, I think his eminence used a name – Sir Geoffroi?'

'That must narrow it down to a few hundred,' sighed the count. 'Did he say how he intended to take Calais back from the English? Or does he expect them to hand it over out of Christian charity?'

'He said something about having the governor in his purse . . .'

The count turned to face her sharply. 'De Pavia? Yes, now that I think of it, I can well imagine it.' So there was more to this than the dreams of some minor French nobleman; here was a plan carefully worked out by someone cynical enough to use bribery rather than a chivalrous attack. And had he not heard Sir Geoffroi de Chargny was in Avignon at the moment?

'He also said Calais would be his by the end of the year.'

'So soon?'

'That is what he said. I did right to tell you this?'

The count feigned disinterest. 'What should I care if the French take Calais back from the English? It is a French town, after all.'

Seeing Katerina's chagrin, he placed his hands on her shoulders and kissed her forehead. 'But no; you were right to tell me. It might have been important.'

The end of the year was less than two months' hence, and England was almost three weeks' journey away. That knowledge filled the count with a sense of urgency which he knew he must conceal; it was a matter of weeks rather than days, and he knew that a couple of hours could make no difference. 'Now, since you have forced me to come here, how do you propose to make my visit worth my while?' he asked her, with a knowing smile.

'I have reviewed all the evidence presented not only to myself but also to Cardinal Adhémar, and all that remains for me to do before I pronounce judgement is to assure all parties concerned that my decision has been reached following careful deliberation on my part and extensive consultation with other experts in canon and civil law.' The presiding cardinal's expression was grave as he surveyed the faces that stared back at him in the court. 'I hereby declare that the contract of marriage entered into by Sir Thomas Holland of Broughton and Lady Joan of Kent was then, and remains to this day, a valid marital union; that the said Lady Joan is to be restored to Sir Thomas; that their union is to be solemnized publicly and *in facie ecclesiae*; and that the *de facto* marriage entered into by Sir William Montague, now Earl of Salisbury, and Lady Joan, is henceforth to be considered null and void.'

Sigglesthorne felt a surge of relief. As the case progressed, he had been increasingly confident of a verdict in his client's favour, but even after Bugwell had admitted his client no longer had any wish to fight the case, there had always been an irrepressible feeling of doubt, a nagging worry that things might yet go against Holland. Sigglesthorne liked the gruff knight, but – more importantly – the case had become so notorious that his whole reputation as a serjeant-at-law now hung on the outcome.

The three attorneys – Sigglesthorne, Vise and Bugwell – shook hands, and then each in turn knelt before the cardinal to kiss his ring before bowing out of the chamber.

In the courtyard outside, Kemp stirred from where he had been dozing in a foetal position on the stone bench as Sigglesthorne emerged, beaming triumphantly. 'I take it you won?' said Kemp.

'Indeed,' said Sigglesthorne. 'However, it is not the simple fact of my victory that gives me cause for celebration so much as the fact that after two years of travelling back and forth between England and the meetings of the tribunal – only to be told that the opposition still had not got their latest evidence prepared, as often as not – this damned case is finally over, and we can all go home.'

'Until your next case here in Avignon,' Vise said with a smile.

'Of course, his eminence's verdict will still have to be ratified by the Pope,' Bugwell pointed out with a sniff. 'However, since that is merely a formality, I must confess that it seems unlikely his Holiness will decide to reverse the cardinal's decision.'

Sigglesthorne, Vise and Kemp made their way back through the crowded streets to del Fiesco's house. The count was waiting for them. 'You will return to England now?' he asked before they had a chance to tell him of the outcome of the case.

Vise shook his head. 'I've always had a hankering to go on a pilgrimage to see the shrine of Saint Peter in Rome,' he explained. 'Before I undertook this case, I gained permission from my bishop to make the pilgrimage as soon as the case was concluded. This coming year will be the jubilee, after all, and I expect the celebrations will be something to see.'

But the count was not interested in the jubilee. His eyes burned with a feverish excitement that made Kemp frown. Del Fiesco turned to Sigglesthorne. 'But *you* will be returning to England? To London?'

'In a few days,' agreed Sigglesthorne. 'I thought I might tarry in Avignon until the Pope pronounces the final verdict of the case. Aren't you interested to know how it went?'

The count glanced about the room to make sure that only the four of them were in earshot. 'There is no time to lose,' he whispered. 'You must leave first thing tomorrow, at dawn.'

'You seem in rather a hurry to be rid of us,' Sigglesthorne observed. 'Have we out-stayed our welcome, perchance?'

'May I have a word with you in private?'

Sigglesthorne followed the count up to his private chamber. The count closed the heavy oak door behind them.

'You seem fevered, your lordship,' protested Sigglesthorne. 'Are you ill? What in the name of the Lord does all this excitement signify?'

The count crossed to his writing desk and picked up a sealed envelope. 'You seem to me to be a loyal and trustworthy subject of King Edward, if I am any judge of men,' he said. 'I beg you to ask no questions but to put your faith in me, and deliver this letter to Canon Reynard of the King's Chamber. Please believe me that in so doing you will be performing a service beyond value for his Majesty the King.'

Sigglesthorne took the letter reluctantly, and turned it over in his hands. The seal was plain, and there was no address on the front. 'To whom do you say I should deliver it?'

'Canon Reynard of the King's Chamber, and none other. Deliver it into his hands, and his hands alone, or else those of the king himself. Speak of it to no one, not even Master Vise or your bodyguard. Tell none that you had it from me, if you value my life. And when you have delivered it, forget we ever spoke of this, or of Canon Reynard.'

Sigglesthorne was not sure if he could trust the count. He could not guarantee he would forget all about the affair, either; but he had certain friends at court whom he could ask about del Fiesco and this Canon Reynard, to cover his own back as much as anything. Treason was an ugly word and usually shortly followed by a phrase that Sigglesthorne had occasionally encountered in the course of his career, although usually addressed to his less fortunate clients: '. . . and may God have mercy on your soul.'

Perhaps it might be better if instead of delivering the letter he burned it as soon as he got the chance.

Sigglesthorne and Kemp reached the village of Corbeil, fifteen miles south of Paris, within two weeks of setting out from Avignon. Instead of a leisurely cruise up the Rhône, Sigglesthorne had insisted they travel up the valley on their horses, a hard ride which left the serjeant-at-law so saddle-sore that Kemp could not understand why he insisted on such a punishing pace. It was only mid-November, and they would be back at Broughton long before Yuletide, as they had originally planned. Much to Kemp's mystification, they had not even waited for the Pope's ratification of the cardinal's verdict.

The afternoon was wearing on when they reached the village and made for the inn there. Sigglesthorne dismounted, and Kemp was about to do likewise when he saw a shield hanging from one of the upper-storey windows, signifying that a nobleman was in residence: a red shield with three white shields emblazoned on it. He leaned down from his hackney to touch Sigglesthorne on the shoulder, and pointed out the shield.

'What is it?'

'The arms of Sir Geoffroi de Chargny,' Kemp told him.

'So?'

'I do not think it would be a good idea to stay at the same inn.'

Sigglesthorne smiled. 'The war is over, Master Kemp.' He sighed. 'However, if this French knight makes you feel so uncomfortable, I'm certain we will find another inn further down the road before nightfall.'

Guilbert emerged from the tavern with one of de Chargny's men-at-arms in time to see Kemp and Sigglesthorne ride on. He froze, staring in astonishment at their backs.

'What is it?' asked the man-at-arms. 'The two Englishmen?'

'How do you know they are English, Baudet?' Guilbert asked sharply.

'Apart from the fact the young one carries an English bow? I have seen them before. I overheard them speaking English.'

Guilbert seized him by the hem of his cape, swinging him around to face him. 'Where?'

Baudet was caught off-guard. 'At Lyon, on the way south, and again in Avignon itself.'

Guilbert rubbed his jaw. 'Can they be following us, I wonder?'

Baudet shrugged. 'If they were travelling from Avignon to England, surely they would follow the same route as us. Our paths would be bound to cross.'

'Perhaps. It is a great coincidence, nonetheless. Sir Geoffroi must be informed of this at once.'

De Chargny was sitting down to supper when the squire and the man-at-arms entered. He listened in silence to what they had to say, his face impassive. 'Do you think they may be following us, Sir Geoffroi?' Guilbert concluded.

'Baudet is probably right,' said de Chargny. 'Doubtless the serjeant-at-law was merely on his way to plead at the Papal Court. I have heard that Holland is disputing Joan of Kent's marriage to the Earl of Salisbury.' He paused, chewing over his last mouthful. 'However, there is too much at stake for me to take a chance on that.' He wiped his dagger on the tablecloth and replaced it in the jewelled sheath at his belt. Then he rose, his supper half-eaten. 'Follow them at once, Baudet,' he commanded. 'They cannot hope to reach Paris before nightfall. Find out where they lodge tonight, and then ride back to meet the rest of us.'

Baudet nodded, and hurried out of the back door, heading for the stables.

De Chargny turned to his squire. 'Have the men fall in and mount up, Guilbert,' he ordered.

Within minutes the remaining seven men in de Chargny's retinue were waiting astride their rouncies in the lane outside. De Chargny swung himself into the saddle of his palfrey while Guilbert held the bridle, and then the squire vaulted astride his own rouncy. At a signal from de Chargny, the nine men galloped out of the village, heading north.

They met Baudet coming back about two miles further on, and reined in their horses. 'There's an inn half a mile away,' explained the man-at-arms. 'They stopped there for the night.'

De Chargny nodded curtly and they rode on, at a more leisurely pace now. Their quarry had gone to ground, but could soon be rooted out.

The inn stood in a clearing in the midst of the woods to the south of Paris, part of Valois' hunting grounds. De Chargny and his men were about to emerge from the shadow of the trees when they saw the door of the inn open, firelight spilling out across the road beneath the darkening sky. There was no mistaking the figure briefly silhouetted in the doorway. Holding a burning brand aloft it made its way around the outside of the inn to the stables at the back.

'Kemp,' Guilbert whispered.

'Kemp is unimportant,' said de Chargny. 'It is the man riding with him who interests me – the serjeant-at-law. Renaud, you stay here and watch the horses. Baudet: you go into the stables and kill the churl.' Baudet nodded, grinning. 'The rest of you come with me.'

Kemp had left the stable door ajar, the light from his brand clearly visible. Baudet peered inside; his quarry stood in one of the stalls, whistling tunelessly to himself as he rubbed down the flanks of a pale grey hackney nag. Baudet pulled back sharply, but Kemp had not seen him. The Frenchman peered through a knot-hole in the stable's wooden walls, waiting until Kemp moved around to the other side of the horse. Then he eased the door open on its leather hinges, entering the stable with practised stealth. He slipped into the stall behind Kemp and produced a slender leather thong, wrapping both ends around the fingers of each hand to make a garrotte.

Kemp was aware of something flickering before his eyes, and then the garrotte was pulled tight around his neck, jerking him back so that his shoulder blades struck the wooden partition behind him. He dropped his brush, clawing at the leather thong that bit deep into his windpipe, choking him.

# CHAPTER THIRTEEN

BAUDET PULLED THE garrotte tighter, the leather thong biting deep into his opponent's neck. Kemp's vision became hazy. Already he could feel his limbs turning to water as he flailed about, his back hard against the wooden partition. Reaching for the dagger sheathed on his belt, he remembered with despair that he had left belt, dagger and sword in the room upstairs with Sigglesthorne. He saw the burning brand that guttered fitfully in the wall bracket and reached out with one hand, but it was too far away.

Baudet gave the garrotte another jerk. A red mist began to fill Kemp's eyes, and he felt the darkness closing in on him. He could just make out the longbow in its canvas case slung from the pommel of his horse's saddle, hung up on a beam nearby. Next to it were his arrows, held together by a leather retainer. He reached up with trembling fingers but they came less than two inches short of the nearest fletching. Straining against the garrotte, he felt it cut into his windpipe, choking off his breath. Baudet pulled back, tightening it even further. Kemp's back slammed against the partition.

Kemp tried again, ignoring the dizzying sickness he felt. Whirling dots and colours filled his vision and he could no longer see the arrows, but still he groped for them as Baudet tried to drag him back. A fletching brushed his fingertips. Making a supreme effort, he gained half an inch, catching the fletching between the tips of his first and second fingers.

Baudet jerked again, and once again Kemp smacked against the wooden partition. Somehow he managed to maintain his tenuous grip on the fletching as he teased the arrow from the retainer. The barbed head caught on the leather and he felt the fletching slip through his fingers. He tightened his grip, and the fletching began to work loose of the shaft. Panic gripped him, but he fought it back, pushing the arrow to free the barb, and then pulling once more.

Then, as the arrow came free, the fletching slipped from his fingers. His open hand arced down, the fingers snapping shut as soon as he felt his palm hit ash, fingers closing around the shaft. He adjusted his grip on the arrow and stabbed blindly over his left shoulder. The steel arrowhead connected with something and he heard Baudet hiss with pain.

The garrotte loosened just enough for him to get the fingers of one hand around it. Baudet tried to tighten it again but Kemp slipped the tip of the arrowhead under the thong and sliced it in two. The arrowhead nicked the underside of his jaw, but he was free. Gasping for breath, he stumbled forward against the side of the nag.

Snarling with frustration, Baudet threw down the two halves of his garrotte and drew a sword from the scabbard at his hip. Before Kemp was able even to straighten, Baudet had moved out of the first stall and trapped Kemp in the second with his horse and drew back his sword to thrust it into the archer's stomach. Kemp reached up, unhooked his heavy saddle from where it hung from an overhead beam and hurled it at Baudet's head. As Baudet stumbled under the weight of the blow, Kemp vaulted over the partition into the next stall and reached for the burning brand. But his assailant recovered swiftly and dodged around the end of the partition, lunging at Kemp with the sword and forcing him back into the corner of the stall, leaving the brand in its bracket.

A shovel for mucking out was propped against the rear wall of the next stall. Kemp reached over the partition and grabbed it. Baudet lunged at him again. Kemp twisted away, as the edge of the sword sliced through the fabric of his sleeve, drawing blood. He swung the shovel like a battleaxe, bringing it down on his attacker's head with all his might. The shovel's iron-edged rim smashed into Baudet's skull, spattering Kemp with gore.

Kemp slumped down beside the man's body. 'It seems the war's not over after all,' he muttered, gingerly rubbing his Adam's apple where the garrotte had chafed his flesh. Bewildered as to who the dead man was and why he should have tried to murder him, Kemp glanced at the corpse once more. Crimson and white: the livery of Sir Geoffroi de Chargny.

Ignoring the sting of the cut on his upper left arm, Kemp rose to his feet and hurried out of the stables. He was about to round the corner of the inn when he spotted another man in de Chargny's livery waiting in front, keeping watch over a number of horses tied to the fence. Kemp drew back, then peered more cautiously around the corner.

The man continued to gaze up and down the road leading past the inn. There were ten horses, which made the current odds nine to one by Kemp's reckoning. He withdrew his head and made his way back to the stables, where he saddled both his own horse and Sigglesthorne's, led them out of the stable and fastened their bridles to a wooden tethering rail immediately outside. Next he thrust his arrows under his belt and took his longbow from its bag, tying on the bowstring.

The man was still on guard in front of the inn. Kemp nocked an arrow to his bow and took aim, letting fly. At that range it was an easy shot, even in the poor light, and the shaft took the man cleanly in the throat. He dropped without a sound. Murmuring soothingly to the horses, Kemp dragged the corpse out of sight, around the side of the inn. Then, crouching before one of the ground-floor windows at the front, he peered through the gap at the bottom of the shutters.

The room was illuminated by the fire that roared in the hearth and by a number of rush candles. De Chargny sat on a bench beside a table, his back to the wall, his long legs stretched in front of him, ankles crossed where they rested on a footstool. Sigglesthorne stood facing him in the centre of the room, his hands tied behind his back, flanked by two men-at-arms. Guilbert and two more men-at-arms also sat nearby, their swords drawn casually.

'... told you, I was going to Avignon to plead at the Curial court on behalf of a client,' Sigglesthorne was saying irritably, although it was clear he understood the danger he was in from the paleness of his usually sanguine hue.

'So you keep saying.' De Chargny's tone was dismissive. 'But how do I know you are not lying?'

Before Sigglesthorne could respond, another man-at-arms came running down the stairs, holding aloft an envelope. 'Sir Geoffroi! I found this in one of the saddlebags upstairs.' Crossing the room, he handed it to de Chargny.

The knight turned the envelope over in his hands. 'No name on the front; no impression on the seal on the back,' he observed, breaking open the seal.

'That's private correspondence!' Sigglesthorne protested, but the knight ignored him as he unfolded the letter and read through it.

Finally de Chargny folded it once more and looked up at Sigglesthorne. 'It seems that someone has betrayed me,' he observed, rising to his feet. 'Well, no matter.' He crossed to the hearth, and tossed the letter into the flames. 'No addressee and no signatory,' he mused. 'Someone was very careful. Who gave you that letter, Master Sigglesthorne, and how did they learn of my plot to recapture Calais?'

Sigglesthorne creased his brow. 'What plot to recapture Calais?'

'Please do not insult my intelligence, Master Sigglesthorne. Do you really expect me to believe you carried that letter for someone without knowing aught of its contents?'

Sigglesthorne sighed. 'What you choose to believe is really no concern of mine.'

De Chargny moved closer to the serjeant-at-arms, holding his nose less than an inch from Sigglesthorne's. 'Oh, but it is, Master Sigglesthorne,' he hissed. 'Believe me, it is.' He turned to one of his men. 'Arnault! You know what to do.'

'Yes, sir.' Arnault crossed to the front door and opened it. Kemp froze but Arnault did not emerge. Instead he began sawing at the leather hinges. 'Hold him down.'

Two of the men-at-arms kicked aside tables and stools, making a space in the middle of the rush-strewn floor. Then they grabbed Sigglesthorne and pinned him there on his back, his arms twisted beneath him.

'See if you can find a cauldron, Gerard,' ordered Arnault, and another man-at-arms stood up and disappeared into the kitchen. Arnault finished removing the door from its hinges and laid it on top of Sigglesthorne's body, so that only his head showed at one end. There was terror in the serjeant-at-law's eyes as he realised what they intended.

Gerard returned from the kitchen carrying a large cast-iron cauldron, and at Arnault's direction he placed it on the door. Sigglesthorne gasped at its weight.

De Chargny looked down at the serjeant-at-law. 'Uncomfortable, isn't it?' he remarked. 'Please believe me, it will get a great deal more uncomfortable before Arnault has finished. He is something of an artist when it comes to inflicting pain. I advise you to save yourself from a great deal of discomfort by giving me some satisfactory answers to my questions.'

Sweat had broken out on Sigglesthorne's brow. 'I wouldn't want to deprive Arnault of his pleasure,' he managed to gasp.

De Chargny shrugged. 'Continue,' he told Arnault.

'I saw a well at the back earlier,' Arnault told Gerard, who nodded and disappeared through the back door, returning presently with a pail of water. He handed it to Arnault, who grinned as he slowly poured the water into the cauldron, which Gerard and the other man-at-arms held steady. When the pail was empty, Arnault went out to refill it.

'Arnault will continue to pour water into the cauldron until your ribcage is crushed under the weight,' explained de Chargny. 'I've seen it happen, and I promise you it is not a sight to be relished. Who gave you the letter, Master Sigglesthorne?' he continued, as Arnault returned. 'To whom were you supposed to deliver it? King Edward himself, perhaps?'

'Go . . . to . . . hell!'

De Chargny nodded to Arnault who began slowly to empty the pail into the cauldron once more. He turned to Guilbert. 'What's keeping Baudet?'

'Louis, go and fetch Baudet,' ordered the squire.

Another man-at-arms headed for the front doorway. Kemp pressed himself flat against the side of the inn. Louis emerged from the now doorless entrance and glanced across to the horses, frowning. 'What the devil in hell?' he muttered under his breath. 'Where's Renaud got to now?'

He began to walk towards the far corner of the inn. Kemp pulled another arrow from his belt, nocking it to his bow and taking careful aim, all in one smooth movement. The shaft struck Louis midway between the shoulder-blades, and he fell with little more than a grunt.

Kemp looped his bow over his head and shoulders and crossed to where Louis lay, dragging his corpse out of sight to lie by Renaud's. Three down, seven to go, he told himself, but the odds were still stacked against him, and he had to act fast, before Sigglesthorne was crushed to death.

A scream came from inside the inn as the weight of water in the cauldron became unbearable.

Kemp fetched his own horse and Sigglesthorne's from behind the inn, tying their halters to the fence and untying the halters of the French soldiers' mounts. They were too well trained to run away, but he slapped them on the flanks, hissing at them as loudly as he dared and chasing them a hundred yards or so down the road.

He climbed up on to the roof of the stables, overlooked by a window at the back of the inn on the upper floor. The window was shuttered, but the flickering light of a burning brand trickled out through the cracks. Bracing his feet on the sloping roof of the stables, Kemp peered through the crack.

A man was searching the room, his back to the window. Kemp unlooped his bow and took another arrow from his belt before breaking open the shutters. The noise alerted the man and he turned as Kemp was nocking the arrow. He opened his mouth to cry out in alarm but Kemp put an arrow in it, killing him instantly. Then he clambered through the window and recovered his sword belt, buckling it around his waist. After draping his saddlebags around his neck, he crept down the stairs, nocking another arrow to his bow. He could hear de Chargny's voice, asking Sigglesthorne another question.

'Anyone who moves is a dead man!'

Everyone turned in surprise to see Kemp standing there, his bow drawn ready to shoot.

'Let him up,' ordered Kemp, nodding to where Sigglesthorne lay.

'I thought you said no one was to move,' said one of the Frenchmen, grinning. Kemp shot him in the eye. The others stared at the man as he seemed to hang there, his head transfixed by the arrow, before toppling to the ground. Then they reached for their swords but Kemp had already taken a fresh arrow from his belt and nocked it with astounding swiftness.

'Does anyone else want to play the jackass?' he demanded.

'Put down your weapon, Master Kemp,' de Chargny said evenly. 'You'll never get away with this.'

'Like I didn't get away with it at Saint-Omer, you mean?' asked Kemp. 'Hold your tongue, de Chargny, else my next shaft has your name carved on it. Let him up and free his hands,' he added to Arnault. 'Now! Otherwise your master dies where he stands.'

Arnault glanced towards de Chargny, who gave a barely perceptible nod. Arnault, Gerard and the other two men-at-arms manhandled the cauldron to one side. Then they pulled the door off Sigglesthorne, helped him to his feet, and began to untie his hands.

Kemp suddenly turned his bow on Guilbert. 'Try it, you whoreson!' he snapped. 'Just God-damned try it, I beg you!' Much to his disappointment, Guilbert stopped reaching for the iron poker propped up beside the hearth.

Freed, Sigglesthorne rubbed chafed wrists, wincing at the pain in his arms where they had been twisted under his body. 'Can you ride?' asked Kemp. The serjeant-at-law nodded. 'Our horses are tied up outside. Don't wait for me.' As Sigglesthorne hurried to the doorway, Kemp nodded towards the far corner of the room. 'I want the rest of you to clasp your hands behind your heads and move into that corner. Bunch up nice and tight now, there's plenty of room for all of you.'

Kemp circled around them towards the doorway, not turning his back on any of them for an instant or even relaxing his draw on his bow. He backed out of the doorway, shot one of the men – it was quicker than removing the arrow from the string – and ran across to where Sigglesthorne was mounting his palfrey, looping his bow across his shoulders. Unfastening his hackney's halter, he swung himself into the saddle, and the two of them dug their heels into their horses' flanks, galloping off up the road just as de Chargny and his men emerged from the inn.

Arnault, Gerard and the remaining man-at-arms were armed with crossbows, but it took them several seconds to span, cock and load their weapons, by which time Sigglesthorne and Kemp were already approaching the edge of the clearing. The three crossbowmen loosed bolts after them. Sigglesthorne's palfrey stumbled, pitching the serjeant-at-law on to the road. The horse rolled over, and did not get up again, moaning eerily as it thrashed its legs in the air. Dazed, Sigglesthorne staggered to his feet while the three crossbowmen hurried to reload their weapons.

Conscious that Sigglesthorne was no longer alongside him, Kemp reined in his hackney and wheeled it, riding back to where the serjeant-at-law was stumbling down the road after him. He helped Sigglesthorne climb up behind him on the hackney, and they rode into the shadow of the trees.

'What in hell was all that about?' Kemp shouted over his shoulder.

'De Chargny seemed to think we were following him, spying on his movements,' replied Sigglesthorne, his arms wrapped about Kemp's midriff as he hung on for dear life. 'Then one of his men found a letter which the Count del Fiesco gave to me to give to some canon at Westminster. Something about de Chargny plotting to recapture Calais?'

There was no time for disbelief. 'Someone has to warn the king,' Kemp decided. 'And with de Chargny and his men close behind us, neither of us is going to make it if we share a horse.'

'It can't be more than ten miles to Paris,' said Sigglesthorne. 'We can soon lose him in the streets of the city.'

Kemp shook his head. 'We'll never make it,' he said, reining in the hackney. 'De Chargny and his men will overtake us before we even get halfway.' He swung one leg over the horse's neck, and jumped down to the surface of the road. 'One will stand a better chance if the other remains here to hold up de Chargny. You've a better chance of getting the king's ear, and a better chance of being believed.'

'What about you?' asked Sigglesthorne, climbing forward over the cantle of the saddle and into its seat.

Kemp unlooped his bow. 'I know what I'm doing. Go on, you're wasting time!' He slapped the horse's rump with the horn of his bow. Sigglesthorne dug in his heels, and set off at a gallop once more.

Kemp hurried into the undergrowth at the roadside. He had not chosen this place to make a stand without thinking. Thick woods crowded on either side. If de Chargny was in pursuit – and Kemp did not doubt that he would be – he would have to come through here. Kemp stood where the bracken reached up to his shoulders, at a point where he could keep a fair stretch of the road covered. Even if de Chargny decided to go around the ambush rather than along the killing ground that Kemp hoped the road would soon become, he would find travelling through the woods at night such heavy going that Sigglesthorne could be sure of reaching the safety of Paris's mazy streets long before de Chargny could catch him.

Bracing his back against the bole of the tree, he checked his arrows: six left. He planted five in the ground at his feet and nocked the sixth to his bow. By his reckoning there were still four men left with de Chargny, which did not give him much of a margin for error.

He did not have to wait long before he heard the sound of approaching hoofbeats. Peering through the gloom, he strained to catch sight of the horsemen. His eyes were beginning to adjust to the darkness and the white patches on their livery showed up quite clearly despite an almost starless night.

They rode at a gallop. Kemp waited until they were a hundred yards away before loosing, aiming at one of the white patches. He did not stop to see if his arrow had found a target, but immediately nocked another. They were still coming on . . . no, there were only four mounted now. A dark shape lay in the road behind them, and one of the others was wheeling his horse.

'Guy's down!'

The other two reined in at a signal from de Chargny, halting less than twenty yards from where Kemp was concealed. Recognising de Chargny's voice, Kemp took aim. De Chargny was the leader, and Kemp had always been taught to aim for the leader. The knight clapped a hand to his head and slid over sideways, falling from the saddle to land in the road.

'Sir Geoffroi's down!'

Kemp loosed again, this time hitting a horse which reared up with a whinny of agony, throwing its rider from the saddle.

'It's an ambush!' De Chargny's voice was calm despite the tension and confusion. 'Make for cover! Get out of sight!'

Those men still on horseback dismounted and ran for the trees on either side of the road, leaving their horses to fend for themselves. Kemp did not loose. He only had three arrows left now and, if de Chargny's wound were not serious, then he had four men to deal with.

Kemp thought of the king, defending an ornamental bridge in that carefully choreographed passage-at-arms at Windsor Castle over eighteen months ago. This was a real passage-at-arms, one man defending a narrow defile against all comers, except here the losers would not walk away to enjoy a banquet with the victors later. People would talk of the king's passage-at-arms at Windsor for years to come; but would anyone remember Kemp's stand after he was dead? A single churl holding a road against five Frenchmen with his peasant's weapon? There was no honour or glory here, just death waiting in the shadows of the forest. But Kemp had the consolation of knowing that if he could hold de Chargny and his men here long enough, Sigglesthorne might just get back to England in time to warn the king of the plot to take Calais. Was it worth it? He had to die some time and, regardless of whether or not he was ready to give his life for his king, the decision had been made.

All was still and quiet in the lane, apart from the five horses which moved about skittishly, sensing something was wrong. The one which Kemp had wounded lay down to die, its breath snorting raggedly between its lips. The cry of a whippoorwill sounded not far away.

'Sir Geoffroi?' The voice came suddenly out of the darkness, startling Kemp. The speaker was no more than twenty yards away. Kemp froze, hardly daring even to breathe. 'Are you injured?'

'I'm all right,' replied de Chargny from further down the road. 'Just scratched, that's all.'

Kemp tried to use the sound of their voices to locate them but, like him, they were too well concealed in the undergrowth and shadows.

'Where are the arrows coming from?'

'Up ahead somewhere,' replied another voice. 'No more than thirty yards.'

'How many of them are there?' asked the first voice, bringing a smile to Kemp's lips.

'It's only Kemp, you fool,' de Chargny called. 'He's trying to keep us pinned down here, while Sigglesthorne gets away.'

Kemp had to fight the urge to call out that he was succeeding; he could not afford to give them any clues as to where he was hidden.

'He isn't shooting at the sound of our voices,' called de Chargny. 'He must be running out of arrows. Gerard! Come here.'

There was a rustle in the undergrowth, and a few fronds of bracken shivered. Kemp toyed with the idea of shooting into them, but with so few arrows left he could not risk using any unless he was sure of a kill. He could hear the muted sound of whispering from about thirty yards in front of him.

'Kemp!' De Chargny's voice again, trying to draw him into

revealing his location by responding. 'I know you can hear me, Kemp!'

Kemp said nothing, his eyes constantly scanning the darkness for any hint of movement.

'How long are you planning to keep us pinned down here, Kemp?' persisted de Chargny.

*As long as it takes, you God-damned whoreson*, Kemp thought to himself.

'We'll get you sooner or later, Kemp. There are four of us, and only one of you. How many arrows have you got left? You must have used at least four back at the inn. How many did you have to start with? A dozen?' De Chargny paused, listening to the silence of the woods. 'We've got crossbows, Kemp, and no shortage of bolts. Who do you think is going to win?' He paused again. 'It doesn't have to end with you dying, you know. You can surrender now with honour. You've given Master Sigglesthorne the head-start he needs. He's probably in Paris by now. There's no need for us all to spend the rest of the night here, no need for you to die. Throw your weapons into the road and show yourself. I promise you I'll spare your life on my word of honour as a man of gentle birth.'

*Kiss the devil's arse*, thought Kemp.

'What is it you want, Kemp? Gold? I can give you gold. Glory, perhaps? There's no glory to be won here. Do you really think that if you sacrifice your life here tonight any one will learn of it back in England? Is it really worth it? To die here, alone? Do you think your masters care whether or not you die? Of course not. They're using you, Kemp. To them you're just a means to an end . . .'

Kemp heard a twig snap a few feet to his right, and whirled around. Gerard stood there, loaded crossbow in hand. He had been advancing stealthily through the undergrowth, while Kemp had been distracted by de Chargny's sibilant tones. As Kemp turned, Gerard spotted the movement and brought up his crossbow, loosing too soon. Kemp heard the distinct click and twang of the crossbow's mechanism and, in almost the same instant, felt pain explode in his left thigh. Then the whole world was spinning, the ground rising up to meet him.

Gerard dropped his crossbow and drew a dagger from his belt. 'I've got him!'

Falling on his back on a mossy bank, Kemp realised he still had his longbow in his left hand and an arrow nocked to the string. He pushed the bowstave towards Gerard and let fly. He could not draw properly while sprawled on his back but at such short range it was impossible to miss. The Frenchman gasped as the arrow entered his stomach and the dagger in his hand slipped out of numb fingers. Staring at the feathered shaft protruding from his stomach, he sank to his knees. Reaching out towards Kemp with a hand twisted into a claw, he fell forward onto his face, driving the arrowhead right through him so that it emerged from his back.

Silence fell over the forest.

'Gerard?' de Chargny called uncertainly.

Kemp wriggled over to the nearest tree and sat with his back to it while he examined the stunted shaft stuck in his own thigh. He explored the wound tentatively with his fingers and immediately regretted it, sinking his teeth deep into his own hand to stop himself from crying out with pain. The head of the bolt was barbed: if he tried to pull it out, half of the flesh and sinew in his thigh would come with it.

'Kemp? Are you still there?'

Kemp glanced towards the road. Even from where he sat he could see the four horses clearly. A plan began to form in his mind.

'Are you wounded, Kemp? I heard Gerard say he'd got you; and Gerard rarely makes mistakes.'

*He made one tonight*, thought Kemp, crawling over to where Gerard had dropped his crossbow, dragging his left leg behind him. He picked up the crossbow and then moved over to Gerard's body to search for his quiver. After pulling out a fistful of bolts, he hauled himself back to the tree.

During the siege of Calais, Kemp had had plenty of opportunities to examine crossbows taken from Genoese captives and he was familiar with their mechanisms. He fixed the spanning-hook to his belt and placed his right foot in the stirrup, pushing the crossbow away from him so the string was drawn back until it caught on the ratchet of the loosing mechanism. Placing one of the bolts in the groove, he then carefully put the crossbow to one side, ready to use.

Next he picked up his bow and his two remaining arrows, and rose unsteadily to his feet, using the bole of the tree to support himself. He could barely put any weight on his left leg, which would not make shooting his longbow any easier, but he had to try. He nocked an arrow, took aim and let fly. The arrow sped home, plunging deep into the chest of one of the horses. It gave a ghastly, eldritch scream before falling. Kemp took a second arrow and shot another horse, fatally wounding it.

'What's he doing?' asked one of the others; either Guilbert or Arnault, by a process of elimination.

'Shooting the horses,' said de Chargny. 'He doesn't want us to ride back for reinforcements.'

De Chargny was always so self-assured that it was a great relief to hear him misguess; to know that even he could make mistakes. Kemp pulled his bow-bag over his longbow and slung it across his back. Then he lowered himself to the ground, picked up the crossbow, and pushed himself back to his feet, fighting the pain of his wound every inch of the way. His leg was sticky with blood.

Only two horses stood in the lane now, Guilbert's rouncy and de Chargny's palfrey. Kemp aimed the crossbow at the rouncy and pulled the trigger. The rouncy seemed to stagger, retreat, and then keeled over as if drunk with a startled neigh.

Kemp had left de Chargny's horse not because it was the finest beast there, and probably the fastest, but because it stood cropping the grass at the edge of the road only a few yards from where he leant against the tree. A couple of yards that might as well have been a couple of miles, considering the state Kemp's leg was in. He took a deep breath, and propelled himself towards the horse.

It was the longest five yards Kemp ever had to cover in his entire life. Half-limping, half-hopping, he staggered out of the undergrowth and seized the palfrey's bridle, moving around the side of it so its body was between him and where he guessed de Chargny, Guilbert and Arnault were hidden. With one hand on the pommel of the saddle to steady himself, he raised his right leg and thrust at the stirrup. His left leg almost gave way underneath him, and in his panic his right foot missed the stirrup. He saw Guilbert and Arnault emerge from the undergrowth about twenty-five yards down the road.

At last Kemp managed to get his foot into the stirrup. Arnault was holding a loaded crossbow, aiming at him. Guilbert had drawn his sword and was charging forwards. He swung his left leg over the horse's rump, ignoring the excruciating pain. The movement was so agonising he felt himself swaying in the saddle, and struggled to maintain his slender grasp on consciousness.

Arnault loosed. Kemp felt the wind as the bolt whistled past his head, only inches away. He reached down and grabbed his left ankle with his hand, guiding it into the stirrup. Arnault was struggling to reload the crossbow. Guilbert was only ten yards away now. De Chargny emerged from the trees, shouting something incomprehensible.

With a final effort, Kemp dug in his heels, gripping the reins tightly. The horse reared, threatening to throw him from the saddle, but Kemp was not ready to relinquish something he had gained with such difficulty. Guilbert drew level, swinging his arm back to slash with his sword at Kemp. Then the horse bounded forward, breaking at once into a gallop. Guilbert's stroke went wide and he almost over-balanced. Arnault finally succeeded in loading another bolt in his crossbow but Kemp was already more than fifty yards away and the shot came nowhere near him. Both horse and rider disappeared northwards, fading into the darkness, leaving only the sound of hoofbeats in their wake.

Arnault threw down his crossbow, swearing. Guilbert rammed his sword back into its scabbard with a grunt of frustration.

Walking down the road to join them, de Chargny glanced towards Gerard's body, which lay partly hidden amongst the bracken, and to Guy's corpse sprawled along with the four dead or dying horses. The three of them would have to walk back to the inn, where they had left the rest of the horses.

'It seems I severely underestimated that young man,' de Chargny observed. It was not a mistake he intended to make again.

'Master Kemp, perhaps you can enlighten us as to whether or not Aquinas's error in failing to recognise the inherent contradictions between reason and revelation are reflected in his commentary on Peter Lombard's *Book of Sentences*, with particular reference to Abelard's *Sic et Non* and his question "Is faith based upon reason"?'

Glancing up from his lectern at the front of a cold lecture hall illuminated by only two candles, Jean de Savoisy, Doctor of Sacred Theology, smiled at his most promising pupil, a young graduate of Oxford University whose scholarship had so impressed a wealthy local clergyman that he had been granted a bursary to help him overcome the fact that he was too poor to pay for his own further education.

Nicholas Kemp rose from his stool, ignoring whispers of 'lecturer's lap-dog' and 'English pig' from his classmates, and began to answer the question in a voice which, though high and reedy, had all the confidence of erudite scholarship behind it. He was precocious even by the standards of his own classmates, begging, borrowing and occasionally even stealing books from his tutors and lecturers to feed his voracious appetite for learning.

Dark-haired like his elder brother Michael, Nicholas shared his younger brother's height but lacked his breadth of shoulder. His face was pale from too much time spent in libraries or in his own chamber, reading. As a child he had never enjoyed fresh air, and any attempts to introduce him to it usually resulted in him catching a cold.

Nicholas had been the runt of the brood. His parents had always been surprised that, unlike his two sisters, he had survived his first year of life. It had always been obvious he would never make a good farmer: he was too much of a weakling and too much of a dreamer. An over-protective mother – still crushed by the death of her second daughter – had persuaded his father to let him go to the local almonry school. Nicholas might be a poor prospect as a farmer, but at least if he gained an education he might be able to supplement the family's meagre income by going into some lettered profession.

At the end of the seminar the students filed out of the hall, paying the lecturer for the education they had received that day. Only Nicholas did not have to pay, because his fees were covered by his bursary. To his fellow students it seemed as if he was receiving his education for free. He often pointed out to them that, if they did not spend so much of their money on wine and women, paying for education would be less of a drain on their finances. But they laughed in his face and replied that it was education that was interfering with their debauchery and not vice versa.

Nicholas lingered until all the others had left the hall before he approached de Savoisy and handed him a parcel wrapped in muslin. 'Thank you for today's lesson, Doctor de Savoisy,' he said with a bow.

De Savoisy unwrapped the parcel and found it contained a plucked capon. 'Why, that's very generous of you, Nicholas. Are you certain you can afford such a splendid gift?'

Nicholas nodded. His bursary included a board and lodging allowance that would have fed a hearty eater, and Nicholas was a long way from being that. This enabled him to save up enough money to purchase gifts for his tutors and, occasionally, theological text books. 'Did you read my essay "In praise of the flagellants"?'

De Savoisy's face grew dark. 'I burned it,' he told Nicholas. 'For your own good. And you will be wise never to mention it again, nor to repeat the opinions expressed within it.'

Nicholas was hurt. 'But why? What was wrong with it?' He had thought it his best piece of work so far, well-thought-out and drawing on a wealth of scriptural authority.

'There was nothing wrong with it,' admitted de Savoisy, as the two of them left the lecture hall and began to cross the courtyard. 'Except that it contradicted the University's call for the suppression of those masters of error. Did you not know that Pope Clement himself has now come out and condemned the flagellants for their heresy?'

'I had heard there were criticisms of the sect, Doctor, but I thought . . .'

'Sometimes it it best to keep one's thoughts to oneself. It was a good essay, Nicholas, and well-argued, I'll grant you that; but the flagellants have been condemned as subversive to the authority of the Church. Even King Philip himself has now forbidden public flagellation on pain of death. If the views you expressed in your essay were to become public knowledge, it would mean an end to your hopes of a career in the Church; perhaps even a trial on charges of heresy.' Nicholas blanched. 'I suggest you learn to keep abreast of current theological opinion as well as those ancient texts you so frequently bury your nose in.'

Nicholas hung his head. 'I have been foolish, Doctor. Please forgive me for my error.'

De Savoisy smiled. 'Not foolish. Rather let us say you were – careless. Now, we'll say no more about it. You've a promising career ahead of you, unless I'm very much mistaken. One day you may even become an abbot, provided you can find some noble sponsor.'

'But how can I do that? I am but a pauper of humble origins, from a country where the Papacy is held in contempt and ridicule.'

'God will provide a way, so long as your faith in Him is strong. Remember: greater men than you were born in humbler circumstances,' he added. 'As for your native land; well, no one can help where they are born. I think people will learn to judge you by where you decide your allegiances lie, rather than the accident of your birth, if you understand me.'

They took their leave of one another, and Nicholas was heading in the direction of his garret when the college gatekeeper approached, calling his name. 'Master Kemp! There's someone to see you.'

'Someone to see me?' Nicholas replied in bewilderment. In the sixteen months he had lived in Paris, no one had ever come to see him. He knew no one in the city apart from his tutors and his fellow students. 'Who is it?'

'A young man, sir. An Englishman, I think. He seemed to be ill.'

'The pestilence?'

The gatekeeper shook his head. 'I do not think so.'

'His name?'

'He would not say.'

Nicholas followed the gatekeeper back to the college entrance, overlooking the Rue Saint Victor in the University quarter on the south bank of the Seine. The man who waited for him was leaning against one of the pillars that supported the gates as if he were too weak to support himself. He was tall, dressed in a black cloak, the cowl raised against the chill November air.

'That's him, Master Kemp.'

The man turned and glanced up at the mention of the name. Nicholas did not immediately recognise the pale and haggard face that stared at him out of the cowl; it had been three and a half years since he last saw it, and those years had not been kind. 'You wish to see me?' he asked coldly.

The face bared its teeth at him in a savage grin. 'Hullo, Nicholay,' said his younger brother, and then he collapsed as his left leg gave way beneath him once more.

'I've removed the bolt, applied some *sang d'amour* and bound it up with fresh bandages,' said the surgeon, as he left Nicholas's garret. 'He should be all right.'

'What's *sang d'amour*?' asked Nicholas.

'The blood of a maiden of twenty taken at the full moon in Virgo, mixed with myrrh, aloes, dragon's blood and powder of alkanet, boiled up with olive oil,' the surgeon explained, adding with a leer: 'I had to use red powder as a substitute for maiden's blood, of course, maidens of twenty being rather hard to come by these days.'

Nicholas wrinkled his nose in distaste at the jest. 'Will he be able to walk again?'

'Oh, yes. The bolt went through the fleshy part of his thigh, and should heal nicely, so long as it is rested.' The surgeon peered at where someone had daubed the words '*Cochon Anglais*' on Nicholas's door, and frowned. 'Don't let him out of bed for a few days, and tell him to take it easy for a couple of weeks. There's always a risk the wound may go bad, in which case you should call me immediately and I'll come round and bleed him. But don't worry. Your friend is strong: he'll survive.'

Nicholas grimaced. 'The last time I saw him he was in a cell waiting to be hanged; the last thing I heard, he was dead of the pestilence. Surviving seems to be something of a talent of his.'

The surgeon nodded absently. Mention of the pestilence always embarrassed him, for he knew no cure for it. 'That'll be fifteen *moutons*, please.'

Nicholas had already taken the precaution of looking after his brother's purse while the surgeon examined his leg, and now he took fifteen gold coins from it. 'You, ah . . . you will be discreet about this, won't you?' he asked, wondering how long he could keep a man in his chamber with a crossbow wound a secret.

'Discretion is the byword of my profession, Master Kemp. Physicians and surgeons are like the three wise monkeys; hear no evil, see no evil, speak no evil. Of course, it couldn't do you any harm to make sure of my silence . . .'

Nicholas gave him another five gold coins, almost emptying his brother's purse; he only held back a couple of coins to cover the expenses he would incur if he was to feed his brother for the next few days. He certainly had no intention of allowing Martin to stay any longer than was absolutely necessary.

The surgeon bowed away, and then turned and descended the narrow wooden staircase that led up to Nicholas's garret.

Nicholas returned inside the cramped room. Kemp was sitting up in the large bed which Nicholas had had to share with two roommates until the pestilence carried them off; God's punishment for their sinfulness, Nicholas had no doubt. A tiny dormer window of translucent waxed parchment let in more cold than light, and there was no fire in the grate. A single table was piled with books.

It was an awkward moment. Neither of them knew what to say; they had detested one another as children, and they had hardly parted on the best of terms. Kemp had been in gaol, awaiting execution for a rape and murder of which he was innocent, and Nicholas had refused to listen to his protestations, sneering that his brother was at last receiving his just deserts.

'You heard about mother?' Nicholas asked at last.

Kemp nodded. 'And Simkin, Thomas Croft and the others. I visited the village last autumn.'

'And where were you at the time?' snorted Nicholas. 'You become a soldier, and yet the one time you could have turned your evil ways to good use, you are not there. Instead you chose to spend a year in London to escape your villeinage.'

'Hold your God-damned tongue!' snarled Kemp. 'Don't you think I haven't thought of that? Don't you think I haven't lain awake at nights tortured by such thoughts? Even if I had been there, do you think things would have been any different? I'd've just been killed along with Croft and the others.'

Nicholas scowled. 'Perhaps it would have been no more than you deserved.'

'I never even knew of that lady I was supposed to have raped and murdered, Nicholay.'

'Perhaps not,' allowed Nicholas. 'But how many wicked deeds did you perform for the King of England during the war? And look at you now.' He gestured at Kemp's bandaged thigh. 'How came you to this pass?'

Kemp rubbed his temples wearily. 'I'm working for Sir Thomas Holland now. I was sent to act as a bodyguard for a serjeant-at-law who was travelling to the Papal Court at Avignon . . .'

'You've been to the Papal Court?' asked Nicholas. To him, Avignon remained the seat of Christianity, a holy place of holy men, the well-spring of the Church which he loved; the closest thing to heaven on earth. That his impious brother should have been privileged enough to visit the city filled him with jealousy and resentment.

Kemp nodded. 'On our way back we were attacked by a French knight called Sir Geoffroi de Chargny. He's plotting to take Calais back for France. We have to warn the king . . .'

Nicholas frowned. 'King Philip?'

Kemp stared at his brother in astonishment. 'King Edward!'

'What for? Calais is a French town. Let the French have it.'

'But when the war breaks out afresh, we'll need Calais as a bridgehead from which to strike at Paris . . .'

Nicholas shook his head. 'Martin, can't you see King Edward's war is wrong? He has no claim on the throne of France. The French succession is governed by Salic Law – it cannot pass through a female line.'

'No loyal Englishman would say such things, Nicholay,' growled Kemp. 'Certainly no brother of mine would say such things.'

'And how do you think I feel, that *my* brother has become a man of war, plying the trade of violence? There is supposed to be a truce between our kings, and yet here you are with a crossbow wound in your leg, making war on some French nobleman . . .'

'If anyone's making war, it's de Chargny,' protested Kemp. 'And what do you mean, "our" kings? Valois is no king of mine.'

Nicholas sighed. 'I can see we are never going to agree on this matter, so there is little point to our argument. Have you eaten recently?'

'Not since yesterday morn.'

'I had best get us some food.'

Kemp reached for the purse at his belt. 'You'd better let me . . .' he began, and then saw it sagging emptily in Nicholas's hand. Blushing, Nicholas stumbled out of the room.

Kemp listened to his brother's feet clumping down the wooden staircase, and then laid his head back on the pillow with a sigh, closing his eyes. He had had no sleep the previous night, and was half-fainting from loss of blood by the time he reached Paris at dawn. He had entered the city from the south, which chanced to place him in the University quarter. There he had found a bookseller setting up his stall on the Grande Rue Saint-Jacques, and asked for directions to the Sorbonne College.

Even as sleep began to creep over him, he was planning his next move. Sigglesthorne was probably riding towards Calais already but, with de Chargny searching for him, there was no guarantee that he would be able to warn the English in time. Kemp still felt it was his duty to do everything in his power to warn the king. He had overheard the surgeon telling Nicholas he was not to be allowed out of bed for a few days; well, he would see about that.

How long he slept he did not know but he was awoken before he was ready when the door suddenly crashed open. He opened his eyes and watched groggily as two men squeezed into the room. Men-at-arms, their swords drawn. Kemp reached for his own sword, propped up beside the bed, but one of the men-at-arms kicked it beyond his reach while the other levelled the point of his blade at Kemp's throat.

'Don't move, Englishman, or you'll die where you lie!'

A pale-faced Nicholas entered the room next, and Kemp stared at him. 'Nicholay? What's going on?'

'I'm sorry, Martin, but I had to do it.' Nicholas stepped aside to allow the next man to enter.

Sir Geoffroi de Chargny ducked his head as he crossed over the threshold, followed by Guilbert. There was a faint smile of triumph on de Chargny's face.

Kemp stared first at his foe and then at Nicholas. Suddenly it all became clear. He had been betrayed by his own brother.

'You lousy God-damned treacherous bastard!' he shouted, launching himself from the bed, his hands reaching for Nicholas's throat. Guilbert interposed himself, lifting his knee into Kemp's stomach and bringing a fist down against the back of his head. Kemp's left shoulder hit the floor, his feet still entangled in the bedclothes, and a spasm of pain shot from the wound in his thigh as his leg twisted against the edge of the bed. He saw Guilbert's foot swinging towards his head, bright lights flashed inside his skull, and he was engulfed by thick darkness.

# CHAPTER FOURTEEN

TYPHAINE WAS DRAWING water from the well in the courtyard of the castle at Saint-Omer when she heard a cry from the other side of the castle walls and hoofbeats echoing against the beams of the lowered drawbridge. She glanced up in time to see the twin portcullises being raised and watched de Chargny ride through with Guilbert and Arnault. The last of the three pulled a fourth horse behind him with something slung across its back. The men reined in in the middle of the courtyard and dismounted, Guilbert leading his own horse and his master's across to the stables.

Typhaine realised with a shock that the object slung across the back of the fourth horse was a man. She ran over to examine him. 'Sir Geoffroi! Is he dead?'

'Get away from there!' snapped Arnault, seeing her raise Kemp's head.

'Arnault!' De Chargny strode to where the man-at-arms stood, and slapped him back-handed. 'You will not address Typhaine in such a rude manner.'

Flushing, Arnault raised a hand to his stinging cheek. 'Aye, my lord,' he said, turning away so the knight would not see his scowl.

Everyone in the castle knew Typhaine had become de Chargny's mistress – her new accommodation in a garret in the keep was tacit acknowledgement of the fact – and, while no one would have dared to admit the fact in the knight's presence, there was nonetheless a feeling she should be treated as the lady of the castle. Most accepted it, but a few, like Arnault, knowing of her humble origins, resented her peculiar status.

When he was in residence at the castle, de Chargny visited Typhaine with mechanical regularity, once a week. If she did not gain pleasure from it, nor did she suffer physical pain; but each time he was as indifferent to her as he had been the first time. She knew he did not see her as a person, but as an object – he lavished more affection on his hawks – and for that reason she had begun to dread his visits, knowing they would leave her feeling diminished and worthless.

De Chargny crossed to where Typhaine stood, trying to revive Kemp with cold water. 'Come away from him,' he said. 'He is dangerous.'

She looked first at de Chargny, and then back at Kemp, studying his dirty and unshaven features, pale beneath the grime. He reminded her of one of a troop of English men-at-arms who had occupied her village in Brittany when she was twelve, in the early months of the Breton Civil War. The English soldier had terrified her at first, but then he won her over by carving her a doll out of chunks of wood, cunningly interlocking the pieces so the limbs were articulated. Since she left Brittany with her husband she had heard people talk of the English as if they were devils, with cloven hooves for feet, and tails, but she knew they were ordinary humans.

She tried not to smile. 'Dangerous?'

He nodded. 'He is an English spy.'

'I thought the war was over.'

'Until it starts again. In the meantime, King Edward's spies would dearly love to learn our secrets.' He turned to Guilbert, who was emerging from the stables, and indicated Kemp. 'Put him in the dungeon.'

Typhaine watched as Guilbert and Arnault hauled the Englishman off the horse's back, each taking an arm and dragging him across to the keep. He was starting to revive now and was trying to support himself, although from the way he hobbled it was clear he was hurt.

'He's wounded!'

'Save your pity,' de Chargny told her coldly. 'He killed seven of my men.'

Ten days later de Chargny and Sir Oudard de Renty stepped out on to the battlements of the castle and gazed over the rooftops of Saint-Omer to the market place, where Sir Eustache de Ribeaumont was marshalling the troops they were assembling for the attack on Calais. 'How many?' asked de Chargny.

'Eighty knights, five hundred men-at-arms and twenty-three hundred foot-soldiers,' replied de Renty. 'Sir Robert de Fiennes should be here before the week is out with another twenty knights, one hundred men-at-arms and seven hundred foot-soldiers.' He gave de Chargny a sidelong glance. 'Do you think it will be enough?'

'Against the garrison of Calais?' De Chargny's face twisted into a sneer of contempt. 'We have enough men to take the town by storm, let alone by stealth with de Pavia to open the gates for us.'

'Supposing the English reinforce the garrison between now and New Year's Eve?'

'Why should they? The truce has been extended until well into next year. They are not expecting any trouble.'

'Supposing Sigglesthorne tells them of our plans?'

'Sigglesthorne knows nothing,' asserted de Chargny.

'We do not know that for certain.'

De Chargny shrugged. 'Then we shall find out.'

The two men made their way into the great hall of the castle, where de Chargny ordered a page to pour them both a goblet of wine. 'Tell Arnault to prepare the prisoner for questioning,' he added. The page nodded, and bowed out of the hall.

A few minutes later de Chargny and de Renty, attended by Guilbert, walked down to the dungeons in the cellars of the keep. The dungeons were illuminated by burning brands set in wall brackets which gave off a noxious smoke. Arnault was already waiting for them and gestured to where Kemp stood with his hands bound behind his back. He was ragged and filthy from his incarceration, with two weeks' growth of beard on his chin. Despite the odds, the wound in his thigh had almost healed, leaving only an ugly scar.

'Master Kemp is a good deal stronger than Sigglesthorne,' de Chargny observed. 'But I doubt we will be interrupted here, as we were at the inn.' He crossed the room to face Kemp. 'I want you to tell me everything you know of our plans.'

'I know naught of your plans,' said Kemp.

'Then why risk your life to ensure that Sigglesthorne got away?' demanded de Chargny. 'You must have felt that he had enough information to make it imperative that he get back to England. Exactly what did the two of you know?'

'Nothing,' insisted Kemp. 'We were going to the Papal Court to plead there. We knew naught of any plans of yours.'

'I find that hard to believe. You forget that I have already seen you acting as a spy for the English. Then an incriminating letter was found in Master Sigglesthorne's saddlebags. Tell me, Kemp: who gave him that letter?'

'I don't know,' Kemp said wearily.

De Chargny turned to Arnault. 'Put him on the *chevalet*.'

The word meant nothing to Kemp. Arnault dragged him across to a stout wooden framework with a roller at either end. He untied Kemp's wrists, and at once Kemp tried to hit him. But Arnault was expecting the attempt and dodged it easily, driving a fist into Kemp's kidneys. Kemp sank to his knees with a gasp, and Arnault hauled him up by the hair, throwing him down across the framework. Two cords were attached to each roller, and Arnault tied the ends of these to Kemp's wrists and ankles.

Now Kemp knew what they had in store for him. He had heard tales of how the Holy Inquisition extracted confessions of heresy from its victims by the use of devices like this, known in England as 'the rack'.

Arnault inserted an iron bar in a hole at the end of one of the rollers, and began to pull on it. The two rollers moved together, interconnected by a series of ropes and pulleys, taking up the slack on the ropes binding Kemp. He felt the cords bite into his flesh, and grunted as his shoulders took the strain.

De Chargny looked down at him. 'Let us take this one step at a time. What were you really doing in Avignon?'

'I was there to protect Master Sigglesthorne.'

'From whom?'

'Brigands.'

'Where did the letter come from?'

'I don't know anything about a letter.'

De Chargny nodded to Arnault, who hauled on the iron lever once more. The ropes cut into Kemp again, and his body was lifted clear of the beams. He cried out in pain, beads of sweat breaking out on his forehead.

'Where did the letter come from?' repeated de Chargny.

'I told you, I don't know anything about any God-damned letter.'

At another nod from de Chargny, Arnault leant on the lever with all his weight. Kemp screamed at the excruciating pain. His arms and legs felt as though they were being torn from their sockets.

'Where did the letter come from?'

'Kiss the devil's arse,' he gasped.

Arnault pushed again. The agony was such that Kemp found himself sobbing.

'Where did the letter come from?' hissed de Chargny, holding his face close to Kemp's.

Kemp spat in his face. The Frenchman straightened, fastidiously wiping the spittle from his face with a sleeve, and then nodded to Arnault once more. Arnault braced his feet and pulled the lever this time, hanging from it until Kemp's arms and legs exploded with searing pain that made him scream. Finally the agony became so intense he fainted.

'Throw a bucket of water over him,' ordered de Chargny.

Arnault left the dungeon and fetched a pail of ice-cold water from the courtyard well. Returning, he tipped it all into Kemp's face. Kemp awoke with a spasm, coughing and spluttering. De Chargny crouched over him so that he could murmur in his ear. 'We're not in any hurry, Kemp. We can keep this up until your arms are torn from your body, and then we can get to work on your legs. Now, where did the letter come from?'

'Kiss the devil's arse, you God-damned whoreson!'

De Chargny backed away, turning to Guilbert. 'Help him,' he ordered.

Guilbert stood beside Arnault, and the two of them grasped the lever, hauling on it with all their might. Kemp stared across at the flickering flames of a firebrand that guttered fitfully in a wall-bracket, focusing all his attention on it, anything to block out the intense agony in his limbs. It was indescribable, driving everything else out of his mind, even his own name. Much more of this, and he was sure he would go mad.

'I do have some idea of what you're going through,' said de Chargny, almost sounding sympathetic. 'Imagine what it will be like, to have no arms?' He smiled. 'It might make it difficult for you to fend for yourself. You'll no longer be able to use a bow or a sword. You'll no longer be able to do anything except beg. You won't even be able to feed yourself. Is is really worth it, just to defend the interests of your king?'

Kemp thought of Lowesby, reduced to begging on the streets of

London by his crippling injury. 'I've already told you everything I know,' he sobbed.

Even de Renty was beginning to appear uncomfortable at this spectacle. 'Perhaps he is telling the truth . . .'

De Chargny looked at him. 'I don't care,' he said simply, before turning back to Arnault. 'Continue.'

'De Chargny is planning to recapture Calais, I tell you!' insisted Sigglesthorne. 'You have to reinforce the garrison, before it is too late!'

'It took the king eleven months to take this town. What makes you think de Chargny can take it in one day?'

'I don't know. But de Chargny seems to think he can, and he's no dreamer. One brave young man has already sacrificed his life so this intelligence may reach England. How many more will die when his sacrifice proves to have been in vain?'

Amerigo de Pavia turned from the window in his chamber which overlooked the harbour of Calais to face Sigglesthorne. The Lombard was sweating profusely despite the cold December air. 'I believe you, Master Sigglesthorne. But I must know more. How did you come by this information?'

Sigglesthorne shook his head. 'I promised not to say. The men concerned are loyal agents of King Edward. I cannot compromise them by revealing their names.'

De Pavia smiled. 'You can tell me. I too am a loyal servant of his Majesty.'

Sigglesthorne opened his mouth and then shut it again. 'Who they are does not matter. I did not even see the contents of the letter for myself, but it does not matter; I have had confirmation from the lips of de Chargny himself.'

'What do you mean?'

'He took me prisoner at an inn a few miles to the south of Paris. When his men searched my saddlebags and found the letter, de Chargny asked me what I knew of his plan to recapture Calais. Up until that moment I had not even known there *was* a plan.'

'You do not have details of the plan? A date? A time? A method of attack?'

'Is it not enough we know such a plan exists? You can reinforce the garrison here and send out scouts to monitor changes in troop concentrations and spies to keep a close eye on de Chargny's activities.'

De Pavia shook his head. 'Sir Geoffroi is a knight who is well-respected on both sides of the Channel for his sense of honour and chivalry. I confess I find it hard to believe he would stoop to such underhand tactics as stealth and truce-breaking . . .'

'And torture,' put in Sigglesthorne, whose ribs were still bruised from his subjection to the torture of *peine forte et dure*. 'The damned rogue tortured me!'

'Are you sure it truly was Sir Geoffroi de Chargny and not some impostor?'

The Lombard's performance was so convincing Sigglesthorne began to question the sense of his own words. He only had Kemp's word for it that the knight was de Chargny. He shook his head. There was a plan to recapture Calais, and de Chargny was behind it; no other explanation made any sense. 'It was de Chargny,' he insisted.

'Fighting men often make plans like this,' de Pavia said dismissively. 'They dream of winning some great victory that will win the war for their liege, and thereby gain great honour. This talk of recapturing Calais is typical of such dreams. They never amount to anything. I'm certain it was nothing more than just talk.'

'So you're not going to do anything?'

'Naturally I shall request more reinforcements from England at the earliest opportunity,' said de Pavia. 'And of course I shall send out scouts to monitor the movements of French troops in the Pas-de-Calais. But purely as a precaution, you understand. I'm quite sure all this talk of retaking Calais is nothing more than that: just talk. I'm most grateful to you for coming to me with this intelligence; I'm certain you thought you were doing your king a great service. But believe me, these things are taken care of by men who know what they're doing. And please: don't go around Calais telling people that the French are going to attack the town. We are trying to repopulate Calais with English citizens, and a story such as yours might scare people away. We need a civilian population to support the garrison, otherwise the town might fall to the French without the need for any plot.'

Sigglesthorne nodded. 'I suppose you're right.'

'Of course I am, Master Sigglesthorne. You'll see. And even if de Chargny does decide to attack in force, he'll find the garrison is already a good deal stronger than it seems. In fact, it would amuse me to see him try such an assault.' He walked Sigglesthorne to the door of the chamber.

'I'm reassured to hear that,' said Sigglesthorne.

'My pleasure, Master Sigglesthorne. That is what I am here for: to defend Calais against the French. If you have any such concerns in the future, I don't want you to have any hesitation in bringing them to my attention.' De Pavia opened the door, and ordered the man-at-arms on guard outside to escort Sigglesthorne out of the castle.

As their footsteps echoed down the spiral staircase, de Pavia closed the door behind them, and wiped sweat from his brow with his sleeve. How the devil had that damned serjeant-at-law found out about de Chargny's plan? De Pavia considered returning to England and telling the king of de Chargny's plot himself; but if he betrayed de Chargny, he had no doubt that the French knight's revenge would be swift and terrible. What should he do? Perhaps he should travel to Saint-Omer to consult de Chargny: he would know what to do.

He stood in the middle of his chamber for several moments, gnawing indecisively on the knuckle of an index finger. Finally he made up his mind. He opened the door and shouted for a servant.

'Pack my bags,' he ordered. 'I'm going away for a day or two on important business.'

When Kemp regained consciousness he found himself lying in a huge four-poster bed with velvet drapes and silken sheets. It was such a contrast to the nightmarish horrors of the dungeon that for a moment his new surroundings seemed unreal.

He tried to sit up, and pain shot through his hips and shoulders. Ignoring it, he tossed aside the sheets and swung his legs out of the bed. The rattle of iron links should have warned him, but the chain attached to the collar around his neck brought him up painfully short before he understood its significance. He retched as the collar cut into his windpipe, and fell back across the bed.

'God damn it!' Sitting on the edge of the bed, he tugged at the chain. The other end was firmly bolted to the stone wall behind the head of the bed. He tried tugging it, but his sore and aching shoulders were not up to the task of pulling the bracket from the masonry. He glanced around the room. It was large, with tapestries hanging from the walls, glass windows, and rugs on the floor; the bedchamber of a nobleman.

He needed to relieve himself, and was about to do so over the rugs by the bed when a thought occurred to him. Peering under the bed, he found a pottery chamber-pot, and used that instead. He chuckled: here he was, a prisoner in France, and he was living in finer style than he had ever known in England.

The door opened and a young woman entered, her black hair hanging down across her forehead in two loose swathes from a centre parting and fastened at the back in a roll. Her long gown was of costly velvet with a gold lamé girdle and her fingers were adorned with jewelled rings. Her complexion, however, was the nut-brown of a peasant rather than the pale fairness of a noblewoman. Kemp hurriedly pushed the full chamber-pot back under the bed with his foot and sat down on the edge of the bed. He watched as she bent down to pick up a salver she had left outside the door, and carried it into the room.

'Good day,' she said, in French.

'Where am I?' he demanded. When she turned her brown eyes on him and shrugged helplessly, he realised he had spoken in English. He repeated his question in French.

'My lord's castle at Saint-Omer.' She displayed no fear as she approached the bed, putting the salver down beside him. It held a wooden bowl full of some kind of pottage, some fresh bread, a spoon, and a cup of watered-down wine.

As she was about to move away, he seized her wrist. 'Who is your lord?' he demanded.

'Sir Geoffroi de Chargny, the Sieur de Pierre-Perthuis, Montfort, Savoisy and Licey.' A trace of fear flickered in her eyes, and Kemp could feel a tremor in her arm, but her voice was bold enough. 'Please, let me go.'

'Where is he?'

'I do not know. He has gone to raise more troops.'

Troops to take part in the attack on Calais, Kemp had no doubt. 'More troops?' he asked. 'How many are here already?'

'I don't know. Many. Very many. More than were garrisoned here during the war.' She tugged her wrist free of his grip, jerking his arm at the shoulder and making him wince with pain. 'Oh! I am sorry! Your poor arm!' She bent over him, her breasts clearly outlined through the fabric of her gown. He pushed her away.

'Why aren't you afraid of me?' he demanded.

'Why should I be?' she retorted.

He rattled the chain attached to his collar. 'This must tell you I am not a welcome or willing guest of your lord.'

'You must forgive Sir Geoffroi. He sometimes seems to forget the war is over.'

Kemp shook his head. 'The war isn't over. It's just a truce.'

She shrugged. 'Eat your breakfast. The physician says you need to build your strength up.'

He stared at her in astonishment. 'Physician?'

'I had a physician called in when I had you brought out of the dungeons. They are not fit for human habitation. I know you English have little love for the French, but do not judge us all by men like Sir Geoffroi.'

'Won't he be angry when he finds me quartered up here?'

She shrugged again. 'Perhaps. But Sir Geoffroi is never angry with me for long.' She headed for the door.

'Wait! Who are you?'

She smiled broadly, the corners of her eyes crinkling prettily. 'I am called Typhaine.'

'I'm . . .'

'Martin Kemp, yes, I know.'

'No chambermaid would be able to order me to be moved up here, yet you're no noblewoman. In what way do you serve Sir Geoffroi?'

She hesitated by the open door and blushed, hanging her head. It was answer enough.

'Doesn't Madame de Chargny object?' Kemp asked bluntly.

'Madame died many years ago. Sir Geoffroi chooses me to . . . comfort him.'

'You love him?' Kemp found it impossible to imagine anyone loving de Chargny.

'Love has nothing to do with it,' she said bleakly, and closed the door behind her.

Outside, she paused facing the door for a moment. She was risking much by having Kemp put in the guest bedchamber. The other servants had obeyed her, fearing that a word from her in de

Chargny's ear could earn them a flogging. But what would de Chargny say when he returned and found his orders countermanded by a woman who was – at the end of the day – no more than a mere chambermaid? She might be his mistress, yet she had seen no sign of any love in him that might permit him to turn a blind eye to her caprice.

Damn de Chargny, she told herself. He had no love for anyone. Least of all for the poor Englishman whose screams of agony had echoed through the castle. She had always known her master was cold and unemotional; but was he really capable of such bestial cruelty as those screams suggested? The injuries visible on Kemp's body when the physician examined him had seemed to confirm it.

She shook her head. No one deserved to be punished like that, not even an English spy. She knew that, regardless of whether or not de Chargny would approve, she was doing the Christian thing by trying to speed Kemp's recovery.

She was making her way down the spiral staircase when Arnault emerged from a recessed doorway and seized her around the waist, pressing his lips against hers. Pushing him away in revulsion, she slapped him hard across the cheek. 'How dare you? If Sir Geoffroi found out he'd have you flayed alive!'

'Sir Geoffroi isn't here, though, is he?' leered Arnault.

'No. But he will be back soon enough.'

'Aye. I wonder how he'll react when he finds out that you've had the Englishman lodged in the guest bedchamber. Why have you done that, I wonder? He is very handsome, isn't he?'

Typhaine refused to give Arnault the satisfaction of a denial. 'He's a man, not a dog to be chained up and forced to live in his own excrement,' she snorted in disgust.

'He's an Englishman. All Englishmen are dogs. You haven't answered my question, Typhaine. Taken a shine to your pet Englishman, have you?'

'I'll justify myself to Sir Geoffroi, not his torturer,' she snapped, turning away and descending the stairs.

Kemp was standing in a room that was strangely familiar yet curiously distorted, the posts of the four-poster bed defying all the laws of perspective, as were the walls and the ceiling. His hand gripped a sword, and it felt comfortable.

It was the bedchamber he was occupying at the castle at Saint-Omer.

Two large brown eyes peered at him over the edge of the bed.

'Come out from behind there,' he heard a voice order. It was his own. 'Show yourself.'

She rose trembling to her feet, but it was not the woman of whom he normally dreamed. It was Typhaine. He walked around to the other side of the bed to face her. She shrank away, but he caught her around the waist, pulling her against him. She cried out, but he pressed his lips against hers, forcing his tongue between her clenched teeth.

She tried to push him away, but he grabbed the front of her dress and ripped it open. She gasped in horror and tried to break away, but he grabbed her by the arm and hauled her back, throwing her against the wall. He slapped her back-handed across the face, drawing blood from the corner of her mouth, then tore the rest of her clothes from her body and held her: one hand on her throat, the other fumbling with the hem of his tunic. He pushed his breech-cloth down over his hips, and was about to force himself into her when a voice screamed 'NO!'

He recognised it as his own.

He was sitting bolt upright in bed, bathed in a cold sweat and gasping for breath. He felt slightly queasy.

The door opened, and Typhaine stood there in a long white nightdress. Her dark hair hung down to her shoulders, lustrous in the yellow glow of the single candle she held aloft. 'I heard you cry out. Are you all right?'

'It wasn't me,' he protested.

'You had a nightmare.'

'Yes,' he admitted, embarrassed.

'Of what did you dream?'

He hung his head. 'The war.'

She nodded. 'Sir Geoffroi has such dreams. I do not think he is the only one for whom the war is not yet over.' She stood staring at him for a moment, but he refused to meet her gaze. Then he raised his head suddenly, and she found herself gazing into flint-blue eyes. In the candle-light, as he sat there naked but for the bed-sheets, chained by the neck to the wall, his eyes no longer seemed empty, but vulnerable and full of pain.

'Perhaps if I fetch you some milk it will help you sleep?' she suggested.

He grimaced. 'I'd rather have a quart of ale.' Only the strongest humming ale, drunk in huge quantities, could dim the memories that haunted his sleep.

She smiled. 'I'll fetch you some milk.' She put down the candlestick on the chest at the foot of the bed and went out.

He sighed, rubbing his clammy forehead wearily. She meant well, he supposed. He turned his attention to the candlestick she had left behind. It was silver-plated, and its broad base would make it a handy weapon. He tried to reach it, to test its weight in his hands, but the chain brought him up a good two feet short.

Waiting for her to return, he studied one of the tapestries on the wall. The tapestries at Broughton Manor displayed the tales of King Arthur and the Knights of the Round Table, which Kemp knew well, but he did not know the stories these tapestries depicted. In the dim glow of the candle he could make out twelve knights surrounded by dozens of black-faced moors in a narrow mountain pass, the knight at the centre of the tableau blowing on a horn as if his life depended on it.

Typhaine returned bearing a flagon and two wooden mazers on a tray, and put it down on the chest. She poured the contents of the flagon into the mazers, handing one to Kemp, keeping the other for herself. He drank the cool goat's milk, and felt it soothe his stomach. Wiping his lips with his sleeve, he indicated the tapestry. 'What tale is that? One from the Bible?'

'Don't you know the Song of Roland?'

He looked at her questioningly.

So she sat down on the edge of the bed and told him the tale of Roland and the Twelve Peers of Charlemagne, of Oliver and Bishop Turpin, of the sword Durandal and the horn Olivant. She told of how Charlemagne had led a crusade across the Pyrenees and inflicted much slaughter upon the paynim armies of King Marsillus; how Roland, leading the rearguard back across the mountains, was ambushed by the moors; how he and his companions fought valiantly until they were all but overwhelmed, when Roland blew Olivant in desperation to summon Charlemagne to their rescue; how Charlemagne, hearing the horn's blast, wanted to turn back, but was persuaded by the traitor

Ganelon that Roland was merely hunting deer, so that Roland was left to his fate. 'And that,' she concluded, 'is the tale of Roland.'

She turned and saw he was fast asleep, his chest rising and falling steadily. She did not wonder how long she had told the tale in vain, feeling only gladness that he seemed to be at peace, his sleep undisturbed by nightmares. She studied his face in the candle-light. He still looked a little brutish, she thought, but perhaps with a wash and a shave . . .

She shook her head, blew out the candle and quietly closed the door behind her.

'I have grave tidings, Sir Thomas,' said the king, when Holland had been ushered into his private chamber at the palace of Havering atte Bower shortly before Yuletide. 'I consider myself a friend of yours, and as such wanted to be the one to break it to you. I have just received word from Upholland . . .'

'My mother?'

'You had already heard?'

Holland shook his head. 'She has been ill for some time, your Majesty.'

'God is merciful, Sir Thomas. She died peacefully in her bed.'

Holland nodded, his face impassive, but the king had not finished. 'There is more. Not so grave, I am glad to say, but nevertheless it requires our joint attention. It concerns your brother, Sir Otho . . .'

Holland closed his eyes as if in pain. Bad news usually did concern his brother Otho.

'As you know, when I entrusted the Count of Eu to the custody of Sir Otho, I imposed only two conditions: that the count should not be allowed to bear arms publicly and that he should not be allowed to leave England.'

Holland sighed. His brother meant well, but he could be infuriatingly foolish at times. 'Permit me to guess, sire. The count has been seen beyond the seas, bearing arms?'

'Aye. As you are probably aware, your brother recently crossed the seas to Calais. He took the count with him, where he has been seen armed and at large. The count is an honourable man, and I do not believe it his intention to flee back to his own territory with his ransom unpaid. However, in allowing this to come about, your brother has failed to comply with my explicit commands, and I cannot allow such a transgression to go unpunished in some way. He must be brought to the bar of the King's Bench to give an account of himself. I trust you understand this?'

'I seek no special favours for Sir Otho because he is my brother, sire. He must learn to accept responsibility for his actions.'

'On the other hand, I do not wish publicly to embarrass Sir Otho by sending the Marshal to arrest him. I'm sure he would be most grateful if you could call on him and suggest that he presents himself to the Chancellor to answer for his negligence, in which case I shall see to it he is treated with fitting leniency.'

It was the Eve of Saint Thomas the Apostle, the twentieth of December. Holland quickly calculated that he could leave for Calais and bring his brother and the count back in time for Christmas. 'I shall set out on the morrow,' he promised.

'There is no urgency. It would please me if you could spend Christmas with us here at Havering. You can set out for Calais after the festivities.'

'Your Majesty is too kind,' said Holland. 'However, I had hoped to spend Yuletide at Upholland with my eldest brother . . . we must bury our mother . . .'

The king shook his head firmly. 'You will spend the Feast of Christmas here at Havering, and leave for Calais in time for the New Year.' He made it sound like a command.

Holland bowed. 'As your Majesty desires,' he agreed, bewildered. He had used up a good deal of the king's goodwill over his petition against Montague; and while he had got away with it so far, he was well aware that if he wished to get on at court it was time to start toeing the line a little more closely.

He was about to leave when the king called after him. 'Wait, Sir Thomas. There is more news. Good news this time, I am glad to say, to temper your grief at your mother's passing.'

'Sire?'

'Two days ago I received a messenger from the Bishop of Comacchio.' The bishop was the Papal Nuncio in England. 'To be brief, his Holiness Pope Clement has decreed your marriage to my cousin Joan was and still is a valid marital union, and that she is to be restored to you. Your marriage is to be solemnized properly *in facie ecclesiae*, of course,' the king added with a smile.

'Of course, your Majesty,' gasped Holland.

'I know I opposed your suit to the Papal Court, and I am always unhappy that a court ruled by a Frenchman should take precedence over my own royal authority; but I could never deny my cousin Joan anything, and you have done me good service, both in the past and, I hope, in the future.' He crossed to the window and gestured for Holland to join him. In the garden below they could see the ladies of the court listen to a *gestour* reciting poetry. Joan was amongst them, her face pink from the cold, framed by the furred lining of her hood. 'Go to her, Sir Thomas. She is yours.'

Grinning, Holland nodded. 'Aye, sire.' He almost ran to the door.

The king called out after him again. 'Sir Thomas! Be sure you look after her, and treat her as one of royal blood should be treated.'

'That I shall, sire.'

'And your feud with Montague ends now, do you understand? If I should hear of any further quarrels between you, then you shall both be expelled from the Companionship of Saint George.'

'I shall seek no further quarrel with my lord of Salisbury, sire; but I cannot guarantee he will not . . .'

'Do not concern yourself about Montague, Sir Thomas. I shall speak to him.'

The king chuckled to himself as Holland left the room. He then turned to the window and watched Holland go into the garden and run to Joan. He picked her up and whirled her around. The other ladies of the court giggled, but Holland and Joan were oblivious to everything but each other.

'Your Majesty?'

The king turned. An immensely fat priest stood in the doorway. The skin was so taut across his fleshy face it was impossible to guess his age, although his tonsured hair remained untouched by grey. His dark brown eyes were myopically watery. 'Ah, Canon Reynard. Come in.'

The canon joined him by the window. 'Well, sire?'

'He seems pleased enough. As well he might be.'

The canon gestured dismissively. 'He will go to Calais?'

'Sir Thomas is loyal.'

'Good,' said the canon. 'For we shall need every good man we can get.'

The king shook his head, chuckling at his chief spy-master's words. 'You worry too much, priest.'

'One of us needs to,' the canon replied sombrely.

Two servants brought a large wooden tub into the bedchamber where Kemp was imprisoned as he finished his breakfast one morning. They were followed by Typhaine and a scowling Arnault.

'What's going on?' asked Kemp.

Typhaine smiled. 'You stink, and your clothes are filthy,' she explained. 'You need to bathe.'

Kemp stared at the tub in horror. 'Bathe?'

She nodded. 'If you want me to keep bringing you breakfast, you will.'

It was the eve of Christmas, two weeks since Typhaine had first had Kemp moved to the bedchamber, and there was still no sign of de Chargny's return. Despite the pampered lifestyle she was able to enjoy since becoming de Chargny's mistress, Typhaine found she had time on her hands. Unable to read, she found de Chargny's surprisingly large library of little use; she could do some embroidery, but that was not enough to occupy her. Kemp's arrival at the castle had been a Godsend, a new diversion, for he was someone she could talk to and thus help while away the hours and days. Though he was not the most communicative person in the world, her persistent questioning had eventually paid off, and she began to draw more detailed answers from him.

She found everything he had to tell her fascinating. Although she was a little disappointed to find that England was not so very different from France, it pleased her to learn that it was not the country of barbarians de Chargny made it out to be. Only when she asked him about the war would he clam up, and she recognised that some experience in his past had wounded him deeply, something he chose not to relive. She was curious what the incident might have been; in a way, it made him even more interesting to her. In time, she told herself, he would bring himself to confide in her.

In return she told him about her own background: the village in Brittany where she had grown up, how she had fallen in love with Pierre when he stumbled into her village after the battle of Morlaix, badly wounded; and how in time he had married her, and brought her back to Saint-Omer. The only thing she did not tell him was how Pierre's serjeant had tricked her into adultery. Why she kept this to herself she did not know, for when she spoke to Kemp she felt as if she could tell him anything. He listened to her attentively, without making fun of her opinions. No one had treated her with that much respect since Pierre had died. It occurred to her that he only feigned interest to win her confidence, or perhaps to seduce her; but would being seduced by him be such a bad thing, she wondered?

For his part, Kemp did not discourage her attentions as long as they seemed platonic. Although his experiences as a soldier had taught him how to cope with long periods of inactivity, he still longed for his freedom. He occupied his time planning his escape. He asked her questions in return: questions about France, about de Chargny, about herself, about Saint-Omer, about the countryside between Saint-Omer and Calais, about the striking force de Chargny was assembling in the town. She knew next to nothing of de Chargny's plans, but what little she did know was enough for Kemp to deduce that the attack on Calais could not be many days away, and the striking force de Chargny was assembling was certainly large enough to carry out its task with ease, unless Calais were reinforced. He knew Sigglesthorne had had plenty of time to get back to England and warn the king, but had he succeeded? Kemp wanted to escape, to make sure the warning got through in case Sigglesthorne had failed. So he bided his time, building up his strength, practising his French with Typhaine, perfecting his escape plans and rehearsing them in his mind.

'Can I trust you?' asked Typhaine, as the two servants returned to the room to pour buckets of steaming water into the tub.

Kemp regarded her uncertainly. 'Trust me?'

She nodded. 'Not to try to escape. Will you give me your word of honour?'

He grimaced wryly. 'I am a churl; I have no honour.'

'I think you do,' she replied. 'Will you promise me?'

He hesitated. He had Typhaine to thank for the fact the past two weeks had been spent in relative comfort, and he had had a hearty diet to help him regain his strength. But if he did not try to escape now, would another opportunity arise?

'I promise.'

She turned to Arnault. 'Remove his collar.'

'I must advise you against this, my lady.' He spat the words 'my lady'.

'You heard him promise not to try to escape.'

'An Englishman's promise isn't worth a fig.'

'I think it is. I command you to remove the collar.'

'I can't be responsible for your safety if he is allowed to roam free,' he said, producing a large bunch of keys from his belt.

'I shall take full responsibility,' she assured him.

'I only hope you don't have cause to regret it.' Arnault glanced out of the narrow lancet window to make sure there was no escape that way – it was a forty-foot drop to the cobbled courtyard below – before using one of the smaller keys to release the padlock holding Kemp's collar in place. He backed away, his drawn sword levelled at a sneering Kemp. 'He's dangerous, I warn you.'

She smiled. 'Not to me. You may all leave now,' she added, addressing not only Arnault but also the two servants, who had finished filling the tub.

'I'll be right outside,' Arnault told her. 'If he tries anything, just yell; he'll be dead before either of you knows I've entered the room.'

Typhaine waited for Arnault to leave, then closed the door and slipped the bolt.

Kemp rubbed his neck where the iron collar had chafed it. 'Are you sure that's wise?'

'I think so.'

'Arnault's right. I am dangerous. To you as much as anyone. Perhaps even more so.'

She shook her head. 'Base-born you may be, but I think you have as much honour as de Chargny. More, perhaps. I do not think *you* would harm a woman.' Her tone implied that de Chargny would.

'You're wrong,' he told her darkly.

'That's a chance I am prepared to take,' she said. 'Aren't you going to take your clothes off?'

He blushed. 'My lady?'

'You cannot bathe fully-dressed, and I have brought some clean clothes for you to wear when you have finished,' she explained, gesturing to where a change of clothing was neatly folded on the chest at the end of the bed. 'They belong to Geoffroi le fitz; you have the same build.'

He felt a sudden pang of jealousy. 'Geoffroi le fitz?'

'Sir Geoffroi's son.'

'Won't he mind?'

She grinned impishly. 'Little Geoffroi would do anything for me; he has said so enough times.'

He found her sense of mischief appealing, and returned her grin. It was the first time she had seen him smile, and in that moment she decided that he *was* handsome, no doubt about it.

Kemp toyed with the idea of asking her to turn away, but dismissed it as childish. He stripped off his clothes.

Six pale weals across his back spoke for themselves, a memento of a flogging, but Typhaine's curiosity was aroused by an old wound in his left side. 'How did you get that scar?' she asked, pointing to it.

'Someone once stabbed me there. I had it cauterised.'

She lowered her eyes.

'And that one I got when one of your master's henchmen shot me with a crossbow,' he added.

She smiled. 'I wasn't looking at that.'

Blushing, Kemp lowered himself into the tub. Producing a razor, she sat down on a milking stool which she placed beside the tub. 'What are you doing?' he demanded nervously.

'Now who's scared? Don't worry, I'm only going to shave you. You can't think that beard suits you. Tilt your head back.' She hacked away at his beard with a pair of scissors, and when she had got the worst of it off she covered his chin in soap and began to scrape away with the razor. 'Hold still.'

Kemp's heart beat faster as she scraped at the underside of his jaw, but it was not so much the proximity of the razor to his throat as her closeness to him. Then she moved behind him, standing over him while she shaved his upper lip. He felt her soft breasts touch the top of his head, and it was too much for him. As she took the razor away to clean it in the water, he seized her by the wrist.

'I can do it,' he told her. Something in his tone startled her, and for the first time she felt fear in his presence. She allowed him to take the razor from her hand. As he finished shaving, she moved across to the window and stared out through the grey glass.

'Is there another?'

'Another what?' he asked, carefully scraping his cheek close to his left ear.

'Another woman in your life.'

He nicked himself, the razor coming away with a single drop of blood amongst the white lather of the soap. 'Hell's teeth!' he hissed. 'No. Why do you ask?'

'Then why do you spurn me? Do you find me less attractive than your English women?'

'No.' He put the razor down on the stool and glanced over his shoulder. She still stood with her back to him. Picking up a towel from the floor nearby, he placed it on the stool, on top of the razor. 'If anything, quite the opposite,' he admitted grudgingly. He ducked both head and shoulders beneath the water.

'Then what?' she asked, when he finally resurfaced and was working up a lather from the soap.

He thought about it. 'You're French. You're the enemy.' He began to wash his hair.

'Firstly, I'm not French, I'm Breton. Secondly, that's nonsense, and you know it to be so. But it has something to do with the war, doesn't it? Something you won't tell me?'

'Yes.' He finished washing his hair and started to soap down his torso.

'Why won't you tell me? I promise I'll never tell another living soul.'

'It's you I don't want to know.'

'I'll understand,' she pleaded. He felt guilty about some dark deed in his past, that much she had guessed; but she too had a guilty secret, and knew all there was to know about shame. 'I promise I will.'

Kemp had run out of excuses, so he ducked under the water again to rinse the soap from his body and hair. Then he stepped out of the tub and reached for another towel to dry himself with.

'The war is over, Martin. It happened a long time ago. But until you accept that fact, you'll always be at war. With yourself.'

'Now you're the one who's talking nonsense. Anyhow, one day soon the war will start again, and I'll be ready for it.'

'Why live for war? Don't you long for peace?'

He shook his head. 'Peace is boring,' he said dismissively.

She gazed at him in horror. 'You're right,' she said bleakly. 'You *are* dangerous.'

He began to dress: a white tunic of silk, a linen breech-cloth to which he fastened a pair of hose a dull-orange in colour. Over the tunic he put on a close-fitting cote-hardie of sherry-coloured velvet fastened down the front with large gold buttons. A pair of soft leather shoes for his feet, and a long cloak with its edges dagged in leaf-shapes completed the outfit. He felt foolish dressed in such finery, but it might help him in an escape attempt if he appeared to strangers as a nobleman. 'Don't you think you should unlock the door now?' he asked, buttoning the cloak at the right shoulder.

She nodded and crossed to the door, sliding the bolt back. He snatched the towel off the stool, seized the razor from underneath and, as Typhaine was opening the door, he grabbed her from behind, holding the razor to her throat. She went very still, and the door continued to swing open to reveal Arnault standing there. Seeing Kemp holding a razor to Typhaine's throat, he reached for his sword.

'I wouldn't, if I were you,' growled Kemp. 'I doubt that your master would be pleased to come back and find his mistress's throat had been slit.'

'You broke your promise,' whispered Typhaine.

'Aye,' Kemp replied. 'Now we're all going to make our way downstairs and out to the stables, where Arnault is going to saddle a horse for me. We'll follow you, Arnault.'

Swearing under his breath, Arnault led the way down the spiral staircase. Kemp and Typhaine were close behind, Kemp keeping the razor's edge close to her Adam's apple. As they emerged into the great hall, de Chargny and his son entered through the main door, accompanied by Guilbert. Kemp's heart sank.

De Chargny stared at Kemp and Typhaine in astonishment. 'What in the devil's name is going on here?' he demanded.

'I am just leaving,' said Kemp. 'Thank you for your hospitality, but I'm afraid that . . .'

'You're not going anywhere,' snapped de Chargny. He turned to Arnault. 'Well?'

'Typhaine thought it would be a good idea to move Kemp out of his cell and into one of the bedchambers,' explained Arnault.

'It seems she is learning just how mistaken she was.' De Chargny sounded amused. 'Drop the razor, Kemp. I've just come back from a long, hard ride, and I'm too tired for this kind of nonsense.'

'Stand aside, Sir Geoffroi, or, by the fire that burns, I'll slit her throat,' warned Kemp.

'Go ahead, then. I've no more use for the foolish bitch. It's no more than she deserves. I was growing bored with her anyway.'

'Geoffroi!' she screamed.

'He's bluffing,' sneered Kemp.

De Chargny was smiling. 'Am I?'

The hand that held the razor was trembling. The smug whoreson, thought Kemp. He had half a mind to call his bluff and open her throat. He had seen throats slit before, and at this range he knew the jet of blood could strike de Chargny in the face.

'Please, Martin . . .' whispered Typhaine.

He sighed, and tossed the razor aside, disgusted by his own weakness. Guilbert, who had been edging around the side of the hall, stepped out of the shadows behind Kemp, pulled him away from Typhaine, spun him around and drove a vicious punch into his stomach. Kemp sank to his knees, clutching his midriff in agony.

'I knew you wouldn't be able to kill a woman,' sneered de Chargny. 'You're weak, like all your race.'

Kemp glared up at de Chargny, his eyes filled with hatred. 'Aye, like we were weak at Crécy, you mean?'

De Chargny turned pale. 'Guilbert! Show him who is weak and who is strong.'

Guilbert grinned. 'Aye, Sir Geoffroi.' He seized Kemp by the collar and hoisted him back onto his feet, driving his fist into Kemp's stomach until Kemp retched with agony. Guilbert threw him to the rush-strewn floor, and was about to kick him in the stomach when de Chargny signalled for him to stop.

De Chargny crouched over him. 'By the way, Kemp, I have some interesting news for you. Your friend Sigglesthorne made it as far as Calais, where he told the governor all about my plan to seize the town. What the two of you obviously did not realise was that my plan involved the governor's complicity. He's refused to grant Sigglesthorne a permit to sail back to England. So all your efforts to foil me have been for nothing.' De Chargny straightened, and then drove his boot into Kemp's head. Kemp lay still, his eyes closed. Typhaine screamed. De Chargny glanced at her and then turned to Guilbert. 'Take him back to the dungeons.'

'Yes, sir.' Guilbert threw Kemp over his shoulder like a sack of grain, and carried him out of the hall.

A little later, de Chargny made his way up to Typhaine's bedchamber, entering without knocking as was his habit; it was, after all, only her bedchamber because he allowed her to use it. She had thrown herself across the bed and was sobbing into her pillow. He sat down on the edge of the bed, and stroked her hair.

'There, there, my child. There's no need to cry. Now sit up and dry your eyes.' He put an arm around her shoulders. 'Arnault tells me that you have . . . certain feelings for this Englishman. Is it true?'

Sniffing, she nodded. 'I know you say the English are all devils, but Martin is no devil. I think deep down he is kind and gentle, if only he would give himself half a chance.'

'Do you love him?' de Chargny asked.

'Yes, my lord,' she whispered.

He sighed, and rose to his feet, shaking his head at the folly of youth. Then he swung round and punched her in the face, throwing her back across the bed. 'Traitorous bitch! Would you see all the work I have done in preparation for the capture of Calais undone?'

He reached across the bed and grabbed a fistful of her hair, dragging her towards him, and slapping her until the rings on his fingers had criss-crossed her face with lines of blood. He thumped her in the stomach, smashed his knee into her face, and threw her against the wall. He went on beating her until he had no more strength to go on. Mercifully, she lost consciousness sometime before he was finished.

Most of the mariners who found themselves loading barrels on board the *Magdalen* in Dover harbour on the evening of the Feast of Saint Thomas had never sailed with her master before, although they knew of him by reputation. It was customary for mariners to contract with a shipmaster for each trading venture rather than becoming permanent members of a ship's crew.

'The wind's getting up,' remarked one. 'It's going to be a rough crossing.

'I don't know why we have to sail at night anyway,' grumbled another.

'Why? Are you scared?' jibed one of his companions.

'Aye,' he snarled. 'Who but a damned fool wouldn't be? No one with any sense sails at night, unless he has to. Surely whatever's in these barrels can wait until the dawn tide?'

'Depends what's in the barrels,' the first one said philosophically. 'It's not wine, that's for sure.'

'Belay that grumbling!' snapped the ship's constable, who was overseeing the loading of the cargo. 'You're all being paid well enough for this voyage, aren't you?'

The master, wearing a dark grey cloak and an outlandish broad-brimmed hat of brown felt at a rakish angle, emerged from his cabin to discuss the worsening weather with the constable.

'What sort of a man is the master, anyway?' one of the mariners asked his companions in a low whisper.

'Jack Curtis?' The first mariner, a grizzled ancient who had sailed with Curtis several times before, paused to scratch his head. 'He's all right, on the whole. He's a bit mysterious at times, like, but he's all right.'

'How do you mean, mysterious?'

'Keeps himself to himself. Always brooding. And he's always making unscheduled landings at foreign ports and stuff like that. Never a word of explanation. But he looks after his crewmen, you can be sure of that.'

A number of horsemen appeared on the quayside, the sound of their hooves alerting Curtis to their arrival. He took his leave of the constable, clapping him briefly on the upper arm and shouting a few instructions over his shoulder to him as he made his way up the gangplank to greet the newcomers.

The horsemen dismounted. Sir Walter Mauny had ridden at their head, accompanied by three other knights, including the Earl of Warwick's brother, Sir John Beauchamp, and a dozen retainers. With them were two tall men, dressed in the brown habits of Austin friars, their faces hidden by deep cowls muffled against the chill December breezes that gusted up the Channel.

Curtis bowed to Mauny, who smiled. 'Permission to come aboard, Master Curtis?'

'Permission granted, Sir Walter.'

'What's the weather looking like?'

Curtis glanced out beyond the harbour mouth where white-capped waves showed in the moonlight. 'Choppy, and it'll get worse before it gets better.'

'You think it dangerous? Perhaps we should tarry until tomorrow night?'

Curtis shrugged. 'The sea is always dangerous. Tomorrow night it could be even worse. I'm prepared to risk it if you are.'

Mauny nodded. 'You must allow me to consult my fellow passengers.' He handed his horse's bridle to Curtis, and then approached the two men dressed as friars, conversing with them in low tones. Watching, Curtis frowned. A man of Mauny's status did not have to consult a couple of friars before making a decision such as this; but Mauny was a gentle knight in every sense, and it would be in character for him to take the safety of a couple of holy men into consideration. On the other hand, there was something odd about those two: they did not carry themselves like friars at all, but had the proud, erect bearing of noblemen.

Presently Mauny returned. 'We cannot tarry any longer. We must take the risk and sail tonight.'

Curtis shrugged. 'As you will, sir.' Turning back to the ship, he ordered some of the more competent mariners to lead the men's horses down the specially widened gangplank and into the stalls that had been built on deck. Mauny followed them down with the men-at-arms and the two friars. As the first of them passed Curtis at the top of the gangplank, the shipmaster could not resist peeking into the depths of his cowl.

Despite his relative youth, Curtis had lived an adventurous life, and was not easily surprised. But his jaw dropped when he saw the man's face.

Seeing that Curtis had recognised him, the man smiled, raised a finger to his lips, and winked, before climbing down the gangplank followed by the friar. Curtis stared after them in astonishment, then shook his head. He had been paid handsomely to make this voyage without asking any questions, and that was exactly what he would do. Smiling as he remarked that the two friars were probably unused to the hardships of a rough sea crossing, he offered them the use of his cabin; he would be engaged on deck throughout the night crossing anyway. The two cowled figures thanked him, raising their hands in benediction.

'*Pax vobiscum*,' they said.

'*Et cum spirito tuo*,' replied Curtis. He opened the door for them with an elaborate bow, and they disappeared into the quarter deck below the aft castle.

Curtis turned to the constable. 'Is all the cargo on board?'

'Aye, Jack.'

'Very well, then. Prepare to cast off.'

Presently the *Magdalen* sailed out of the harbour mouth with the wind on the starboard tack, crossing the Strait of Dover towards Calais.

De Chargny awoke full of excitement on the morning of New Year's Eve. He forced himself to be calm, attending mass in the castle's chapel with Geoffroi le fitz, de Ribeaumont, and Sir Robert de Fiennes. Afterwards, the four of them had breakfast in the great hall. They were almost finished by the time de Renty entered, bowing low.

'What news from Calais, Sir Oudard?' demanded de Chargny.

De Renty was smiling. 'My spies tell me that there have been no attempts to reinforce the garrison. It seems the English remain quite oblivious to our intentions.'

'And de Pavia?'

De Renty pursed his lips. 'He's scared.'

De Chargny nodded. 'Scared of me, and rightly so. He'll play his part.' He turned to de Ribeaumont. 'Order the men to cut their lances down to five feet. Any fighting that takes place will be in the streets of Calais itself, where fourteen-foot lances are apt to be unwieldy. Then have them form up into a column on the road to Calais.'

De Ribeaumont bowed, and left the hall. The knights loaded their armour on to packhorses for the journey to Calais. It would be a hard day's ride. They would halt a few miles from the town so the men could eat and don their armour before the attack. De Chargny ordered Guilbert to go to the stables and saddle the horses and Geoffroi le fitz left the castle with de Renty, while de Chargny turned to Arnault. 'You're in charge here while I'm gone. I've taken all the guards; we're going to need every man we can get to be certain of success. As soon as I've left you're to raise the drawbridge and lower it to none but me or King Philip himself. Oh, and I've locked Typhaine in the guest bedchamber.'

Grinning, Arnault nodded. 'Yes, Sir Geoffroi. God be with you, sir, and good luck.'

'Thank you, Arnualt. If God is willing, tomorrow night we shall dine in the great hall of Calais castle with Sir Amerigo de Pavia.' Buttoning his cloak at his right shoulder, he headed for the door, then paused on the threshold before turning back. 'You have the keys of the castle?'

Arnault patted the large bunch of keys that hung from his belt. 'Aye, my lord.'

De Chargny looked thoughtful. 'Good. Kill Typhaine.'

'My lord?'

'You heard me, man. She is no longer to be trusted. Make it as slow and as painful as you like.'

'Yes, sir.' Arnault looked as though he could hardly believe his ears.

'And dispose of Kemp while you're at it,' de Chargny added, as an afterthought. 'Nothing fancy – he's too dangerous to take chances with. No trying to prove yourself the better man. A crossbow bolt through the grille in his cell door should suffice.'

# CHAPTER FIFTEEN

ARNAULT WATCHED AS de Chargny made his way down into the courtyard where Guilbert awaited him, holding the bridle of de Chargny's massive black courser. The knight swung himself up into the saddle and took the foreshortened lance Guilbert handed up to him. Then Guilbert climbed into the saddle of his own rouncy, and the two of them rode out into the streets of Saint-Omer on their way to join Geoffroi le fitz, de Ribeaumont and de Renty at the head of the column slowly forming up on the road to Calais.

Arnault descended to the gatehouse and operated the mechanism to raise the drawbridge. Returning to the keep, he found de Chargny's steward clearing up the debris of breakfast in the great hall. 'Sir Geoffroi's left me in charge,' said Arnault, revelling in his new-found power.

The steward nodded. 'Yes, he told me.'

'Good. Go to the gatehouse and keep watch.'

Arnault watched from the entrance of the keep until the steward had entered the gatehouse. Then he locked the heavy oak door and ran up the spiral staircase to the upper level, taking the steps three at a time. He let himself into the guest bedchamber.

Typhaine was lying in bed, her eyes red-rimmed from crying, her face covered in scratches and ugly blue-black bruises. A pity she wasn't looking her best, thought Arnault, but he would not let that spoil his fun. The sight of her dishevelled state inflamed his lust at once.

She sat up as he closed the door behind him. 'How dare you come in here! Get out!'

He grinned. 'Didn't Sir Geoffroi tell you? You're not the queen of the castle any more.' Pulling up the hem of his tunic, he unfastened his breech-cloth as he approached the bed.

She shrank away from him. 'Stay away from me!' she warned.

He laughed. 'Or you'll tell Sir Geoffroi? Sir Geoffroi doesn't care about you any more, bitch. He says I'm to kill you; and I'm to take my time about it. And I will, believe you me. But first I'm going to have some fun with you.'

She jumped out of the other side of the bed, but he ducked around the chest at the foot of the bed and grabbed her around the neck, throwing her across the mattress. She screamed.

He laughed again. 'Scream all you want. There's no one to hear you except me, and I like it. I want you to scream. I want to hear you beg for mercy, you jumped-up whore.' Climbing astride her, he ripped open the front of her nightdress. She tried to strike him, but he seized her by the wrists, pinning them to the bed, then dipped his head to lick her breasts with a coarse tongue. She felt sick with revulsion.

He squirmed back off the bed, releasing her wrists to grab her calves, forcing her legs apart as he leaned over her, poised to force himself into her. 'I've been looking forward to this for a long, long time.'

'Not as much as I have,' she spat in reply. He started to frown, but she had already grabbed the heavy candlestick from the chest by the bed and smashed it against the side of his skull. The sheer force of the blow knocked him off her. She raised the candlestick above her head and brought it down with all her might, again and again, until there was nothing left of his head but a bloody, pulpy mess.

Then she crawled off the bed and was sick in a corner of the room.

She sat hunched on the floor for a moment, looking at anything but Arnault's corpse. Now what?

Only one course of action was left open to her. She took a gown and a mantle from the chest at the end of the bed, dressed, and then helped herself to the keys from Arnault's belt, before making her way down to the dungeons.

Kemp was sitting in the far corner of his cell. He glanced up as she opened the door, and stared at her in the dim torchlight. 'Hell's teeth! What happened to your face?'

'De Chargny.'

He looked grim. 'He's got a lot to answer for.'

'He's left for Calais. Nearly all his retainers have gone with him. They won't be back for a few days. We can be long gone by then.'

He pushed himself to his feet. 'My sword?'

'De Chargny's chamber.'

'Lead the way.'

Kemp found his sword-belt with his scabbarded broadsword and his dagger in its sheath still attached in the room. 'You said de Chargny writes about chivalry?' he asked as he buckled the belt around his waist. Typhaine nodded. 'Where are his books?'

She pointed to a parchment manuscript on the desk. 'That's what he's working on at the moment.'

Kemp snatched the manuscript off the desk and was about to throw it on the embers that still smouldered in the hearth when a thought occurred to him. There would be no point in burning the manuscript. Kemp wanted de Chargny to know what had happened to it, to know it had been deliberately and maliciously destroyed. The pressure on his bladder gave him a better idea.

'What are you doing?' Typhaine asked him in astonishment.

He grinned, shaking off the drips. 'Exactly what I intend to do to de Chargny himself before the day is out.'

'I told you: he's left for Calais.'

Kemp fastened his breech-cloth once more. 'I know. I'm going after him.'

She stared at him in astonishment. 'You . . . you're mad! He has over three thousand men with him. Are you going to take them all on single-handed?'

'If needs be, aye. A force that large moves slowly. If I can find a good horse I can be in Calais ahead of him.'

'Minutes rather than hours ahead of him. What good can that do?'

'Time enough to alert the garrison, and make sure the gates of the town are closed. I spent the best part of a year sitting in the swamps around Calais when we besieged it. I'm not going to let de Chargny win it back in a single night.'

'You're mad,' she repeated. 'You wooden-headed dozy-beard! You'll be killed.'

He shook his head. 'I died a long time ago.'

The two of them made their way down to the courtyard. 'You fetch some horses from the stables,' ordered Kemp. 'I'll open the gate.'

He slipped into the gatehouse and studied the mechanism for lowering the drawbridge. It worked on exactly the same principles as the one he had operated at Château Gaillon, when Holland's company took part in the assault on the castle during the march to Crécy. He released the ratchet and the drawbridge swung down, the counterweights slowing its descent so it did not break when it touched the ground at the other side of the moat. Kemp was about to leave the gatehouse when the steward, who had been on guard on the battlements above, came down the stairs. Recognising the former prisoner, he pulled his dagger from his belt and lunged.

Kemp dodged the thrust, seized the steward's wrist with his left hand, and smashed his right elbow into his face. The man collapsed, and Kemp finished him off by plunging the steward's own dagger into his heart.

Typhaine entered the gatehouse, and a look of horror crossed her face when she saw the steward's corpse. Of all the staff at the castle, he alone had been kind to her. 'You've killed him!'

'Aye,' Kemp responded. 'The horses?'

'There's only one left in the stables.' There was a hint of panic in her voice.

'There must be somewhere else in Saint-Omer where we can find another horse,' urged Kemp. 'Think!'

She bit her lip. 'Would they have stables adjoining the garrison's barracks?'

'If there are mounted troops, aye.' They went into the castle stables, where a single pony stood in its stall. 'You take this,' he said, helping her to put on its saddle and harness. 'Where will you go?'

'Rennes, in Brittany. I have kinsmen there.'

'It's a long way to Brittany. Are you sure you'll be all right?'

She led the pony out into the courtyard. 'I'll be fine. It's you I'm worried about. For God's sake, Martin! Calais is as good as recaptured. If you try to stop Sir Geoffroi you'll be riding to your death.'

He shrugged. 'Maybe. I have to try, though. It's my duty. You understand, don't you?'

She nodded wearily. 'There's nothing I can say that will dissuade you?'

He shook his head, and she swung herself into her saddle. 'God be with you, Martin Kemp.'

'And also with you,' he echoed. He slapped the pony's rump, and it cantered out of the courtyard and across the drawbridge.

She was several miles away from Saint-Omer before she realised that of all the things she had considered saying to Kemp to dissuade him from his intention of committing suicide, she had never thought of telling him she loved him.

Kemp watched her ride down the main street of Saint-Omer. He wondered briefly if he was making a mistake in letting her ride out of his life; well, perhaps, he decided, but there were more important matters to take care of.

He walked briskly to the barracks, remembering the way well enough from the day when he entered the town as a spy with Preston and Conyers. The barracks were almost deserted, except for a few men-at-arms and foot-soldiers running to join the column preparing to move off from before the walls of Saint-Omer. They were too busy to pay any attention to Kemp. He slipped into the large stable block where a few rouncies remained. A man-at-arms, wearing a chain-mail habergeon and a 'kettle' helmet, was saddling the nearest. He nodded at Kemp as he began to lead the horse out of its stall. Kemp nodded back, and waited until the man was almost past him before speaking.

'Excuse me . . .?'

The man-at-arms turned, and opened his mouth to ask Kemp what he wanted. Before he could speak, however, Kemp had smashed his fist into his face. The man staggered back and Kemp followed him down, punching him until the man lost consciousness, his face covered in blood. He rolled the man over on to his front and stamped on the back of his neck to break it.

Kemp worked quickly, dragging the body to the end stall and unbuckling his sword-belt before removing the man's habergeon. He had not imagined that it could be such hard work to remove a habergeon from a corpse and he found he was sweating despite the chill December air.

But at last he succeeded. There was no time to take off the man's quilted gambeson as well. Kemp pulled the habergeon over his head and shoulders until the chain-mail coif was snug against his scalp, and then buckled his sword-belt on again, before placing the helmet on his head. Then he strapped on the man's greaves to protect his calves, and picked up his foreshortened lance.

He led the rouncy out of the stables to the yard outside, where two dozen men-at-arms were forming up into a troop while their serjeant-at-arms inspected them. Kemp tried to lead the rouncy out of the yard without any of them noticing, but the serjeant called after him.

'Hey, you! Where do you think you're going?'

Sir Thomas Holland arrived in Calais with his retinue shortly after noon, and they made their way directly to his house adjoining the White Lion inn. He found the door bolted from within, and hammered on it with his fist until it was answered by a young page.

'What can I do for you?'

'What can you . . .?' Holland almost exploded, but managed to control his temper. 'Tell me, boy, whose house is this?'

'Why, Sir Thomas Holland's, sir, but I'm afraid he's not in. If you will state your business, I shall inform his brother Sir Otho, and see if he can help you.'

'Can you describe Sir Thomas to me?'

'I've never seen him, sir, but they say he wears a white patch over one . . .' The page's voice trailed away, and he blushed bright scarlet.

Holland turned to Preston and his men. 'Quarter yourselves in the inn,' he commanded. As Preston and his men headed for the White Lion next door, Holland pushed past the page and mounted the steps to the hall, where he found Sir Otho dining with the Count of Eu. Astonished by the unannounced appearance of his elder brother, Sir Otho rose to his feet.

'Hullo, Tom! What a pleasant surprise! I thought you were going to spend the New Year with mother and John at Upholland.'

'So did I,' Holland said heavily. 'But I was summoned into the king's presence, and he asked me to come here, to Calais.'

'What in the world for?'

'Search your memory, Otho. See if you can dredge from the depths of what is laughingly referred to as your brain the instructions which his Majesty gave you as regards keeping Raoul in your custody,' said Holland, gesturing towards de Brienne.

'He said that Raoul was not to leave England, and not to be seen bearing arms publicly.' Otho looked puzzled.

'Where are we, Otho?'

Otho considered the question. 'Calais?' he hazarded.

'And where, pray, is Calais?'

Otho grinned sheepishly. 'In France, geographically, but I thought now it's an English possession, it must be part of England . . .'

'It is not an English possession, it is a possession of his Majesty the king, like Gascony. Would you describe Gascony as part of England?'

Otho squirmed in his seat. 'Well, not as such, no.'

The count rose to his feet. 'Do not be so harsh with Otho, Sir Thomas. I was well aware of the conditions imposed on my custody. I am as much to blame as him . . .'

Holland held up a hand for silence. 'Please, Raoul. It was not you the king ordered to carry out such a simple set of instructions. While you are in my house you are my guest, and will not be held responsible for the failings of my brother. God forbid anyone should have to bear that burden other than Otho himself,' he added. 'Could I have a few moments alone with him?'

The count nodded, and bowed low, heading for the door. 'I'm a guest in your house, too,' he heard Otho plead as he closed the door behind him. 'Stop hitting me, Tom!'

'And for the thousandth time, stop calling me Tom, as if I were some God-damned peasant lad!' snapped Holland, clipping Otho across the back of the head once more. 'I am Sir Thomas Holland of Upholland, not Tom the village swain. Friends and –' he grimaced – 'relatives call me Thomas; but never Tom. Do you understand?'

Holland explained to his brother – slowly, avoiding words of more than one syllable wherever possible – that he would have to return to England at the earliest opportunity to present himself at the King's Bench, and throw himself on the marshal's mercy. Otho nodded miserably, and Holland left him, making his way to the tavern next door where he found Preston and the others having a reunion not only with Brewster but also Sigglesthorne. They all rose to their feet as he entered. 'Good afternooon, Sir Thomas,' Brewster said cheerfully. 'Can I get you a drink?'

But Holland was staring at Sigglesthorne, his face as dark as thunder. 'Tell me, Master Sigglesthorne, why I should pay you a small fortune in fees, and then not hear of the success of my petition until the king himself tells me?'

'I had to leave Avignon before the Pope confirmed Cardinal d'Albi's verdict. You must have heard about what happened to Kemp and me? I would have returned to England almost a month ago, but I couldn't get a pass to leave Calais.'

'What happened to Kemp?' asked Conyers.

'Never mind what happened to Kemp,' snapped Holland. 'Why did you have to leave Avignon early? When I pay you for your time, I expect you to use it in my service not the service of . . .'

'The king?' put in Sigglesthorne.

Holland creased his brow. 'The king? What are you talking about? Explain yourself, man!'

Now it was Sigglesthorne's turn to look puzzled. 'But surely you must have heard? About de Chargny's plot to seize Calais? De Pavia assured me he would inform the king . . .'

'What plot? I was with the king less than two weeks ago, and he made no mention of de Chargny or of any plot to seize Calais. Hell's teeth!' he exclaimed suddenly.

'Sir Thomas?' said Sigglesthorne.

'Wat: if you were Sir Geoffroi de Chargny, and you planned to seize Calais back from the English, how would you go about it?'

Preston pulled back his chain-mail coif to scratch his head. 'If it were me, sir, I'd make sure I had someone on the inside, to open the gates at the right moment.'

'And who would be able to do that?'

Preston shrugged. 'Anyone with access to the keys, sir, from the governor right down to . . .'

Holland shook his head. 'The acting governor, Wat. A Lombard knight who would sell his own mother for a fistful of florins.' He turned to Sigglesthorne. 'Come on. I think it's time you and I had words with de Pavia.'

Holland left his men with Brewster at the White Lion and marched to the castle while Sigglesthorne trotted behind him, struggling to keep up.

The castle gate was shut. Holland hailed the gatekeeper.

'State your name and your business!'

'Sir Thomas Holland of Broughton and Master Robert Sigglesthorne of Beverley. We have urgent business with the acting governor.'

'What business?'

'That's for the acting governor's ears. Open up!'

There was a long pause while the gatekeeper consulted someone who was out of sight in low tones. Then the drawbridge was slowly lowered. 'You may enter.'

Holland and Sigglesthorne crossed the drawbridge, Holland looking about him with a puzzled expression. 'There's something wrong here. Something very wrong,' he muttered to Sigglesthorne.

They were met in the courtyard by a page. 'If you would follow me, sirs?' The page led them into the keep and up a spiral staircase, opening a door for them near the top. He ushered them inside.

Holland and Sigglesthorne entered the room, and found themselves surrounded by armed men.

De Chargny's column halted at the walled town of Guînes towards nightfall. He glanced to where the sun was setting over the Heights of Sangatte. 'We'll break our march here,' he told de Ribeaumont. 'Tell the men they have one hour to eat and rest before the final leg of our journey. Then send de Werre and de Mortagne ahead to Calais to see if it is safe for us to advance. We'll meet them at the bridge at Nieullay in three hours.'

'The men are weary,' warned de Ribeaumont. 'We've already covered over twenty miles today, and we've another six miles to go.'

'That can't be helped,' said de Chargny. 'We must reach Calais before sun-up.' He smiled. 'Once there, they'll have nothing to do but take possession of the town and castle.'

'I hope you're right, Sir Geoffroi. I have little liking for this stealthy approach. The sooner we get this business over with, the happier I'll feel. The more blood is spilled in the taking of Calais, the more likely King Edward is to declare the truce broken.'

De Chargny gestured dismissively. 'He'll declare the truce broken; but he would have done so sooner or later anyway. At least this way, we make it harder for him to renew the war. Fear not, Sir Eustache; there'll be little or no blood spilled tonight. I'll wager we can take Calais without so much as a blow being struck.'

De Ribeaumont turned away to pass on de Chargny's orders.

'It seems Sir Eustache has little stomach for our enterprise,' murmured de Renty. 'Can we rely on him, do you think?'

De Chargny shrugged. 'I share some of his misgivings about our approach. But this is war, Sir Oudard, war against an enemy with little understanding of chivalry. If we fight by the rules while they ignore them, we are certain to be beaten. Sir Eustache, like myself, will never stand by and allow that to happen.'

Sitting uncomfortably close to de Chargny and Guilbert, the brim of his stolen helmet tilted low across his brow to hide his face, Kemp overheard them speak. The thought of Calais falling without a blow being struck filled him with frustrated rage. He was the only man who could warn the garrison of the town, and here he was unable to act, unable to get away.

It had been fortunate that the French serjeant-at-arms believed Kemp when he explained away his accent – now slight – by claiming to be a Breton; although what had at the time seemed like good luck now seemed like bad. He was riding to Calais just as he had intended, but as a member of the attacking force rather than as its saviour. The irony of it almost made him choke on the salt-fish he was eating.

Some of the men wandered away from the camp-fire to answer the call of nature, and Kemp strolled after them, hoping to use the opportunity to escape; but he bumped into the serjeant again.

'Where do you think you're going?' the serjeant demanded. 'The camp's back that way.' He narrowed his eyes. 'You were trying to slip away again, weren't you?'

Kemp said nothing. He had said as little as possible all day, knowing the more he said the more likely he was to betray himself.

'I know what you are,' snarled the serjeant.

Kemp felt his stomach twist itself into knots.

'You're a damned coward!'

Kemp almost vomited with relief.

'Let me tell you something, my friend. You're coming with us to Calais, and you'll fight the English whether you like it or not. I'll make a man of you yet, and if I don't I'll see you die in the attempt. Don't you love your king?'

'More than you can possibly imagine,' Kemp could not resist sneering.

The serjeant raised a gauntleted hand as if to strike him, but then thought better of it. 'Hold your insolent tongue, damn you! I've got my eye on you, so don't try slipping away again.'

De Chargny and the other knights had donned their armour by

the time Kemp and the serjeant got back to the camp. De Chargny was wearing the new style of 'pig-faced' bascinet, with a pointed visor. He ordered the men to mount up, and presently they set out marching once more, skirting the marshes to approach Calais from the west. It was dark by the time they reached the bridge at Nieullay, where the two knights de Ribeaumont had sent ahead were waiting for them. Smiling, they greeted de Chargny.

'De Pavia is ready to let us in,' reported one. 'There are no sentries posted anywhere in the town.'

'The Lombard has played his part well,' de Renty admitted.

De Chargny grunted. 'We shall see. Any problems?' he asked the two knights.

One of them grinned. 'An English knight stumbled into us. We took him prisoner, gagged him, and put him in the stocks.'

De Chargny smiled. 'And you are certain it is not a trap?'

The two knights nodded. 'We searched the castle. All is quiet.'

'Good.' De Chargny turned to Sir Robert de Fiennes. 'You stay here with your men and some of my crossbowmen and hold this bridge. I'll send word as soon as the town is taken.' De Chargny detached some of his men, leaving a force of about six hundred men-at-arms and crossbowmen behind to guard the western approach. Then the rest of the column, still over three thousand strong, continued on its way, marching along one of the causeways through the marsh around Calais.

The walled town looked dark and forbidding in the moonlight. There was no sign of any activity. But for the host of armed men gathered outside the Boulogne gate to the west, all seemed quiet and peaceful.

'It's quiet,' said de Ribeaumont.

'Too quiet,' replied de Chargny, and turned to de Renty. 'You have the gold for de Pavia?' De Renty nodded. 'Take a dozen of your knights and a hundred men-at-arms to take control of the castle. Once we have that, the town is as good as ours. The rest of us will wait here. Take Guilbert with you. As soon as the castle is in your hands, send him to bring word to us.'

Guilbert looked up from where he sat on his rouncy. 'Sir Geoffroi?'

'Go with them, Guilbert. If de Pavia has betrayed us in any way, I want you to make sure he is the first to die.'

Guilbert grinned. 'Yes, my lord.'

De Renty picked twelve of his best knights and singled out five troops of men-at-arms. 'You men will come with me. The rest of you, wait here with Sir Geoffroi.'

'Come on, lad, that's us,' the serjeant-at-arms told Kemp. 'Remember, I've got my eye on you.'

The Boulogne gate was opened from within by agents of de Chargny who had been waiting for them. There was no sign of any sentries, and de Renty's small force entered the town unchallenged. As they rode through the dark and deserted streets, Kemp looked about in desperation. There had to be some way to alert the garrison. He thought about simply shouting. The men would kill him, but he considered his life of little value now, and it would be worth it, to save the town. But a mere shout might not be enough; and if he must die, he did not want his death to be in vain.

Then they were passing the Church of Nôtre Dame.

Kemp dismounted from his horse and crouched down to examine his rouncy's fetlocks. The serjeant was on to him in a moment, riding around to where he stood.

'What the hell do you think you're playing at?' he hissed.

'My horse is lame, serjeant.'

'There's no time for that now!' snapped the serjeant, pointing to where the rest of the column was riding on down the street towards the castle. 'We're almost there.'

Kemp shook his head. 'This is as far as you go,' he said, and thrust the point of his foreshortened lance into the serjeant's throat. The serjeant gurgled, coughed blood, and then half-fell out of his saddle. His horse whinnied in fright.

De Renty glanced over his shoulder at the sound and saw the dead serjeant with the lance still stuck in his throat and Kemp running towards the door of the church. 'What the devil in hell . . .?'

'Kemp!' exclaimed Guilbert. He could not see Kemp's face at that distance, but some sixth sense told him it was none other.

'What?' De Renty looked baffled.

'Ride on to take the castle, Sir Oudard,' said Guilbert. 'I'll deal with him.' He wheeled his horse and began to ride back down the column.

Kemp reached the door of the church and opened it. Inside, he paused only momentarily, trying to adjust his eyes to the darkness within. Only the faintest starlight filtered through the stained glass windows, but Kemp knew his way around the inside of a church sufficiently well to hurry down the aisle of the nave. He dodged around the altar until he came to the door leading to the bell-tower. It was locked.

'God damn it!' Kemp threw himself against the sturdy oak door. It held fast, but there was enough give in it to instil him with hope.

'Kemp!' Guilbert's voice echoed around the interior of the church. Kemp froze, his hand creeping to the hilt of his sword. He heard footsteps as Guilbert strode down the aisle. Kemp tip-toed across to stand behind one of the pillars and eased his sword out of its scabbard.

Guilbert had stopped moving now. He too was keeping quiet to listen for some sound that would give Kemp away. Kemp saw moonlight glisten on the blade of a sword and held his breath, fearful it might betray him.

The squire was moving again now, walking towards the pillar where Kemp was hiding, keeping his footfalls soft. As he passed the pillar, Kemp suddenly swung his sword at him.

But Guilbert was ready for the blow, his own sword raised to parry it. He grinned in the darkness as the two of them backed away from one another. 'Let's see how well you fight without your bow, Englishman!' He charged forward, swinging his sword at Kemp's head.

As de Renty approached the postern gate of the castle with his men, the drawbridge was lowered slowly, its chains rattling and clanking noisily in the silent town until the wooden beams touched the far side of the moat with a dull boom. The portcullis was already raised. De Renty gazed into the courtyard beyond with narrowed, suspicious eyes. Then de Pavia appeared at the other end of the drawbridge with his young son, beckoning them forward. De Renty signalled the advance once more, and the knights and men-at-arms rode into the courtyard, where they dismounted.

'My son as hostage, as was agreed,' said de Pavia. Despite the chill air of the winter's night, sweat was pouring off him.

De Renty gave orders to his men. 'You two: take the boy. Serjeant: take six men and seize the gatehouse. The rest of you come with me.' He pulled the bulging saddle-bags from his horse and slung them over his shoulder, following de Pavia into the keep of the castle. The place seemed deserted, the torches guttering in their wall-brackets only adding to the silent and empty atmosphere. 'Search the castle,' he ordered his men, when they reached the great hall. The serjeants split their men into search parties and began to check every room.

'Here are the keys to the castle and the town,' said de Pavia, handing over the same bunch of keys that Jean de Vienne had given to Sir Walter Mauny over two years earlier. 'Where is Sir Geoffroi?'

'He's not far away,' de Renty replied gruffly. 'He'll be here shortly.' He took the saddle-bags from his shoulder and handed them to de Pavia. They were heavier than de Pavia had expected, and his arm sagged under the weight. 'Ten thousand *écus d'or*, as agreed,' said de Renty. 'You'll get the other ten thousand when the town is securely in our hands.'

'Will you follow me to the great tower so that you may become master of the castle at once?'

De Renty nodded and turned to the two men holding de Pavia's son. 'Follow me. Bring the boy.'

Guilbert was as good with a sword as he was with his fists, and his immense strength steadily drove Kemp back down the side aisle with a succession of powerful blows that Kemp was hard-pressed to ward off with his own blade. The clash of steel against steel rang out in the darkness of the church, each stroke accompanied by a blood-thirsty roar from the French squire. Kemp retreated before this onslaught, too busy defending himself to strike any blows in return. Then he tripped, and landed sprawling on his back. Guilbert whirled his sword above his head. Kemp rolled out of the way a split second before Guilbert's blade struck sparks from the flagstones where he had lain.

Kemp rose on one knee, raising his sword to parry another stroke from the squire. The blow was so powerful that it jarred his arm badly, knocking his sword from his grip. He tried to snatch it from the floor, but Guilbert put his foot on the blade, pinning it to the ground. Grinning in triumph, he swung at Kemp's head once more. Kemp threw himself backwards, landing against the side of a pew. He vaulted over the backrest to stand on the seat. Guilbert raised his sword again. Kemp tried to dodge aside, lost his footing, and fell into the space between two pews as the squire's sword came arcing down. The blade bit deep into the back rest of the pew. Guilbert tried to tug it free, but it was caught fast. Kemp was back on his feet in an instant, diving over the pew, his hands reaching for Guilbert's throat. Guilbert went over backwards and Kemp was on top of him at once. The two of them grappled on the floor. Guilbert rolled on top, pinning Kemp to the flagstones, repeatedly driving his fist into his opponent's stomach.

Kemp lashed out with a fist. He caught Guilbert on the side of the jaw and snapped his head around. With a roar of fury, Guilbert seized him by the throat and began to beat his head against the floor. Kemp brought his hands up between Guilbert's arms. He clasped them behind the squire's neck, at the same time lifting his knee into Guilbert's crotch. Guilbert howled in agony and rolled away, clutching at himself.

Kemp picked himself up and ran towards where his sword had fallen. Guilbert was back on his feet in an instant, running after him. He caught Kemp from behind, driving him past the sword and slamming his body against a wall. With one hand on Kemp's neck, he drove the other into his kidneys. Gasping in agony, Kemp twisted free. He pulled his dagger from his belt and thrust it at the squire's eyes. Guilbert was fast, though, and caught him by the wrist, knocking the dagger out of his grip to clatter on the floor somewhere in the darkness.

Guilbert punched him in the stomach. As Kemp doubled up, the squire lifted his knee into his face. He sank to his knees, barely conscious. Guilbert bent over, picking him up by the harness of his habergeon, and slammed him back against the pillar. Kemp gasped as the back of his head cracked against the masonry. In some way, the pain seemed to revive him. He seized the collar of Guilbert's tunic and pulled him forward, at the same time butting him on the bridge of his nose with his forehead.

Guilbert staggered back, shaking his head muzzily. Blood streamed from his nostrils. It was the first time Kemp had seen the squire's blood and the fact it could be spilled proved he was not as invincible as he seemed. Kemp dodged around the dazed squire, running for his sword once more. Seeing his intention, Guilbert forced himself to recover, and he seized Kemp by the back of his collar and his belt as he ran past. Giving a mighty roar of effort, he lifted him clear above his head. Kemp struggled helplessly while

Guilbert turned, staggering under the weight of his burden, and then hurled him with all his might into the midst of the pews.

Kemp felt pain explode in every part of his body as wood splintered and smashed beneath him. He could feel a darkness even blacker than the gloom of the church descending over him.

Guilbert picked up Kemp's sword and began to make his way to where the archer lay amongst the wrecked pews. Kemp had to force himself to keep his weakening grip on consciousness. He tried to get up, but one of the pews had fallen across his left ankle, trapping him. Then Guilbert was standing over him, panting heavily, the sword in his hands.

Kemp grabbed blindly for the first object that came to hand, one of the planks that was part of the smashed pew. He struggled to pull it free, but the break was not clean and it refused to come away in his hand.

Guilbert reversed his grip on the sword and raised it above his head, aiming for Kemp's heart.

With a sob of desperation, Kemp wrenched at the plank. Suddenly it came free. He thrust the broken, jagged edge up at Guilbert, the splintered end catching him in the throat. Even as the squire's blood gouted onto Kemp, he brought the sword down. Kemp saw the glint of steel as it descended and twisted aside. Then the sword fell from Guilbert's lifeless grip on to the flagstones as the huge squire toppled forward.

Kemp blacked out.

How long he was unconscious for he did not know, but it was still dark and silent in the church when he came to. He had a feeling that he had not been out for more than a moment or two.

There was something he had to do. Something important. Then he remembered de Chargny's plot. He had to alert the garrison. It might be too late already, but he had to try.

Ignoring his exhaustion, ignoring the pain of his bruises, cuts and grazes, he summoned all the energy he could muster and lifted the pew from his ankle with a grunt of effort, freeing his foot. The ankle felt a little twisted, but it was not sprained or broken.

He was wasting time, worrying about himself when the whole of Calais was at stake. He pushed himself to his feet and staggered across to the door leading to the bell-tower. It was still locked, but Kemp had not survived his fight with Guilbert only to be defeated by a mere piece of wood. Summoning up reserves of strength he had not known he possessed, he threw himself against it until his shoulder was numb, so many times he lost count. Suddenly the door burst open and he staggered into the tower.

The bell ropes hung down in the centre of the room, disappearing into the pitch-black darkness above. When all the bells of a church pealed back in England, that was the signal that the French were invading. Nearly all of the new citizens of Calais were from England. Kemp could only pray they would understand. The noise should at least rouse them from their beds.

He seized one of the ropes and twisted it around both hands, preparing to pull on it with the whole weight of his body. He would set the church bells tolling so loudly they would rouse the dead from their graves.

'Pull that rope and you're a dead man!' a voice from behind warned him in French, and he felt the hard point of a sword press against the neck of his coif.

# CHAPTER SIXTEEN

DE RENTY AND DE PAVIA ascended a spiral stairway, followed by the two men who held de Pavia's son. They passed several groups of French men-at-arms, going from room to room as they searched the castle but otherwise the place seemed deserted. De Pavia opened a door on the top floor and flung the saddle-bags full of gold into the room beyond.

De Renty looked amused. 'Aren't you going to count them?' he asked.

De Pavia shook his head. He was sweating more profusely than ever. 'I'll take your word for it as a man of gentle birth they are all there,' he said, locking the door to the room with his spare set of keys. 'I haven't time to count them now. It will be daylight in a few hours.'

A serjeant with half a dozen men arrived. 'Have you searched everywhere?' demanded de Renty.

'Just about, sir. We were just going to check through yonder door.'

'What's through there?' de Renty asked de Pavia.

'The great tower,' the Lombard told him, unlocking the door with his set of keys and pushing back the bolt. 'Won't you go in?' he asked, and flung open the door.

It was as if he had opened the gates of a dam to let out the flood waters. Suddenly dozens of armed men were pouring through. De Renty and his men did not even have time to draw their swords. Sir Walter Mauny stepped forward, and pulled de Pavia's son away from the two men who held him hostage. They were too astonished to resist.

'Sound the tocsin!' ordered Mauny.

The rest of de Renty's men were reassembling in the courtyard when the tocsin rang out. At the same moment, a false wall that had been built there collapsed, revealing another hundred knights and men-at-arms who charged forward with swords and battleaxes. Panicking, de Renty's men turned and ran back towards the postern gate, but at that moment a large stone dropped from the battlements smashed through the drawbridge, which had been partly sawn-through in preparation. The portcullis crashed down, cutting off their escape.

More men were emerging from the entrance of the keep now, led by Mauny shouting his battle-cry: 'Mauny! Mauny to the rescue!'

'What!' exclaimed another Englishman, a tall figure dressed in 'all-white' armour, unemblazoned with any coat of arms. 'Do these Frenchmen think to conquer Calais with such a handful of men?'

De Renty's men put up only the briefest resistance before throwing down their weapons and surrendering.

'I'm sorry, I thought you were French . . .' began Curtis, and then broke off in astonishment. 'Good God above! Martin Kemp!'

'For Christ's sake, Curtis! I have to sound the alarm! The French are inside the walls!'

'Yes, I know,' Curtis replied.

'We have to do something about it!'

'Don't worry, it's being taken care of.' Curtis was picking lint off his cloak. 'The king knows all about it.'

'What?!'

'It's an ambush. That's why you mustn't ring the bells. There are over a thousand English troops concealed in and around the castle. I'd say de Renty's in for a very nasty surprise.' The sound of the castle's tocsin clanging sounded faintly a short way off. 'Sound's like he's getting it right now,' added Curtis.

'Only a thousand?' Kemp demanded.

'Isn't it enough?' asked Curtis.

'De Chargny has over three thousand men waiting outside the town walls.'

'Indeed?' Curtis grinned. 'Perhaps tonight will not be as dull as I'd originally feared. Come on,' he added, leading the way out of the bell-tower. 'We don't want to miss any of the fun.'

As they made their way through the church, Kemp picked up his broadsword and slotted it back into his scabbard, but there was no time to search for his dagger. Exhausted by his fight with

Guilbert, he was hard-pressed to keep up with the long-legged Curtis as they marched down the street towards the castle, heading around the moat to the main entrance.

'You recovered from the pestilence, then?'

Kemp nodded, and then frowned. 'You do not seem surprised.'

Curtis smiled. 'I have always found lancing the buboes and applying an ointment of Armenian clay surprisingly efficacious. If only more people would listen to me, instead of condemning it as a paynim pratice . . .'

Kemp stared at him in astonishment. '*You* cured me . . .?'

'Aye. As I failed to cure my wife, because I was absent on a trading venture when I should have been at her side,' Curtis said bitterly.

Kemp knew exactly how Curtis felt. 'I heard about Mistress Curtis. I'm sorry.'

It appeared that Curtis did not wish to discuss it. 'How do you know how many men de Chargny has, anyway?' he asked, changing the subject.

'Because I rode here with them, that's how!' said Kemp. 'I was trying to escape to warn the garrison here, but I was mistaken for a French man-at-arms, and had to keep up the pretence to stay alive. I've been trying to get away all day.'

'Good for you. Fortunately your services weren't needed. The king already knew of de Chargny's plan.'

'Marvellous,' Kemp muttered. 'Next time I shan't bother. I was almost killed just now!'

By the time they reached the main gate, the drawbridge was being lowered, and a number of knights rode out under Mauny's banner, including Sir John Beauchamp, Holland, and two tall figures in 'all-white' armour. The taller of the two unidentified knights seemed to be giving instructions to the rest. Behind them, companies of men-at-arms and mounted archers were forming up into troops.

Holland glanced towards Curtis, and seeing Kemp he performed a double-take. 'Kemp? How the devil did you get here? Sigglesthorne told me you were dead.'

'I feel as if I am, sir,' Kemp admitted ruefully.

'It seems Master Kemp was not sure whose side he was supposed to be on this day, and came here with the French,' Curtis explained with a chuckle.

The taller knight in 'all-white' glanced up at Curtis's words, turning the eye-slits of his visored bascinet on Kemp. 'You came to Calais with de Chargny?' he demanded.

'Yes, sir, but I'm no Frenchman. I got caught up with . . .'

'Never mind that now. How many men does he have?'

'Apart from the men who came here with de Renty, sir? About three hundred knights and men-at-arms, and about twenty-seven hundred foot-soldiers. There are also six hundred men-at-arms and crossbowmen at the Nieullay bridge.'

The knight laughed. 'Is that all?'

'Wait, sire!' protested one of the other knights. 'How do we know if we can trust this man? He may be one of de Chargny's agents.'

'I'll vouch for him,' said Holland. 'He's a trusted member of my retinue . . .'

The knight in 'all-white' held up a hand for silence. 'You've no need to vouch for this young man, Sir Thomas. I know him.' From the eyes that twinkled behind the eye-slits of his visor, Kemp fancied that the knight was smiling. 'We met at Saint-Vaast-la-Hougue, did we not?'

Kemp frowned, trying to remember which knights he had met at Saint-Vaast, but the knight was no longer paying any attention to him. 'Sir John, take Sir Roger and Sir Guy and three hundred archers, and attack the men posted at the Nieullay bridge. Sir Walter, take my son, a hundred men-at-arms and a hundred and fifty archers and sally out of the eastern gate of the town. The rest shall come with me, and we shall attack de Chargny from both sides.'

As the men-at-arms and mounted archers formed up in the square in front of the castle, Kemp saw Preston ride out with Conyers and the other men of Holland's retinue. Even Brewster was there, dressed in a habergeon of mail and a steel bascinet. Seeing Kemp, he called out.

'Martin! God be praised!'

'How did you come here?' demanded Preston. 'We heard you were dead.'

'There'll be plenty of time for telling of our adventures when the fighting's done,' called Holland. 'Are you coming with us, Kemp? You look as though you've had a hard time of it already.'

Kemp shook his head. 'I'm coming, Sir Thomas. I've a number of scores to settle with de Chargny.'

'De Pavia's taking his time,' grumbled de Chargny, while he waited with Geoffroi le fitz, de Ribeaumont, and the rest of his force outside the Boulogne gate. The breath billowed from their mouths in the chill air of the winter's night. 'He is making us die of cold!' They had dismounted from their horses to stretch their legs.

'In the name of God, the Lombards are avaricious people,' said another knight. 'He is looking over your *écus*, Sir Geoffroi, to make sure none are false, and they are all there.' There was general laughter amongst the men who were close enough to hear.

De Chargny did not laugh, however. Frowning, he suddenly waved the men around him to silence. 'What's that noise?'

From somewhere inside the town, they could hear the clop of hooves on cobbles. 'At last,' said de Ribeaumont.

The gate opened, and suddenly a trumpet sounded the charge. Armed men were surging out, knights, men-at-arms and archers, hundreds of them, all under the banner of Sir Walter Mauny. They turned, bearing down on de Chargny and his men, the hooves of their horses pounding the frozen soil.

'Mauny to the rescue!'

'Havoc! Havoc!'

The causeway was barely wide enough for twenty men to stand abreast; there was not enough room for a mounted charge, and the land on either side of it was too marshy for horses. The English dismounted, knights and men-at-arms along with the archers, and began to move towards the French.

De Chargny drew his sword. This was not the town's pathetically small garrison. 'Betrayed!' he hissed to de Ribeaumont, and then turned in his saddle to address his men. 'Gentlemen! If we retreat now, we shall lose all. It will be better for us to fight valiantly, that the day may yet be ours.'

'By Saint George, you speak the truth,' jeered an English man-at-arms who had been close enough to hear him. 'The Devil take anyone who thinks of fleeing!'

Everything seemed to happen at once. In all Kemp's previous battles there had been a build-up, a pause while he and his companions awaited the attack of the French, their inner fears stoking them up into a fever-pitch of nervous excitement. But tonight it was the English who charged. Kemp and his companions found themselves swept along the causeway by the fast-flowing tide of events, thrust at once into the thick of battle without being given a chance to muster their courage.

Led by Mauny, the English knights and men-at-arms charged along the causeway on foot, wielding their swords and battleaxes above their heads. The French outnumbered them over ten to one, but there was not enough space on the causeway for them to bring the full weight of their numbers to bear. De Chargny had been caught off-guard, and had no time to adopt any coherent formation. The English smashed into the enemy ranks, gouging a path through the closely packed bodies. The silence of the night was shattered by the clash of steel, shouted war-cries, and the screams of the wounded. Men fell dead or mortally wounded on both sides, and it was not long before the corpses lay so thick on the causeway that those who still fought stumbled over the bodies of their comrades.

Then the two sides disengaged, the French withdrawing a short way while the English rallied for another. Positioned behind the knights and men-at-arms, Kemp could see Sir John Beauchamp leading his forces along the beach to the west of Calais, to take the bridge at Nieullay from de Fiennes' men and cut off the French retreat.

But de Chargny had seen how few the English who attacked him were, and ordered one of his trumpeters to rally his men. He formed his men-at-arms into a line across the causeway, four ranks deep, their foreshortened lances levelled to receive the next charge.

The unknown knight in 'all-white' armour was still in command of the situation. Seeing the French rally, he turned to Holland. 'Take those archers over there to yonder island,' he commanded, indicating an area of more solid ground in the middle of the marsh, to one side of the causeway. 'I'll take these over there. We'll catch the French in a cross-hail.'

'Aye, sire.' Holland hurried away, and the unknown turned to the two platoons of dismounted archers who stood around him. 'Who's in charge here?'

Preston and another serjeant-at-arms stepped forward. 'We are, sir,' said Preston.

'Bring your men and follow me.'

'Says who?' demanded the other serjeant.

'I do,' replied the unknown, raising the visor of his bascinet, and it was not until that moment that Kemp recognised him. 'I am Edward of Windsor.'

Abashed, the serjeant went down on one knee before his king. 'My apologies, your Majesty. I did not realise . . .'

'Nor could you be expected to,' the king replied kindly. 'Take your men to yonder spit of sand, and shoot at the French from there.'

'Aye, sire.' As the two serjeants descended into the marsh, followed by their men, the king ran to join the men-at-arms further down the causeway to encourage them to greater efforts. The archers stripped off their habergeons, holding their bows above their heads as they waded through the mire.

'Christ's body!' grumbled Jarrom. 'I thought we'd seen the last of this God-damned swamp!'

'Stop grumbling! snarled Preston. 'Nails and blood! Come back, Jankin Newbolt, all is forgiven.'

'Who the hell is Jankin Newbolt?' Jarrom muttered under his breath.

'He was in our platoon before you came,' said Kemp, holding aloft a bow that Conyers had found for him as he stumbled waist-deep through the morass. 'He was always grumbling too, but he was a better man than you, aye and like.'

'Was?'

'He died at Crécy.'

Jarrom laughed. 'He can't have been that good. Even I survived Crécy.'

'More's the pity,' jibed Conyers.

They reached the area of dry sand and hauled themselves out of the marsh, clambering up the muddy bank to the drier ground at the top of the spit, shivering. The frozen wet sand beneath their feet was too hard to stick their arrows in, so they took them out of their retainers and thrust them under their belts.

They had only brought two dozen arrows each. 'Make every shot tell,' ordered Preston. 'Shoot at will. In your own time.' They had no mounted charge to hold off; it was simply a matter of killing as many of the enemy as they could from their vantage point.

The French provided an easy target, a close-packed body of

men on the causeway barely two hundred yards from where the archers were positioned. At the front, the French were still engaged with the English men-at-arms, but the foot-soldiers straggled out behind the French men-at-arms, far enough back for the skilled archers to be in little danger of hitting their own countrymen. Kemp nocked an arrow to his bow and loosed, quickly reaching for another. He was back in his element, doing what he did best. His eyes searched constantly for de Chargny's distinctive jupon as he sought out fresh targets but he could not see the French knight anywhere.

Aware of the killing hail that harried their flanks, many of the French foot-soldiers climbed down the sides of the causeway to advance on the archers. As they waded through the morass, however, their heavy armour weighed them down and they were vulnerable targets.

The sky was growing lighter with the coming of the false dawn, making it easier for the English archers to see their prey. The king was at the centre of the mêlée on the causeway, swinging his sword left and right under Mauny's banner. Seeing de Ribeaumont hacking away at his opponents, the king pushed his way through the press of men to face him and the two engaged in single combat in the midst of the confusion. De Ribeaumont was as tall and strong as the king, and beat him back with savage blows which the king countered with difficulty. He sank to his knees under the onslaught. But as de Ribeaumont tried to bring his sword down against his opponent's head, the king parried his blow, holding the tip of his blade in his gauntleted left hand, and driving the fist that clutched the hilt of his sword into de Ribeaumont's stomach. Winded, de Ribeaumont staggered back as the king rose and hacked at him repeatedly, each blow accompanied by cries of: 'Ha! Saint Edward! Ha! Saint George!'

Engaged with a man-at-arms nearby, de Chargny recognised the war-cry, and glanced towards the knight in 'all-white' armour who was fighting de Ribeaumont. Certainly the man had the right build, and yet it seemed incredible . . . but he had often heard that the English king liked to fight incognito at tournaments. If he could capture or kill the King of England, the day might not yet be lost . . .

He dispatched his opponent with a sword-thrust to the throat, and tried to push his way through the crush to where de

Ribeaumont fought the English king. Three men-at-arms blocked his path. He drove his sword into one's chest, ducked as the second swung at him with a battleaxe, and lashed out at the third with one foot, hearing the man's kneecap smash. As the man went down with a scream, de Chargny withdrew his sword from the first and swung at the second, his broadsword biting deep into the man's side.

But now there were even more men between him and King Edward. Surrounded by his own troops, de Chargny paused to take command of the situation once again. 'You, you and you!' he snapped at three Frenchmen-at-arms. 'I want a path cut through to where Sir Eustache is fighting that knight in "all-white", understand?'

The archers had exhausted their supplies of arrows by now, and Preston led them back through the mire to join the fight on the causeway with their swords. Kemp followed him willingly; he did not consider himself particularly brave, but he found it intolerable to stand by as a spectator while the battle was being decided only a few hundred yards away. Jarrom, Elliott and Gower did not see it the same way: they were archers and, when their arrows were gone, considered the rest was up to the men-at-arms. When Preston wasn't watching, they slipped back down the other side of the sand spit, leaving Preston, Kemp, Conyers, Brewster, Hamo Newton and the archers of the other platoon to advance on their own.

A few crossbowmen remained on the causeway, and they loosed a few shots at the advancing archers, but most of them were caught up in the hand-to-hand fighting with the English knights and men-at-arms.

Kemp hauled himself from the marsh and scrambled up the side of the causeway, drawing his sword as he plunged into the foray. He was beyond exhaustion, his mind so numb it ignored the signals his body sent it to tell him he had had enough for one day. He struck at a Frenchman from behind with his broadsword, the blade cleaving through mail and flesh, and then ducked as a foreshortened lance was thrust at him. Pulling his blade free of the first man, he stabbed the second, and barely had time to parry as a third man slashed at him. Struggling to keep his footing on the edge of the causeway, he thrust at the third man's face, stabbing him in one eye.

Glancing around for another victim, he struck at a man, his blade glancing harmlessly off a steel bascinet. The knight turned with a roar and thrust at Kemp's midriff, but he did not have enough room in the crush to move fast enough, and Kemp dodged the blow. He lifted his broadsword, hacking at the man's face and slicing into his visor. Blood gouted through the eye-slits, and the knight fell to the ground to be trampled underfoot.

'Kemp!' Conyers had seized a knight from behind in an armlock, holding his victim's arms out so he could not use his sword. There was no room for Kemp to use his own sword, so he took the dagger from the knight's belt and jabbed its slender blade through the eye-slit of his visor.

Then a French man-at-arms in turn grabbed Kemp from behind. As another man-at-arms moved in front of him to stab him while he was helpless, Kemp kicked the man in the chest, sending him sprawling back so Conyers could hack at his head with his short sword. The kick also knocked the man holding Kemp off-balance, and Kemp broke free, whirling round to slash at his throat.

'Look out!' Conyers' voice again. Kemp ducked instinctively, and a lance aimed at the back of his head passed over him to plunge into a Frenchman's neck. Kemp turned, swinging his broadsword, and the blade sliced through to the bone of his attacker's arm. More blood spurted, and the man staggered back with a scream of agony, lost his footing and tumbled down the side of the causeway.

But the English were growing weary and at last the weight of numbers was beginning to tell on the side of the French. De Chargny's men had cut a path through to where the king fought, and de Chargny himself was about to go to de Ribeaumont's aid when Kemp saw his jupon and recognised his coat-of-arms. 'De Chargny!' he roared.

De Chargny's pointed visor turned. The last time he saw Kemp, he had been a prisoner in the dungeons of the castle of Saint-Omer. He remembered giving Arnault specific instructions to kill the churl without any risk to himself. How had he survived, and come here? It did not matter: Kemp's survival could swiftly be remedied. De Chargny tapped two of his men on the shoulder, pointing to Kemp. 'Kill him!'

As the two men-at-arms moved to block Kemp's path, de

Chargny turned back towards the king and de Ribeaumont. At that moment, one of Kemp's companions, Hamo Newton, seized the French knight from behind in an arm-lock.

'Serjeant Preston!'

Preston turned and saw Newton holding a visored knight. He raised his sword to bring it down on the knight's head. De Chargny swung his foot up between Preston's legs, his steel sabaton catching the serjeant in the crotch.

'Nails and blood!' Preston gasped, sinking to his knees in agony. De Chargny flipped Newton over his shoulder so the archer landed on top of Preston, knocking him out. Then de Chargny reversed his grip on his sword, and plunged it down into Newton's chest with both hands.

The first of the two men-at-arms, meanwhile, spun his sword around his head and swung at Kemp. Kemp parried the blow, and kicked at the man's kneecap, shattering it. As the Frenchman fell, Kemp brought down his sword on top of his head, knocking off the man's 'kettle' helmet. Kemp was forced to parry a blow from the second man-at-arms, swinging his sword at the man's side. His blade did not penetrate his assailant's mail, but the blow was strong enough to knock the man off-balance. That gave Kemp a moment to hack at the first man's head before he could stab up at him. The blade cleaved through the steel links of his coif, and then went on through his skull, killing him.

The second man was aiming another blow. Kemp tugged his blade free with a roar of effort, and stabbed with all his might. The point of his sword pierced the man's habergeon, and blood spurted as the blade penetrated his stomach.

'Mauny to the rescue!' Just as de Chargny was about to go to de Ribeaumont's aid, the English battle-cry was renewed, and he looked up in time to see another knight in 'all-white' armour come riding into the fray at the head of another two hundred mounted men.

That swung it for the French. Panicked by the arrival of these English reinforcements, they began to throw down their weapons. Knocked on to his back, de Ribeaumont reversed his grip on his sword, offering the hilt up to his opponent. 'Sir knight, I surrender myself as your prisoner, for the honour of the day must fall to the English.'

De Chargny ran to where his horse was tethered and swung

himself up into the saddle. If he could fetch de Fiennes and his men from the bridge at Nieullay, the French might yet win.

Brewster ran up and seized the bridle of his horse. 'Yield, sir knight! The battle is lost.'

'It's not lost until I say it is,' de Chargny replied coolly. 'And as for yielding to a churl . . . I would rather die.' He swung his broadsword down at Brewster's head. The blade did not penetrate his steel bascinet, but the force of the blow was such that it knocked him senseless. De Chargny dug his spurs into his horse's flanks and galloped away in the direction of the bridge.

Soon it was all over on the causeway. De Renty, de Ribeaumont and de Chargny's son were all prisoners, while the French soldiers were disarmed by the English men-at-arms and archers. Holland found Preston pinned under Newton's body, and helped him to his feet. 'What happened to you?' asked the knight.

'He got kicked in the bollocks.' Conyers grinned with the relief of a hard-fought victory.

'Oh aye, very funny,' Preston grumbled hoarsely. 'Where's Kemp?'

The king was also glancing about. 'Where's de Chargny?'

Riding along the causeway towards the Nieullay bridge, de Chargny saw pockets of fighting taking place all over the marsh, although everywhere he turned the English were now gaining the upper hand. He approached the bridge in time to see his own crossbowmen wavering under the concentrated and repeated volleys of the English archers under Sir John Beauchamp. On the far side of the river he could make out de Fiennes' banner being carried away as he escaped on horseback with a couple of squires. The French crossbowmen saw it too, and lost heart. Some of them fled towards Boulogne, but most threw down their weapons and called for quarter. The English quickly seized the bridge, cutting off any hopes de Chargny might have had of escaping in that direction. He wheeled his horse about, and began to ride back along the causeway towards Calais. Perhaps he could still challenge the English king to single combat . . .

He was almost halfway there when he saw a single figure, a mere archer, bare-headed and unarmoured, standing in the middle of the causeway, blocking his path. The archer stood with his hands resting on the crossguard of a broadsword, the point resting on the ground between his feet. De Chargny sighed. Some commoner, intent on making his fame and fortune by capturing a French knight in an impromptu passage-at-arms. He drew his own broadsword, and charged.

Then he recognised it as Kemp, and urged his horse into a gallop, roaring his own battle-cry. 'Chargny!'

Kemp hefted his sword in both hands, bracing himself to receive the attack.

De Chargny lifted his sword back, aiming a stroke that would lop Kemp's head from his shoulders.

Kemp chopped at the horse's head, ducking as he was spattered with the animal's blood and brains. De Chargny swung and missed, so he was already off balance when the horse stumbled and fell, tumbling him from the saddle.

The Frenchman was on his feet in a moment, charging at Kemp and swinging his sword at his head. Kemp parried the blow with surprising ease.

So, the churl knew how to use a sword. So much the better: it would make killing him all the more enjoyable.

Kemp swung at de Chargny. The Frenchman met the blow almost without thinking about it. He thrust at Kemp's chest. Kemp twisted aside and the blade lanced through his sleeve, drawing blood from his arm. He tripped, and de Chargny was standing over him in an instant. The Frenchman brought his sword down with all his might. Kemp parried again, but his arm was badly jarred. He rolled out of the way as de Chargny came at him again and, scrambling clear, rose to his feet. De Chargny followed him, dangling his sword negligently and waiting until Kemp was ready before swinging once more. Kemp thrust at de Chargny's head, but his sword glanced harmlessly off the pointed visor. De Chargny slashed at Kemp's chest, the tip of his sword slicing through the fabric of the archer's tunic, scoring a line of blood across his chest. Kemp swung at de Chargny's side, but the Frenchman turned the blow aside with his own blade. Then he thrust at Kemp's leg, slicing him along the side of one thigh.

Kemp was exhausted, bleeding in three places, and limping. The ache of his shoulders from his torture on the rack had returned as a result of constantly wielding his sword. He whirled it above him, swinging at the side of de Chargny's head. De

Chargny raised his sword to parry, but it was a feint, and Kemp thrust at the Frenchman's midriff. The knight twisted aside, and the tip of Kemp's sword was turned by his chain-mail habergeon. De Chargny reacted swiftly and brought his sword down against Kemp's blade. He forced it to the ground and stamped on it close to the hilt so it was torn from Kemp's grip.

Disarmed, Kemp backed away. The knight advanced implacably. Holding his sword with both hands, he lifted it above his head to hack at Kemp's skull.

Kemp threw himself forward, catching de Chargny around the waist before the Frenchman could bring his sword down and knocking him off his feet. The two of them tumbled off the causeway, rolling down the slope into the morass below.

De Chargny lost his sword in the fall. They grappled in the slime, the knight smashing a gauntleted fist into Kemp's stomach and punching him on the jaw. Kemp was thrown back into the mud. De Chargny waded through the mire, grabbing the Englishman by the collar and lifting him up to punch him again. The front of Kemp's tunic came away in his hand. He pulled his dagger from his belt and tried to plunge it into Kemp's chest.

Kemp raised both hands to defend himself, catching de Chargny's wrist. The Frenchman put his free hand on Kemp's throat and forced his head under the morass. Kemp kicked his legs desperately, suffocating in the slime. Unable to hold his breath any longer, he opened his mouth and mud filled it at once. He was choking, suffocating, dying. Terror paralysed him.

He fought against the fear. He was not dead yet.

The only thing he had a grip on was the cuff of de Chargny's right-hand gauntlet. He began to twist it, turning it and the hand within with all his might. De Chargny cried out in pain, releasing his grip on Kemp's throat to clutch at his wrist. Kemp managed to get his feet on firmer ground at the bottom of the morass. He rose up out of the mire, his hands pulling free of de Chargny's grip. With his left hand he pushed up de Chargny's visor, driving his right fist into the knight's face. Blood gouted from the knight's nose as it broke under the force of the blow, and he staggered back, stunned.

Wrenching off the knight's helmet, Kemp punched him again, and again and again, until his own knuckles were raw and de Chargny's face was nothing but a mass of bruises. Then he put his hands behind de Chargny's head, and kneed him in the face with all his might.

'That's for Typhaine,' he said.

De Chargny slumped back, defeated. But Kemp had not finished with him yet. Summoning up his last reserves of strength, he dragged the barely conscious knight out of the mire, back on to the side of the causeway. Then he kicked him savagely in the side. De Chargny parted bloodied lips to scream in agony. 'That's for Master Sigglesthorne.'

He kicked him again, in the head this time. 'That's for me.'

Then, standing over de Chargny, he unfastened his breech-cloth and pissed in the unconscious knight's face. 'And that's for sheer spite.'

Only then, when it was all over, did his mind accept the signals his body had been trying to send it for over an hour. His eyes rolled up in his head, and he collapsed to lie unconscious beside the knight.

# EPILOGUE

ON THE FIRST day of January, 1350, Sir Geoffroi de Chargny, Sir Eustache de Ribeaumont and Sir Oudard de Renty dined with Amerigo de Pavia in the great hall of the castle at Calais, just as de Chargny had predicted; but the three French knights were captives of King Edward III. De Chargny had had his wounds tended by his personal physician, whom he had brought with him, and sat with a face that was too bruised and swollen to scowl, in fresh new robes provided by the king, as the Prince of Wales and the knights of England served the first course of the banquet in honour of their brave and noble captives.

When they had all dined, the tables were removed, and the king, bare-headed but for a fine chaplet of pearls, made his way around the room, talking to French and English knights alike. Only when he spoke to de Chargny himself did the expression on his face darken a little.

'Sir Geoffroi, Sir Geoffroi,' he said, shaking his head sadly. 'I think that I owe you but little love, since you wished to steal from me by night what I obtained at very great expense. You wanted to have it at a cheaper price than I did, when you thought to win it for twenty thousand *écus d'or*. But God has helped me by making you fail in your intention. If it is His will, He will aid me to fulfil my entire plans.'

De Chargny said nothing, his face expressionless, and the king turned to de Ribeaumont. 'Sir Eustache, of all the knights in the world, you are the one whom I have seen attack his enemies and defend his own body with the greatest skill and valour.' The king was smiling again now. 'I never yet faced anyone in close combat who gave me as much to do as you did last night. I therefore award you the prize of valour, and all my knights agree with me in this decision.' And so saying, he took off the chaplet of pearls he was wearing and placed it firmly on an astonished de Ribeaumont's head. 'I present you with this chaplet, for being the best fighter of the day on either side, and I beg you to wear it all this year for love of me.' He grinned. 'I know you are lively of spirit, and enjoy the company of ladies and damsels,' he said with a wink, 'therefore wherever you go, tell of how King Edward gave it to you. And although you are one of my prisoners, I give you in addition your liberty, free of ransom. You may set out tomorrow, if you choose, to go wherever you like.'

'Noble sire, you do me greater honour than I am worthy of. May God reward you for the courtesy you do to me,' replied de Ribeaumont, bowing low. 'I am a poor man who desires to improve himself, and you give me an example after which I may willingly strive. I shall carry out all you have instructed me to do, sire, both loyally and openly; for, after the service which I owe to my own much-loved and much-revered lord the king, I know of no other king whom I would more willingly serve, nor with so much love, than I would serve you.'

That same night, Curtis found Kemp getting drunk with Preston, Conyers and Brewster in the White Lion inn. 'Do you mind if I join you?'

'Not at all,' said Preston, indicating a spare stool with a magnanimous gesture. 'We were just toasting the hero.'

'Bollocks,' said Kemp. His face was a mass of bruises and, below the clean new tunic he wore, his body was covered in grazes and bandaged cuts.

'I hear you captured Sir Geoffroi de Chargny,' said Curtis.

'Aye, though I'll not get a farthing,' Kemp replied bitterly. 'He's the king's captive, and the king gets the ransom.' Kemp would not even get the glory of de Chargny's capture to his credit: while he had lain unconscious, a knight from the West Country had ridden up and found de Chargny, claiming him as his own captive.

'Aye, and ransoms from all the other French knights captured last night,' said Curtis. 'Add to all that money the twenty thousand *écus* de Chargny brought for de Pavia, and all in all it was a very profitable night for his Majesty. And as a bonus, he gets to keep Calais.'

'Just how did the king get to hear of the plot, anyway?' asked Kemp.

'Sigglesthorne didn't know de Pavia was central to de Chargny's plan, so when he reached Calais what more natural than that he should warn the acting governor?' explained Curtis. 'When Sigglesthorne came to him, de Pavia panicked. How many other people knew of the plot? If the king heard of it from anyone other than de Pavia first, de Pavia would have been for the chop. So he decided to hedge his bets and warn the king in person, slipping incognito across the Channel. The king told him to send a message to de Chargny, telling him that Sigglesthorne knew of the plot, but that he had told no one but de Pavia, so de Chargny would think it safe to go ahead. Then the king prepared his response, smuggling men and arms to Calais in preparation. Hardly anyone knew of the ambush. Even Sir Thomas Holland was not let in on the secret until yesterday afternoon, when he and Sigglesthorne marched into the castle demanding to speak to de Pavia, only to find themselves shown into the room where the king and the prince were lying in concealment with Sir Walter Mauny and his men!'

'So everything I did was for nothing?' asked Kemp.

'I wouldn't exactly say that, lad,' said Preston. 'If you hadn't held de Chargny and his men on the road to Paris, Sigglesthorne would never have made it to Calais to panic de Pavia like that.'

'So even you can claim a share of the credit for saving the day,' said Curtis, taking an apple from the bowl of fruit Brewster had placed on the table and biting into it.

'What about that letter Sigglesthorne had, that de Chargny's men found in his saddle-bags?' asked Kemp. 'Where did that come from?'

Curtis shook his head vigorously until he had swallowed his mouthful of apple. 'Forget it. It never existed.'

Kemp frowned. 'I don't understand.'

'You don't have to. Suffice to say whoever wrote that letter is a loyal servant of King Edward, whose identity is best kept secret for his own safety.'

Kemp stared at him. 'What about you? You're not just a shipmaster, are you?'

Curtis grinned. 'Let's just say I've had occasion in the past to act as a courier for his Majesty, carrying out the kind of mission his knights and noblemen consider below their dignity.'

'By the way, did you hear that the Pope confirmed Cardinal d'Albi's verdict annulling the Lady Joan's marriage to the Earl of

Salisbury in favour of Sir Thomas?' asked Conyers. Kemp shook his head. 'They're finally living as husband and wife now.'

'What about that?' asked Curtis. 'Is it true what they say of that business?'

'That depends on what they say,' Preston said carefully.

'That there was no clandestine marriage between Holland and Joan of Kent,' said Curtis. 'That they only met one another after Holland was appointed steward of Montague's household at Mold in Flintshire, and became lovers; and concocted the story of the clandestine marriage so Joan could leave Montague for Holland. Come on, Master Preston, you've been with Holland for a long time now. You *must* know the truth of the matter.'

'It's because I've been with Sir Thomas for so long that I refuse to dignify your slanderous accusation with a response,' growled Preston.

Curtis laughed, and slapped his knee. 'I knew it! There's no smoke without fire.'

Kemp sighed, and shook his head. 'Nothing is ever what it seems, is it?'

'Aye,' agreed Curtis, smiling. 'But bear that in mind, Master Kemp, and I think you'll go a long way in life. A very long way indeed.'

'Never mind that,' said Conyers, grinning lecherously. 'I want to know more about you and this Typhaine lass. Did you . . .?'

'No,' Kemp cut in firmly, scowling.

But that night he dreamed of her, and for once they were pleasant dreams.

# HISTORICAL NOTES

Some of the situations and events I have described in this book are so outrageous and far-fetched that I would never have dared to use them were it not for the fact they are completely true.

Michael Packe has described King Edward III's ambush of de Chargny at Calais as 'surely the most irresponsible adventure ever undertaken by a king of England'[1]; and any student of English history can tell you there are plenty to choose from. Packe takes a very cynical view of most of the famous episodes I have described, and I have generally accepted his viewpoints as more realistic than the simple anecdotes of chivalry that Froissart relates in his chronicles.

Packe argues that 'the pantomime whereby the leading burgesses were brought out [*of Calais*] with halters round their necks, and Queen Philippa save[*d*] them from his wrath by pleading mercy on her knees'[2] was stage-managed, partly to impress on the people of Calais King Edward's rage at being kept so long besieging the town, and partly to cover the fact of his indiscretion with a mistress – Alice Montague, perhaps – by playing up publicly his susceptibility to his wife's entreaties. Pantomime or not, one cannot detract from the courage of the six burghers of Calais who offered to sacrifice their own lives for the lives of the rest of the townspeople.

Packe also deals admirably with the bizarre quarrel between Holland and Montague over which one of them was married to Joan of Kent. It seems incredible that Joan of Kent should have made no mention of her marriage to Holland when she was wedded to Montague (although she was only about twelve at the time of the first wedding), and more incredible still that Holland should subsequently have been appointed steward of their

[1]M. Packe, *King Edward III*, p.197 (ed. L. C. B. Scaman, Routledge & Kegan Paul, London, 1983)

[2]Ibidem, p.171.

household on his return from Prussia. 'It is possible that the whole tale was cock-and-bull,' suggests Packe; 'that they had simply become lovers quite lately, while Holland was serving as her steward in Montagu's [*sic*] household'[3]. Montague does not seem to have been desperately upset by the loss of the fairest woman in England as his bride, but then he did have his earldom to console him, and he married Elizabeth Mohun about a year later.

Although Sir Thomas Holland's star continued to rise at court, King Edward cannot have been pleased that the marriage he had arranged between the son of one of his old friends and his ward and cousin should be annulled by a French pope. Perhaps it is significant that a little over three years later the parliament at Westminster passed the Statute of Praemunire, forbidding appeals to the papacy.

Both Hollands – Thomas and Otho – were founder members of the Companionship of Saint George. Most scholars now accept that the order was founded on or around April 23 1348, although Froissart – described by some as the first ever journalist, and certainly as inaccurate as most members of that breed – puts the year as 1344, confusing it with the foundation of the Order of the Round Table, a precursor to the companionship which never quite got off the ground in the way that the Companionship of Saint George did. The order exists to this day, although it is of course better known as the Order of the Garter. The story as to how the order got its motto – *Honi soit qui mal y pense*, 'Evil to him who evils thinks' – is apocryphal, but quite in keeping with the morals of the time. Which lady at the ball at Calais actually lost her garter while dancing with the king – or indeed whether the ball was at Calais, Windsor, or somewhere else – is open to debate. For many years it was said to be Joan, the Fair Maid of Kent (who, according to another legend, was raped by King Edward III at the castle of Wark while her husband was out campaigning against the Scots). Once again it requires the scholarship of Packe to untangle the many threads of legend and argue quite convincingly that it was Alice rather than Joan Montague (or should that have been Joan Holland?) who danced with the king at Calais[4].

1348 was also the year the Great Pestilence, known to later generations as the Black Death, reached England. Some people

[3]Ibid., p.152.

[4]See ibid., pp.105-123, 170-178.

did contract the pestilence and survive, including Guy de Chauliac, Pope Clement VI's personal physician; although it seems more probable that, like Kemp, he contracted bubonic plague, rather than the pneumonic plague which was confused by fourteenth-century medicine with the bubonic. Bubonic or pneumonic, it seems that roughly a third of the population of western Europe died of the pestilence during this period. The learned blamed God and the stars; the unlearned – including the flagellants – blamed the Jews and, whatever Pope Clement VI's faults, he must be praised for doing his best to protect the Jews against the pogroms that were carried out in those years. If no such pogroms were carried out in England at this time, it was simply because those Jews who had not converted to Christianity had already been expelled from the country.

When I first began writing about Martin Kemp, his life and his times, I had not intended to feature so many real people so prominently; but once I placed him in Holland's company in the first book, it became not only logical to do so, but inevitable, as I found my story increasingly entangled with that knight's. Sir Hugh Despenser and Countess Margaret of Kent both died at this time. Sigglesthorne and Vise did actually exist, but if their names are passed down to us, it is thanks only to the Papal records of Holland's petition. I have also found reference to an English spy at the Papal Court in Avignon by the name of Count Niccolino del Fiesco, although I have yet to find either scholarly reference to him or documentary evidence to back up the claim.

There really was a vintner named John Chaucer living on Thames Street, in the Vintry Ward of London, and he did have a son named Geoffrey. Young Geoffrey went on to make a name for himself in his own lifetime scribbling verses, and if it should seem like pure self indulgence to introduce him here, all I can say is that since his path is destined to cross Martin Kemp's at least twice more, I had to introduce him sooner or later.

Raoul de Brienne, Count of Eu and Constable of France, was another real character, who was indeed sold by Holland to the king, apparently so that the king could persuade him to sell him his estates around Guînes in the Pale of Calais; for which crime the count was beheaded by Valois' son, John II, shortly after his succession in 1350 on the count's return to France. The story that Sir Otho Holland was brought to the bar of the King's Bench for allowing the count to be seen at large and armed in Calais is also true. He admitted his culpability, putting himself upon the king's favour, and was thereupon committed to the custody of the marshal. His name was not struck from the membership of the Order of the Garter, however, so he was most likely forgiven his crime.

But of all the characters whose names I have shamelessly hijacked, none is more fascinating than the villain of the piece, Sir Geoffroi de Chargny (or Charny), governor of Saint-Omer and Sieur de Pierre-Perthuis, Montfort, Savoisy and Licey. None of the characters I have encountered in my studies of the period so far have better illustrated the dichotomy between the chivalric ideals of the nobility and their ignoble behaviour, except perhaps Edward III himself. Described by contemporaries as 'the perfect knight', de Chargny is best known to historians as the author of a number of tracts on chivalry; and when John II of France founded the Order of the Star to rival the Order of the Garter, his close friend Sir Geoffroi was one of its founder members. Can this really be the same de Chargny who sought to bribe the governor of Calais into handing the town over to him? The same de Chargny who, quickly paying his ransom to escape English captivity, hunted de Pavia down to a small castle King Edward had given him outside Calais, surprised him in bed with a mistress sent to him from England, and had him cut into pieces in the crowded market place at Saint-Omer? But that, as they say, is another story . . .